BELOVED ANGEL

"Wha…what do you want?" she stammered, thoroughly disconcerted by his assessing gaze and the caressing tone of his voice.

"You," he told her bluntly. "I want you, Tori, but not until you want me too, just as much."

"Don't say such things, Jacob!" she gasped, her entire body trembling violently now, her fingers shaking so badly she could scarcely retain her hold on the gown that shielded her quivering body from his view. "Please! It's sinful! You musn't even think such things!"

One dark eyebrow cocked upward as he answered softly, "Why not, angel? *You* were. You were wondering what my hands would feel like on your body."

"No!" she screamed, denying his words. "No!"

"Oh, yes, my little liar. That look in your eyes was a woman dreamin' of her lover's touch."

CATHERINE HART

HART

Fallen Angel

LEISURE BOOKS **NEW YORK CITY**

I dedicate this book, with love and gratitude, to:
My Mom and Dad,
Who instilled in me the belief that a good education
was
the road to my success;
and to
My lovely Mother-in-law,
Who lives her religious beliefs more honestly than
anyone I have ever met.

A LEISURE BOOK®

June 1996

Published by

Dorchester Publishing Co., Inc.
276 Fifth Avenue
New York, NY 10001

Printed in the United States of America.

Chapter
1

It was late, a couple of hours before dawn, when Jake Banner rode up to the ranch. He was dead tired, and had nearly killed his horse pushing it so hard. In less than five days, he had covered what should have taken at least seven to travel, but he was here.

In the early morning darkness, it was impossible to judge the extent of the damage to the ranch. He could tell there had been a fire, but what he could see at first glance didn't look too bad. The main part of the house still stood, looking much the same as the last time he had seen it. The barns and stable were still there.

He stabled his horse, making as little noise as possible, not wanting to alert anyone to his presence. Then he let himself quietly into the house. Creeping through the kitchen, he started stealthily down the hallway toward the main living area, the room Carmen always called the *sala*, only to draw up short when the barrel of a rifle poked him sharply in the back.

"That's far enough, stranger," he heard a man growl from behind him. "Hands over your head! Real careful like!"

"Gill?" Jake asked hopefully, guessing that the voice belonged to the older ranch hand.

"Jake?"

"Yeah."

"Well, goldurnit, boy! Why'd ya come sneakin' in here like a thief in the night?"

Gill lowered the rifle and Jake turned to face him. "'Cause I just got in and I didn't want to wake the whole house, is why," Jake explained in a loud whisper, embarrassed that Gill had gotten the drop on him so easily. He must be more tired than he'd thought, to be so careless. "I didn't expect you'd be roamin' around playin' guard dog at this hour."

"I been sorta watchin' over the place 'til you got here."

"How's Carmen?" Jake wasn't sure he wanted to hear the answer, but he had to know. He barely remembered his own mother, but he loved his stepmother as dearly as if she had given birth to him. She and Tori, his young stepsister, meant the world to him.

In the shadow of the hall, he could barely see Gill shake his head as he replied, "Bad, Jake. Real bad. Doc says he doesn't know how she's made it this long. Mostly it's her lungs. She breathed in a lot o' smoke, and now she has trouble breathin' and coughs a lot. She's as weak as a newborn kitten."

"And the burns? Was she badly burned?"

"Her hands mostly, and her feet, too. It happened in the night, and she didn't think to put anything on her feet. She burned her hands tryin' to open the door to your pa's room. As thick and heavy as that door is, it was blisterin' hot when she touched it."

"How'd the fire start?"

Gill sighed and shook his head sorrowfully again. "Don't know for sure, but we think maybe your pa had been smokin' in bed again, and maybe dropped a live ash off o' his cigar or something. Everything's too charred to tell, but it looks like the fire started in your pa's room. It's the one with the most damage."

Tears stung Jake's eyes and he blinked them back. "Carmen warned him so many times about that," he reflected gruffly. "Stubborn old man should've listened to her." A moment later he said softly, "He never stood a snow-ball's chance in hell of gettin' out of that room alive, did he?"

Gill shook his head as he and Jake both

recalled the gruff old man who had stubbornly run his ranch from his wheelchair. Roy Banner had run the Lazy B with an iron hand, and Jake had always wondered why his dad had called the ranch the Lazy B when Roy had seen to it that not one living soul, human or animal, had ever had a truly lazy moment on it. Now the irascible old man was gone, never again to raise his voice in supreme authority over one and all.

"Yeah, well," Gill said uncomfortably. "Why don't you go try to get some sleep?"

"Where?" Jake asked, not knowing how much of the house was now uninhabitable.

"Your old room is still okay, and Miss Victoria's. Just the one wing where the master bedrooms were got ruined, though most everything in the house still smells like smoke. The guest rooms are all right. We put the Missus in the big one next to yours."

Jake nodded. "Thanks, Gill. I think I'll look in on Carmen first, and let Tori know I'm home."

"Uh." Gill scratched his head and shifted his feet. "Miss Tori ain't here, Jake. Rosa's been lookin' after Carmen."

Jake swung back around and stared at Gill as if the man were daft. "What do you mean, Tori's not here? Where is she?"

"She's still at the convent, as best we know," Gill said.

Jake frowned. "Well, when is she coming home? Why hasn't she arrived already?"

Gill shrugged helplessly. "I don't rightly know. We sent a message right away, same time as we sent yours, and one since, but she ain't answered either one. Don't sound like Miss Tori, ignoring her mama when she knows she's so bad off and askin' for her little girl."

"No. No, that doesn't sound like Tori at all," Jake agreed with a scowl. Taking charge, he said, "I'm going to look in on Carmen. You go wake Zeke and send him up to the house. I want him to ride over to the convent with another message. This one I'll write myself, and I'll make damn good and sure Tori knows just how serious things are with her mother. Maybe she doesn't realize it's this bad."

"Jake," Gill said hesitantly. "She has to know it's pretty bad. We buried your dad five days ago. That's about as bad as it gets."

Jake nodded, his face grim. "You just go get Zeke."

Jake tiptoed quietly into the guest room where Carmen lay sleeping. Nodding a mute greeting to Rosa, he approached the bed and stared down at the woman who was all the mother he could remember or ever have wanted. She looked awful. Even in sleep, her age-lined face was twisted in pain, and more pale than he'd ever seen it. Her hair was more gray than black now, just in the year since he'd last seen her. It was brushed back from her face in an untidy mass. Rosa, or someone, had washed her and dressed her in a clean night shift, and for this, at least, Jake was thankful.

His gaze shifted to her hands, wrapped in layers of cloth and laid stiffly at her sides. Beneath the thin sheet, he supposed her feet had been likewise bound. Gill had said the doctor had been here to treat her.

Just now it was her breathing, so harsh and labored, that bothered Jake. Her wheezing filled the room. Only once in his life had Jake heard such a sound. Though he had shoved the memory far back in his mind, suddenly it came clear to him. This was how his real mother had sounded just before she died. It had scared him then, when he was seven, and it scared him even more now, twenty long years later. He closed his eyes against it, fighting for control.

"Dear God, I don't want to lose you, Mamacita," he prayed softly.

"Jake." The sound was thin, raspy, yet he heard and opened his eyes to see her looking up at him dazedly.

"I'm here, Mama," he assured her. "I'm home, and I'll take care of everything."

"Your papa?" she asked, then went into a fit of coughing that brought Rosa rushing to the bedside.

Catching Jake's eye, Rosa frowned and shook her head. Jake knew what she was trying to tell him. Carmen had yet to be told of Roy's death.

When the coughing spell passed, Carmen lay exhausted on her pillows, which had been piled high beneath her head to ease her difficulty in breathing. Quickly, Jake bent and kissed her cheek. "Everything else is being seen to, Mamacita. You just concentrate on getting well. Don't worry about anything."

"'Toria?" she wheezed pitifully.

"She's coming. Rest easy. She'll be here soon," Jake promised. *Or I'll know the reason why*, he added to himself with a deep frown.

Jake awoke to a tapping on his bedroom door. Wrapping the sheet about him, he rose and went to answer it. Rosa stood just outside, a worried look on her face. "Señor Jacob, I hate to disturb you, but Zeke has just returned from the convent. As you told him to do, he insisted upon speaking with Señorita Tori personally, and to give her the note you sent. He says they refused to let him see her. They took the message, but would not call her to speak with him. I know he was supposed to try to bring her home with him. He is very upset that he has failed you, but it could not be helped. What are we to do?"

Jake rubbed his eyes and tried to come awake. "I'll take care of it, Rosa. Tell Zeke I know none of this is his fault. He tried. I guess I'm just going to have to take the bull by the horns and go there myself to find out what the problem is."

Stifling a huge yawn, he asked, "What time is it? How is Carmen?"

"It is a little past noon," she said, confirming his suspicions that he had gotten very little rest. "Señora Carmen is resting a little better. I think she is not so fretful now that you are home to take care of things. She knows that you will bring Tori home to her."

Jake's face hardened in determination. "She'll be home before supper, Rosa. I can guarantee it."

"Will you see the doctor before going to get Señorita Tori?" the woman asked. "He is due to come soon, and I know you wish to speak with him."

Jake nodded. "Yes, Rosa. I'll talk with him before I go."

Doc Green was not very optimistic. As Gill had said, he was surprised that Carmen had lived this long. "I can't begin to predict what might happen from here," he told Jake. "It can go either way, I suppose."

"How are her burns?" Jake asked.

"I've seen worse, but any burn is serious, especially when it covers a large area. Carmen is fortunate she did not burn more of herself. Her night shift caught fire and burned the lower part of one leg, but one of your ranch hands caught it and managed to douse the cloth before it did further damage. Her hands might heal the best, though you never can tell about these things. They may never be the same as before; if the skin heals too tightly and doesn't want to stretch with movement, she may have limited use of them in the future."

"And her feet?" Jake questioned worriedly.

The doctor shook his head. "I just don't know. If the injuries don't putrefy, she'll be one very lucky woman."

"And if they do?" Jake knew the answer before the doctor gave it.

"Then I'll have to amputate."

The very thought made Jake sick. "You've told Rosa what to do for her? How to treat the burns?"

Doc Green nodded. "And I've given her something to ease Carmen's pain. It's not the burns that worry me just now, though. It's Carmen's lungs. They've weakened from all the smoke she inhaled. In short, she has literally singed her lungs from the inside, breathing all that hot, smoky air. I can't say if they will be able to heal themselves or not. We will just have to wait and hope for the best."

"There isn't anything you can do for this?"

"Not a damned thing, I'm sorry to say. I'm just a country doctor, Mr. Banner, but in all my years, I've never heard of or read of any sort of cure for this type of thing. Sometimes nature just has to take over and let the body heal itself, if the patient is strong enough?"

"And do you think she's strong enough?"

"That is a question only time and God can answer, but I would advise not telling her about her husband's death for as long as you can, unless she becomes so agitated that it is upsetting her more not knowing. The longer you can avoid it, the stronger she will be when you finally do tell her—hopefully. If the worst happens, she'll know he's gone when she sees him in the hereafter."

"Yeah," Jake muttered. "If the two of them happen to end up in the same place." It was an irreverent thing to think, let alone say, but Jake wasn't sure his father had been good enough to make it to heaven. Carmen, he was certain, would spend her eternity with the angels.

"And try to get her daughter home," the doctor added. "It will ease Carmen's mind a good deal to have her near."

It was mid-afternoon when Jake rang the bell outside the convent walls. He rang it three times, with increasing force, before a middle-aged nun finally arrived to answer his summons. Trying to hold tightly to his swiftly rising temper, Jake stated firmly to the white face looking out at him from the small square hole in the gate, "I'm here to see Victoria Fernandez."

"I am sorry, sir, but our novitiates are not allowed to speak with anyone from the outside," the sister told him.

"She's my stepsister, and I've got to talk to her," Jake replied. "Her mother is badly injured and may be dying. She is asking for Victoria, and I mean to see that her wish is fulfilled."

"I am sorry," the nun repeated. "Sister Esperanza cannot leave the convent. It is against the rules."

Jake was fuming inwardly, but tried not to show it. "Is this why she hasn't answered any of our urgent messages?" he questioned.

A queer look crossed the sister's face. "I cannot say, sir," she answered softly.

Jake had had enough. "Open this gate," he ordered quietly, his tone quite mild, though firm.

"I cannot do that, sir."

"You'll do it or I'll bust the blasted thing down," he informed her, the dark glint in his gold eyes telling her he meant what he said.

"Please, sir," the woman said, her wary eyes wandering from his face, noting the gun tied down on his thigh. A flicker of fear crossed her features. "We want no trouble. We strive for peace here."

"You'll get more trouble than you've ever imagined if you don't open this gate immediately," he promised.

She hesitated, and he saw her chewing her

lip in indecision. Finally she offered, "If you will wait here, I will speak to the Mother Superior about your request. If she says you may enter, I will return to let you in."

"You do that," he said. "And if you're not back in five minutes, I'm letting myself in, invited or not, so you'd better hightail it. Do I make myself clear?"

"Perfectly, sir."

Evidently she had impressed his adamance on the Mother Superior, because the same nun was back in less than the required time. After opening the gate, she stammered with false bravery, "I must ask you to remove your gun, sir, and leave it here at the gate."

To Jake, this was tantamount to asking him to remove his arm. For the past seven years he had lived by this gun. He made his living with it, and he was never without it. Even when he slept, it was within easy reach. After all this time it was almost a part of him, like a third hand, and he would have felt naked without it. The suggestion that he remove it now irritated him, and he glowered. "No, ma'am. Where I go, it goes."

"Then I'm afraid . . ."

Jake cut her off. "No need to be afraid, Sister. As soon as I collect Tori, we'll be on our way, and you can go back to your prayers and such."

With an apprehensive frown, she turned to lead the way, instructing him in a slightly wavering tone, "Follow me, please. The Mother Superior will speak with you now."

Mother Superior was waiting, and quite prepared to meet him head on. This was her territory, and she ruled it with all the supreme control and regal dignity of royalty. "Sister Sarah has informed me that you wish to speak with Sister Esperanza," she said by way of greeting, indicating that he might sit in her presence.

She waited until he seated himself before continuing. "We have strict rules forbidding this. I hope you will understand that I must deny your request, though I quite sympathize with your circumstances. I was very distressed to hear that Mrs. Banner is so ill."

"I imagine Victoria is pretty upset herself," Jake said with a humorless smile, "especially since you seem to be refusing to let her come home when her mother lies next to death."

"Which is precisely why Sister Esperanza has not been told of this," the woman surprised him by saying. "Nothing of the outside world must interfere with her training at this stage of her instruction."

He sat there staring at her, aghast and unable to speak for several seconds. Then he came up out of his chair with an exclamation that made the poor Mother Superior's face turn red. "Do you mean to tell me that Tori knows nothing at all about what's happened to her family? Is this why she hasn't rushed to her mother's side to comfort her? Is this why she's answered none of our summons, didn't even attend my father's burial?" he shouted. "Damn it all, woman! We're her family!"

"No," the nun replied quietly, regaining her composure. "You are wrong. Now that Sister Esperanza is with us here, we are her family, her sisters in Christ."

Jake gritted his teeth in the face of such calm opposition. "Lady, you are tryin' my patience and my temper to their limits," he grated out. "I understand your stupid rules, and maybe under other circumstances I'd be willing to abide by them, but I've promised her mother that I'll bring Tori home. If you have any compassion in you at all, you'll grant Victoria leave to return home, either until her mother recovers or, God forbid, until she dies. Then Tori can come back if she wants."

"I'm sorry, sir . . ." the woman began.

"So am I," Jake interrupted tersely. He walked to the desk behind which the Mother Superior had sat, and leaned down to bring his face on a level with hers. "Let me put it to you this way. Either you bring Victoria to me now, and let her leave peaceably, or I'll find her myself, if I have to search every inch of this place."

"I cannot let you do that," she replied a bit breathlessly, her eyes straying to the gun tied low on his hip.

"You can't stop me," he intoned in the same soft manner. "Send for her."

She eyed him imploringly. "I can't."

"You mean you won't."

"It is one and the same, Mr. Banner. Please understand."

"Oh, I do. I just hope you understand." He straightened. "I don't suppose you'll tell me where I might find her in this rabbit's warren?"

The woman shook her head.

Jake shrugged. Then he marched from her office, heading with determined strides down the hallway in the opposite direction from the outside entrance. Fearing for her flock, the Mother Superior was fast on his heels. "Please! You mustn't do this!" she implored.

Jake did not reply. He merely lengthened his stride, making it impossible for her to keep up with his pace without half-running. "Tori!" he hollered. "Victoria Fernandez!"

If he had been in any mood to appreciate it, Jake might have been amused that the further he went into the confines of the convent, the more followers he collected. The nuns hurried along behind him like so many penguins, and had he a flute, Jake could have been the Pied Piper of Hamelin.

The further he went, through the kitchen, the chapel, hall after winding hall, the more exasperated he became. To add to his problem, the sisters all dressed alike, all in black habits with either black or white head pieces, and he was forced to slow his pace in order to study individual faces. Of course, unless she was deliberately hiding herself; or unless she was beyond the sound of his voice, which was now booming and echoing off the bare walls; or unless Sister Sarah had been instructed to spirit her away, Victoria surely would recognize his voice and not ignore it. Where the devil was she?

Jake was reluctant to go out into the yards and gardens until he had searched every nook and cranny within the main building, for he felt sure that once he stepped outside the doors, they would promptly be shut and bolted behind him. He was about to search the sisters' private sleeping quarters on the upper level when he caught sight of Tori at last. On his way up a long, narrow flight of stairs, he saw her on the top landing. On hands and knees, a bucket at her side, she was diligently scrubbing the hard stone floor.

"Tori!" he bellowed. Startled, she whirled about on her knees and nearly tumbled headlong down the steps. Catching her balance, her big green eyes wide with surprise and disbelief, she exclaimed, "Jacob! What are you doing here?" Her puzzled gaze shifted to the entourage of sisters clambering up the stairs behind him, a grim-faced Mother Superior in the lead. "Oh, dear! Jacob! What have you done?"

Now towering over her, his legs braced wide, hands planted squarely on his hips, and looking very strong and tall as he scowled down at her, he commanded authoritatively, "Get your things together, Tori. I've come to take you home."

Chapter 2

Sinking back on her heels, Tori stared up at him with a dumbstruck expression. "You what?" she squeaked. Then, in total exasperation, she berated him. "Jacob Banner, have you lost your mind coming here and making such ridiculous demands? What on earth has possessed you?"

He merely stared down at her, unmoved and unmoving. "Do as I said, Tori," he directed.

"No, I most certainly will not! This is my home now, Jacob, and I have no desire to leave it. I thought I explained all this to you last summer. I thought you understood how I feel."

"Things have changed," he told her solemnly. "Something has happened."

She barely heard his words, her mind bent on convincing him. "You shouldn't be here, Jacob. It's against the rules."

"When I leave, you're comin' with me."

"That, too, is against the rules," she said, glaring at him.

"Damn the rules," he cursed, causing several sharp gasps behind him, and Tori to blush in embarrassment.

"Jacob! This is not the place for such talk!" she remonstrated sharply.

His scowl deepened, his gaze sweeping over her critically. "Will you please get up off your knees?" he snapped at her. "Just look at you! Your hands are nearly raw from scrubbing, and I'm willin' to wager your knees are even worse! Is this what you came here for, Tori? To labor away washin' floors and walls and stairs like a charwoman? If this is what it takes to make you happy, we'll gladly put you to better use at home."

Were it not for so many eyes and ears taking in every word, Tori would have screeched at him. Instead, she eyed him with as much dignity as she could manage in the circumstances. "I'm here to learn piety and humility, and this is a part of my training, Jacob. If you don't care to see me on my knees, then I suggest you depart immediately."

His patience at an end, he reached down

and jerked her to her feet. Through his teeth, he muttered darkly, "Pack what you need to bring with you, Tori, or leave it behind. Either way, we are leaving—together! You're needed at home."

Wrenching her arm from his grasp, she glared openly at him now. "You are not my keeper, Jacob!" she hissed.

"That remains to be seen," he countered smoothly. "Now, are you comin' nicely, or do I have to carry you out of here over my shoulder?"

"You wouldn't dare!"

"Wouldn't I?" Quick as a striking snake, he grabbed her and tossed her head-first over one broad shoulder and started swiftly down the stairs. "Your mother needs you. She's been askin' for you."

"I don't believe you," she panted, her ribs knocking hard against him with each step. She closed her eyes against the dizziness that assailed her. "Mother understands. Unlike you, she accepts my choice. Why, after all this time, would she ask for me?"

Pushing his way through a sea of black robes, he answered, "She's sick, Tori. Very sick."

Tori went deathly quiet. "Jacob?" she said in a tiny, frightened voice. "Put me down, please."

He did so immediately, drawing her about

to face him as he eyed her somberly. Large green eyes searched his face, mutely asking what she did not want to put into words.

His hands stayed about her arms, not to detain her, but to offer support as he announced quietly, "She may be dyin', Tori. I didn't want to tell you this way, believe me. I wish there was some easier way."

"Oh, dear heaven!" She clung to him now of her own accord. "What happened?"

"There was a fire. Carmen was burned, and the doctor is very worried about the condition of her lungs. She breathed in a lot of smoke."

Tori closed her eyes tightly, as if to shut out his words. Tears crept from between her clamped lids to stream down her face. Pitiful mewling sounds came from her throat. Drawing her close, Jake folded his arms about her shaking body, both of them now totally unconcerned with the watching crowd of sisters, many of whom were openly sharing Tori's grief.

"Cry, little angel face," he crooned, unconsciously using his old pet name for her. "Cry it all out."

One by one, quietly and unobtrusively, the sisters melted away until only the Mother Superior was left to witness their sorrow. At length, when Tori had calmed somewhat, Jake said uneasily, "There's more, Tori."

She nodded, her face still hidden against his

chest. "Tell me," she requested, bracing herself against him.

"Dad's dead. He died in the fire."

"Oh, God, Jacob!" she wailed. "I'm sorry! I'm so sorry!"

"So am I, darlin'," he admitted softly. "More than I ever thought I would be."

"You loved him," she choked out. "As much as the two of you fought, I know you loved him as dearly as I did. And he loved you, whether you believe it or not."

"Yeah, I reckon he did, in his own way," Jake conceded sadly.

It was several minutes more before they became aware of the Mother Superior standing quietly to one side, waiting. Drawing the tearful girl into her own embrace, she offered her condolences. Then she asked with a resigned sigh, "I suppose you will be going now, Sister Esperanza?"

Tori nodded. "Yes, Mother. I'm sorry, but I must go home."

Giving her young novice a gentle smile, the woman said, "Come back to us, little sister. Our love goes with you, until you can return to the fold."

If Tori was stunned to learn that the fire had occurred more than a week before, and her fellow sisters had willfully withheld the news from her, she was even more shocked upon seeing her dear mother for the first time in almost two years. She gazed in tearful distress at the pale, pain-racked face framed by lank gray hair. Could this truly be her mother, the woman who had always been so robust, so unfailingly energetic and cheerful? When had her beautiful dark hair turned so gray? Was it just the pain that creased her face so, or had the years begun to add lines of age to her beloved features?

"Oh, Mama!" she breathed. At the sound of her daughter's voice, Carmen stirred and murmured, "'Toria," but she did not waken. Her eyes swimming with tears, Tori pulled a chair close to the bedside. "I'll sit with her," she whispered to Rosa, who stood looking on.

Rosa nodded and crept from the room. Jake stayed, standing unnoticed in the doorway, gazing longingly at mother and daughter, his heart in his eyes. After a while, he said softly, "I'm glad you're home, Tori. If anyone can give her the will to live through this, it'll be you."

For two long days, Tori kept a constant vigil at her mother's bedside, rarely leaving the room for even long enough to eat; most of the time she asked Rosa to bring her a light tray in the sickroom, where she would barely nibble at the food provided her. She slept in a chair next to the bed, ignoring the discomfort of aching neck and back. Jake lost count of the number of times he would check on Carmen and find Tori on her knees in prayer. He put up with it as long as he could, and then he put his foot down.

On the morning of the third day, he entered Carmen's room and announced to a bleary-eyed Victoria. "Beginnin' now, you'll eat all your meals at the table, Tori. I've told Rosa not to bring you any more trays." Walking to where she sat slumped in her chair, he took her arm and pulled her to her feet, leading her toward the door.

Stumbling, Tori tried in vain to pull from his firm grip, but she was so weary that her efforts were puny at best. "Jacob, I can't leave her!" she cried out softly, not wishing to wake her mother, who had suffered a restless night.

"She'll be fine," Jake assured her. "Rosa'll watch over her while you eat and get some rest—in your own room, in your own bed," he added. He guided her into a chair before a plate full of steaming eggs and bacon. "Eat," he commanded.

When she sat dumbly, almost too tired to comprehend, he placed the fork in her trembling fingers and repeated, "Eat, Tori. If you keep on the way you have been, you'll be too sick to tend to your mother. You're so thin your bones are about to poke through your skin, and the hollows under your eyes are not becomin' to you. It's a wonder you don't scare

Carmen witless when she sees you. You're startin' to resemble a vulture hoverin' over the sickbed."

Tori grimaced at his description. "Such flattery, brother dear! It's no wonder you haven't married yet, if you spout such flowery compliments for all the ladies."

He returned her look with a wry grin. "In my profession, I don't have much to do with real ladies, Tori. Usually they draw their skirts aside and turn their delicate noses up if they actually do notice me, and they're more likely to swoon in fear than at the sight of my handsome face. Gunfighters don't often appeal to genteel women. Still, I've managed to turn more than one interested head in my time."

Giving a disdainful sniff, she said, "Painted ladies, no doubt. The sort that want to be paid for their time and affection."

Jake's grin widened devilishly. "Jealous, pet?" he taunted. "If you'd get rid of that ugly, shapeless black sack you call a habit, you could attract a man's eye again pretty easily, even without painting your face. Lord knows, all you'd have to do is bat those long eyelashes at him and he'd stumble all over himself to please you. It's beyond me why you want to hide yourself away in some dreary convent when you could have a husband and children of your own."

With a sigh, Tori set her fork aside. "Jacob, we've been through all this before. I'm content with the life I've chosen for myself. When you decided to go after Caroline's killers and avenge your sister's murder, I didn't condemn you for it. I didn't stand in judgment of you. Don't do so now with me, please."

"As I recall," Jake answered, thinking back to that dark time in his life, "you did your share of tryin' to talk me out of going, though. You cried and argued and threw a right proper fit."

"For all the good it did me," she pointed out. "Off you rode, paying no heed to any of us. Dad ranted and raved for a solid month after you were gone, and Mama always had tears in her eyes and a prayer for you on her lips. It was miserable around here. I felt as if I was walking on eggshells half the time, and we worried continually about you. We were sure we were going to be notified of your death at any moment. With poor Caroline and her family barely cold in their graves, it was quite a burden for us."

Grimly, Jake replaced the fork in her hand and motioned for her to eat. "I had to go, Tori. I know it was hard for you to understand then, being so young. What were you, eleven then?"

"Yes," she concurred, "and I knew why you went. If I had been a man, I would have gone with you. I loved Caro too, you know, but I loved you more, and I was so afraid for you. You were only nineteen, and you were going after several killers who were much more experienced with guns than you were."

"I managed all right by myself," Jake said, his eyes darkening to the color of old gold as he recalled his first mission of revenge. Caroline, his older sister by two years, had been shot down in the street by a band of drunken, wild outlaws. She'd had her baby in her arms at the time, and when she'd fallen, the child's head had struck the boardwalk. Both had died. Stunned and enraged, Caroline's young husband, Charlie, had drawn his gun. Before he could fire, he had been shot by one of the gunmen. Three innocent people all senselessly met their deaths that day, one young family snuffed out in a matter of minutes.

After shooting up several Santa Fe stores and terrorizing the citizens in their drunken spree, the outlaws had promptly left town. The sheriff, who had been cowering behind his desk the entire time, hesitated to go after the rowdy band.

Jake had no such fears or doubts. He had ridden home, cradling the tiny baby's stiff little body in his arms, tears racing unashamedly down his face as he led a horse with his sister's and brother-in-law's bodies tied across it. By that evening, his bedroll and provisions were packed, his horse saddled, and his gun strapped on. Deaf to the frantic pleas of his stepmother and young stepsister, and to the harsh admonitions and threats of his father, he had gone after the desperados, murder in his heart.

That had been the beginning of his profession as a gunfighter, seven long and lonely years ago. Since then he had honed his talents to perfection. The man who now sat across the table from Tori hardly resembled the laughing, carefree boy she had grown up with. Gone was the confusion of youth, replaced by a hard cynicism that put a cool glint in his golden eyes and a resolute set to his shadowed jaw. The brother she had known all her life was practically a stranger to her now.

Lost in her own thoughts of that terrible time, Tori sat staring at Jake, wondering how much of himself he had lost in the past several years. How many men had he killed? Jacob had never said whether or not he had managed to track and kill all of Caroline's murderers, and neither Tori nor her mother had ever dared to ask. In the time since, Jacob had returned to the ranch only twice, and the last time Tori had already entered the convent. She'd seen him for a few minutes that one day, and he'd spent much of their short time together trying to convince her to quit the convent, while she had tried to make him understand why she could not. She hoped he would not continue his arguments now, while she was home nursing her mother, but she knew he would not let the opportunity pass.

"Jacob," she said tentatively, knowing she was opening a subject best left closed, "I'll need more clothes if I am to stay with Mama. I only have this one habit with me. We were in such a hurry the other day, and my mind was in such a state that I didn't think to pack my things. Do you think you could send one of the ranch hands to the convent to collect some of my belongings?"

Hard golden eyes glared at her. "You have clothes in your room, Tori," he told her tersely. "Mama has kept most of your old things. Your wardrobe and dresser are the same as you left them."

A weary sigh shuddered through her, but she steeled herself for the argument ahead. "I can't wear my old dresses, Jacob. I must have my other habits. Will you send for them please?"

"No." One word, short and harsh, and war was declared between them.

"Then I'll ask one of the men myself," Tori responded, staring at him determinedly, though her voice remained soft and calm.

Jake shook his head. "No, you won't. Any man who goes against my orders won't be working for the Lazy B for long, and I don't think any of them are gonna risk losing a good job just to please you."

"They wouldn't risk the wrath of such a

formidable gunslinger, is what you really mean, isn't it, Jacob?" Her tone had a distinct bite to it now, her resentment overflowing.

Jake merely grinned and shrugged. "It amounts to the same thing, sweetheart."

"You are despicable, Jacob Banner! Well, your tactics won't work with me. I'll collect my own things from the convent."

"And leave your mother unattended?" he suggested with raised eyebrows.

At this she hesitated, then countered, "As you've said, Rosa will be here, and it's only a short ride. I can be there and back in a few hours."

"Forget it, Tori. You're not going back to that place anytime soon."

His smug tone irritated her all the more. "You can't stop me, Jacob."

"Can't I, angel face?" he taunted. For long minutes they glared stubbornly at one another, the seconds counted off by the loud ticks of the grandfather clock in the hall. "How old are you, Tori?" he asked conversationally, suddenly seeming to change the subject. "You'll be having another birthday soon, won't you?"

Tori frowned across the table at him, wondering what he was up to now. "Yes, I'll be eighteen the end of August."

Nodding, he said, "That's three months from now, little darlin'." He paused, the gleam in his golden eyes unholy. "Until then, according to Dad's will, I'm your legal guardi-an. I have full control over you and everything you do. Not to mention the fact that I have full control of your funds, including that plump little trust Dad set up for you, until you reach the age of twenty-one or marry, whichever comes first."

"Are you going to be around that long, Jacob?" she asked, giving him a sugar-and-vinegar look. "The only time you came back for long enough to hang your hat was when Dad had his stroke and Mama needed you to run the ranch. Then, as soon as Dad was well enough to take over again, you were off and running again, off to parts unknown, back to your guns and your glorious reputation as a big, bad gunslinger."

Jake glared at her across the tabletop. "You're still a razor-tongued little witch when the mood strikes you, aren't you?" Then he sent her a lopsided grin that set her insides tumbling. "Don't you fret, though. I'll be around long enough to cure you of that habit. A big, bad gunslinger like me ought to be able to handle a sassy-mouthed brat like you with one hand tied behind my back. Besides, things have changed now. Dad isn't here anymore. He's not going to get better this time and take charge of things again like before."

"Will that make the difference, Jacob? Is it just that Mama and the ranch need you full-time now, or is it the fact that Dad isn't here to ride you and yell at you about how he wants things done? Are you home to stay this time?"

With a lazy shrug, he covered the hurt her words brought him. There was a lot of truth to what she'd said. "Maybe. We'll see how things go. Now maybe I can try some of those ideas of mine that Dad never agreed with. As big as this ranch is, it was never big enough for the two of us."

"That's because each of you wanted your own way, and neither of you would give an inch."

"That's not entirely true, Tori," he reminded her. "You know how it was with us. All my life I tried my damnedest to measure up to what the old man expected of me, but it was never enough. No matter how hard I tried, it was never good enough for him. Christ!" he groaned disgustedly, "I could have walked on water and he would have complained because I didn't turn cartwheels, too!"

Tori winced. "Will you please not take the Lord's name in vain in my presence, Jacob. It's bad enough that you've dragged me home to begin with. Don't make it worse by cursing and carrying on."

He raised a dark eyebrow at her in that insolent manner of his. "Don't tell me you're not glad to be here, Tori, to see Carmen again, even as bad as things are now."

Nodding, she agreed. "I've missed Mama so

terribly these last couple of years. I hate seeing her like this, in such pain, but I love being near her again. It seems strange, though, with Dad gone," she added, tears shining in her eyes. "I miss him."

"So do I, pet," he sighed. "So do I."

"Is it just because of Dad that you didn't come home to stay sooner?" she asked. "If you would have given up that life of violence, he would have welcomed you back at any time, you know."

"You don't just *give up* being a gunfighter, Tori," he said, shaking his head at her naivete. "You don't just go home and hang up your guns and have everything be the way it was before. Folks just won't let you, no matter how badly you might want to. You make a lot of enemies along the way, and those you don't kill will dog you for the rest of your life. Your reputation clings like a dirty shadow, following wherever you go, and you can't shake it no matter what you do. There'll always be someone out there waiting to prove that he's faster on the draw, a better aim. There's always someone with a grudge to settle, an axe to grind. I wouldn't have to go out looking for danger, honey; it would find me soon enough. That's why I've hardly ever come back. I didn't want to endanger all of you."

"And now?"

"Now I've got no choice. I have to stay." He pinned her with his sharp golden gaze. "So do you, Tori. We both have our responsibilities to those who need us, to those we love. I'm warning you fairly, here and now. I'll do everything in my power to keep you from going back to that convent. You belong here, and I mean to see that you stay. I won't let you leave."

"You can't make me stay, Jacob," she told him, her chin jutting out defiantly. "Once Mama is well again, you can't keep me from going."

His smile was the most arrogant, devilish smirk she'd ever seen. "I can and I will, if I have to tie you to my side and watch you every minute of the day. You're home to stay, Tori, like it or not, so you'd better get used to the idea. With Dad gone, I run this ranch now, and everything on it, including you. My word is law here, and no one will dare help you. I'm your guardian, your keeper, your—"

Tori's face was livid, her cheeks blazing and her green eyes snapping. "You're a hateful, rotten devil!" she cried, interrupting him. "As much as you raved about Dad being a tyrant, you're twice as bad as he was at running other people's lives. You despised that about him, Jacob, yet you're fast becoming just like him, only worse!"

Had he not become so accustomed in past years to not showing his feelings, Jake would have visibly flinched at her angry words. Tori had hit him in a very vulnerable spot, and he knew she had done so deliberately. Comparing him to his father was one of the most hurtful things she could have done, especially now, with Roy so newly in his grave. Jake and his father had been at one another's throats for the better part of Jake's twenty-seven years, but just now he was grieving for the old man in a way that surprised him greatly. He had not yet worked through all these confusing and conflicting feelings that had assaulted him since Roy's death.

"That was uncalled for, Tori, and pretty damned small of you. If this is how they're teachin' you to behave at that convent, to be so spiteful and mean, then I'm sure it's not the proper place for you."

"You are the one being mean and hateful, Jacob!" All at once Tori was much too tired for this. The past few days had been almost more than she could bear. Her mother lay deathly ill in the other room, and Tori was worried sick for her. She had not yet felt strong enough to confront her grief over Roy's death, the man who had been a father to her all her life, since her mother had married him when Tori was just a few months old. Her heart ached for Jacob and the pain she knew he, too, must be feeling. She felt betrayed by her sisters at the convent, that they would keep such momentous news from her. In the past sixty hours she'd had little sleep, and everything was such a tangle in her mind, in her heart. Now to have this insane argument with Jacob! It was just too much!

The first loud sob caught them both unaware. It was quickly followed by several more, and try as she might, Tori could not stop them. They tore from her throat in raw, ragged bursts as hot tears burned salty paths down her face. She sat staring helplessly at Jake, horrified that she could not control the emotions tearing through her.

Then he was kneeling beside her chair, and her arms reached out to him, seeking the comfort she had always found there. Gathering her into his arms, he carried her swiftly down the hallway to her bedroom. Seated on the edge of her bed, he cradled her to him, rocking her to and fro as they shared their misery.

"Oh, Jacob, it hurts! It hurts so much!" she sobbed, burying her face in his neck, seeking his strength for her own.

"I know, angel. I know," he croaked hoarsely, tears thickening his own throat. His arms tightened convulsively about her as they clung together.

Some time later, when her crying had eased to an occasional shaky sob, he eased her back onto her pillows. With shaking hands, he wiped the tears from her face, gazing tenderly down into her swollen, red-rimmed eyes. "Sleep for a while, Tori," he said, placing a gentle kiss on each of her eyelids and watching them close.

On a deep, weary breath, she implored softly, sleepily, "Don't be so mean and angry, Jacob. It hurts me when you are angry with me. I love you."

Had her eyes been open, she would have seen the pain her simple words caused him, she would have seen him wince as if struck. "I love you, too, angel face," he told her. "I don't want to cause you pain, ever, but I think I'm bound to. I don't think there's any way to avoid it." Unable to stop himself, he leaned down and kissed the last shimmering droplets of tears from her lush lashes. Already she was deeply asleep.

"Oh, Tori," he sighed, looking down at her. "What am I gonna do about you? What am I supposed to do about my feelings for you? You say you love me, but I know you're talkin' about the love a sister feels for her brother. But I'm not really your brother, you know, not by blood. How will you feel when you learn that I don't love you in a brotherly way anymore, that I love you the way a man loves a woman, that I have for a long time now?"

Dragging a weary hand over his face, he whispered softly, "I hope you don't come to despise me, little angel. I need your love so damned much that I think it'd kill me if you ever came to hate me. You, my innocent little nun, are my greatest weakness. This might be my last chance to save us both from disaster, love, and I'd be a fool to let it pass."

Gently he reached out to remove the heavily starched white veil from her head, careful not to awaken her. The sight of her shorn hair, though he had been expecting it, still came as a shock to him, and he drew in a sharp breath of dismay. Her long, silken tresses were gone, replaced by a sleek cap of dark brown hair nearly as short as his own. Pain twisted in his stomach as he ran his fingers through the uneven lengths that layered her head. If they had severed her arms, he could not have felt worse, for to his mind they had deliberately mutilated her, destroying something fine and beautiful in his world. "Damn them for doing this to you!" he cursed quietly.

His original intent had been to make her more comfortable, so that she might rest better. The sight of her chopped hair made him angry. Then, when he could not easily remove the heavy, ugly button-up shoes, his temper frayed further. Too infuriated to search for a button hook, he drew the knife from his boot top and proceeded to slice the offending shoes from her feet. Next came the hot woolen stockings, much too warm and uncomfortable to be worn this late in the New Mexican spring weather.

Standing back, Jake debated his next move for just a moment, arguing with a conscience he was surprised to find he still possessed. "Oh, what the hell!" he muttered finally. "I might as well be hanged for a wolf as for a lamb, I suppose."

Chapter 3

While Rosa and Ana, another of the maids, took turns tending to Carmen, Tori slept around the clock and then some. Jake had ordered that she not be disturbed, that she be allowed to awaken when her body was ready. She did so slowly and groggily, her mind and body reluctant to face the trials she subconsciously knew awaited her. Finally, as her eyelids drifted lazily open after several jaw-popping yawns, she realized that she was in her own bed in her old room. It took a few moments to recall how she came to be here, and several more to recognize the fact that, beneath the thin sheet, she was completely naked!

Suddenly wide awake, Tori pondered this. Couldn't Rosa find her nightgown after undressing her? Or had the woman merely been afraid she would awaken her if she tried to put the night dress on her? Tori shrugged. It really didn't matter that much, she supposed, and it did feel sinfully delicious to wake up so unhindered by yards of cloth that tended to bind about her as she slept.

When she failed to find her habit, Tori assumed that Rosa was having it laundered for her, and she blessed the woman for her thoughtfulness. "I really have to try to find a way to lighten Rosa's workload," she thought to herself. "She is so devoted to us; such a warm, wonderful person."

It felt strange, indeed, to be dressed in something light and colorful after nearly two years in a heavy black habit. Though she had chosen the least colorful garment in her closet, a simple green dress she used to wear to garden in, she still felt as light as a feather in it, as if she might fly away at any moment. It also felt distinctly odd to have her head uncovered, to feel neither the weight of her veil nor that of her hair upon her shoulders. Searching through her dresser drawers, Tori finally found a shawl to drape over her head in place of her missing veil. Feeling a bit more comfortable, she ventured out of her room.

She found Rosa just coming out of Carmen's room. "How is Mama?" she whispered, poking her head inside the room and seeing that her mother was asleep.

"Señora Carmen is resting well this morning, Señorita Tori. The doctor will be pleased to hear of this, I think."

"Good. Thank you for watching over her while I slept. I will sit with her now."

"Oh, no, Señorita Tori. Ana is just putting the noon meal on the table, and Señor Jacob will have our heads if you do not sit down and eat. It has been more than a day since you have had any food. You must eat, and then you will sit with your mama."

Staring at the woman in astonishment, Tori echoed, "A day? I slept for an entire day?"

"*Sí*. You were ready to faint, I think, if Señor Jacob had not made you rest. You must take better care of yourself, *niña*, or you will be of little use to your mother."

"Yes, yes," Tori agreed vaguely. "You are right, Rosa." She reached out and gave the kindly woman a hug. "You take such good care of us, and you must be tired from all the extra work of nursing Mama. I can't thank you enough, but I'll say an extra prayer just for you."

Rosa blushed with pleasure. "*Gracias*."

Starting toward the dining room, Tori suddenly recalled her missing clothes. "Oh, Rosa! I hate to be a bother, but could you let me know as soon as my habit is ready for me again? I really can't go around in these clothes for long."

"Your habit?" Rosa asked with a frown.

"Yes, and I couldn't find my shoes this morning either. What did you do with them?"

"Señorita Tori, I know nothing of your shoes or your clothes," Rosa said, shaking her head confusedly.

Tori froze, an awful thought taking hold in her head. "Didn't you undress me?" she asked the other woman in a small, hesitant voice.

"No, *niña*. I did not."

The two women stood staring at one another, the same thought racing through their minds. Two faces turned bright red.

"That snake!" Tori hissed, when at last she found her tongue. "That rotten, lousy snake!" As she stomped off to find Jake and confront him with his actions, all the careful training of the past two years fell away from her like a discarded cloak. Caught up in her anger, she gave no thought to prayers or turning the other cheek. Lost were all the teachings of the good sisters. Her voice was strident, not soft and quiet; her footsteps swift, not measured; her broiling emotions far from serene, her features not the least composed.

"Jacob! I'm going to murder you with your own gun!"

She found him sitting at the dinner table, a roguish grin etching his mouth. "Problems, Tori?" he asked mockingly.

Trembling with anger, she could hardly speak. When she could, she shrieked at him. "I want my habit, Jacob, and I want it now!"

"Nun's garb for a screeching shrew? Nope, I just don't think so. I see the good sisters didn't have much luck taming your temper."

"You beast! You undressed me!"

Managing a nonchalant shrug, he said simply, "So? It sure wasn't the first time, and I doubt it'll be the last. I was only makin' you more comfortable."

"And getting an eyeful in the process! Don't you have an ounce of respect for my privacy, Jacob? Have you no shame?"

"Very little," he answered, chuckling at her embarrassment.

"How dare you do such a thing!" she ranted.

"Why are you making such a big deal of it, Tori? I used to change your diapers. Besides, it certainly isn't the first time I've seen a naked woman, and just a few years ago you had quite a habit of shuckin' all your clothes for a cool dip in the river. Dad tanned your hide many a time for that, if you recall."

"That was different. I was a child then, and now I am a woman."

"So I noticed," he concurred wryly.

"You are lower than a snake's belly in a wagon rut! I ought to scratch your eyes out!"

"You can try, little one. You can try, for all the good it will do you."

Hands balled into tight fists at her sides, she literally shook with impotent fury. Blast him for being so calm about this! And so darned superior! Both of them knew her threats carried little weight. Next to Jacob, Tori looked like a starving orphan. She stood no taller than his chin, and was a good seventy-five pounds lighter than he. Over the years, as they were growing up, Tori had lost count of the times she had prayed to be his size for just five minutes so she could beat the tar out of him! Now was one of those moments!

Drawing deep breaths, Tori struggled to rein in her temper. As she began to collect her senses once more, she was aghast at how easily she had lost control of herself. What would her sisters at the convent think if they could see her now? And Mother Superior would have been shocked and dismayed! How shameful! Tori grimaced as she thought of her next confession and the penance this day's sins alone would bring. If she did not learn to control her temper and her tongue, she would be a lowly novitiate until her dying day!

Forcing herself to speak quietly, she said meekly, "I'm sorry I lost my temper with you, Jacob, but you must agree that it wasn't right for you to undress me. You must never do such a thing again, regardless of your good intentions." He met her gaze with a silent, steady look that baffled her. "If you'll please return my habit, I'd like to dress properly now."

"You look fine in what you have on," he answered. "Sort of drab, but better."

"My habit?" she repeated stubbornly.

"I got rid of it," he told her, calmly spearing a piece of meat from the plate before him.

"You did what?" she screamed.

"Don't fret yourself over that old rag, Tori. My God, I've seen old saddle blankets in better shape! Make do with what you have in your closet until we can get you some newer things. You have decent, pretty clothes to wear, so don't make such a fuss."

"Jacob, you can't do these things!" she groaned. "It's wrong! Do you have any idea how many hours of fasting and meditation you are causing me?"

"There won't be any fasting in this house, Tori," he assured her, gesturing toward her empty chair. "Sit down and eat before your meal gets cold. Then we'll see what we can do about that mess on your head that used to be hair. What in hell did they whack it with anyway, a dull machete? Your hair looks like something I've seen on the south end of a northbound goat!"

Her hands flew reflexively to the shawl that covered her head, and she blushed to the roots of her sheared strands, but she managed to say piously, "Vanity is a sin, Jacob."

"What the devil has vanity got to do with it, Tori? Your hair was a thing of beauty. Since when has beauty been evil? Is a sunset sinful? Is a newborn foal? What about the perfection of a summer rose or a shimmering rainbow?"

"That's different," she muttered, her brow furrowed in confusion.

"How? How's it different? It gave others joy to see your hair falling in dark waves about your shoulders, flowing like shining satin down your back or streaming out behind you as you raced along on your horse. And the feel of it slipping through my fingers like silk!" His eyes glowed like molten gold as they gazed into hers. "Do you remember how I used to brush it for you when you were little?" he asked softly, the seductive quality of his voice causing shivers to chase over her flesh. "I want to do that for you again. I want to run my fingers through your hair and watch it shimmer like a midnight waterfall, to see it flow gently across your breasts."

Unable to speak, Tori merely stared, her eyes lime green and wide in confusion. What was happening to her? Why was she reacting in this way to the mere sound of Jacob's voice? How was it that his eyes could hold hers captive and cause butterflies to take wing in her stomach with just a look? Why did her skin burn so, and her heart start to race?

Sensing her confusion, Jake hid a smile. Good. Tori was beginning to react to him as a man, though he suspected she did not realize the source of her inner turmoil as yet, and probably wouldn't like it when she did. More likely, she would fight it at first, thinking it wicked and forbidden. At least it was a start, a sign that she was not immune to his male charm, and that was enough to begin with. With careful timing and effort, things might work out between them yet.

Stepping out of her bath, Tori stood dripping on the towel. It felt good to just let her skin dry in the cool night air that drifted through her bedroom window. The day had been hot and tiring, despite all the sleep she'd had. She had sat for long hours at her mother's bedside, waiting for those rare moments when Carmen awoke and was lucid, praying for her and hurting for her when she cried out in pain.

The doctor had come again, and though he still cautioned them not to get their hopes up too high, he had seemed pleased that Carmen was doing as well as she was. He had left more ointment and pain medication, and more instructions on the patient's care and feeding. Now that Carmen was awake more often, she could begin to take in more liquids, so very necessary to someone who had been burned.

Carmen still had not been told of Roy's death, but with each passing hour it was becoming more difficult to hide the fact from her. They would be forced to reveal it to her soon, and Tori could only pray that her mother was strong enough to take the devastating news. It helped that both she and Jacob were home, for Carmen seemed calmed by their presence, much more willing to fight for her life, knowing they were home with her.

Even now, knowing what she did, Tori found it hard to believe that the sisters and Mother Superior had kept her mother's condition from her. If not for Jake and his overbearing insistence, she might still be at the convent, blissfully ignorant of the tragedies that had hit the Banner household, and her mother would still be crying out for her, wondering why her only daughter did not come to her in her need. A hundred times a day, Tori thanked God for Jacob's stubbornness. Not for anything in the world would she have her mother suffer so and not be here to comfort and care for her.

Though she tried to understand the strict rules that had forbidden messages from the outside world to be passed along to her in the convent, under such dire circumstances, with one's mother near death, keeping her uninformed seemed cruel and unfeeling. How could they have done such a thing? Carmen could have died calling out for her, never knowing that her daughter did not rush to her side because she knew nothing of the fire or her injuries, thinking perhaps that Tori did not care enough to come, wondering how her loving daughter could ignore her so. And Roy had been dead and buried days before Tori had learned of his death.

It all seemed so unfair, and every time she

thought about it, Tori could not help the fierce anger that surged through her. She could not help the resentment she felt, though she prayed daily for the anger to leave her, that she might return to the convent without any ill feelings toward her sisters. It simply would not do to go back still holding a grudge in her heart, and Tori did still want to return once her mother was well again, regardless of Jake's threats.

For the past two years she had made her home there, and she cared deeply for her fellow nuns. She loved the quiet hours, the serene atmosphere, the loving fellowship. The peace she gained through prayer more than made up for long hours spent in kneeling. Aching back and knees were forgotten in the calm that filled her soul. Even penance and all the hard work were worth a single smile from one of the orphan children she helped to teach. This was what she had tried to explain to Jacob when she had spoken with him last summer, but somehow she had failed to make him understand. Perhaps during this time at home with him, she could convince him, but he seemed so determined to keep her here.

Reaching for her night shift, Tori caught a glimpse of herself in the long mirrors that fronted the doors of her wardrobe. It seemed strange to see her reflection in the various mirrors scattered about the house, since there were no mirrors at the convent. Now it caught her by surprise to see her own face looking back at her from the glass, to see not only her face, but her entire body, sleek and naked, reflected there.

She knew she should look away, but somehow she could not bring herself to do so. She was drawn closer, despite herself. A few small steps brought her even with the mirror, and she stared as if mesmerized. A smile crept over her lips as she saw her hair and recalled Jacob's diligent efforts with the scissors earlier that afternoon. Refusing to let Ana or Rosa help, he had tackled the chore himself, muttering and cursing under his breath all the while, but the result wasn't bad at all. At least now her hair was evenly cut, instead of all jagged edges poking out in every direction— but goodness, was it short!

Now freshly washed and nearly dry, her hair curled softly about her head in a short bob. Left uncovered, without the weight of the heavy veil, it was not matted down to her skull, but light and fluffy, like the puffy fur of a fat puppy she'd had as a child. It framed her small oval face, making her eyes seem larger and brighter than ever.

Of their own, her eyes now strayed to her nude form, and a rosy blush tinted her flesh. It had been months since she had surveyed her own body this way, and as she did so now, it was with an odd excitement and embarrassment. This was what Jacob had seen when he had undressed her last night. What had he thought of her body, now that she was no longer a child but a full-grown woman? Had her breasts seemed small to him, compared to those of other women he had seen? Were her legs too short, her knees too rough? Did he think she had ugly feet or fat ankles? Had the sight of her body pleased him at all?

It was hard to judge one's own body critically, but she tried to do so now. A frown creased her brow as she saw how thin and pale she was. Gone was the soft golden glow her skin used to have, for it had been months since her flesh had last felt the warm kiss of sunshine upon it. Though her hips were still gently curved, and her waist as tiny as ever, her breasts did seem smaller. She had lost weight, her arms and legs were too thin, her ribcage too bony. Even the bones in her face stood out sharply, with hollows beneath her cheekbones and dark bruises beneath her eyes. The skin on her elbows and knees was rough, her hands no longer smooth but red and worn.

With a mind of their own, it seemed, her hands caressed the long line of her throat, weaving a path to her breasts, where they stopped. It was as if she stood outside herself, watching a stranger in the mirror, seeing the other woman's dusky nipples rise as slender fingers brushed lightly over them. But it was she who felt a gathering within herself as she wondered what it might feel like to have a man's hands upon her body, Jacob's hands touching her there.

As if in a dream, her hands drifted over her quivering stomach and across the curve of her hips, ventured to the soft inner flesh of her thighs. She was trembling now, and feverish as she envisioned Jacob's large, dark hands upon her pale skin. Would he delight in the velvet feel of her soft, warm flesh? Would she find pleasure in his touch? Would he be . . .

Abruptly, Tori came to herself. What in heaven's name was she doing? What was she thinking, to allow such ideas to enter her mind? Her hands flew to her flaming cheeks in dismay as shame at her behavior washed through her, drowning her in self-recrimination. In a fit of denial, she forced her eyes back to the figure in the mirror, striving to view it realistically once more, faults and all; trying to convince herself that no man, and certainly not Jacob, would find anything pleasing in what she saw there, and that this thought did not bother her in the least.

"This must be one of the reasons why there are no mirrors at the convent," Tori murmured sternly, "so we won't have to confront our own ugliness and shortcomings. We won't know how pale and thin we become, so we won't care. And the veils must be to disguise from one another these horrible haircuts, so we don't frighten each other as we pass in the halls, or catch a stray glimpse of ourselves in the shiny bottom of a cooking pot and realize how awfully homely we are."

"You're far from homely, pet."

That deep, familiar voice seemed to echo through her bedroom as Tori spun about to find her stepbrother standing just inside her room. With a startled cry of mortification, she grabbed for her night shift, holding it before her to hide her body from his glowing golden eyes. Jacob shoved the door shut behind him, closing the two of them in a room that seemed to shrink in size with his presence. "You've got a beautiful body, Tori, and a face so lovely that angels must envy you."

Finding her tongue at last, Tori gasped out, "Jacob! How long have you been standing there?"

His heated gaze traveled the length of her body before he answered with a lazy drawl, "Long enough."

"Wha . . . what do you want?" she stammered, thoroughly disconcerted by his assessing gaze and the caressing tone of his voice.

"You," he told her bluntly. "I want you, Tori, but not until you want me too, just as much."

"Don't say such things, Jacob!" she gasped, her entire body trembling violently now, her fingers shaking so badly she could scarcely retain her hold on the gown that shielded her quivering body from his view. "Please! It's sinful! You mustn't even think such things!"

One dark eyebrow cocked upward as he answered softly, "Why not, angel? You were. I watched you touching yourself, thinking of me as you did. You were wondering what my hands would feel like on your body."

"No!" she screamed, denying his words. "No!"

"Oh, yes, my little liar. That look in your eyes was a woman dreamin' of her lover's touch."

"You're wrong! How could I think of you that way? You are my brother, Jacob! To even consider such a thing is evil!"

"But I'm not your brother, Tori, so there's nothing wrong in it. There's no blood between us. There's no guilt in your wanting me, or in me desirin' you. Lightning won't instantly strike us dead. Our souls won't be condemned to everlastin' hell by our being attracted to one another."

"But you are my brother," she said shakily. "I've always thought of you as my brother! I always will."

He shook his head slowly. "I don't think so, love. Deny it all you want, but we both know better, and the sooner you face it, the happier you'll be. Don't eat yourself alive with guilt, darlin', over somethin' as good and natural as desirin' a man, and especially if that man is me."

Suddenly he grinned. "And for heaven's sake, don't heap imaginary sins on yourself.

As it is, you've told enough lies just in the last five minutes to make your Mother Superior wring her hands raw."

Closing her eyes, she begged, "Please, Jacob. You're wrong. Don't do this to me. It's insane, and I don't want to discuss it any further. Just leave me alone."

"All right," he conceded easily, so easily that her eyes popped open again in surprise. "We'll talk about it again later."

"No we won't. I refuse to hear another word from you about this."

"We'll talk later," he repeated. "In the meanwhile, sleep sweet and dream of me, Tori." He had his hand on the doorknob when he grinned again and nodded toward the mirror behind her. "By the way, your front side might have been covered, but I've had a delightful view of your backside this whole time. Very encitin', pet, and most distracting!"

Tori inhaled sharply as his parting words shot flames of acute embarrassment through her. With an angry shriek, she grabbed the nearest object, which just happened to be the hand mirror on her dressing table, and hurled it at his dark head. It smashed into slivers against the hastily closed door, making a satisfying crash but missing her target. His mocking laughter floated back to her, grating on raw nerves.

Furious and totally humiliated, Tori stared

dumbly at the shards of glass at the base of her door. Hot tears raced down her cheeks. "Damn you, Jacob Banner!" she cursed recklessly. "Now look what you've made me do! As if I don't have enough problems already, now I have seven years of bad luck to look forward to!"

Chapter
4

Tori was deliberately ignoring him. Jake knew it, and for a while it amused him. It was a sign that she was disturbed by him, but after two whole days, his humor was fast waning.

If he had known the extent to which he was confusing Tori, Jake would have been a good deal happier. Tori was in a dither, and she had no one to confide in, no one to help her sort her jumbled thoughts and feelings. Her mother was too ill to burden with such matters, even if Tori could have found a way to explain it.

She decided to ignore the whole dilemma for the time being, and that meant staying as far from Jacob as she could manage. During the day, and often during the evening, she sat with her mother, barely seeing Jacob except at mealtimes. Then she spoke only when addressed, and tried desperately to keep her eyes on her plate. It seemed each time she dared to look at him, she met golden eyes full of knowing, masculine laughter. For the most part, she succeeded in ignoring his taunts and jibes, escaping to the solitude of her own room or to her mother's as soon as possible.

Still, they were living in the same house, and it was difficult not to run into him at odd times, and each time she did, her heart would leap into her throat and her pulse would begin to pound like a war drum. Her initial anger, which had sustained her through that first awkward breakfast with him the morning after he had walked in on her after her bath, soon waned beneath her own confusion.

Jacob wanted her. He had said so very bluntly, and there was no mistaking his meaning. He wanted her as a woman. But that was only a part of Tori's problem. Because of their confrontation, Tori was thinking more and more of Jacob as a man instead of a brother. She was suddenly seeing him through new eyes, and she wasn't sure she wanted to. It was so much simpler to think of him as her older brother, the one who had bandaged her knees when she was small, the one who had taught her to climb trees and to ride her first pony, the one toward whom she had taken her first faltering steps.

Now, to think of him as a man, to look at him and see the desire blazing in his eyes, was almost too bewildering. She didn't want this! She didn't! Over and over she told herself that if she ignored it, it would go away, like a bad dream. She had her life at the convent. She was content there. Why did Jacob have to come home now and ruin everything? Why did her breath catch in her throat and her hands begin to shake whenever he was near?

Why did everything have to change? A fire, a death, illness, and suddenly Tori's safe little world had been turned upside down and inside out, and she wasn't sure of anything anymore. If only she could turn the clock back a few short weeks! If only Jacob had not turned into a stranger before her eyes! She needed time to think, to sort things out in her mind. She needed her brother back again— her brother, her confidant, her teacher—only now he wanted to teach her vastly different things, things Tori was not at all sure she wanted to learn.

"Lookin' for somethin', love?"

Tori's head jerked up and she banged it hard on the lid of the heavy chest she was busily searching. "Ouch! Darn you, Jacob! Do you have to sneak up on a person like that?" His deep chuckle grated on already frayed nerves.

"Looks like you're the one sneakin' around, Tori. That's my trunk you're goin' through, and my room," he added as he glanced about at the half-open drawers of his dresser and the boxes pulled out from under the bed. "Find anything interestin', besides my longjohns?"

Her face blazed as red as a summer rose. "I couldn't care less about your clothing. I'm looking for my habit."

"Aw, shucks," he taunted, giving her a crooked grin. "And here I thought you were tryin' to find out if I wore a nightshirt."

"Aren't you supposed to be doing something outdoors?" she groused, rubbing the rising lump on the back of her head.

"I was just takin' a break and thought I'd look in on Carmen for a minute. If I'd known I'd catch you in my room, I'd of come in sooner."

"Well, you can just go right on out again."

In answer, he gave her a lewd wink. "Now, honey, don't go gettin' all embarrassed. Curiosity's a natural thing. All you had to do was ask, and I'd have told you I sleep in the raw. You didn't have to go to all this trouble lookin' through my things. Anything else you want to know?"

"Yes!" she hissed, her cheeks and neck on fire. She stood facing him, her hands balled into tight fists at her sides. "When did you become such a despicable snake? And where in blue blazes did you hide my habit?"

Shaking his head at her, he gave her that irritating grin again, his teeth flashing white in his deeply tanned face. "You'll never find it, sweetheart. But I'll give you this, for a small ransom." From the pocket of his shirt he drew her rosary, dangling it before her.

When she reached for it, he held it just beyond her reach. "Uh-uh, sugar. First you have to pay the price."

Suspicion clouded her face as she glared up at him. "What price?"

"A kiss."

"A kiss?" she echoed stupidly, her heart beginning to hammer against her ribs.

"Yeah," he chuckled, eyeing her with open amusement. "Don't tell me you've forgotten what a kiss is. First you pucker your lips and—"

"I know what a kiss is, Jacob!" she interrupted angrily.

On an exaggerated sigh, he said, "That's a relief! I was beginnin' to worry there for a minute what they might've done to your mind with all their holy teachin's in that convent."

"You are a sacrilegious beast!" she retorted.

"If I'm the Beast, you're the Beauty. Do you remember how the story goes? Beauty kissed the Beast, just like you're gonna have to kiss me if you want your prayer beads back."

Her legs felt like overcooked noodles as she stood staring up at him, but she held her ground. Finally, knowing he was not about to barter with her, she said meekly, "You win, Jacob. A kiss. One kiss."

Before she lost her shaky courage, she reached up to plant a quick, sisterly peck on his cheek. But Jake had read her intentions and immediately turned the tables on her. Before her pursed lips could touch the side of his face, he turned his head and swiftly captured her mouth with his own. His arms came about her, shackling her own helplessly to her sides.

A startled shriek was trapped in Tori's throat. For just a second, she tried to pull back from him, only to feel his strong fingers come up to clamp about her neck and hold her face to his. Then her knees were turning to heated jelly as his warm lips caressed hers, cajoling, teasing, tempting her in a way she had never dreamed possible. His features blurred dizzyingly, and her lashes drifted closed, bringing her remaining senses into play. Acrobats were turning somersaults in her stomach; she couldn't seem to catch her breath; there was a loud thumping in her ears. Vaguely, she recognized it as the frantic beating of her own heart.

The pressure of his lips forced hers apart, just slightly, but enough for Jake's tongue to slip between her teeth and into her mouth.

His tongue touched hers, and a flame ignited in her belly. A whimper escaped her; a shiver danced down her spine as his teeth nibbled lightly at her lower lip before settling back to claim her lips more fully. Desire clawed at her with wild fingers, wicked wonderful desire such as she'd never known, never even dreamed of.

Senses swimming, Tori surrendered herself fully to the strange new emotions assaulting her. Her knees gave way beneath her, allowing Jake to pull her more closely to him, and Tori felt as if her very bones were melting into his. Even through their layers of clothing, the heat of his body seared her, fanning the flames of her yearnings.

Jake felt her melting into him, yielding to him, as he guided her through her first real kiss. The tiny mewling sounds she made as his lips played over hers nearly drove him mad with longing. The first tentative venture of her tongue against his, those first novice movements of her untaught lips, sent his blood thrumming through his veins like wildfire in a dry forest. Through the years he'd had many women, most of them well-versed in the arts of pleasing a man, yet Tori's innocent lips now gave him more pleasure, more joy and spearing desire, than he'd ever before experienced.

A wave of pure possessiveness surged through him, and he caught her more tightly to him. She was his; she belonged to him just as surely as the sunrise belonged to the morning sky. He would have it no other way. He needed her so badly, all of her—her heart, her body, her mind.

Very slowly and oh-so-carefully, with all the wavering control left to him, Jake eased his lips from hers, breaking the kiss as tenderly as possible. Want her though he did, with a passion that amazed him in its intensity, he was also aware that all this was very new to Tori. Above his own needs, he did not want to frighten her; he dared not press her too hard or too fast. She was so young, so innocent and wary, likc a colt not yet broken to the bridle. She needed time to accustom herself to the idea of wanting him, to thinking of him as a lover. She needed time to think of herself as a woman instead of a nun, and as much as it pained him to do so, he would try to allow her this time to come to terms with her own awakening desires.

As Jake's lips left hers and he set her slightly away from him, Tori's senses grasped frantically for reality. Gulping air into her straining lungs, she stared up at Jake in astonishment. So shaken was she that she could not decide whether it was anger, frustration, or disappointment that she felt the most, or a mixture of all three combined with a growing dose of guilt.

The kiss had been wondrous, like riding a falling star through the heavens, but now that it was over, Tori was more confused than ever. She was angry that Jacob had tricked her, that he dared to take such liberties, liberties she would never have given otherwise. Vying with the anger was lingering desire, and a sense of loss. She had wanted that glorious feeling to go on and on, Jacob's arms hard about her, his warm lips over hers.

But now, thinking of how she had responded to his kiss, recalling how readily she had yielded to his will, Tori was furious with herself. How could she have done such a thing? How could she surrender so easily to passion, to the earthy call of his flesh toward hers? Were all her mother's teachings, and those of the convent, so easily cast aside? This was not right; it was sinful! She was mere months from taking her first binding vows as a Sister of Mercy, and this was how she showed her faith as a prospective Bride of Christ?

Disgusted at her own behavior, as well as his, Tori turned her tormented gaze from Jake's. "Jacob, you should not have done that," she said in a trembling voice.

Work-roughened fingers grasped her chin and turned her eyes toward his once more. "Why not, Tori?" he asked. "We both enjoyed it. You're a liar if you tell me you didn't."

"It was wrong," she told him, anguish bringing tears to her eyes and making them shimmer like fireflies on a warm night.

"'Cause you still want to think of me as your big brother?"

"No. Because I am going to be a nun, Jacob. I must enter into my vows pure in heart and spirit and body."

Pain and anger glowed in his eyes, his jaw tightening, as he jeered, "And my touch sullies you? Is that it, Victoria? My hands and my lips make you dirty?"

The very fact that he called her Victoria was an indication of just how angry Jacob was with her. He never called her that unless he was furious with her. She shook her head, trying to deny his words. "You are twisting my words, Jacob. I don't think of you that way at all. It is just wrong for me. I must not do such things."

"Kissing? Touching?" he questioned tightly, seeing her nod her head in agreement. Reaching out, he grabbed her arms again, this time to shake her so hard that her teeth nearly rattled. "You're a woman, Victoria. A beautiful, desirable, flesh-and-blood woman! Damn it all! Can't you admit that to yourself?"

"You may have the face of an angel, but God gave you the body of a woman. It's *meant* to come alive at a man's touch. You're *supposed* to feel desire and longings. None of that is wrong; it's the way God meant it to be. Desire isn't sinful; it's good, and it's right. Your breasts are meant to suckle babes, your arms to hold them. Your body is fashioned to receive a man's, to shelter his seed and bear his children, not to wither away in some moldy old convent until your beauty fades and your soul dries up."

"My soul is more threatened here than in the convent, Jacob. There it soars; there my heart sings with joy. That's what I've tried to explain to you, but you refuse to understand. Can't you see that I love my life with the sisters? My days are filled with prayer and praise for my Lord, and an inner peace that defies description. Only the other sisters can truly know what I'm trying to tell you. The serenity is so beautiful, the calm so fulfilling, the devotion so complete that I need nothing else. And the satisfaction I get from working with the orphans, seeing those little faces light up with delight and laughter, is worth any sacrifice I may be making."

"You should have children of your own," he continued to argue with a frown, hating the serene glow that had come into her face as she spoke of her life at the convent. How was a mere man supposed to compete with such devout faith, especially a man like himself?

"The orphans are my children. I love each and every one of them."

"I know you love them, honey," he said more reasonably, "but it's not the same as bearing sons and daughters of your own flesh and blood, born of your own body. You would never feel a child grow and move inside you. Won't you yearn for that, Tori? Won't you feel cheated? Can you imagine holding a baby of your own in your arms, knowin' it was born of a love between you and the man who loves you? And I *do* love you. I want to give you those babies, Tori. I want to see you grow round and full with them, to feel them move in your belly. I want to look into the faces of my sons and daughters and see your eyes, your nose reflected in their tiny features."

Gently, regretfully, with tears shining on her face, Tori reached up and laid her fingers over his lips to still them. "Jacob. Oh, Jacob, don't do this to me! Don't do this! Please, I beg you! You're making me doubt all that I know is right for me, everything I have wanted and been so content with for so long. You're shaking the very foundations of my world, of my faith."

"I don't want to destroy your faith, little angel," he assured her softly, his golden gaze intense as he held her face in his hands. "You want to pray, then pray. You want to go to church, then go. You want to teach the children at the orphanage? Teach them. I don't want your faith for myself. I want your love, Tori. Give me your heart, your mind, your body, and God can keep your soul." Settling a tender kiss on her forehead, he dropped his hands from her face. With a final, searching look, he turned and left her standing there, dazed and thoroughly shaken.

Knowing that Jacob wanted to speak with Doc Green after he had examined Carmen, Tori went in search of him. When she failed to find him in the main part of the house or the immediate outbuildings, she thought perhaps he had ridden out to check on the cattle. She was on her way back into the house, passing the burned wing of the house, when she spotted him. Through the gaping window of his father's gutted bedroom, she saw Jacob standing inside. Only when Caroline had been killed had Tori ever seen Jacob look so utterly despondent, and her heart went out to him in shared sorrow.

Disregarding debris and charred wood, Tori quietly made her way toward him. He was half turned from her, and she saw his slumped shoulders quake with a silent sob. Tears filled her eyes as she witnessed his pain. She was nearly upon him before he noticed her. Jacob's own eyes were brilliant with unshed tears, his anguish creasing harsh grooves into a face already lined by twenty-seven years of hard living.

Their eyes met and locked for a timeless moment. Wordlessly, Tori held her arms open to him, inviting him to share his pain with her, to seek comfort in her embrace. For just a heartbeat, Jake hesitated, ashamed that she had caught him in such a vulnerable state, his masculine pride holding him back from her. Then each took one final step toward the other, and she was holding him to her, her arms wrapped tightly about him.

Beneath her palms, his big shoulders shook as she cradled his head on her own slim shoulder. "It's all right, Jacob," she crooned softly. "It's all right to cry for him. He was your father, and you loved him. He loved you, too." Gently she urged him down, until they were both sitting on the soot-blackened floor, but neither noticed the dirt as she pulled his head onto her breast and held him close to her heart. Her hands stroked his dark hair as she rocked him to and fro, murmuring to him.

Then he cried, great shuddering sobs racking his broad frame as he clung to her like a child. His tears soaked her bodice, while hers fell like raindrops atop his bent head. Tori's heart felt as if it were cracking open in her chest as she shared his grief, his aching loss.

Eventually his sobs eased, but when he would have pulled away from her in embarrassment, she refused to loosen her hold on him. "No, Jacob. Let me hold you. Let me give you my strength now."

He relaxed against her once more, and for endless minutes they just sat quietly together, holding one another. At last he spoke, his voice gravelly. "I guess I loved him more than I thought," he said. "I'd never have guessed his death would hit me so hard. I miss the old coot." His voice broke as he fought fresh tears.

"I know, Jacob," she soothed. "I know."

She held him a short while longer. Then, remembering why she had been searching for him to start with, she brushed a light kiss on the top of his head and whispered, "Jacob, the doctor will be leaving soon. Do you still want to speak with him about Mama?"

With a deep sigh, Jake drew himself slightly away from the pillow of Tori's breast. He tried to keep his face averted to hide the ravages of his grief from her view, but his voice sounded gruff and raw as he answered, "Yeah. Why don't you go tell him I'll be there in a few minutes."

Small, slender fingers stroked his hot cheeks, gently turning his face to hers, despite his wishes. With a tenderness that took the breath from his body and nearly made him want to cry again, she lightly brushed cool lips across his swollen eyes. Then, in a gesture so unexpected and beautiful, her tongue swept out to lap gently at the salty tracks his tears had left on his face. Like a mother cat cleaning her kitten, Tori soothed him with her warm, wet caresses.

If he lived to be a hundred, Jake knew he would never forget this moment. He would treasure it in his heart always, and he regretted the moment when Tori finally realized how intimate she was being, when her embarrassment overcame her wish to console him and she pulled away. Color rode high and brilliant on her cheekbones as she stumbled to her feet and mumbled, "I'll go tell Doc Green you'll be right in." Then she dashed from the room, unwilling and unable to meet his bemused golden gaze.

Chapter 5

The doctor was more concerned than ever about Carmen's condition. "Her lungs are weak, and it sounds to me like they are filling with fluid," he told Jake gravely. "I'd say she's headed for some kind of crisis soon, and whether she'll make it through is anybody's guess." As he prepared to leave, he added. "Send for me if you need me, and I'll do what I can. Meanwhile, I've instructed Rosa to make a tent of blankets around Carmen's bed. She's to place steaming pots of mullein leaves and water inside the tent to ease the congestion, and I've left directions for a camphor mixture to be applied directly to Carmen's chest."

Gulping back her tears, Tori asked in a

small voice that tore at Jake's heartstrings, "Do you think we ought to send for Father Romero?"

Wishing he could give her some other answer, the doctor nodded. "It wouldn't be a bad idea, but since I'll be going right by the church on my way to the Shadley place, I'll stop and tell Father Romero to come out."

The young priest arrived that afternoon. Just his presence and prayers seemed to bring Carmen more comfort, and Tori was glad they had sent for him. He stayed until after dinner, and Tori found time to talk with him privately and have him hear her confession. Then, since Carmen was getting no worse, the good Father left. As the doctor had done, he told Tori to call him immediately if Carmen needed him again. "Whatever time of day or night it might be, I will come," he promised.

Tori prayed desperately for her mother's life. She knew she should accept God's will, whatever it might be, but it was so hard right now. This was her *mother*, and she loved her so very much. In the short time that Carmen had been responding so favorably to treatment, they had become close once more, like they'd been before Tori had left for the convent. As hard as it was for Carmen to talk, she had asked about Tori's life with the sisters. She had wanted to know if Tori was happy, what her dreams were, if she missed her home and all her old friends, if she had any regrets.

Tori had talked with her mother for many long hours, always trying to hide her growing confusion, her exasperating new feelings about Jacob, and his for her. She studiously avoided all references to Roy, knowing instinctively that Carmen was not yet strong enough to bear the news of his death. Instead, she read to her, brushed her hair, chatted about neighbors and friends. She told her every interesting detail she could think of about her time at the convent, and when Carmen wanted to talk, Tori asked what had gone on around the ranch in her absence.

Now Carmen's chest was so congested that breathing was almost impossible, let alone speech. All Tori could do was sit by her mother's side and pray for her, to hold her hand and offer what little comfort she could. Though she tried to be grateful for their short time together, Tori was greedy. She wanted more—so much more. She wanted her mother to get well again. This became her primary prayer, repeated over and over again from trembling lips, and despite her faith, she feared that prayer might not be enough this time.

Jake thought nothing of it when Tori did not eat her dinner that evening, merely keeping him and Father Romero company at the dinner table. She was upset and terribly worried over her mother. She seemed so quiet, so subdued, and she would not quite meet Jake's eyes as they spoke. Jake suspected she was also feeling embarrassed again, but then so was he. This morning had been the first time he had broken down and cried over Roy's death. The release had been long overdue, and he'd prefer it be in private if he was going to cry like a baby; but she had been so sweet, and it had felt so good to be held like that and know that she shared his grief.

When Tori did not show up at the breakfast table the next morning, nor for lunch, he tried to dismiss it, but when dinner came around again and her chair at the table remained empty, Jake cornered Rosa and asked her what was going on. Rosa shrugged her shoulders and said, "I know only what I see, Señor Jacob. Since Father Romero comes, Señorita Tori does nothing but pray and sit with her mother. Always she is on her knees, her head bent over her beads. Even in the night, when she should be sleeping, I hear her awake in her room, still praying."

Jake's mouth stretched into a thin line. "Go get her. Tell her I want to talk to her, now."

When Tori walked into the room, Jake nodded toward her chair. "Sit down and eat while the food is still hot, Tori."

She sat, but did not eat. "I can't, Jacob."

"You can and you will," he countered stubbornly. "Do you want to get sick? What's wrong with you?"

"Nothing is wrong. I just can't eat yet."

"Why not?"

She sent him a glare that told him to mind his own business, but when he returned her glare with a more severe look of his own, she relented. "I'm fasting, Jacob. It is part of my penance, if you must know."

"What penance?" he insisted gruffly.

"The penance Father Romero gave me after hearing my confession yesterday. I told you it was not right that I should be dressed like this. I asked you to return my habit to me. Now I must pay the penalty for your stubbornness, as well as my own sins. Father Romero has promised to bring me another habit when he comes again, and he is not too happy about your part in all this, either."

"That's too bad, 'cause I'm about to make him even more unhappy," Jake said firmly. "I told you before that there'll be no fastin' in this house, and I meant it. You're gonna eat, Tori, if I have to tie you to that chair and feed you like an infant." When she looked as if she might defy him, he warned. "Try me, Tori. I dare you."

With a sullen pout, Tori picked up her spoon and began to eat her soup. Once she started, her appetite went wild, and within minutes she was wolfing down the rest of her meal, trying to ignore Jacob's chuckles and dry comments. "Don't eat the pattern off the plate, darlin'. Rosa has more food in the kitchen, if you want."

When Tori had finished her meal, she pushed herself away from the table, her guilt already building again at her own weakness. Accurately reading the look on her face, Jake said, "If you really need to punish yourself, I think we can work somethin' out without havin' you starve. Seems to me you have a likin' for kneelin' and scrubbin', and after the fire, this place could really use a good cleanin'. Since you're on your knees day and night anyway, we might as well kill two birds with one stone. You can clean and pray at the same time." He pushed back his chair, gave her a nasty grin, and started from the room. "Start in the *sala*, and be sure you do it right, 'cause I'm gonna inspect it when you're done."

She glared after him. "You're a tyrant, Jacob Banner!" she called after his retreating back. "Why don't you buy your own island and start your own country? You'd make a magnificent monarch!"

Jake laughed. "Get busy, Tori. Just don't touch anything in Roy's room until I tell you."

Jake had his reasons for not wanting Roy's room disturbed any more than it had been already. There was something about that room that disturbed him, but he couldn't quite put his finger on what it was. As he stood once more in the center of his father's bedroom and looked around, he frowned. Something was not right here; something was out of place. What was it that set his teeth on edge and caused the fine hairs on the nape of his neck to stand on end?

Jake's narrowed eyes swept the room, taking in every detail one by one. The bed was where it had always been, the bedding and mattress just charred lumps amid the burned, lopsided framework. The nightstand stood next to it, handy for Roy to reach his reading glasses and lamp at night. Walking closer, Jake saw that Roy's glasses were merely melted metal and cracked glass, melted right into the top of the stand. A metal ashtray was no more than a misshapen lump, the burned remains of a cigar trapped in its folds. The lamp lay in jagged shards on the floor on the opposite side of the bed. But where was the little bell that always sat on the stand, Roy's means of summoning aid in the night should he need to? Why hadn't he used it that night? Or had Roy been overcome by smoke before he'd had the chance?

Searching the room, Jake finally spotted the partially melted bell in the far corner of the room. What was it doing way over there? Had Roy rung the bell, then become agitated when no one responded? Had he thrown the bell there? If so, he had to have been awake. But if he had been awake, why hadn't he called for help? Why hadn't someone heard? And when had the lamp fallen to the floor? Had Roy accidentally knocked it from the stand, starting the blaze that way, not by smoking in bed as everyone thought? Then Jake's eyes widened as it hit him—the lamp was on the floor on the wrong side of the bed! If the lamp had fallen from the stand, it would be on the right side of the bed, not on the left where the broken pieces were lying now.

More puzzled than ever, Jake continued to scan the room for clues to his growing suspicions. Dark brows came together when he noted that Roy's wheelchair was across the room from the bed. How and when had it come to be there? When they had removed his father's body from the bed, had the ranch hands moved it from its usual spot next to the bed, within easy reach so that Roy could lever himself into it whenever he wished? Upon examining the chair, tilted pathetically now on burned wooden wheels, Jake did not think so. He would ask, but the chair did not appear to have been moved since the fire.

And why was there still such a strong smell of kerosene in the room? Sure, the oil from the lamp had spilled out when the glass had broken, perhaps starting the fire, but the odor seemed so strong. It seemed to be all about the room, from end to end. Even the walls on the opposite side of the room reeked of it, almost as if the entire room had been liberally doused in it, then set aflame.

Could that have been? Was that what had been nagging at the back of Jake's mind all this time? Could someone have entered the room unnoticed, perhaps through the court-yard doors, and deliberately set the fire, kill-ing Roy beforehand, or rendering him unconscious and leaving him to burn to death? Had the killer been the one to throw the bell across the room, maybe when Roy had awakened and tried to summon help? Had Roy struggled with his murderer? Had this person tried to make the fire seem like an accident by breaking the oil lamp, but done it clumsily on the wrong side of the bed?

Jake was sick—literally sick at the thoughts whirling through his head. Unless he was badly mistaken, his father had been mur-dered! Someone had set this fire, moved Roy's wheelchair out of the invalid's reach, and left him to die a horrible death. Jake could only hope that his father had not been conscious at the time.

Gasping for air, Jake reeled from the room in a stupor, his mind and stomach rebelling at the very idea, yet he knew in his gut that he was right. This fire had been no accident, as they had thought. Someone had deliberately murdered Roy Banner; someone who thought he'd gotten away with it. But who? And why? For what purpose? Jake was going to find out, and when he did, that person would pay dearly, just as the men who had murdered Caroline had paid, with their lives.

For the next couple of days, Tori cleaned furiously and Jake brooded angrily. In her sullen mood, Tori did not immediately recognize that something was preying heavily on Jake's mind. Between caring for her mother, whose condition was gradually worsening and causing Tori untold heartache, and performing the chores Jacob had assigned to her, she was busy from dawn to dusk. Actually, it was a blessing to be so occupied. By the time her head finally hit her pillow at the end of the day, Tori fell into an exhausted sleep that left no room for worries.

She was never aware of the number of times Jake crept quietly into her room to check on her, often standing for long minutes just gazing down at her in silent longing. He was torn between wanting to confide his suspicions to her and wanting to shield her from added worry. The weight of his own problems rested heavily on his shoulders—the constant fretting over Carmen and Tori, the burden of the ranch, trying to figure out who could have murdered Roy.

He had quietly questioned some of the more reliable ranch hands, but no one had seen anything suspicious the night of the fire. Neither had anyone moved Roy's wheelchair to its present location. Other than helping to put out the fire before it gutted the entire house, they had done nothing more than remove Roy's body and give him a proper burial. Since then, none of them had gone back into that room. There had been no need, for everything in it was burned beyond use.

They were surprised when Jake told them what he suspected, for all had assumed the fire to be a tragic accident, probably caused by Roy himself. No one had any idea who might have set the fire or killed Roy. Every one of the men he asked was as mystified as Jake. As far as they knew, Roy didn't have any enemies—at least none who hated him enough to want him dead.

"You sure about this, boy?" Gill had asked skeptically.

"As sure as I can be without more proof, yeah," Jake had replied wearily. "Gill, everything in that room had been thoroughly doused with kerosene, and the lamp had been thrown on the floor on the opposite side of the bed from where it usually sits. Now you tell me, how did it get that way? Dad couldn't have done it. And what was his chair doing all the way across the room, for God's sake? I'm tellin' you, Gill, someone set that fire and made sure the old man was trapped in that bed like a rat in a cage! I know it as well as I'm standin' here. I feel it, damn it! I haven't lived by my instincts this long just to be wrong now."

"Then we're gonna have to be real careful, Jake. Whoever did this got clean away, but he could come back. Maybe he was lookin' for somethin' he thought Roy had, and maybe he didn't find it. I don't think anyone would just come in and kill Roy like that for no reason, or just 'cause he didn't like him."

"Neither do I, Gill, and I have a hunch we're in for some more trouble ahead. I've been thinkin' about it. If the killer just wanted Roy dead, why set fire to the house? Why not sneak in and knife him, or choke him in his sleep? Whoever did this wanted the house destroyed, and wanted it all to look like an accident. What I don't know is why."

"Or who," Gill added worriedly.

"Right, and until we find out, we're gonna have to keep our eyes peeled and our ears to the ground. Carmen's hangin' on by a thread, and Tori could be in danger now, too. We all could, so from now on we're postin' guards day and night. And I'll personally skin alive the first man I catch drunk or sleepin' when he has watch duty, so pass the word along. I don't want to hear any lame-brained excuses if trouble comes and we're caught with our britches down because some jackass wasn't payin' attention."

Carmen kept her eyes closed, pretending sleep, until she heard Tori walk softly out of the room. Then she opened them, her eyes searching through the gloom of the blanket tent about her bed. "Rosa?" she croaked.

Rosa immediately materialized at her bedside. "*Sí*, Señora? What is it you need? Another pillow, perhaps? Some water to drink?"

Carmen shook her head slightly, trying to stem the fit of coughing that seemed to jar her entire body. "Tell . . . tell me about 'Toria," she wheezed.

"Oh, Señorita Tori is fine, just fine," Rosa assured her gently. "Don't worry yourself over her. You just get better. Tori worries only about you."

Again Carmen shook her head. "Some . . . thing is wrong. Bothers her."

"Only that you are ill," Rosa insisted. "You must get well again for her, for all of us."

"Do not lie to m . . . me, Rosa. Something else. Jac . . . ob? You know. T . . . tell me." Carmen's eyes implored her servant and old friend to be truthful with her.

Rosa sighed, wondering how much she should tell her mistress. "They argue, Señora. Señor Jacob, he does not like the idea of 'Toria belonging to the church. He wants her home to stay. And 'Toria, she loses her temper, too, so quickly, just like before, when she was small and Jacob would tease her so. They are like a cat and dog, those two."

"Love each other," Carmen said weakly.

"*Sí*," Rosa agreed, not quite meeting Carmen's avid gaze. "Of course, they do. Always, they have been so close to one another."

"No, Rosa," Carmen corrected with a smile. "Hear things. Know. Love . . . real love." Again her eyes asked Rosa for confirmation. Sick she might be, but a person would have to be either dead or stone deaf to have missed all the arguments going on in the house lately, or not to have some idea of what they were about.

Rosa shrugged. "You may be right," she conceded. "At least for Jacob. It is in his eyes for all to see, and 'Toria knows this now, I think."

Carmen tried to speak again, but her words got lost in a severe coughing spell. At last, so softly that Rosa had to lean over her to hear her words, she choked out, "Confuses her."

Rosa nodded, patting her friend gently on the arm. "*Sí*, it is very confusing for her, Carmen. She has seen herself for so long now as a nun, and before that as Jacob's little sister. Now, suddenly, she is seeing herself through Jacob's eyes, as a woman, and she does not know what to think of this. I think sometimes she likes this idea very much, but too often it scares her, and it makes her feel guilty, you know."

Carmen sighed, as if she understood perfectly and agreed. "Will work out," she managed. In the next breath she was already asleep, but Rosa thought she saw a small smile curving Carmen's lips ever so slightly.

Chapter
6

When Carmen's condition worsened, it did so in the bat of an eye. One minute it looked as if she might finally be winning the battle over the congestion in her chest, and the next she was fighting for her life, every breath likely to be her last.

Tori had been dozing in the chair by her mother's bedside when she suddenly jerked awake, not sure at first what had awakened her. Then she realized that it was the sound of her mother's breathing, so awfully labored, so much worse than ever before. A quick glance at her mother's face told the rest of the story. Carmen's face was almost purple with the effort to draw breath into her body, and her chest was rattling ominously. This was what they had all feared, what Doc Green had repeatedly warned might happen. As incongruous as it seemed in the stifling heat of late June, Carmen had contracted pneumonia.

Tori laid her hand on her mother's forehead and confirmed what she already knew. Carmen was burning with fever. She was flame-hot with it, and shivering with chills, all at the same time. Tori was out of the room and racing for Jacob as fast as her shaking legs would carry her. Knocking but once, she did not wait for a reply but threw the door wide and burst into his room. "Jacob! Come quickly! I think she is dying!"

Hastily pulling the sheet up over his nude body, Jake blinked in confusion. As many times as he had dreamed of Tori being in his bedroom, and in his bed, it took a moment for reality to register. Then her frantic words penetrated the fog that clung to his brain, clearing it instantly. "Go back to her. Let me pull my pants on, and I'll be right there."

"Hurry, Jacob! Please hurry!" Tori cried hysterically. "I'm scared! Oh, dear Lord! I just don't know what to do for her! She's burning up with fever!"

"I'll send one of the men for the doctor. You wake Rosa. The two of you try sponging her down with wet cloths. Maybe that will bring the fever down."

She dashed from the room, and Jake was halfway out of bed when she ran back in. "Jacob, you'd best send for Father Romero, too!" She turned for the door, then spun about just in time to see the sheet drop away from his body as he reached for his trousers, but she was too upset to register what she was seeing. "I think she has pneumonia! Won't the cool water make her worse?"

"Tori!" he yelled. "Just go do it and get the hell out of my room so I can get some clothes on! Get a hold on yourself, woman! At this point, what harm can a little water do?"

He immediately hated himself for screaming at her when she was so distraught. "Go on, love," he said more gently. "Go on. I'm right behind you, darlin'."

They worked frantically trying to reduce Carmen's fever, doing what little they could until Doc Green finally arrived. Close behind him came Father Romero. Jake and Tori, who was practically frozen with fright and next to useless by now, were ushered from Carmen's room. Rosa, at the doctor's request, stayed to help him and Father Romero.

Endless minutes dragged by as Tori and Jake sat helplessly waiting in the *sala*. The delicate bones in Tori's fingers protested as she fitfully wrung her hands together, and Jake resorted for the first time in years to cracking his knuckles.

"Will you please stop that awful noise!" Tori

exclaimed snappishly. "That and your constant pacing are setting my teeth on edge!"

"Sorry," he muttered, flopping himself down on the divan and running shaking fingers through his tousled hair. In retaliation, as he watched her gnawing on her third fingernail, he could not help but remark smartly, "I thought nuns were supposed to be schooled in patience. Did you fail that lesson, too, Tori?"

To his absolute horror, she burst into tears, making him feel like the lowest of beasts. "Oh, Lord, honey! Don't cry," he begged. "I don't think I can handle it on top of everything else right now. Pray! Scream! Throw somethin'! Just please don't cry!" He reached across and dragged her from her chair into his lap, cuddling her close and absorbing the hard sobs that jarred them both.

"I . . . I'll c . . . cry if I w . . . want to, Jake B . . . Banner!" she wailed, beating her small fists against his chest.

He captured her fists in one large hand, drawing her more firmly against him, crooning softly to her as she cried. "We're makin' an awful habit of this, little one," he told her. "If we don't stop soon, we'd better start buildin' a boat."

What began as a hesitant laugh ended in a hiccup. "An ark," she countered with weak humor.

"Now, honey, I like animals as well as the next man, but let's not get carried away."

She'd stopped crying, but made no move to leave the quiet comfort of his arms. That was how Rosa found them when she dashed into the room. "Come quickly!" she panted. "Carmen is asking for both of you."

Tori blanched as white as new snow, and without the support of Jacob's arm about her, she would never have made it down the short length of hall to her mother's room. Just outside the doorway, she suddenly balked. "Jacob! I'm frightened! I can't go in there! I can't watch my mother die!"

"I'll be with you," he promised. "I won't leave you for a minute." When her shaking legs still refused to move, he said, "Tori, she's askin' for you, honey. She needs you with her now. If you don't do this, you'll never forgive yourself. You know that."

She nodded and edged closer to him. "Stay with me, Jacob. Stay with me."

"I will."

Trembling so badly that she had to clench her teeth to keep them from chattering, Tori entered the room, Jacob at her side. Hesitantly she tiptoed to the side of the bed. "Mama?" she whimpered.

The bandaged hand near hers fluttered slightly, and Tori grasped it gently in her own. She felt Jacob's strong hands come down on her shoulders, lending her his support as she said, "I'm here, Mama. Jacob and I are both here. We won't leave you."

Carmen whispered something in a frail voice, and Tori glanced across at Doc Green, who sat at Carmen's other side. "What did she say?" Tori whispered.

"Marry," Carmen repeated softly, the word wavering from her lips.

"Mary?" Tori repeated questioningly, gazing down into her mother's pale face. "The Virgin Mary?"

With effort, Carmen shook her head slightly. "No. You. Jacob. Marry now. Here." She was caught in a spasm of coughing, and did not see the shock of her words register on her daughter's features.

Tori's eyes grew huge in her face, her gaze swinging up to catch Father Romero watching her intently. To her astonishment, the priest repeated what she surely thought had been a mistake of her own hearing. "She wishes the two of you to marry, to become man and wife before she dies."

For long seconds, only the sound of her mother's labored breathing and Tori's own heartbeat echoed in her ears. Tori could not believe this was happening. Her own dear mother was asking her to marry Jacob! A deathbed request! How could she deny her mother this final favor? Yet how could she, in all good conscience, agree to it? Would it be fair to Jacob, to herself, to agree to such a thing? It was too sudden, too soon. But there was no time; she must decide now, this minute!

Carmen groaned and clutched at her hand —and Tori's decision was made. "Yes, Mama. If Jacob agrees, we will be married."

Jake's hands tightened convulsively on Tori's shoulders. Carmen had just handed him his fondest wish. He couldn't help but wonder if she knew how much he had wanted this, how often he had dreamed of it. Yet he, too, wondered if this was right, to force Tori into a marriage she was not prepared for. It might be too soon. With all his heart, Jake wanted Tori for his wife, but he wanted her to come to him willingly, wholeheartedly, without doubts or reservations. But time had just run out. As if in a trance, he heard himself say, "I agree, Mamacita. I'll take good care of her. I promise you this."

"If you will join hands, we will begin the ceremony," Father Romero suggested, a sense of urgency in his voice.

"Here? Now?" Tori asked in confusion. "What about the banns?"

"There is no time, child. Under such circumstances, the banns can be waived."

Tori swallowed an hysterical sob and signaled her agreement by placing her shaking hand in Jacob's outstretched palm. There, beside her mother's sickbed, with Doc Green and Rosa acting as their witnesses, she became Jacob's wife. Kneeling in her nightshift, her short hair sticking out in all directions and her bare feet poking out beneath her hem, she vowed to love, honor, and obey, till death should part the two of them. And Jake, bare-chested and barefoot, wearing only his trousers, promised to love and cherish her, to protect her all the days of their life together.

No ring, no gown, no flowers; just a chaste kiss to seal their vows, and the deed was done. No throng of happy friends to congratulate them; just a grim-faced doctor looking on, and a tearful hug from Rosa for each of them. Yet the most elaborate wedding in the world could not have meant more to Tori than hearing the contented sigh her mother gave from her pillows, or seeing the tiny smile that crossed her pain-racked features, making her look almost young again for just that one second. "I love you, Mama," Tori murmured, placing a kiss on Carmen's flushed cheek. "I love you."

"Make him happy," Carmen whispered back.

"I will."

"G . . . give him babies."

Tori blushed to the roots of her hair, but nodded. "Beautiful babies, Mama. Babies for you to rock in your arms when you are well again."

Jake bent down and brushed a kiss on

Carmen's brow. "Rest now, Mamacita. Don't try to talk anymore. Just rest and save your strength."

They sat with her until she fell asleep. Tori almost panicked, thinking her mother had died at that moment, but the doctor quietly reassured her that Carmen was only sleeping. He suggested that she and Jake try to get some rest themselves. "It might be a long night," he told them. "I'll have Rosa wake you if there are any changes in Carmen's condition."

They spent the remainder of their wedding night as strangely as it had begun, huddled silently together on the divan in the *sala*. He held her without talking, knowing how confused she must be, feeling her pain and offering his arms as a shield against it, gently stroking her softly curling hair with his big, rough hand.

Gradually she relaxed in his embrace, taking comfort in his greater strength, deliberately pushing aside the awful awkwardness that made her view him as a stranger. This was Jacob, whom she had known and trusted all of her life. The only thing different was that he was now her husband. He was still the same man he had been half an hour ago, just as she was the same woman. At least that was what Tori tried to tell herself—it helped to quell the nervousness that threatened to choke her each time she thought of herself as his wife. She had nothing to fear from him. Jacob would never hurt her. Mama knew that. Mama had wanted this. Mama was happy now. Mama was dying.

Tori awoke stiff and cramped, her limbs entangled with Jake's longer ones. They were still on the divan, Jake stretched out on his back and Tori lying half over him. The dark mat of curls carpeting his chest tickled her nose as his chest rose and fell with each deep breath. Sometime during the long night they had both fallen asleep. Now it was light out. Morning had come, and so far no one had come to awaken them, and Tori wondered if that was good news or bad.

Pushing herself upright, still seated across Jacob's thighs, she unwound her legs from Jake's, tugging the skirt of her nightshift out from under his knee. But her thoughts were not centered on their intimate sleeping position, or even their hasty, middle-of-the-night wedding. Her mind was slowly coming alert, and she wondered if the doctor was still here. Was he still tending to her mother? Was her mother still alive, or had she died while Tori slept? Where was Father Romero? Had he administered last rites? What was Rosa doing? Why had no one come to wake them?

Her glance fell on Jacob's face. Her husband—how strange to think of him that way after all the years she had spent seeing him through the eyes of a younger sister, looking up to him, admiring him, idolizing him to the point that no other man had ever measured up to her ideals. Even in sleep, his features were hardened, his overnight beard lending added harshness. Only the dark hank of hair falling across his forehead lent a false look of youth to his face, a youth so hastily stolen from him.

She reached out and tenderly brushed the stray tendrils back from his face. A deep sigh rose in her chest as she wondered what surprises this day might hold for the two of them. Surely they'd had enough shocks already to last them both a lifetime.

Easing herself from his lap, careful not to wake him, Tori went in search of Rosa. Upon peeking into Carmen's room, she spied the doctor slumped in a chair next to the bed, snoring softly. It took all her limited courage to approach the bed, but when she did, she heaved a silent sigh of relief. Her mother was sleeping, her breathing much easier now than the night before.

She found Rosa in the kitchen, preparing breakfast for Father Romero. As she entered the room, both of them looked up at her with red-rimmed eyes that testified to their lack of sleep. Taking pity on the other woman who had done so much for all of them, especially lately, Tori suggested softly, "I can take over now, Rosa, if you would like to get some rest."

Rosa nodded gratefully. "*Gracias*, Señorita

Tori." Immediately she caught herself and corrected her blunder. *"Perdóname*. It is Señora Tori now. I must remember that."

"It will take a little getting used to for me, too, Rosa," Tori said with an awkward shrug and a weak smile, waving the weary woman out of the kitchen.

She served the priest his plate of eggs, potatoes, and bacon, then poured a cup of strong black coffee for each of them. Self-consciously, she seated herself across the table from him. "I want to thank you for all you have done, for coming out here in the middle of the night to be with my mother. I'm sure it helped to set her mind at ease, having you here."

Father Romero cleared his throat nervously. "Sister Esperanza," he began, then caught himself with a flushed face and a little laugh. "I am as bad as Rosa, aren't I? And I performed your wedding ceremony!"

Tori returned his smile. "I suppose I should wear a sign around my neck, to remind myself as well as everyone else of my new name. It might be easier just to call me Tori and be done with it."

Father Romero nodded. "Tori," he began again, "I wanted to speak with you about your sudden marriage last night. Forgive me if I am speaking out of turn, but I have the feeling you were pressured into this by your mother's request, thinking it might be her last wish. I know you were happy at the convent, and I want you to know that I understand that what you have done you did out of love for your mother. You are a good and loving daughter, but the deed can be undone if you wish. You need not stay married to Señor Banner, you know. Once your mother is well enough, I am sure she will understand and rescind her wish, if this marriage makes you unhappy."

Tori's mouth flew open in surprise, her eyes wide and green as she stared at the priest. "You are suggesting an annulment?" she squeaked, the word practically sticking in her throat.

"*Sí*. As long as the marriage is not consummated, it can be dissolved as if it never existed, if that is what you wish."

Jake stood unnoticed in the doorway of the kitchen, his face thunderous. As he waited for Tori's reply to the priest's suggestion, his heart seemed to lodge tightly in his throat, threatening to choke him. He wanted to barge into the room, yank Father Romero from his chair, and beat the man senseless, but something kept him rooted where he stood. In his heart, he knew he needed to hear whatever Tori would say next. His future—their future together—might depend on her reply.

Slowly Tori shook her head, denying the priest's solution. "No," she said, and across the room Jacob's heart began to beat again. "I know you are thinking of my happiness, Father, but I cannot do such a thing. This is what Mama wants for me. Deep in her heart, I think this is what she has always wanted. Even if she lives, which is my most fervent prayer, she has told me she wishes me to give Jacob children. I have promised her this, if it is God's will that I be a mother. I have pledged my life and my love to Jacob, and I will not take back the vows I have made."

"But is it your wish, too, Tori?" Father Romero argued. "Can you be happy married to this man? You were studying to be a Sister of Mercy; he is a gunfighter, a killer. Can you ever truly come to love such a man?"

A smile crept over her lips. "I already love him, Father," she told him sincerely. "I have always loved him."

"But as a brother, not as a husband. Can you love him as a wife should?"

Again Jake waited anxiously for her reply, hardly daring to breathe. "It should not be so difficult. Jacob is the most wonderful man I have ever known. All my life I have measured other men against him, and they always seem lacking. Perhaps this is one of the reasons I decided to enter the convent, because no other man has ever come up to the standards Jacob has set in my mind."

"But that was before he became a gunfighter. Can you live with what he has become now?"

The priest had touched on Tori's greatest

worry. In her heart she was not sure she could stand it if Jacob were to continue his gunslinging ways. She hated violence. It made her ill even to think about it. But Jacob was home to stay now. He had already taken over running the ranch. Surely there would be no more bloodshed, no more reason for him to kill, no more worrying that Jacob might be killed himself someday. If he could try to put his past behind him, surely she could, too. "I can try, Father," she answered softly.

"What about your work with the children?" the priest persisted.

"Jacob is not unreasonable," Tori said in defense of him. "He has told me that I can continue to work with the orphans, if I wish, once Mama is well again."

Tori graced him with another sweet smile. "Please, Father. You must not worry over me. Everything will work out as God has planned it. Perhaps it is His wish, too, that Jacob and I marry. Perhaps I was never meant to be a Sister after all, and God knew this all along, while you and I could never see it."

"You are wise beyond your years, *niña*," the young priest said, shaking his head and smiling back at her. "Your husband is a fortunate man to have found such a woman for his wife."

Jake echoed that sentiment. Not much for prayers as a rule, Jake offered up silent thanks as he backed quietly out of the doorway, still unnoticed. His heart had never felt so light in his chest as it did now, after hearing Tori's answers. She intended to stay married to him! She meant to have his children! She had actually admitted that she had compared other men to him and found them lacking!

Jake felt like singing, though he couldn't carry a tune worth spit.

They would make it! Their marriage would work! He would do everything in his power to keep her safe and happy and see that she never regretted becoming his wife.

"Thank you, God," he whispered softly. "Thank you, Carmen. And thank you, Tori, my own darlin' angel."

Chapter
7

Tori walked into her bedroom and stopped short. "Ana, what are you doing?"

The young servant turned and smiled as she continued to gather clothing from Tori's dresser. "Good morning, Señora Tori. How is your mother feeling?"

"She is much better this morning, *gracias*. Why are you removing my clothes from those drawers?"

"Oh! Señor Jacob asked me to help move these things to your new room—his room. He knew you would want to spend most of your day with your mama."

"I see," Tori murmured disconcertedly.

"Well, I suppose he is right. Thank you for doing this for me." In a daze, Tori turned to leave, not even remembering why she had come to her room. Ana's words had brought a whole new set of confusing thoughts flooding into Tori's brain. With all else going on in the house, Tori had not even thought that tonight, being a new bride, she would share her husband's bed for the first time. Now she could think of little else!

For the next few hours, Tori was a bundle of nerves. Where was that calm, wise, reasonable woman who had spoken with Father Romero so confidently this morning? Tori had never felt so young, so unsure of herself, as she did now. Raised on a ranch, Tori was not entirely ignorant about procreation, though her knowledge was limited strictly to animals. Even what she knew was not much, for Roy had tried to shield her from that aspect of ranch life, barring her from the barns and paddocks when the mares were put to stud and trying to make sure she was busy elsewhere when the cattle were mating. He had not been altogether successful in his attempts, but her knowledge was still sadly lacking when it came to humans, and now her imagination was running away with itself.

How she wished she had someone to talk with! She didn't feel she could ask Rosa, even as close as she was to the woman who had been with the family since Tori was a baby.

None of Tori's former girlfriends had been by to visit, either not realizing that she was home, or out of respect for Carmen's illness. Carmen was too sick to advise her, and by the time she'd be well enough, Tori was certain the advice would no longer be necessary. Jacob obviously intended that she share his bed tonight!

Tori tried keeping her mind occupied with other tasks. Though her mother slept most of the day, Tori sat by her bedside and read to her anyway. By the middle of the afternoon she was as fidgety as a bachelor at an old maids' tea party. Desperately needing something more active to do, she dragged buckets and brushes and long-handled brooms into the front library, which also doubled as a second sitting room, and proceeded to clean the fireplace.

She was still at it when Jake walked into the room, took one look at her, and burst into laughter. "What in the world are you doing, darlin'? You look like a little chimney sweep!"

Tori scowled up at him, her eyes glowing green in her soot-blackened face. Her hair was wrapped in an old bandanna to protect it from the worst of the dirt, but it hadn't helped much. She was filthy from head to toe. When she opened her mouth to throw him a scathing retort, her teeth gleamed like white beacons, and he let out another roar of mirth. "I take back what I said before," he snickered.

"You look more like an organ grinder's monkey!"

"Go ahead and laugh, you big galoot! You're the one who told me to clean!"

"Aw, honey," he said, trying to stifle his chuckles. "Don't get your cute little black nose bent out of shape. I just came to tell you that Carmen's awake and wants to see you for a minute."

"Now? This minute?" she squealed in dismay, yanking the kerchief from her head. Her short dark hair sprang out in a riot of curls.

Another hoot erupted from Jake. "I'd take the time to wash my face at least, honey, or your mama might not recognize you," he suggested.

Drawing her shredded dignity about her, Tori swept past him. "Try to control yourself, Jacob. I may look like a monkey, but you are sounding more and more like a braying jackass all the time."

A few minutes later, Tori stood at her mother's bedside. Jake had been asked to come, too. This time, however, it was not an urgent summons.

Gesturing toward the bedstand, Carmen said softly, "Open it." When Tori had done so, Carmen murmured, "The chain. Hand me the gold chain."

As Jake watched Tori open the drawer in the nightstand, something nagged at his brain but was gone too swiftly for him to grasp it.

Rummaging through the drawer, Tori found the chain her mother had always worn about her neck. In all her life, Tori could never recall a day, until the fire, that Carmen had not worn it. Now, instead of the crucifix she had always assumed lay hidden under her mother's bodice, she found a ring dangling from the chain. It was beautiful. A glistening square-cut ruby crowned a circlet of intricate silver filigree.

Carmen took the ring and held it in her bandaged hand, tears gleaming in her pale brown eyes. "Your papa gave me this ring, 'Toria," she rasped. "On our wedding day. Since the day he died, I have worn it close to my heart."

Her tears ran over, streaking down her cheeks. Slowly, and with great reverence, she held out the chain to Jake. "I cannot unfasten the clasp," she said.

Jake's long fingers worked at the tiny gold clasp until it came undone, but when he would have handed it back to her, Carmen shook her head. "Only the chain, Jacob. I would like for you to take the ring." Carmen paused a moment to catch her breath, then continued. "It would please me if you would give this ring to 'Toria now, as her wedding ring."

Jake didn't know what to say. In fact, he couldn't have spoken at that moment if his life depended upon it, so he merely nodded, letting his eyes tell Carmen how deeply touched he was. When his gaze met Tori's, he could see that she felt the same. She was biting her lip to still its quivering.

As Carmen looked on, Jake tenderly took his bride's small hand in his and slid the ring onto her finger. Still holding her hand, he brought it to his mouth and kissed her fingers, his warm lips sending tingles all the way to Tori's toes. "With love, Tori," he promised softly. "Always."

As his eyes held hers, Tori's heart skipped in her chest. "Always," she repeated on a shaky whisper. Salty tears raced down her cheeks as she looked from her new husband to her mother, her heart almost bursting.

Suddenly it struck Tori that here she stood, for the second time in as many days, making solemn vows in the most unconventional attire. She'd been wed in her nightshift; now she received her wedding ring dressed like a filthy ragamuffin. Her dress was black with soot, her hair a mess, the very finger now adorned with the beautiful ring was still grimy with dirt. It made her wonder if all the important events of her life were destined to follow along similar lines. She surely hoped not! She could half envision herself at her child's christening dressed in rags and riding boots. Why, even her wedding night had been spent on the divan!

Bright spots of color flooded to her cheeks

as she was reminded of the night to come. Already it was nearly time for dinner, and she certainly didn't want to resemble a chimney sweep when Jacob claimed his husbandly rights!

With a kiss to her mother's cheek, Tori voiced her love and gratitude. "Thank you, Mama. The ring is as beautiful as you are. I will cherish it always, as you have done." Then she hastily excused herself. She had to take a bath and get cleaned up. Oh, why had she decided to clean that fireplace today, of all days?

Tori lay in Jake's big bed, quivering with nervous anticipation. Her mind was in a whirl, and her body threatened to shake itself apart before he got here. This was torture in the extreme! Gazing about the room, Tori could recall times, when she was very small and frightened of thunderstorms, when she had crawled into Jacob's bed and huddled under the covers next to him until the storm had passed. It all seemed so long ago now, looking back on it. Now the room felt strange to her, and her older stepbrother was her bridegroom! How had her life taken such a sudden, drastic turn?

Tori might have felt a little better had she known that, at that very moment, Jake was almost as nervous as she. He was pacing back and forth in the courtyard garden, heedlessly trampling flowers underfoot and puffing at his cigarette as if it were his last before his execution. This brave, bold gunfighter, who'd lost count of the number of women he'd bedded, was nearly a blithering idiot now.

Of all the women he'd had, not one had been a virgin, and the thought of hurting Tori was almost more than he could bear. He'd wanted her for so long, but now that the moment was at hand, Jake Banner, lover extraordinaire, was a mass of nerves as he made his way through the house toward his waiting bride. Could he arouse her sufficiently to counter what pain she might feel? What if she froze up at the last, crucial moment? Maybe a glass of wine or brandy was in order—just enough to relax her, but not enough to get her drunk.

With his hand outstretched toward the doorknob of his room, Jake pivoted about and headed for the liquor cabinet in the study. Halfway there, he wiped the perspiration from his brow, pushing at a lock of hair still damp from his bath. Damn! He was sweating like a pig! And he felt like a raw youth about to take his first woman!

Tori had tensed when she heard Jake's footsteps outside the door, then had nearly collapsed in frustration as they faded away again. Blast! Didn't the man realize what this endless waiting was doing to her? If he didn't come soon, she was sure she would break out in nervous hives. Then wouldn't she be a sight! Her eyes riveted to the doorknob, she waited, almost fainting when she saw it turn at long last.

Jake closed the door softly behind him and almost chuckled at the sight of Tori with the bedcovers pulled up to her chin. Never, in all of his many fantasies about finding her in his bed, had he pictured her like this. He'd imagined her in revealing French silk, in clinging satin, even completely nude, but never this way. Her mint-green eyes were huge and wary, her fingers clutching the covers so tightly that her knuckles had turned white. Compassion flowed through him as he realized that, as nervous as he was, she was practically terrified, and most assuredly less certain of what to expect than he was.

Walking to the side of the bed, Jake sat down on the edge of the mattress. "Here," he said softly, holding out the goblet of wine. "This might help settle you a bit. Just don't gulp it, or you'll be drunk as a cowhand on a Saturday night before you know what hit you." He hadn't failed to notice how she had merely picked at the food on her dinner plate.

Tori took a tiny sip and managed a tremulous smile. "Th . . . thank you, Jacob. I know it's silly of me to be so nervous, but I can't seem to help it."

He took her other hand between his, warming her cold fingers with his own. "Poor baby," he crooned. "Everything has happened so fast for you that you must feel like you are in the middle of a stampede. I understand, darlin', and it's perfectly natural for a bride to be nervous on her weddin' night. It happens all the time, so I hear."

While Tori sipped her wine, Jake took the opportunity to begin to remove his clothing. At first, Tori's eyes never left his fingers as he released the buttons of his shirt one by one. She watched with wide eyes as he sat on the edge of the bed to pull off his boots and socks. But when his hands reached for the buckle of his belt, her gaze fluttered down to the glass of wine in her shaking hands and stayed there. She stared long and hard at the shimmering liquid, while Jake removed his britches and crawled under the covers with her.

He couldn't help but chuckle inwardly. With feigned curiosity, he leaned toward her stiffly held body. "Somethin' floatin' in there, honey?" he teased, eyeing her goblet. She didn't answer, merely shook her head, but Jake saw a glimmer of a smile curve her lips. His silly attempt at humor had served its purpose, and the tension surrounding them was considerably relieved.

Gently he released her clenched fingers from the delicate stem and placed the glass on the nightstand next to the bed. "Come here, sweetheart," he urged, gathering her into the curve of his arm and laying her head on his bare shoulder. "Let's just cuddle a while, all right?"

He felt her nod, then she heaved a sigh of relief and some of the stiffness left her limbs. Ever so gently, Jake began to stroke her soft, feathery hair. "It's growin' out already," he commented easily.

"By this time next year you'll never know it was cut," she answered, her warm breath tickling Jake's bare skin.

By this time next year Tori could bear him a child. The thought pleased him, but he kept it to himself, not wanting to say anything that might cause her to tense up again just as she was beginning to relax a little. His hand eased down to caress her shoulder and upper back through her cotton nightshift. Gently he kneaded the tight tendons at the back of her neck and along her spine. His lips feathered along the top of her head and found the pulse at her temple. Even as they rested there, he felt her heart begin to pound a little faster. "Trust me, angel," he whispered. "You know I'd never hurt you."

In answer, she raised her face toward his, just enough to meet his gaze. "Jacob, you held my hand while I took my first steps. You taught me how to ride my first pony. Whenever I had to learn something new, you were the one to guide me through it. Now," she sighed tremulously, "you must show me how to become a woman, because I don't know the first thing about how to do this. I'm not so much afraid as I am unsure of what to do."

Her childlike honesty, her implied trust, touched the very depths of his soul. "Just relax and let me love you, Tori," he told her. "Let me touch you and kiss you. That's all you need to do. I'll do the rest."

"But what do I do with my arms—with my hands?" she asked. "Good heavens, I feel so awkward! Like I'm all elbows and knees!"

Laughter rumbled through his chest. "Feel free to touch me back whenever and wherever you want, little darlin'," he told her. "Believe me, I won't mind at all!" With that he kissed her before she could think of any other girlish questions. Knowing Tori, she could have spent the entire night just talking about it, while he was practically dying to show her what it was all about.

Jake's mouth claimed hers with a white-hot heat that chased every other thought out of Tori's head. Only his lips over hers, his hands caressing her, existed now. As his mouth widened in invitation, she parted her lips for him, and his tongue speared into her mouth. Oh, heaven could not be sweeter, she was sure! She felt a river of heat stream through her as his tongue twisted itself about hers, inviting her to play the game with him.

Tori arched closer, wanting to melt into him. When her fingers came up to tangle in the soft mat of dark hair that pelted his chest, it was as if lightning had seared them both. Jake groaned in delight, and Tori gasped with the wondrous shock of it. Beneath her tingling palms, she felt the firm nubs of his male nipples harden even more, and she wondered momentarily what it would feel like to have his hands caress her breasts.

Almost as if he had read her thoughts, Jake's hands curved gently around the undersides of her breasts, cradling them within his palms. His thumbs brushed her nipples through the cloth, creating a delightful friction that brought a strangled moan of desire to her lips. Tori felt as if he'd just set fire to her. When his mouth left hers to search out one pouting peak, the hot, wet tugging sent streaks of pure flame straight to her belly. She didn't even think to object when Jake tugged her nightshift over her head and tossed it to the floor. By now, her one objective was to get as near to him as was physically possible.

Now, when his mouth sought her breast, there was nothing but heat between them, and the pleasure was unbelievably sweet. Tori's fingers twined into Jake's dark hair, holding his head to her breast, almost unable to breathe for the desire sizzling through her. Vaguely, her passion-fogged mind registered the hot length of his desire pressing against her thigh, his hair-roughened legs against her silken ones. Everywhere their bodies touched, her skin seemed seared, every inch of her flesh more alive and sensitive than ever before.

One large palm came to rest on her belly, an incredibly intimate and possessive gesture that sent fresh shivers through her and caused her toes to curl. His other hand was slowly stroking the length of her body from shoulder to thigh, pausing along the way to tease at the breast his mouth had now abandoned. His lips were charting a new course along her throat, nibbling a tingling path along her shoulder, nipping at her earlobe.

All the while he murmured endearments to her, telling her how sweet she was, how perfect, how desirable, and Tori was melting beneath his touch and his sweet praise. Her hands stroked the length of his hot, bare back, feeling his muscles tense at her touch, reveling in the pure masculine strength beneath her fingertips.

"Oh, angel!" he whispered, his voice husky with desire. "How beautiful you are! How soft and smooth, like sun-warmed honey!"

Tori was totally spellbound by the time his hand strayed to her inner thigh, tracing a trail of fire to the juncture of her legs. His fingers delved through the dark curls to find the heart of her desire, that throbbing point of passion hidden there. A gasp lodged in her throat at this new invasion, this burning touch where no hand had ever ventured. She forgot to breathe as he gently caressed her silken flesh.

Her blood felt as if it were boiling in her veins, the pleasure growing and growing until she feared she would go insane with longing. His name became an endless chant upon her lips.

Of their own, her legs fell further apart, granting him easier access as his long, lean fingers prepared her to accept him into her body. Tori arched into him, pleading with him now to end this blissful torment, this aching emptiness within her. "Jacob! Please!"

"Soon, love. Soon." Then she felt him levering himself over her, felt him gently prodding for entrance as he introduced her to womanhood. Her body tensed, just as he had feared, and Jake spent precious moments and untold patience to ease her fears, to whisper softly to her, to kiss her tenderly until she was trembling eagerly beneath him once more.

One sharp lunge—a single moment of pain, and he was sheathed tightly within her. Another slight pause to allow her body to adjust to his intrusion, and then he was moving within her—long smooth strokes that brought building sensations of yearning and made her forget the brief pain that had come before. Instinctively, she rose to meet his thrusts, holding him tightly to her and glorying in the fiery cloud of passion that was engulfing them.

Then, suddenly, her body seemed to explode with rapture. Together they were spinning crazily inside a pinwheel of blazing flame, sparks flying all about them, around them, within them. Tori cried out, hearing her cry echoed by Jake's. She clung dizzily to him as the world slowly righted itself once more.

Breathless, astounded, they had no words to describe the passion they had just shared. For all his previous experience, Jake was stunned speechless. Tori simply did not try to describe what she had felt. She merely looked up at him with awe-filled eyes and whispered, "Oh, Jacob!" Then she drew his lips to hers for a kiss more sweet than any he had dreamed possible this side of heaven.

Chapter 8

Tori awoke in the most delightful way. Something soft and fragrant was tickling her cheek. Her lids fluttered open in time to watch Jacob trail the velvet petals of a rose across each of her breasts, finally nestling it in the valley between them. Lambent golden eyes greeted hers, a lazy smile curving his lips. "Wake up, sleepyhead. After all the trouble I've gone to to bring you breakfast in bed, you should eat it while it's hot." Sending her a suggestive wink, he reached for the tray at the foot of the bed. "You need to keep up your strength, angel face."

"Breakfast in bed! Goodness sakes, Jacob!

What has come over you?" Tori sniffed appreciatively. Coffee, hotcakes, and crisply fried bacon—and fresh wild strawberries! Jacob must have gotten up early to go and pick them himself. If breakfast tasted half as good as it smelled, she was going to relish every single bite. She was ravenous!

"Let's just say I'm courtin' you, honey. After all, everything happened so fast, and a woman needs courtin' at least once in her life, doesn't she?" he answered with a self-conscious shrug and a grin.

Tori smiled back, her whole face lighting up. "I don't know if they *need* courtin', but they surely do appreciate it. I expect I'm going to love being courted by you."

It felt strange to be entirely naked under the thin sheet, sitting there eating her breakfast with her bare breasts exposed to Jacob's avid gaze, and the rosebud still tucked between them. Jacob had refused to let her retrieve her nightshift from the bedroom floor, insisting that he was enjoying the view too much to let her ruin it. While she ate, he lay across the foot of the bed, never once taking his eyes from her.

When she had eaten all but the strawberries, Jake moved up on the bed next to her. Removing the tray, he proceeded to hand-feed the succulent fruit to her, one by one. Sweet, sticky juice covered her lips and dripped onto her exposed breasts as Jacob held the lush berries just far enough from her that she had to reach for them, managing only a tiny nibble each time. With every bite, more juice dribbled down her chest until it ran in red-pink streaks all across her breasts, and between.

It was the most sensual experience Tori could imagine, especially when she saw the light of desire growing steadily in Jacob's eyes. Her own senses were achingly aroused. "Aren't you going to eat any?" she asked, her voice trembling with longing.

"In a minute, love," came his low promise. "In a minute."

The last strawberry almost stuck in her throat as Jacob's tongue snaked out to lap at the sticky liquid painting one bare breast. "Delicious!" he declared softly.

Tori could utter only a strangled moan in return as his teeth gently captured a pink-tinted peak. He nipped lightly, then soothed the small hurt with light lashes of his tongue. Inch by inch, Jake meticulously licked the sticky nectar from her tingling flesh, until Tori was nearly delirious with desire. Stroke after stroke, nip after nibble, until she cried out against this tantalizing torture, begging him to come to her.

Her hands joined his to tug at his clothes, tearing them from his hot, hard body. Then he was over her, plunging deep inside her, filling the emptiness and satisfying the deep craving he had lit within them both, and creating more. Their passion built, carrying them relentlessly upward to dizzying heights, toward a beckoning peak of unbearable pleasure.

Then, miraculously, Tori was flying—flying on wings of rapture, soaring through rainbow clouds of ecstasy and brushing the heavens themselves. Breathless with wonder, she clung tightly to Jacob, her only anchor on this glorious, gossamer flight. When they had flown as high as their hearts would reach, they hovered for a timeless eternity, then drifted slowly downward, sheltered in one another's sweet embrace.

Tori was thoroughly enchanted. If this was Jacob's manner of courting, she certainly could not complain! Her good mood was doubled when she looked in on her mother and found Carmen much improved from the previous day. Everything was going well for once. Outside the sun was shining, the birds were singing; God was in His heaven, and all was right with the world!

Tori thought that, today at least, nothing could destroy her sunny outlook on life, but she was mistaken. Shortly after lunch, Ana came to tell her that Millicent Moore, one of Tori's oldest and dearest friends, was waiting for her in the *sala*. Delighted that her girlhood friend had come to visit, Tori hurried to greet her.

No sooner was she across the threshold than Milly leaped from her chair and began pelting Tori with questions, not even allowing Tori to welcome her properly. "Is it true, Tori? Rumors are flying all over town that you have quit the convent and married your brother! Your *brother*, of all people!"

Taken aback, Tori managed to nod and say, "Yes, I have married Jacob, but—"

"How could you?" Milly interrupted with a frantic squeal. "It's illegal! It's immoral! My stars, Tori, have you lost your mind entirely? It's a sin, not to mention against the law!"

"Milly, please!" Tori shouted back. "Settle down and just listen to me for a minute, will you?" She motioned toward the chair Milly had vacated, and the other woman sank into it with a despondent sigh and a look of helpless disbelief.

"There is nothing wrong with my marrying Jacob," Tori hastened to explain. "Jacob is not my brother, though many people tend to forget that. He is only my stepbrother, and now he is my husband. Lands! I can't believe how people love to gossip, always making mountains out of molehills and stretching the truth until it's bent beyond all recognition. Did you honestly think I would do such a thing, Milly? Can you even imagine Father Romero condoning such a ceremony, let alone performing it?"

Milly heaved a heartfelt sigh of relief and shook her head. "No," she admitted, "but the fact remains that you *did* leave the convent, and he *is* still a gunfighter. Why, you could have knocked me over with a feather when I heard! I still can't believe you did it, stepbrother or not!"

Tori wanted to throttle her friend. Why did people always have to poke their noses into other people's concerns? Milly should be happy for her, not standing first in line to condemn her, and Tori promptly told her just that. "I thought you were my friend, Milly," she said reproachfully. "You had hissy fits when I decided to enter the convent, and I distinctly recall you telling me how I was throwing my life away. Well, now I'm home again, and the least you could do is wish me well in my marriage."

"I *am* your friend, Tori, and I *do* want to see you happy. That's why I'm so concerned about you now. I love you like a sister, and I don't want to see you hurt."

"Jacob would rather die than hurt me," Tori argued. "You know that."

"Do I? Tori, that was a long time ago, when we were small. Yes, he was a loving brother then, but what about now? People change, and I'm afraid Jacob might have changed more than most. He's a killer, Tori. That's how he earns his money, by shooting men down in the street! How can you, of all people, live with that? You can't just shut your eyes and ears to it and pretend it isn't so."

Hurt and angry, Tori snapped at her former friend. "I ought to toss you out of here on your bustle, Milly Moore! But before I do, I'll try once more to convince you that Jacob is not the devil people are painting him to be. Doesn't anyone remember what led Jacob to become what he is? Can't you recall how devastated he was when Caroline and Charlie and the baby were killed by those drunken outlaws? He was the only one with gumption enough to go after them, even as young and frightened and inexperienced as he was. Yes, he took vengeance into his own hands, but what else was he to do? Was he to sit around and watch the sheriff do nothing, and let those murderers get away with their crime?"

"All right, but in doing so, Jacob became just like them, didn't he?" Milly pointed out.

"No! I don't believe that. I'll never believe that about him, and I won't listen to anyone who says so. Besides, Jacob has given all that up now. He is home for good, and he is going to run the ranch. He is putting his past behind him, and I am going to help him do it."

Milly shook her head resignedly. "Then I wish both of you good luck, because you've got quite an uphill road ahead of you. Sweetie, as much as you wish it were different, people just aren't going to let Jacob forget that easily. He's got quite a notorious reputation. Even folks who've known him all his life are going to back away from him. Even if only half of what they've heard is true, it's enough to make them shy off. It's gonna make it rough for you, for both of you, but it will especially hurt you, Tori."

"What about you, Milly?" Tori asked hesitantly, knowing that her friend had spoken the truth. "Will you turn your back on him, too, without giving him a chance to prove you wrong? Are you going to turn your back on me and pretend our friendship never existed all these years?"

Milly rose from her chair, tears glistening in her eyes as she reached out to enfold her friend in her arms. "How could I do that to you, Tori? It would hurt me more than it would hurt you, I think. I just want you to know what you are up against, what people will say, so you can be prepared for it. And I hope you're not wrong about Jacob, honey. I pray you are right about him."

Jake jerked awake, sitting straight up in bed. His heart was thundering in his chest and his mind was racing as he recalled the dream that had wakened him. He was out of bed and pulling on his pants before Tori had time to realize what was happening. Her head had been resting on his shoulder as they slept, and he'd nearly toppled her onto the floor when he sat up so abruptly.

Tori rubbed her eyes, squinting at him in the darkened room. "What's wrong, Jacob? What time is it? Where are you going?"

"It's okay, darlin'. Go back to sleep."

"What's going on?" she mumbled sleepily.

"I just remembered something I have to check on. Nothin' to fret about."

"But it's the middle of the night," she argued. "Can't whatever it is wait until morning?"

Halfway to the door, he backtracked and kissed her hastily on the cheek. "Keep the bed warm, and I'll be back before you know it," he promised. Then he was out the door and gone before she could protest further.

As Jake's long strides carried him rapidly toward the other wing of the house and his father's gutted bedroom, he remembered the dream and the reason he had suddenly jerked awake. In his dream, he had been seeing again the afternoon when Carmen had given Tori her wedding ring. Carmen had pointed toward the drawer in the nightstand, and Tori had stretched out her hand to open it. But instead of pulling out the gold chain and ring, Tori had drawn forth a gun. Then, as dreams tend to do, Tori suddenly turned into Roy, holding the ivory-handled Smith and Wesson .44 that he'd carried through the Civil War.

Jake's mouth thinned into a straight line as

he thought of his father and the gun that had been Roy's pride and joy. It was a seven-shot revolver, and Roy had replaced the ordinary grips with a pair made of carved ivory. His initials were engraved in intricate script on the outer grip. Roy had been immensely proud of that handgun.

Jake knew his father had kept it handy, especially since his stroke had disabled him. At night, it was kept in the drawer of Roy's nightstand. It should still be there, but Jake had somehow forgotten about it and thoughtlessly failed to check, until the dream had reminded him. Now he knew what had been nudging at his brain that afternoon in Carmen's room. When she had gestured toward the drawer, he'd been foggily reminded of the drawer in his father's bedstand.

As Jake reached for the drawer, blackened and warped from the fire, he wondered why Roy had not awakened and armed himself that fateful night. With the gun so close at hand, he might have prevented his murder, if there actually had been an intruder as Jake suspected.

The drawer was jammed, and Jake twisted and pulled until he finally managed to get it fully open. He felt all around the inside of the drawer, but did not find the revolver. Frowning, he pulled a match from his pocket and struck it, holding it over the drawer. Inside, he found charred papers, a half-burned book, several burned matches and similarly charred cigars, all victims of the flames that had demolished the rest of the room. The gun was missing.

Unwilling to give up the search for such a vital item, Jake brought an oil lamp from the study and continued to look. Before he was finished, he had searched every nook and cranny, every drawer and corner of the room. The Smith and Wesson was not to be found. In the morning he would ask the others if any of them had seen the pistol, but standing there at that moment, Jake was willing to bet everything he owned that whoever had killed Roy now had the gun. Knowing how Roy had treasured that special weapon, it infuriated him that his father's murderer had taken such a favored possession, but in a strange way he was glad, because now it would make his search a little easier. When he found the possessor of that ivory-handled .44, he would most likely find his father's killer.

"I'll find him, Dad," he said softly to the empty room. "I swear to you, I'll find him." With one last, grim look at the fire-charred remains of walls and furniture, Jake spun on his heel and stalked out.

After his thorough search of the master bedroom, Jake knew there was nothing left in it to point to the murderer or give added clues. Tomorrow he and his men would begin repairs to the burned section of the house, starting in that room. Jake didn't think he could bear to walk past the room again, let alone enter it, until it had been cleared of all reminders of his father's tragic death. Maybe when it was fully rebuilt, spotlessly white-washed, and filled with different furniture, he and Tori could move into it and fill it with fresh, happy memories of the new residing master and mistress of the Lazy B ranch.

With any luck, by then Roy's murderer would be burning in hell, as Roy had burned here, and the memories of what had happened in this room would not torment Jake so severely.

In order to proceed with the repairs to the house, Jake had to make the ten-mile trip to Santa Fe for supplies and building materials. Since the doctor had visited again and been very pleased with Carmen's recovery, Tori felt it would be safe for her to leave her mother in Rosa's capable hands for this one day. It had been so long since she had been out of the house for longer than a few minutes, let alone into Santa Fe. Besides, she had some shopping of her own to do, and she could scarcely recall the last time she had gone shopping for herself. She had been at the convent for nearly two years.

Jake was thrilled to have Tori accompany him. He had intended all along to suggest that she come with him, but he had thought she would refuse, wanting to stay near Carmen. It was nice to have her sitting next to him on the wagon seat, his own ray of sunshine to brighten a boring ride. From the corner of his eyes, he saw her pat her short, curling hair self-consciously. Realizing how long it had been since she'd been to town, a trip the average ranch wife made about once a month, Jake suddenly realized how nervous she was about her appearance.

He grinned over at her. "You look right pretty today, honey," he assured her.

She grimaced and fiddled with a stray brown curl. "My hair is too short. Everyone will notice and stare."

"If they do, it'll only be because you're the most beautiful woman in the territory."

"Jacob!" she exclaimed with a wry chuckle. "You are a flirt!"

He laughed and leaned over to kiss her lightly on the lips. "Only with the most beautiful woman in the territory."

"That's real smart of you," she bantered back, poking him smartly in the ribs. "Especially if you want to stay healthy, Mr. Banner."

People did indeed stare as their wagon progressed through town. But it had little to do with the length of Tori's hair. Jake tried to ignore it, as did Tori, but neither could help but notice how nearly everyone they passed stopped dead in their tracks, stared, then hastily moved on as if they could hardly wait to spread the news that the Banners were in town. Tori could almost hear the wagging tongues over the noise of the wagon wheels. Her heart felt heavy in her chest. Milly had been right.

She didn't realize how right until Jacob stopped the wagon in front of Alder's Mercantile and helped her down. Three women on the boardwalk immediately pulled their skirts aside and turned their backs to her, openly snubbing her. Tori was appalled, and her face must have shown it, though she hastily tried to cover her shock with a sunny smile for her husband's benefit.

Jake's brow furrowed in disgust and anger. "I'm sorry, Tori," he apologized softly in her ear. "I should have realized this would happen. I guess I'm just so used to it myself that it doesn't bother me much what people think of me. But when they cut you, that's a different matter."

She raised a gloved hand to his cheek, touching it gently. Her eyes, though shadowed with sadness, also glowed with love. "It's all right, Jacob. I half expected it after Milly's visit. It will just take time, that's all. Besides, this is a good opportunity for me to discover just who my true friends are, and those who are just paying lip service to the word."

"Father Romero is right," he told her, shaking his head in wonder. "You are wise beyond your tender years."

Her eyes widened perceptively. "Jacob! You were eavesdropping!"

Having given himself away, he nodded. "And I learned some very interesting things that morning, too."

"I'll talk with you more about this later," she promised. "Now, why don't you go on about your business and let me get to my shopping, or we'll never be finished in time to get home before dark."

"You sure you'll be all right alone?" he asked, his gaze wandering to the other women standing nearby.

"I'll be just fine. Go on, Jacob. Trust me to handle this in my own way. Please?"

"I'd trust you with my life, darlin'," he told her solemnly, then left her standing there with a bemused smile on her lips.

Once inside the store, Tori met with much the same treatment, though some of the ladies had the finesse to cover their feelings a bit more gracefully. A few actually greeted her with taut, polite little smiles and asked about her mother's health. All surreptitiously glanced at her ring finger to see if the rampant rumors might actually be true.

Tori felt torn. On the one hand, she felt as if she should be wearing a sign about her neck reading "Jacob Banner Is Not My Brother, and Yes, We Are Married." On the other hand, she and Jacob owed these gossiping geese no explanations. Some of them had been her friends and friends of her mother for most of Tori's life, or at least they had professed to be their friends. Now they were certainly showing their true colors! She hoped they all strained their blasted necks trying to get a good look at her hand, her hair, and her infamous husband.

As she stood at the counter to have Harriet Alder fill her order, a small group of curious women gathered about her, their ears almost sticking out from their heads as they strained to hear what Tori might have to say. "Mornin', Victoria," Mrs. Alder said. "Been a spell since you've been in here."

"Yes, ma'am, it has," Tori agreed shortly. She proceeded to read off the items she needed from her shopping list.

As Harriet scurried about filling the list, she commented casually, "We all heard about the fire out at your place. Sorry to hear about your pa." After a short pause, during which Tori remained silent, deliberately not correcting the woman's glaring error in referring to Roy as her father, Harriet continued. "How is your ma doing now? Doc was in a few days ago and said she'd been through a real rough time of it."

"She's doing much better now," Tori answered. "Thank you for inquiring after her. I'll be sure to tell her you asked."

"You do that, dearie." Harriet placed an armful of goods on the counter in front of Tori and eyed her slyly. "Hear tell there's more news out your way. Word has it you've quit the convent and married that scoundrel son of Roy's."

Tori's chin went up defensively. "You must have heard wrong, Mrs. Alder. Roy Banner had only one son, and to my mind, Jacob has never been a scoundrel."

Harriet's laugh was grating. "Well, then, missy, our opinions differ a mite. I seem to recall that Jake Banner has quite a reputation with that fast gun of his, and if that don't make him a scoundrel, I don't know what does."

Tori stared the older women straight in the eye, her own eyes blazing with righteous fury. "I don't remember asking for your opinion, Mrs. Alder. Nor do I care what you think. You have a small mind and a big mouth, and that's a pitiable combination! Your husband has my condolences!"

That said, Tori shoved the items on the counter back into Harriet's limp arms, and told the flabbergasted woman and all others who cared to hear, "I will be taking my business elsewhere, where I do not have to contend with idle gossip and wagging tongues." She swept from the store with regal poise. "Good day, ladies," she said, aiming her parting shot at them all. "I do hope you serve your poor husbands more than simpleminded gossip at the supper table this evening."

Chapter
9

Though it would have been easier to get most of what she needed from Alder's Mercantile, instead of having to search several other establishments for the various goods, Tori managed to find the items on her list. Along the way, she was forced to endure added snubs, but her anger held her in good stead. It also helped that she met several women, most of them dear friends in the past, who chose to disregard the nasty rumors being circulated about her and Jacob. Their pleasant greetings, their welcome invitations and good wishes, were a balm to Tori's battered spirits. It warmed Tori's heart that she could still count so many townspeople as her friends, despite the spiteful attitudes of some.

Meanwhile, Jake was having problems of his own in trying to deal with the merchants of Santa Fe. Old boyhood friends pretended they'd never met him. Clerks and store owners clearly wished he would take his business elsewhere, though their fear of him made them serve him politely and promptly. This was not a new experience for Jake, but it made him impatient. Why couldn't they at least give him the benefit of the doubt? After all, nearly everyone knew that he was home for good, that he owned the ranch and intended to stay, especially now that he and Tori had married. Hell! Did they all have to walk around like timid rabbits, acting as if he were about to shoot them between the eyes the minute they did something that displeased him?

As he crossed the street, headed for the lawyer's office, he tried to rein in his temper. Tori was right when she said it would take time. The people of Santa Fe were not ready to welcome him back with open arms. At least not yet. But when they saw that he really meant to settle down to a normal life, that he wasn't going to go off half cocked and shoot up the town, surely they would come to accept him again.

Wayne Neister had asked Jake to stop by his office when he got the opportunity. There were some legal papers he needed Jake to sign. Now, as Jake sat across the big oak desk from his father's lawyer, he decided to confide some of his thoughts to Wayne. He needed the other man's opinion on what had happened at the Lazy B, about who might have been responsible for Roy's death. However, until he knew Neister better and was sure he could trust him, Jake decided not to say anything about the missing gun.

"Well, let's see," Neister drawled, the fingers of both hands pointed up under his ample chin in an attitude of thought. "From what you've told me, it would seem that the fire might not have been an accident, as we all assumed. But you haven't got much to go on, boy. Could it have been someone out to get back at you? In your profession, you're bound to have made a slew of enemies."

The old lawyer's straightforward attitude was refreshing, if not pleasing. At least Neister wasn't going to beat around the bush and walk on eggs around him. For that, Jake admired him. "No," Jake answered with a shake of his head. "I don't think so. Why would they bother, when I wasn't even home? Hell, I've only been back about three times in the last seven years. And I sure don't go around advertisin' where my family lives. I can count on one hand the number of men I'd trust enough to tell, and three of them are dead."

Neister's eyebrows rose. "And the other two?" he asked.

Jake's grin was wry. "A friend of mine in Arizona, and you. Blake I'd trust with my life. You I'll trust with my legal needs, until you prove different."

The lawyer threw back his head and laughed, his belly jiggling. "I like you, boy!" he announced. "You may not have seen eye to eye with your dad, but you remind me of him. He had a lot of grit."

Jake nodded. "I want you to draw up a will for me," he said, changing the subject.

Neister frowned. "You expectin' more trouble?"

"Yeah, and I'm not sure what kind," Jake admitted. "Whoever killed Dad might try it with me, and regardless of the rumors, I don't have eyes in the back of my head. Then, too, like you've pointed out, I've made a lot of enemies. Word's bound to get out that I'm livin' here now, and a few of my old rivals might take it into their heads to pay me a not-so-friendly visit. I want to make sure that if anything happens to me, Tori inherits everything. I also came here today so that someone else would be aware of what is goin' on. If I do get killed, I want someone lookin' out after my wife."

"Good plannin'," Neister approved. "I'll get right on it, and I'll be thinkin' about who might have killed your dad. By the by, does Victoria know any of this?"

"Not yet. I don't want to tell her unless I have to. With Carmen sick and everything else happenin', Tori's got enough to worry over."

"Well, I'll ride out your way sometime next week then with that will. And congratulations on your new bride. That's one sweet little gal you've got there, Banner."

Jake was just coming out of the bank when someone came up from behind and pounded him smartly on the back. Swinging around, fists balled, Jake came face to face with Ben Curtis, a boyhood buddy he hadn't seen in at least four years.

"Jake, you old rascal! I couldn't believe my ears when I heard you were back!"

The broad, open smile on Ben's face made Jake relax his guard. "Ben, you always were a foolhardy sort," Jake said, shaking the hand Ben extended. "Don't you know better than to sneak up behind a man as mean as I'm supposed to be? You could have gotten your face bashed in."

"Naw," Ben drawled, unconcerned. "You think I believe all those tall tales? I ain't as dumb as I look. Hey! How about joinin' me for a drink? I sure could use somethin' to wet my whistle about now."

"You sure you want to be seen talkin' to

me?" Jake asked, his tone telling Ben how serious he was despite the grin on his face.

Ben shrugged. "I'd druther talk with you than get dragged through that dress shop with Nancy Ellen and those two little hellions we have for kids," he joked. "Now that is pure torture, old buddy!"

With a laugh, Jake admitted, "I reckon I'll find that out for myself soon enough."

"Yeah, I heard you married Tori. Jesus, Jake! You should hear the talk goin' on around town about you two. You'd think no one has the sense to remember that you're not really her brother. And to hear them tell it, you practically kidnapped her from the convent and dragged her home by the hair and made her marry you."

Jake's eyes narrowed, his jaw tightening in anger. "Damn busybodies," he snarled. "They couldn't mind their own business if they were sewed into a sack."

"Don't let it bother you," Ben advised. "Next week they'll be gossipin' about somethin' else, and you'll be old news."

"Sure, but in the meantime, Tori is the one bein' hurt the most by all this. Some of those self-righteous old biddies have already started turnin' their noses up at her."

"Then I hope it rains—a real gully washer. Maybe they'll all drown before they can get their snoots out of the air."

Jake was laughing again as he and Ben

walked into the saloon. Suddenly, all the talk stopped, and you could have heard a pin drop as everyone watched Jake and Ben make their way to a table and sit down. "Dang, Jake," Ben said in a voice loud enough to carry. "You quiet a place down better'n old Father Miguel ever could!"

They were sitting at a table drinking and minding their own business, talking over old times and catching up on more recent days, when a drunken cowboy stumbled up to them. Behind the stubble of beard and the red-rimmed eyes, Jake recognized another acquaintance from his youth, but Ed Jenkins wasn't in a mood to be polite.

"Well, well, if it ain't the high and mighty Jake Banner," he declared drunkenly. The whiskey fumes from his foul breath were enough to ignite the room. "The big, bad gunslinger come to honor his home town!"

Ed belched and drew himself as erect as he could manage in his inebriated state. "But, I ain't afraid to face ya. No, sir, I ain't!"

Jake cursed under his breath. He and Ed had never been friends, especially once Ed had taken a shine to Tori and Jake had been forced to cool the young man's ardor. "H'lo, Ed," he drawled, pushing himself back slightly from the table and getting ready to rise in a hurry if need be. "Somethin' I can do for you?"

"Yeah, you dirty bastard," Ed growled.

"You kin cart yer rotten carcass out o' town as fast as ya came in, and you kin take that little whore of a sister with ya when ya go. Nun, my sweet ass! Boy, that's a laugh if I ever heard one!"

Jake was on his feet and towering over the table faster than Ed could blink. Beside him, Ben stood too, ready to fight at his side. "You're drunk, Ed," Jake hissed through bared teeth. "Stinkin' drunk. If you were sober, I'd probably kill you for what you said about my wife. As it is, I reckon I'll just rearrange your nose for you. Again."

The table went tumbling as Jake pushed it out of his way, whiskey glasses and all. Ed just stood there, blinking stupidly at him for a long minute, while the crowd in the saloon waited to see who would throw the first punch. Then Ed lurched forward, swinging wildly, and the fight was on. While Jake sidestepped and landed two solid blows, one to Ed's face and another to his stomach, one of Ed's drinking buddies decided to join the fracas. Ben took him in hand, but by now several more men had jumped into the free-for-all, and the entire saloon became a battleground, with no clear sides drawn.

Fists were flying indiscriminately, glass was shattering, tables and chairs were hurled across the room. Curses colored the air as flesh pounded flesh and bones crunched in protest. Finally, having taken enough of this nonsense that was wrecking his tavern, the saloon keeper raised his double-barreled shotgun toward the ceiling and pulled a trigger. Everyone froze. Several of them comically examined their own bodies for a bullet wound as the owner roared, "There's another shot left for anyone who wants to go on fightin' in my place! You want to beat each other's brains out, do it outside!"

Amid the grumbling that followed, most of the men preferred to stay and drink peaceably. Tables and chairs were retrieved and turned upright again, and fresh drinks ordered. Jake and Ben had had enough. Ed lay groaning on the floor, his head half buried under a broken chair, his broken nose bleeding profusely.

"Let's go," Ben said, leading the way toward the swinging doors.

Jake agreed. "Yeah, before anyone else gets any bright ideas." He followed, rubbing his bruised jaw where someone had landed a lucky punch.

They were halfway to the doors when the short hairs on Jake's neck rose like hackles. Ed's cry of "Hey, Banner!" still rang in the air as Jake's spine began to tingle. Jake spun on his heel, his gun drawn and firing almost faster than the eye could see. The gun Ed had leveled at Jake's back went spinning out of his hand as the man grabbed his stinging fingers and yelped.

"Consider that a warnin', Jenkins," Jake snarled, his eyes narrow slits of gold in his chiseled face. "I don't give 'em twice."

Shaking his head in awed disbelief, Ben traipsed after Jake. Behind them, they could hear the whispered comments of the stunned cowhands. *I ain't never seen anyone clear leather that fast! Did you see that? He didn't even take aim, but he blew that gun clean out o' Jenkins' hand just slicker than a whistle! Didn't even nick Ed's fingers! I don't ever want to tangle with him. That's for sure. That Banner is one mean rattlesnake! Heard tell he killed four men at one time in a shootout down in El Paso once, and had two shots left in his gun!*

"More grist for the gossip mill," Jake grumbled.

"Why didn't you kill him?" Ben asked shakily. "Christ knows, he sure did ask for it, and no one could've faulted you."

"You think not?" Jake asked ruefully. "Before supper there'll be twelve different versions of what went on in there, and ten of 'em will have me deliberately pickin' a fight with good ol' Ed. Shit! If I'd've killed the drunken fool, the whole town would've been ready to lynch me before the smoke had cleared. And wouldn't Tori just love havin' to live that down, on top of everything else?"

By the time he met up with Tori, Jake was in a foul mood. As he tossed her bundles into the bed of the wagon behind the seat, he told her grumpily, "I hope you bought a new dress or two while you were at it. Maybe seein' you in something bright and pretty will help cheer both of us."

He was boosting her up into the seat when he caught her grimace. "Okay, darlin'. What's the face for?"

"Well," she confessed hesitantly, "I *did* buy two new dresses, but I don't think they are quite what you have in mind, Jacob."

Jake placed her back on her feet beside the wagon. "Where are they?" he demanded. "We're not movin' from this spot until I see them."

Tori pointed out the package and chewed her lip as he reached for it. "Jacob, this is ridiculous! Let's go on home."

Tearing the wrapping away, Jake held the drab dresses up for inspection. His scowl deepened. "Why in blue blazes did you buy these? These are only fit for old ladies and the poorhouse!"

"Stop exaggerating," she argued, her hands on her hips as she faced him. "Those are perfectly proper dresses for a married woman. Ladies aren't supposed to wear bright colors and frothy dresses once they are married."

"Oh?" Jake cocked a raised brow at her. "You mean once they catch their man, they don't have to look pretty anymore?"

"Quit twisting my words, Jacob. You know very well that I am right about this. It is unseemly to dress so . . . so—"

"Attractively?" he supplied when she could not find the proper word. "Sweetheart, you're a young, beautiful bride. You're not an aging matron or a prim old maid. I want to see you in light, lovely colors. You should be dressed in frills and lace, with flowers in your hair." At her stubborn frown of disapproval, he said sternly, "Victoria Banner, are you going to please your husband or this petty-minded little town?"

Voiced that way, there was little she could do but agree. A good wife always tried to please her husband in all things, and Tori was too new to married life to strain at her traces as yet. At least not over the purchase of a couple of dresses which she, too, considered ugly. She'd only bought them because she thought it was expected of her to dress more conservatively now.

With Tori in tow, Jake marched her straight back to the dress shop where she had bought the dresses. Within minutes, he had helped her select three lovely little day dresses that flattered her huge green eyes and petite figure. Then, much to her surprise, and the shock of several women inside the milliner's shop, he steered her past the hats and bonnets and insisted on inspecting the newest in the line of French silk undergarments and nightwear.

Tori was mortified! Her face felt on fire as Jake bought a seductive red satin gown and a peignoir of filmy peach silk. She nearly fainted when he purchased several sets of sheer undergarments, never even having to question the size!

But Jacob was not yet satisfied. Before they left the shop, he watched as she selected a perky bonnet to match the prettiest of her dresses. Tori wondered how she could ever face anyone in town again, once the news of Jacob's latest escapade had gone the rounds, as it surely would the moment they stepped out of the store!

Tori was still fuming later that evening. The day, which had started out with such promise, had ended in disaster. First to meet with such vile behavior in town, especially when she had done nothing to deserve it. Then to have Jake embarrass her by choosing her unmentionables in full view of half the town!

Jake watched Tori toy with her dinner. He'd dragged the entire story from her on the ride home, including the confrontation with Mrs. Alder. He felt terrible, knowing that he was mostly responsible for the way Tori had been treated, but he was immensely proud of her, too. She had stood up for him again, and for herself. More and more, Tori was shedding that shy-mouse attitude she had assumed in her role as a nun. Day by day, she was becoming the Tori he used to know—sweet and darling, but also full of spunk.

He hid a grin as he heard Tori grumble under her breath about "hateful old biddies" and "nosy busybodies". He swallowed a chuckle as she muttered something about "infuriating, bossy husbands." It eased his mind that she was handling these problems as well as she was. Instead of dissolving into tears and crawling away to lick her wounds, Tori was angry. She was fighting mad, and that was so much better than acting like a hurt little defenseless animal. Jake sensed that he'd have to be careful not to get in her way when she really began to let her temper fly.

In fact, she had become almost as angry with him as with the townspeople when she noticed the purpling bruise on his jaw. Then he'd had to tell her about the argument with Jenkins and the resulting brawl in the saloon, though he did not repeat Jenkins' insults to her. Knowing she would learn all about it from someone else, he had told her how Jenkins had tried to shoot him, and how, instead of killing the man, he'd merely shot the weapon from his hand. At least this part of his confession pleased her. It proved that he was trying to put the violence of his past behind him.

As they were getting ready for bed, Jake thought he had the remedy for Tori's anger. Seating her on the edge of the bed, he told her, "Close your eyes, darlin', and don't peek. I have somethin' for you, but I don't want you to look until I say."

Tori complied with an exasperated sigh. "Jacob," she complained, "I'm much too wrought up for this sort of thing." She listened as he pulled something out from under the bed, unwrapping the crisp paper noisily, and her curiosity was piqued. Against her will, she found herself anxious to see what Jacob had brought her.

"You can look now," he said finally.

Tori opened her eyes to behold the most beautiful shawl she had ever seen. It was of the finest, most delicate white lace, so filmy that it looked like an intricate gauze cobweb. Fine silver threads ran through the snowy fabric, catching the light and making the shawl glimmer in a thousand places. "Oh, Jacob! Where did you ever find it? I have never seen one so lovely," she breathed, reaching out to finger the lace.

Ever so tenderly, Jacob draped the shawl across her head and shoulders. "It was surely made for you, sweetheart. No other woman would ever be able to complement its beauty the way you do." His eyes told her how beautiful he thought she was.

Gazing back at him with her heart in her

eyes, Tori murmured, "But, Jacob. It must have cost the earth! You really shouldn't be so extravagant."

"It's your weddin' present, Tori. A man only gets married once, if he's lucky enough to find the right woman and keep her safe, and he has a right to spend a little extra on a gift for his bride."

"But I didn't get you anything," she protested.

"Oh, but you did, angel face. You stood up to those old biddies today and spoke for me, when I'm probably not worthy of the defense you gave me. You give me your sunny smile to brighten my dreary days. You gave me yourself, sweetly and passionately. That's more than enough for any man, Tori, and much more than I deserve or ever expected to have."

Tears sparkled like emeralds in her eyes as she reached out to draw him near. "Oh, Jacob! I do love you so very, very much!"

His voice was slightly gruff as he said, "Do you know, I think that is the first time you've spoken those words to me in just the way I've waited for so long to hear you say them—the way a woman says them to her lover, to her husband."

"You are more than my lover, Jacob, and more than just my husband. You are my heart. My dearest darling. You are my love."

Then, in the privacy of their room, she set

out to prove to him the deep, abiding truth of her words; giving herself to him fully, sweetly, with no reservations. She held nothing of herself back from him, but offered him the full glory of her body and her heart, asking nothing in return but his own love to warm her soul.

Chapter 10

Trouble seemed to follow them like a dark storm hovering on the horizon. When Jake saw one of the hands galloping hell bent for leather toward the ranch yard, he knew it had struck again. He felt it in his gut as he watched the man rein in his lathered horse so sharply that the animal reared up on its hind legs, nearly unseating its rider. Jake met the man halfway.

"Boss!" Red hollered excitedly. "We got trouble! Real bad trouble!"

Jake's face was grim. "What is it?"

"The water hole in the far north pasture! It's been poisoned!"

"Damnation!" Jake couldn't think of anything worse that could have happened right now. They had just driven some of the herd onto that range to fatten through the summer. This time of year the grazing was good there, and the water plentiful. "Any cattle dead?" he asked anxiously.

"Two down and about a dozen more actin' peculiar," Red declared with a glum look. "And the fish are all bloated and floatin' on top o' the water."

Turning to Gill, who had approached in time to hear Red's solemn announcement, Jake said, "I want ten men mounted and ready to ride out with me. Send three more out to check the other herds and watering areas. I want a report on anything unusual." Jake headed for the ranch house at a trot, calling back over his shoulder, "Tell 'em I want them all carryin' their guns."

By the time they reached the north pasture, five head were dead. Several others were staggering about and bawling pitifully. Jake's face grew dark with anger as he spat out orders. "Keep the herd away from the water. Round 'em up and head 'em east. Jeb, you and Swifty round up all the sick ones and shoot 'em. Willy, you and Rooster drag the carcasses into that hollow. I reckon we'll have to either burn or bury 'em. Sam, I want you up on that ridge standin' guard."

Jake stalked to the edge of the water hole and stood staring morosely at the sea of dead fish. "Hell fire!" he muttered. "What I'd give to get my hands on the bastard responsible for all this!" Fury in his eyes, he started walking the bank, carefully checking the area around the small pond. He'd gone about a fourth of the way around when he spotted the patch of white crystals at the edge of the water. Bending down for a closer look, Jake knew he'd found the poison that had been used. "Lye!" he snarled. "The lousy sonovabitch put lye in the water!"

When he told them what he'd found, the men shook their heads in dismay. It was a miserable thing to do to a dumb animal. Lye caused severe inflamation, burning and swelling the victim's insides, until it finally died. A bullet was quicker, and much more merciful. The snake who'd done this deserved the same death he'd dealt these poor beasts.

With grim resolution, they set to work putting the cattle out of their misery. There was no help for it. More toil lay ahead, when that task was done. The water hole had to be fenced off or filled in so that no more animals could drink from it. Since fence could be too easily cut, allowing the same thing to happen again, Jake decided that the hole had to be filled.

Then, if they were to continue using this land for grazing, fresh water had to be supplied. If they dug other ponds or wells, the culprit could poison those, too. Jake wasn't willing to risk it. Instead, he decided that now was the time to put an old idea of Roy's into play. It would mean a lot of hard labor, for he and his men would have to dig a channel from the Santa Fe River, which ran almost dead center through the Banner property.

It wasn't probable that anyone would chance poisoning the new channel since the poison could contaminate the river water, too, and the Santa Fe River was the main supply for dozens of ranchers and farmers, and the town as well. Jake suspected that whoever was behind this only wanted to bring disaster to the Lazy B. It was doubtful that he'd risk harming others. Jake needed to find out why this culprit had targeted the Banners for his revenge. Why? What possible reason was there?

The stench from the dead fish, already growing rank in the heat of the sun, was so bad that the men had to wear their bandannas over their noses. Jake knew he should be thankful that the putrid stench had caught Red's attention and led him to investigate as soon as he had. Otherwise, they might have lost a good many more cattle before they had discovered the poisoned water.

Working alongside his men, Jake tried to block out the wretched bawling of the suffering animals. Even when the last one had been mercifully shot, the bawling continued. Several young calves had lost their mothers and were crying out in fear and confusion. Adoptive mothers would have to be found for them. Those that would not be taken to teat by another cow would have to be weaned immediately or bottle-fed until they were old enough to graze on their own.

At length, another of the hands was sent up on the ridge to change places with Sam. When Sam rode into view, he was not alone. Across the saddle in front of him, he carried a quivering little fawn. "Found its mama dead in a patch of tall grass," he explained. "This little mite was curled up next to her body and makin' the most pitiful sounds. Guess the doe must've managed to get back to him somehow after she come down for a drink. What we gonna do with him, boss?"

Jake sighed heavily. "If the fawn drank her milk before she died, then he's probably a goner, too."

"I looked him over real good, boss," Sam said. "I don't think he's sick. He's just mighty lost and hungry, and mournin' his mama."

"Then we'll take him back to the ranch with us," Jake decided, taking pity on the poor orphaned deer. "Maybe Tori can feed him until he's old enough to be turned loose on his own again."

A smile crept into Jake's tawny eyes for the first time that day. "I'll bet she'll take to him like a bee to clover." The smile melted instantly as he wondered how many more animals would die before this was over. Hanging was too good for the man or men who had done this!

It was long past dark by the time the weary cowhands rode into the ranch yard. They had buried twenty-seven cattle, nine of them calves. It had been a long, gruesome day, and for some it was not yet done. Four armed men had been left to guard the water hole so that no more cattle would wander back and try to drink from it. It would take three days or more to fill it in safely. A half-dozen more cowhands would ride the boundaries of the Lazy B, on lookout for anyone intent on doing more evil. Still others would keep a special watch over the herds. Tomorrow morning, Jake would ride into town to notify the sheriff of this latest attack on Banner property.

When she heard the men ride in, Tori went out to the stable. There she found Jake unsaddling his horse. Her heart went out to him. He looked so tired, almost asleep on his feet. He didn't even notice her standing outside the stall.

"Your supper's warming on the stove," she said softly, not wanting to startle him.

He turned to find her watching him, a warm concern glowing from her eyes. "Thanks, honey."

"How bad is it?" she asked.

Jake shook his head. "Almost thirty head

lost. It could have been worse, though, so I reckon we can count ourselves lucky."

Hearing the awful bawling coming from a pen outside the barn, Tori winced. "Are more dying?"

"No. Those are orphaned calves. We'll try to place them with new cows tomorrow."

He finished rubbing down his horse and came to take Tori's hand. "Come with me. There's somethin' I want you to see." He led her down the row of stalls, then stopped before one and pointed inside. "There. What do you think of that little fella?"

Squinting through the dark shadows, Tori saw something move. It had spots and long, spindly legs. As her eyes adjusted, Tori almost squealed in surprise and delight. She had never seen anything so adorable! "Oh, my lands!" she whispered excitedly. "It's a fawn!"

Jake's arm came across her shoulders, drawing her close to him. "Think you can mother him for a while?" he asked. As she turned wide, questioning eyes up to his, he added, "Sam found him next to a dead doe. She must have taken some of the poisoned water."

"Oh, the poor darling!" Tori was immediately overwhelmed with sympathy. Her second emotion was a deep-welling anger. "Who could be so unthinkably evil, to put poison in the water like that? Lord only knows how many other animals are suffering and dying because of this one act of violence." Her mind was filled with horrible pictures of small animals curled up in agony, dying a terrible death.

"I know, but we saved this one at least. And most of the new calves. You'll probably have to bottle-feed him for a while. Looks to me like he's only a couple of weeks old. Think you can manage that?"

Tori nodded, her gaze fixed on the tiny animal curled up in the stall. "I'll heat some milk right away. Poor thing is probably starving."

As if aware of what she had said, the fawn lifted its head and let out a weak, soft little bleat that tore at Tori's heart. "Oh, Jacob! He's calling for his mama!" she said with a catch in her voice.

"You're all the mama he's got now, darlin'." Jake gave her a quick hug and pulled her away from the stall. Side by side, they headed toward the ranch house. "You see to your little orphan while I clean up."

He wrinkled his nose at his own odor, wondering how much of it was his and how much he had absorbed from the dead animals he'd helped bury. "God, it's been one hell of a day! I'm almost too tired to eat."

Tori would have pampered her husband a bit, but Jake was more capable of seeing to his own needs than the little orphan in the barn, so she hurried to heat the milk and pour it into one of the big bottles they sometimes used to feed baby calves. By the time she returned to the stable, the fawn was bleating more loudly, demanding to be fed, and most likely bawling for his lost mother.

"Come here, little one," Tori crooned, seating herself on the straw and pulling the trembling animal half onto her lap. She held his head and pushed the nipple up to his mouth, but the fawn suddenly decided not to open his mouth. It took several tries before Tori could get him to accept it, but once he smelled the milk and sampled a few of the drops Tori had managed to work onto his tongue, the fawn grabbed at the nipple with such force that he nearly pulled the bottle from her hand.

Tori chuckled, holding the bottle while he suckled hungrily. "Greedy little baby, aren't you?" she teased. As he nursed, she stroked him gently. His nose was like black velvet, and his spotted coat still had a downy texture to it, less coarse than it would be soon. His front legs were curled under him, his hind quarters sprawling. He had the longest ears, and the most soulful brown eyes, with long dark lashes fringing them to perfection.

Tori was enchanted, thoroughly and totally. She petted the fawn long after he had finished his meal and drifted off to sleep, and in those few precious minutes a bond was formed between her and the velvet-eyed baby on her lap.

By the time she tore herself away and made her way back to the house, Jake had eaten and gone to bed. He was sprawled on his stomach across the bed, buck naked. He had fallen asleep before he had found the energy to pull the coverlet back and crawl between the sheets.

Tori walked up to him, sympathy welling up as she saw the dark circles beneath his eyes. "Another poor baby who needs some loving care," she sighed to herself. When she tugged at the covers and tried to move him into a better position, he groaned and flexed his shoulders, as if they were bothering him in his sleep. Tori could only imagine the labor he'd done today.

Running her hands over the bunched muscles of his shoulders, she could feel how tense he was. Probably sore, too. Quietly, she tiptoed out of the room, returning with a small bottle of liniment. Hiking her nightdress up out of her way, she straddled his bare buttocks and poured a generous amount of the liniment into her palm. "Jacob Banner," she told him softly, "you are about to get the best rubdown you've ever had in your life, and you won't even be awake to appreciate it!"

He moaned, he groaned, he grunted in oblivious pleasure, but he never awakened as she worked the tension from his back and thighs. As her hands and the liniment worked their magic, he melted further into the mattress, sighing with contentment. When she was finished, Tori blew out the lamp, fitted herself crosswise on the bed alongside him, and pulled the extra blanket from the foot of the bed over them both. Within seconds, her deep, even breathing joined his.

In the next few days, the fawn, which Tori named Velvet, took to following Tori around like a puppy. In the midst of their busy, troubled days, she and Velvet were the one bright spot around the ranch, bringing a smile to many a weary face, both young and old. Velvet had been well and truly adopted, and if Tori were not careful, the little rascal would even follow her into the house, his sharp little hoofs clicking along the tile floors and making Rosa throw up her hands in dismay.

Velvet took all his meals from the bottle, guzzling the milk like a glutton. When he thought Tori was a bit slow about getting his dinner to him, he would butt her legs and bleat softly, as if to say, "Hey, remember me? Isn't it time to eat yet?"

At night he slept on his bed of straw in the stable stall, but during the day Tori let him loose, and he faithfully dogged her every footstep, hardly straying from his new "mama"'s side. Tori lavished him with attention, which the fawn lapped up like honey, each filling a spot in the other's heart. He was her "baby," at least for now, and by the time he was big enough to fend for himself, Tori hoped she would be carrying another kind of child to take his place—a child conceived of the love shared by her and Jacob.

Carmen was recovering rapidly from her terrible bout with pneumonia. Her lungs, which had been through the worst of trials, were finally starting to clear. Her burns were beginning to heal nicely, and the doctor was thrilled with her progress. At long last he deemed Carmen well enough to tell her about Roy's death. This sorrowful chore fell to Tori.

Tori chose a quiet morning when Jake and most of the men were gone. They had begun digging the new channel from the river to the north pasture, and because every hand was needed there, repairs on the house had come to a halt. The house and immediate ranch yard were unusually void of activity.

Tori entered her mother's room carrying a tray with tea and toast. She doubted that either of them would want anything to eat or drink once she had broken the news to Carmen, but it gave her something to do with her hands and a good excuse for visiting with her mother, as if she really needed one.

One look at her daughter's face, and Carmen was not fooled into thinking this was an ordinary visit. "You may stop trying so hard to smile, 'Toria," she told her. "It is not working very well to disguise your troubled face." She gestured toward the chair at the side of the bed. "Come tell me what is wrong. Is it Jacob? Is he making you unhappy?"

"Oh, no, Mama!" Tori denied quickly. "Jacob is wonderful to me." She sat down and took her mother's hand in her own. "It is something else, something I must tell you that will make you very sad."

Carmen's hand came up to stroke her daughter's cheek, her eyes full of understanding and sorrow. "If it is about Roy, I think I already know what you are trying so hard to tell me, what you have avoided saying all this time. He is dead, isn't he?"

Tori nodded miserably, tears flooding her eyes. "We didn't know how to tell you, and you were so sick before that the doctor thought it would be best to wait. I'm so sorry, Mama."

"I am sorry, too, 'Toria, more than I can say. He was a good husband to me, and a good father to you. I miss him very much, but it is Jacob I grieve for most. Losing his father has been a great blow to him, more than he could guess. I am glad he has you to console him, 'Toria. He needs you so just now."

"I am glad, too, if I can help him through his sorrow," Tori admitted. "But how did you know about Dad?"

Carmen's smile was sad but wise. "How could I not guess?" she asked. "If he were alive, he would have come to talk with me, to sit with me, to argue and tell me to hurry and get well so I could make his favorite meals. In his own gruff way, he would have urged me to get better, trying to make me think it was just to make his life easier that he wanted me well again."

Tori nodded in agreement, and for the next few minutes the two women sat silently recalling the irascible man who had wormed his way into both their hearts. "Do not fret, 'Toria. Yes, I am saddened by his passing, but already I have had time to start to come to terms with my grief. It is not so sharp a pain now, not so fresh. As my body is healing, so will my heart, and so will yours and Jacob's. In time, it will not hurt so much to think of Roy. There will only remain treasured remembrances of the man we all loved."

Jake returned to the house in mid-afternoon that day to find Tori gone. From Rosa he learned that she had spoken with Carmen about his father's death, and he supposed that Tori was upset because of this. In past years, whenever Tori was deeply troubled she'd had a habit of wanting to be by herself, to work through her problems in solitude. Jake guessed that was what she had done now, but where would she have gone? He hadn't actually told her not to leave the ranch yard, but because of their recent problems, he had assumed she would have the good sense to stay nearby. Apparently he was wrong.

Worry nagged at him. He had to go after

her! Evidently, because he had put off telling her his suspicions about the fire and Roy's death, Tori did not fully understand the perils of going off by herself. At this very moment, she could be in danger. But where to look?

It was Carmen who gave him an idea of where to search. "There is a meadow in the hills that Tori loves. Before she left for the convent, it was her favorite place. She told me once that to her it is nature's cathedral, the most perfect spot on earth."

"Do you know where it is, Mamacita?"

"Not exactly, but I can describe it to you as Tori did to me. It is ringed with pine trees, and the mountains loom up on two sides. A stream runs there, clear and cold from the mountains. I know it is not far, for Tori could ride there and back in the same afternoon. I'm sure that is where she must have gone, Jacob. Do not look so worried. She has visited there many times and will not lose her way. Just wait; she will be home soon. You will see."

But Jake was not about to sit calmly back and wait while Tori's life could be in danger. While he said nothing to alarm Carmen, since she knew nothing of any of the problems going on around the ranch, Jake was fast becoming frantic to find his wayward wife. Saddling his horse again, he rode out toward the mountains, having a good idea now where Tori's meadow might be. At least he knew the general area in which to look, and when he found her he was going to give her the spanking of her life for being so blasted reckless and for worrying him so!

If Tori weren't so blindly trusting, she would have known better than to ride off alone. Knowing her aversion to guns, Jake was also willing to bet she had also broken another cardinal rule of the ranch, that of never going anywhere without a loaded gun, if only for protection against varmints and wild animals. Damn, if he wasn't going to tan her hide when he caught up to her!

But Tori was not alone. She had ridden slowly to her meadow hideaway, deliberately dallying so that Velvet could keep the pace. She wanted to share this lovely spot with the dainty, timid fawn. She wanted Velvet to be able to run safe and free among the flowers, to chase after butterflies and bees and stretch his gangly legs to their limit. He was a wild thing, and it was not right that he be confined to the ranch so much. He needed to stay in touch with nature, even while Tori looked after him, so that he would know what to do when she set him free.

While Velvet romped happily close by, Tori lay flat on her back in a field of wildflowers so thick they looked like a rainbow carpet. In a flight of fancy, she had plaited a garland of blossoms and placed them about her head like a crown. Their scent surrounded her with a fragrant perfume unmatched by man's most concentrated attempts.

Above her, the sky was a brilliant cerulian blue, with only a few puffy clouds floating serenely in its limitless expanse. A light breeze ruffled through her hair, carrying the scent of pine needles her way. Nearby, a small stream gurgled merrily, adding its song to that of the birds and bees. Behind her and to one side, the ageless mountains stood sentinel over this special place, this magic meadow where peace and beauty reigned supreme.

Jake sat astride his horse, shaking in relief. She was here. He had found the meadow and Tori, and she was fine. At the moment, he didn't know which urge was stronger, to beat her until she cried for mercy, or to kiss her until she did the same. He was glad as heaven that he'd found her unharmed, and mad as hell that she'd led him on such a goosechase.

What infuriated Jake the most was Tori's complete disregard for her own safety. Here she lay, with a garland of wildflowers bedecking her shiny black tresses, looking like an elfin princess off on a holiday, completely at ease and humming contentedly to herself. Anyone or anything could have come upon her here, just as he had, and she had no means of protecting herself.

Jake eased from the saddle and crept silently forward, intent on teaching his careless young wife a well-earned lesson. Neither the baby fawn nor Tori's horse became alarmed at his arrival. He crept to within inches of her, careful to keep his shadow from falling upon her and alerting her to his presence. At the very moment that Tori seemed to sense that her privacy had been invaded, her eyes widening suddenly in wary surprise, Jake pounced.

Tori shrieked, panic streaking through her like a lightning bolt. Kicking and clawing for all she was worth, she fought for several seconds before she realized that it was Jake she was fighting, Jake who was holding her captive, his big body firmly atop hers. His eyes blazed down into hers with the fury of a hundred suns, his hands clamped about her wrists to stop their flailing. For long moments he said nothing, merely glared at her. Finally he spoke. "Victoria Elena Marianna Banner, you don't know the extent of the trouble you're in."

Beneath him, Tori's heart lurched and her limbs began to quiver. Lord in heaven, what had she done to deserve the fury she saw on Jacob's face? Whatever it was, it must be pretty awful! Jacob had used her full name, and she could only recall two times in all her life when she had made him angry enough to do that. Both times he had paddled her bottom until she'd had trouble sitting for a week. But surely she was too old to spank now! Or was she? From the dark frown on Jacob's face, she wouldn't bet her last dollar on it!

Chapter 11

"Jacob!" Tori exclaimed breathlessly. "What in the world? Why are you so angry with me? Lands, but you scared the daylights out of me!"

"I'm beyond angry, Victoria. I'm downright furious!" His smile was deliberately sinister as he said, "And I meant to scare you. Maybe it will knock a little sense into that feather-twitted head of yours! How you can be so stupid, coming all the way up here alone and unarmed, is beyond my understandin'!"

"But, Jacob, why shouldn't I? I've come here for years, and no one has ever bothered me."

His face came close to hers, his jaw twitching with barely bound rage. "Are you just naturally dense, or is that another thing they taught you in that convent? I don't recall you bein' quite this damn stupid before!"

Without another word, he hauled Tori onto his lap and kissed her soundly. "That is for being safe and whole when I found you," he announced, as her head continued to spin from the force of his kiss, her lips tingling delightfully. "And this is for goin' off and worryin' me half to death!"

With a deft move, he swiftly flipped her face first over his lap and anchored her there, tossing her full skirts over her head. As he jerked her pantalettes down to her ankles, Tori regained her breath. "Jacob! No! You can't!"

"Oh, yes, I can!" he ground out, administering a sound whack with the flat of his hand. Her muffled shriek of pain and outrage barely fazed him as he released his pent-up emotions on her bared bottom. "You are never . . . *never* to leave the house alone again unless I say you can! Is that understood?" Another whack followed the first.

Through her skirts, Tori was yelping, "Stop! Jacob, please! I'll never be able to ride home!"

The punishing hand ceased smacking her bare flesh. "Do you understand that you are not to go off by yourself again?" he repeated.

"No!" she sobbed. Then as his hand came down hard a third time, she shrieked, "Yes! Yes!"

"Which is it, Tori?" he asked, pausing once more. "Yes or no?"

"Yes, I will stay at the ranch," she gulped tearfully, "but no, I do not understand why it's so blasted important to you all of a sudden!"

Jake groaned, as if he had been the one to take the spanking. "Tori, Tori, what am I to do with you? How do I get through to you how much I love you and how dangerous it is for you to roam about like this?" Not waiting for an answer, he bent and placed his lips gently on the tender flesh he had abused just moments before.

Expecting another whack, Tori jerked when she felt Jake's lips touch her smarting bottom. Beneath her skirts, her already flushed face turned even brighter as he proceeded to lavish kisses on her bared posterior, murmuring apologies for having spanked her in anger. Her breath caught sharply as his tongue came out to lave the faint marks his fingers had left there. A new heat rose to her cheeks, chasing through her veins, as his hand soothed the hurt, then strayed between her quivering thighs.

A strangled moan tore from her throat as his fingers found her, stroking and arousing until she was trembling with sudden, searing longing. Still dangling across his knee in the most humbling, humiliating position she could imagine, her embarrassment was overshadowed by acute desire as his long, lean fingers slid smoothly into her, finding her wet and warm and throbbing. Her muscles clenched about him, holding him there while her body exploded into spasms of ecstasy.

Before she had regained her senses, still trembling, Tori found herself once more on her back in the flowers. Her skirts had become lumped about her waist, her rosary twisted into a knot of beads at her throat, the scooped neckline of her blouse loosened to bare her breasts to his seeking mouth. Hot, eager lips suckled, making her gasp with renewed passion as Jake loomed over her. Crazed with desire, her shaking fingers tore at his shirt, ripping the shoulder seam in her haste. "Come to me, Jacob! Come to me now!"

Cradling her burning bottom in his hands, Jake plunged into her, her cries echoing his own as he made them one and took them on a soaring ride upon the spinning tail of a comet. It was a very long time before they returned to their shaken earthly bodies.

Tearing his lips from hers, Jake stared down into her glimmering green eyes and flushed face. "You make me crazy, Tori. Are you an angel or a she-devil, to bewitch me like you do?"

Her answering smile was as old as Eve. "If

I'm an angel, as you've always said, then I'm a fallen angel. Your own fallen angel, my darling.''

His big hand came up to straighten the coronet of blossoms that had somehow stayed about her head all this time. He laughed. ''Your halo is crooked, angel face.''

''Yes, and you have clipped my wings, my love. I could not fly from your arms if my life depended upon it.''

Tori's words were almost prophetic as they rode slowly home a little while later. With every bounce of her sore bottom upon the stiff saddle, Tori was reminded of the spanking she had received, and what had come afterward, but Jake had still not explained everything to her. He'd said he wanted to get her home safely first, and then he would tell her all the reasons behind his anger and his worry.

Tori rode beside him, carrying the tired fawn before her on her horse. For as young as he was, Velvet had had quite a day in the meadow, and now he was almost too tired to protest being carted about like a sack of potatoes. His long lashes fluttered in a losing battle with sleep.

Suddenly a sharp report rang out, and the bark flew from a tree just inches from Tori's head. Tori screamed in terror, frantically trying to control her startled mare, even as Jake grabbed her horse's bridle and tugged the frightened animal along behind his into the thick brush beside the trail. More shots rang out, whistling through the air, barely missing them as they fled for cover.

They thrashed through the trees and under-growth, limbs and thorns tearing at their clothes and the horses' hides. Behind them they could hear the sounds of pursuit. When Jake spotted an outcropping of rock that looked like a good place to take cover, he pulled their horses to a halt and yanked Tori from her mount so quickly that she barely had the presence of mind to grab Velvet in her arms. She sat huddled behind the rock where Jake had pushed her down, and watched with wide eyes and trembling limbs as Jake drew his Colt and prepared to fight for their lives. Velvet bleated softly in fear, ceasing only when she hugged him tightly to her in false security.

"Jacob?" she whispered fearfully. "Who is shooting at us?"

His eyes scanning the surrounding area, Jake did not spare her a look. His face was grim and alert, his gun ready. "I don't know," he answered softly. "Probably the same per-son who poisoned the water hole and set fire to the house. The same man or men who killed Dad and caused your mother such agony."

As frightened as she was, his words still rang clear in her mind. "What do you mean? Are you saying that someone deliberately set fire to the house that night?"

Jake nodded, still not looking her way. "I can't really prove it yet, but yes."

Tori was stunned at this new thought. "But who?" she repeated shakily. "Could it be Ed Jenkins? You fought with him in town just a few days before the water hole was poisoned."

"That could have been his doin', but I sort of doubt it. Besides, I don't think he would've had any reason to kill Dad. I wasn't even home then, and not plannin' to be."

Catching a glimpse of a plaid shirt through the trees, Jake fired, but his target had moved too quickly and was now hidden again. Several more shots rang out. Jake dodged a bullet that whined past his ear. More bullets ricocheted wildly off the rocks. "Damn! They've got us pinned down here like rabbits in a pen! All they have to do is wait, and sooner or later I'll run out of ammunition."

"They?" Tori questioned. "There are more than one?"

"Yeah," Jake snarled, returning another volley. "One man may be callin' the shots, but he has help. I'd say there are at least three of them out there, and that makes our situation even more dangerous. While one or two keep our attention occupied, the others can try to double around behind us."

Jake's next shot was followed by a loud howl of pain. "That's one we don't have to worry about anymore. I just wish I could get to the body and find out who the bastard is. I also wish there was more than one way down from here, besides the trail we were on, since they're between us and it."

"But there is, Jacob!" Tori exclaimed softly.

His head swiveled about and he stared at her, barely avoiding a bullet that whipped his hat from his head. "What?"

"There is another trail, just an overgrown path really, but it leads practically right to the river. I've used it as a shortcut to the ranch when I've lost track of time and had to hurry home."

Jake took a moment to shoot back at their ambushers. "Can you get to it from here without having to go past these bushwhackers?" he asked.

Looking around her, Tori nodded and pointed to the south. "That way."

"I'll hold them off while you make a run for it," he told her solemnly. "Ride for the ranch as fast as you can, and send help back. I may not need it, but as long as you are here, I can't chance anything too risky."

"No," she said, shaking her head at him. "I won't leave you here alone. I won't go without you."

"Tori, get out of here!" he hissed. "Don't get stubborn on me now. Can't you see that I need to know that you're safe? As soon as I'm certain of that, I can concentrate on getting rid of this vermin, one by one!"

"And get yourself killed needlessly, when

we can both escape right now!" she argued back.

"I promise you I won't get myself killed," he told her. "I just need to know you are out of danger. Then I can find out who is causing us all the trouble and take care of the problem once and for all."

"And what if these are just hired assassins?" she pointed out. "What if the main source of our problems is down there waiting? What if one of them is out there now, just waiting for us to make a break for it? What if he catches me? What then, Jacob? What if you sacrifice yourself for nothing?"

She had a point, and Jake decided it was too much of a gamble to let her try alone, with no way to defend herself. If he'd been by himself, he might have stood a decent chance of eliminating the few men out there. He'd been in tighter spots than this, and come out the winner. But Jake had Tori's safety to consider, and he knew that if these killers got Tori in their clutches, they would have him hogtied. She couldn't and wouldn't go alone, and the two of them couldn't stay here much longer.

They waited until the shooting slowed and the lack of return fire would not be so noticeable right away. Then, leading their horses, they quietly sneaked away. Tori led the way, with Jake keeping a sharp lookout for their assailants. "It'll be dark soon," he whispered.

"If you can find that path before then, maybe we can lose them altogether."

As good as her word, Tori found the faint path as the last rays of daylight were fading. For a short distance more they crept quietly along, not mounting their horses until they were certain their attackers had not found the path and were not following. Only then did they ride, when there was no chance of immediate discovery.

Jake had never been so happy to see the Lazy B, though he still didn't draw a decent breath until they were safe within the bounds of the ranch buildings. His only regret was that he had failed to identify their assailants. By this time, Tori was so shaken that she could not dismount without his aid, and stood quivering within the safe haven of his arms for long moments afterward. "Oh, Jacob! I have never been so frightened in my life!" she declared tearfully.

"Now do you understand why I was so upset when I found you gone this afternoon?" he asked, cradling her head against his thudding heart. He felt her head nod against his chest. "I'm holdin' you to your promise. I don't ever want you to leave the ranch yard without an armed escort personally approved by me. If I'm too busy, and if I know about it, another of the hands might go with you, but you are never, ever to go off by yourself again—at least until we catch the maniacs behind all these attacks. It's just too dangerous, honey, and I swear I'd go mad myself if any harm ever came to you."

Frightened beyond anything she had ever experienced, Tori readily agreed, but the following morning when Jake insisted she learn how to handle a gun, Tori balked again. "No, Jacob. I have agreed not to leave the ranch by myself, and I fully understand the danger now, but I cannot do this. Dad tried to teach me once, after you were gone, but I was hopeless at it. He finally gave up and admitted that I was more of a hazard with a gun than I would ever be a help."

"Well, I'm not as willin' to give in as Dad evidently was." He handed her a rifle and said firmly, "We'll start with this. I've set targets up behind the barn. Let's go."

Jake started off ahead of her, but when he looked back to see if she was following and found himself eye to eye with the barrel of the loaded rifle, his heart nearly stopped. "Jesus, Mary, and Joseph!" he shouted. "Don't ever point a loaded weapon at anyone unless you intend to kill them!"

"I'm sorry!" she shrieked back at him, startled by his shout and what might have happened if the gun had gone off while it was aimed his way.

"You'll be a damn sight sorrier if you ever turn a gun on me again!" he promised gruffly, his eyes flashing golden flames. "You think your sweet little arse is sore now, just pull that trick again and I can guarantee you won't sit for a month!"

The rest of their morning passed in like manner, with Jake shouting at her and Tori pouting, her bottom lip sticking out sullenly and her eyes clouding to murky green slits that reminded Jake of cat's eyes.

"Holy shit, woman! Aim at the target! The target! I won't have to worry about feedin' those last few calves if you don't stop peltin' lead their way!"

"Don't scream at me, Jacob! That watering hole won't be the only thing around here poisoned if you don't watch your step!"

"You threatenin' me, sugar?" he asked with a dire look.

"That was no threat, mister! It was a solemn promise!" she spat back, returning his look in full.

On it went, until Jake finally had to admit defeat. Tori was more of a threat than most of his enemies, and it would probably be safer all around not to let her within ten feet of a loaded gun. There just was no determining what she might hit, or not, as the case may be. He'd just have to keep her safe without arming her.

Tori was vastly relieved. Not only was she terribly inept, but it scared her silly to be in charge of such a lethal weapon. Besides that, everything she believed in, all her religious teachings, went against having to kill someone. Tori simply did not think she would ever have the heart to deliberately harm another living person, regardless of what they had done to deserve it.

The men continued their work on the river channel to the north pasture, and Carmen continued to improve daily. As she did, some of her friends began to come out to the ranch to visit with her. This cheered Carmen greatly, and it made Tori happy, too, since she was now forbidden to leave the house.

Most of Carmen's visitors were dear friends, not prone to spreading gossip or believing idle rumors. If a few women whom Carmen had thought were close friends did not make an appearance, she seemed not to notice their absence, or if she did she did not comment upon it.

Inevitably, however, Carmen learned of the gossip about Tori and Jake, and how a number of the townspeople had treated them on their last trip into Santa Fe. Not only did she hear about Tori's encounters, but also about Jake's fight with Ed Jenkins. It dismayed her to know that her daughter and the man she had raised as her own son were having such trials. As ill as she still was, Carmen staunchly defended them, like a mother bear with her cubs.

"People can be so stupid, and so cruel," she

commented sadly. "They have such small minds that they cannot see what is before their eyes. Always, they see only what they want to see, and hear only what they want to hear. No matter that it makes little sense, or that it might be wrong. Their lives are so dull that they must invent things to worry over, and they leap at any bit of gossip that comes their way. They are to be pitied, I suppose, but it is difficult not to resent their vicious tongues."

"The Bible says that we are to love those who despise us, and to love our enemies," Tori reminded her gently. "Are we not taught to turn the other cheek?"

"*Sí*," her mother agreed, "but nowhere does it say we must abide them endlessly, take them to our bosoms, or put up with them for company. People like that are best avoided, 'Toria. They are not true friends, nor will they ever be. They only cause trouble and strife."

"Snakes in Eden is what they are," Alvina Garcia, one of Carmen's dearest friends, decreed. "Fiendish devils with no good to do or say for anyone but themselves."

Milly, who was also visiting that day, added to Alvina's statement with a giggle, "And they speak with a forked tongue, as all snakes do, just as the Indians have always suspected."

"Do not take their hateful comments to heart, 'Toria," Carmen advised. "Do not let them hurt you with their words or deeds. Do not allow them to mar your happiness with Jacob, or they will have succeeded in their vile attempts. Just because they cannot find such joy as you have found, they let their jealousy eat at them and try to destroy the happiness of others more fortunate than they."

"I won't, Mama," Tori vowed. "Nothing they might think or say can destroy the love Jacob and I have found together. Our love will stand strong and true against them."

Little could Tori know that her brave words would be severely tested in the not too distant future.

Chapter 12

It took just over a month of back-breaking work before the new water channel was completed. After the attempt on Jake's and Tori's lives, nothing further occurred to cause alarm. Still, Jake was not about to believe that all was well. He suspected that this reprieve was merely a deceptive calm before the storm, and he warned his men not to let down their guard. Danger was still lurking about, just waiting for the right time and opportunity to strike at them again.

Everything was going smoothly, almost too smoothly. The repairs to the house, put off for so long, could be resumed. Suddenly Jake was eager to see the wing repaired and move into the master bedroom with Tori. Not that their present room was uncomfortable. Still, it seemed more fitting, more permanent some-how, that they move to the larger room de-signed for the master of the Banner ranch and his wife. It even had a private bathing and dressing area connected to it, which would surely be much more pleasant, especially for Tori.

When two more weeks had gone by and no more trouble had reared its head, Tori announced that she would like to go to church. "I don't want you going into town by yourself yet," Jake told her.

"Fine, then come with me," she suggested, not to be deterred.

"I think that is a lovely idea," Carmen put in from her chair by the big *sala* window. She was now allowed to be up and about a bit during the day, and was thoroughly enjoying every moment of regained activity, though it would be weeks yet before she could resume her usual routine once more. She still tired easily, and the burns on her hands and feet were still tender, the new skin shiny and sensitive.

"It's a terrible idea!" Jake could only hope the two of them were merely teasing him. "Why, I'd be as out of place as a burro in a horse race. Besides, the roof would probably cave in if I set one foot inside the door. Do either of you realize how long it's been since I've been to church?''

Tori shot him a wry look. "I have some idea," she told him mockingly. "Your first confession would probably go on for three days. They'd have to bring in food and drink to sustain Father Romero, but the sheer variety of your sins would guarantee that he'd stay awake, if only out of shock and curiosity.''

"You're linin' up quite a list of indiscretions yourself there, honey," Jake shot back with a grin. "Make sure you include your sassy mouth, especially toward your husband. That ought to earn you a few extra prayers, at least.''

In response, Tori stuck her tongue out at him. "You are sadly irreverent, Jacob Banner,'' she declared.

"And you're an impudent brat. Don't point that tongue out at me unless you intend to use it for somethin' besides lookin' silly.''

Coloring to the roots of her hair, Tori shot a quick, embarrassed glance at her mother, who merely shook her head at their antics. "Take her to Sunday Mass, Jacob," Carmen advised. "You could both benefit from a little piety.''

On Sunday, Jake escorted Tori to the door of the mission chapel, but refused to go in with her, despite her pretty pleas. "Maybe another time, Tori. I'm just not ready for that yet, and neither are the other parishioners, I'm thinkin'."

Standing on tiptoe, she brushed his lips with hers in a quick kiss. "I'll say a special prayer for you, Jacob."

"You do that, darlin'. A prayer from an angel is bound to get results." He straightened the white lace shawl, his wedding present to her, about her dark halo of hair. "I'll be here to meet you when you come out. Now mind, if I'm a little late, don't go wanderin' off. Stay put right here until I come for you."

Jake watched until Tori entered the church, then went off in search of a saloon that might be open this early on a Sunday morning. Maybe in the course of downing a few beers he could pick up some interesting tidbits about who was behind all the troubles at the ranch. Men, even those up to no good, tended to brag about their deeds, especially when drunk. It was amazing, the things a bartender or barmaid learned and were often willing to pass along, for the right price, of course. A dollar down the front of a barmaid's dress could buy a lot more than a good tumble in an upstairs room.

Jake's hunch paid off, though not as well as he had hoped. He'd wanted to run into someone from the feed store or the lumberyard, both places where lye was sold; he'd wanted to find out if anyone had purchased a quantity of lye lately. Instead, he learned that Harold's

Feed and Grain had been broken into about a month and a half back, and among the missing merchandise was an entire keg of lye. The thief had not been caught, and no one had the faintest notion who might have done it.

More disturbing was the news that several strangers had been seen around town lately. A couple of the drifters were real rough-looking desperados that no one wanted to lock horns with. Upon closer inquiry, Jake identified the two men. One was Rafe Mendez, a Mexican bandit noted for his fancy silver-trimmed saddle.

The other was known only by the name of Reno. He sported a long, jagged scar down the left side of his face, which turned one corner of his mouth up in a permanent grimace. He was a hot-headed young gunslinger looking for a fast reputation and an even quicker death. Jake had heard of him. Reno was out to impress the world with his bad mouth and his fast gun, both of which spelled trouble. He was always spoiling for a fight, and always ready to prove himself faster on the draw than any other man, particularly another gunfighter with an established reputation—and Reno had been asking around town about Jake.

Trouble was, Reno hadn't arrived in Santa Fe, as far as anyone knew, until about a week ago. Not that he couldn't have been somewhere in the area sooner than that and just not shown his face around town until lately.

Jake wasn't going to rule him out as a suspect in the attack on him and Tori, but it just didn't seem like Reno's style. The cocky gunslinger was too vain to sneak around behind a man's back. No, Reno preferred the glory of goading a man into an open fight and shooting him down before a crowd of wide-eyed spectators. Reno enjoyed strutting about like a peacock and seeing the fear build in people's eyes.

Jake also doubted that Reno would stoop to something as underhanded as poisoning cattle. That was something done by a man who wanted to remain nameless, and Reno was out to claim every victory he could. He was one of those brash young braggarts who actually notched the butt of his gun for every man he killed, and Jake suspected that Reno added more notches than he could truthfully account for just to make himself look meaner than he was. In truth, Reno probably wasn't as fast on the draw as he claimed to be.

However, Reno's supreme vanity made him as dangerous as a snake with no rattles, and Jake was not fool enough to disregard his presence in town. While Jake doubted that Reno was behind the attacks, he suspected that Reno was looking for him, wanting to draw him into a showdown, wanting to add yet another notch on his gun by cutting down the legendary Jake Banner. The foolish young gunslinger was just another worry to add to Jake's growing list of worries, just another problem he would prefer not to have to deal with just now.

For Tori, entering the mission again after such an extended absence was like coming home. It was like a reunion, every face so dear and familiar to her, especially those framed by the stiffly starched veils of her former sisters. Tears stung her eyes as she was embraced lovingly time and again, drawn into their midst and their hearts. After the cruel rejection of several of the townspeople, this warm, heartfelt welcome was doubly sweet to her.

Her heart swelled with gladness. As she let the cleansing peace of the service wash through her, it seemed that the weight of her worries lifted from her slim shoulders. Once more she found solace in prayer and devotion to the Supreme Creator. With sincere gratitude, she offered up thanksgiving for her mother's recovery, and for the love she had found with Jacob.

By the time Jake returned to the mission to take Tori home, he found her in the connecting schoolyard, surrounded by children. Her face was aglow with joy and peace, and a stab of envy shot through Jake that Tori's faith and these children could so easily give her such a look of absolute contentment. Rarely did *he* bring her peace; rather, he brought her love, passion, anger, frustration, and lately a lot of worry. As he stood silently observing her, he hoped he gave her happiness as well.

In complete disregard for her dress, Tori was kneeling in the dirt, showing several little boys how to shoot marbles. Hovering nearby, a group of giggling girls clamored for her attention. "Come, Sister Esperanza! You promised to turn the rope for us to jump!"

"*Momento, niñas*," Tori chuckled indulgently. "You must learn patience, little ones. The boys asked first."

It struck Jacob, as he watched Tori with the children, how very good she was with them, so patient and gentle and caring. He could see the love shining from her face, reflected in the bright eyes of the youngsters clustered about her. He could see the open trust on the young faces as they hung on her every word. As he watched, he had a vision of Tori with children of her own, his children and hers. She would be a wonderful mother, he was sure. The thought brought a slight smile to his lips.

The only disturbing thing was that Jake wasn't certain he would make a very good father. Those years when he had helped to raise and guide Tori seemed a lifetime ago, part of a distant, hazy past that often seemed no more than a dream to him. So much had happened between then and now, and he had changed in many ways. Would he still have the patience and humor with his own children that he'd had when teaching Tori? Or would he be a stern, domineering father, following the pattern his own father had set with him?

Tori scored a hit with her marble and the boys cheered her success, but Tori was confused when their piping voices suddenly stopped in mid-stream. Glancing up, she saw the tension in their bodies, the tight-lipped fear on their faces as they stared at something behind her. Even the girls had fallen silent, now huddled together with silent, anxious looks. Turning slowly on her heels, Tori was relieved to find that Jake was the source of their wariness. A smile lit her face as she held a welcoming hand out to him, inviting him to come nearer.

"Niños," she called gaily, noting how carefully they watched him, how their eyes seemed to take in the size of him, the fluid way he walked as he stepped closer, and especially the intimidating gun strapped low on his thigh. They seemed to hold their breath as Jake reached out to take her hand and pull her to her feet. Letting her fingers rest within his, she said calmly. "Come meet *mi esposo, niños.* This is Jacob Banner, my new husband, who I was telling you about earlier."

For a long moment, none of the children moved, just stared silently at Jake as if frozen in place. Then six-year-old Tomás bravely stepped forward, his hand outstretched toward

Jake in a manly gesture. *"Mucho gusto, señor,"* he intoned gravely, his voice quavering only slightly. "I am called Tomás."

Jake bit back a grin as he hunkered down to Tomás's level and shook the boy's small, trembling hand. *"El gusto es mío, Tomás,"* he said, returning the greeting. "I am glad to meet you."

"Tomás is becoming a very good player at marbles," Tori announced. Jake almost chuckled as Tomás drew himself up proudly at Tori's praise, his small chest puffing out like a banty rooster's.

To Tomás, and the other children who were witnessing this exchange, Tori said, "Jacob is the one who first taught me how to play the game. I still cannot beat him."

At this, the boys, at least, stared at Jake in awe, their big eyes wide with new admiration. "Really?" they chorused.

Jake grinned and shrugged sheepishly. "Yeah, really," he chuckled. "Do you think I should let her win once in a while, just to make her feel better?" he asked, as if he truly wanted their advice.

Several dark heads shook from side to side. "No," one little fellow said seriously, quickly switching his alliance to this new hero. "That would only make her more uppity."

As Tori's eyes widened in surprise, Jake laughed. "You're right," he agreed, "and girls can be a real pain in the neck when they get too full of themselves." Several small heads nodded in vigorous agreement.

"So I'm uppity, am I?" Tori huffed in mock anger, hands on her hips and eyes traveling from boy to boy.

The chorus of varying answers brought more laughter from Jake: "Well, only sometimes." "No, but you could get that way, I guess." "He didn't mean nothin' bad, Sister. Don't be mad."

Tori wagged a finger at them, her stern demeanor completely ruined by the grin that teased at her lips. "I see where your loyalties lie. I may be vain, but at least I'm not a fickle puss like the lot of you!"

Tori still had the girls on her side, and they were not so swiftly won over by Jake's charm. One pigtailed darling piped up in Tori's defense, "Can he jump rope better than you, Sister?"

Casting a smug grin at Jake, Tori declared, "Definitely not!"

The little girl smiled in satisfaction, turning up her pert nose in disgust. "Then he's not as good as he thinks, is he?"

Tori almost choked on a very unladylike hoot. "No," she chuckled, then winked and whispered loudly as though confiding a secret, "but we women always try to make the men think they are, anyway. It makes them feel good to think they are smarter and better than us, even if they're not."

The girls all giggled at this and nodded wisely. The boys and Jake frowned, but Jake's golden eyes twinkled up at her from where he knelt, promising retribution for her sassy remarks. Tori returned his teasing look, her face glowing with anticipation, her heart beating more rapidly in her chest.

"Jacob, I want to go back to teaching at the orphanage." Tori sat brushing her hair, which caressed the tops of her shoulders in soft, dark waves. "Mama is well enough now."

Jake hid a sigh. Ever since they had returned from church, he'd been waiting, knowing that Tori would soon broach the subject. Buying time, he sat on the edge of the bed and tugged his boots off. Finally he met her waiting gaze. "No, Tori. Not now; not yet. It's too dangerous. I want you here at the ranch, where I know you're safe."

She returned his look with a frown. "It's been well over a month since we've had any trouble. Perhaps whoever was making the problems has given up, now that he knows you are home for good."

Shaking his head, he repeated more firmly, "No."

"Is that all your word is worth to me?" she accused, her face a mask of hurt. "You promised, Jacob. You said once Mama was well, I could teach again."

"I'm sorry, but it's too big a risk. Be reasonable, Tori. Surely you don't expect me to let you go back and forth to the convent school every day when a killer might be lurkin' out there just bidin' his time and watchin' for the right opportunity to strike again."

"Oh, but you expect me to just sit here until donkeys fly, twiddling my thumbs and quaking in fear, when the danger might be long gone, when I could be doing something good and useful instead. Is that it?" Her eyes flashed pale green fire at him.

A muscle twitched in his jaw as Jake tried to keep a rein on his rising temper. "You've got plenty to keep you busy right here," he pointed out. "When I'm sure it's safe, you can teach again."

"And when might that be?" she persisted hotly.

Jake exploded. "How the hell should I know? Damn it, Tori, give it a rest! I'll decide when the time is right, and you'll be the first to know. All right? Have you forgotten already what it felt like to have bullets flyin' past your head? To be pinned down behind those rocks and wonder if you were gonna come out of there alive?" He hated feeling so helpless in this situation. He hated not knowing who was behind the attacks. He hated dictating to Tori and refusing her requests; and he hated not being able to do anything about any of it.

"No, I haven't forgotten," she assured him stiffly. "And I haven't forgotten how you killed a man that day, either."

He winced at that, but would not back down. "Am I supposed to apologize for killin' a man who was out to do the same to you and me?" he asked sarcastically. "Well, you'll wait a long time to hear that, sweetheart."

"You could send someone with me to the school," she suggested, switching the conversation back to the original vein. "Just mornings and afternoons, to and from. I could go just two or three days a week, and I'd be safe with the sisters at the convent during the day."

"Right," he jeered. "What could the sisters do to protect you, Tori? Pray your attackers away? Throw a rosary at them? Threaten them with reading primers and scrub buckets?"

"I was safe there before."

"That was before. Now you are the wife of a gunfighter. Now you live here at the ranch, where all the trouble started. Besides, I can't spare a man to escort you right now. I need all the hands we have just to guard the ranch, get the regular work done, and attend to the repairs to the house. And God knows, you can't protect yourself worth beans!"

Tori's chin rose defiantly. "Perhaps I ought to move back to the convent, then, if you're so concerned," she said stubbornly. "I could teach the children, I'd be away from any trouble that arises here, and you could come and get me when all the problems are solved to your satisfaction."

His smile was just a twist of his lips. "Over my dead body," he answered softly, the dark, quiet tone of his voice more of a warning than if he had shouted.

She had no reply to that. As much as she wanted to argue her point, she did not want anything to happen to any of them, not to Jacob, her mother, herself, or anyone else on the Lazy B. There seemed no ready solution, and she would just have to wait a while and swallow her disappointment.

She and Jake were at an impasse, and in the next few days it created a small rift in their relationship. Help was to come from an unexpected source. One morning, just as they were sitting down to breakfast, a shout was heard. "Banner! Get your carcass out here and call off your blasted watchdogs before someone gets hurt! Is this any way to welcome guests?"

Chapter 13

Tori scampered after Jake as he hurried toward the front of the house. There she stopped short, dumbfounded at the sight before them. Astride his horse, his pistol trained on three anxious ranch hands, sat Jake's best friend, Blake Montgomery. Next to him, astride her own mount, sat his lovely wife, Megan. Even as she urged her horse sideways to the armed men before her, shielding the infant hanging from the pommel of her saddle in something that resembled an Indian cradleboard, Megan leveled her own gun at the men who threatened her and her child.

Spotting Jake, Blake threw his friend an

exasperated look. "Nice welcoming committee you have here, Banner. Bet they keep the beggars away, not to mention practically everyone else. Got many friends left these days?"

Jake laughed and waved his men away. "It's all right, fellas. This is Blake Montgomery, one of the finest men you'd ever want to meet and the fastest gun in all of Arizona, now that I've left his territory."

"Still as modest as ever, I see," Blake commented dryly, dismounting and tossing the reins to one of the men. As he assisted Megan from her saddle, he asked, "What in tarnation is going on around here?"

"We've had a little trouble lately, so we're taking a few extra precautions."

Jake had sent a telegram to Blake and Megan shortly after he and Tori were married, telling him about the fire, Roy's death, and Carmen's injuries. Now Blake's brows rose as he questioned, "Besides the fire, you mean?"

"Yeah, but we can discuss all that later. Right now, I'd like both of you to meet my new bride, Victoria Banner, or Tori as we all call her."

Megan's smile was wide and friendly as she stepped forward to give Tori a warm hug. "It's good to see you again, Tori," she said. "Last time we met, you were Sister Esperanza, and I felt so sorry for Jake then. He was so alone."

"Last time we met, there were only two of you," Tori answered softly, eyeing the baby in Blake's arms with eager anticipation.

Blake laughed and handed the baby over to her. "Watch her, Tori," he warned with a grin. "She makes a habit of wetting on anyone and everyone."

Megan chuckled. "You'll be lucky if that's the worst of it. She's teething and fussy, and thoroughly put out with us for making her ride in her cradleboard."

"Oh, Tori has a way with children," Jake assured them, watching as Tori bent to rub her cheek against the soft skin of the baby's face.

"That's good," Megan said as Blake nodded in agreement, "especially since you are Alita's godfather. If anything ever happens to Blake and me, you two will be expected to raise this little darling for us, and I might as well warn you now, Alita likes to have her own way most of the time."

"Like mother, like daughter," Blake teased, earning himself a sharp elbow to the ribs.

"Well," Jake said, "let's go on inside. Then you can tell us what brings you all this way. Breakfast is on the table."

At this, Megan nearly groaned in gratitude. "That sounds wonderful! Blake rushed me so this morning that I barely got a bite of breakfast at Aunt Josefa's, and I could swear I smelled hotcakes and sausage all the way from the river!"

"Don't mind my wife, folks. She's always been a bit forward, and she's always swearing. I've tried to break her of that habit, but—" Blake ducked as his wife swung a playful fist at him and missed. Catching her arm, he swatted her on the bottom as he steered her through the open door. "Tsk, tsk, Megan," he taunted. "You really should stick to throwing frying pans. Your aim is so much better."

Tori wasn't sure, but she thought she heard Megan mutter, "You should know, dear!"

Over breakfast, the Montgomerys informed Jake and Tori that they would be in Santa Fe for a few weeks. Blake's Aunt Josefa had been living with them on their ranch near Tucson since before Alita's birth. Only now could they finally find the time to make the trip back to Santa Fe to collect more of Josefa's belongings. "She has decided to sell her little house and stay with us permanently," Blake told them. "She and her menagerie of animals."

Megan nodded. "She's a sweet old dear, a bit batty at times and terribly forgetful, but she loves Alita, and the baby simply adores her. However, I am not looking forward to sorting through sixty years of collected miscellaneous papers and recipes and books. The woman is a veritable pack rat! It took over a week for Blake and me to search through things just looking for proof of his parents' marriage. Packing Josefa up and closing the house will take much longer, I'm afraid."

"Perhaps I can help," Tori suggested. Her generous offer met with a deep frown from her husband.

"What's the matter, Banner?" Blake teased. "Don't want your new bride away from your side?"

"It's not that exactly," Jake said, as Tori tried not to blush. "I just don't want her away from the ranch right now, with all the problems we've had lately." He went on to outline for his friends all the trouble that had occurred.

With a sigh, Tori added, "Now Jacob is afraid to let me out of his sight. He won't even let me teach at the orphanage anymore, until all this is settled."

Megan surprised them all by agreeing with Jake. "He's probably right, Tori. You shouldn't go around unprotected. Still, if Blake and I were with you, you'd probably be safe enough." Arching a brow at the two men, Megan asked, "Well, what do you think?"

Blake shrugged. "I'm willing, if Jake agrees."

To refuse would cast a slur on his best friend's abilities, and Jake had been the one to teach Blake how to fastdraw in the first place.

He knew Montgomery was every bit as capable of protecting Tori as he was. "I'll think about it," he conceded. "Maybe we can work somethin' out. I know Tori is gettin' sick of bein' confined to the ranch yard day in and day out." The hopeful glow on Tori's face made it hard for him not to agree, even though he still had serious doubts about the wisdom of letting her go. "We'll try it and see how it goes."

Tori was out of her chair and throwing her arms about his neck almost before the words had passed his lips. "Oh, Jacob! Thank you! You won't be sorry! You'll see, everything will be fine."

"I hope so," he muttered with a frown. "God, I hope so!"

In the end, it was decided that the Montgomerys would stay at the Lazy B and ride into town on the days they needed to help Aunt Josefa. Josefa's tiny little house was too small for the two of them and the baby, and this way they would be on hand to escort Tori into Santa Fe. Blake would also be handy in case of another attack at the ranch, a welcome and very valuable addition to Jake's small army of defenders.

Tori could have danced on air, she was so happy! This gave new meaning to the phrase "Having your cake and eating it, too." Not only did she have Jacob and her life at the ranch, but she could now see her friends in town and teach a couple of mornings a week as well. The only thing better would be to discover who was causing all the trouble and see them locked up in jail where they could do no more harm.

In the meantime, Tori was quite content with the present situation and her newfound freedom, and when she was at home with Jacob, she made certain he knew just how much she appreciated him and his love. If they spent less time together, the time they did have was well spent, with hardly a minute wasted and rarely a cross word between them.

In Megan, Tori found a new and valued friend. She had never met anyone quite like the vivacious, outspoken redhead. She said what she thought, no matter how outrageous, and she was quite the opposite of the soft-spoken, timid nuns Tori had been accustomed to associating with. While she was a good mother and a loving wife, Megan was also her own woman, secure in who and what she was. If she felt like riding astride, she did so, and the devil take whoever didn't like it. If she wanted to carry her baby on her back like a papoose, she dared anyone to criticize her. She also carried her own weapons and knew how to use them.

"I've been through too much to chance

losing those dear to me now," Megan told a wide-eyed Tori. "If it ever comes down to it, I'll kill anyone who tries to harm my family."

"Did your husband teach you to shoot?" Tori asked, relating how both Roy and Jacob had attempted to teach her, and how miserably she had done.

Laughing at Tori's experience, Megan said, "Blake didn't exactly teach me. I sort of have a natural talent for it, I guess. He did give me some instruction, though. I'm no quickdraw, but I can generally hit what I aim at."

"I don't think I could ever take another life, no matter what," Tori confided. "I hate guns and violence. I don't mean to sound self-righteous or anything, but doesn't it bother you to think about spilling another person's blood?"

"Tori!" Megan exclaimed with a giggle. "I'm not going gunning for anyone, dear. I merely want to be prepared to defend my loved ones if need be."

Considering this a moment, Tori conceded reluctantly, "Maybe I should learn to use a gun. Chances are, I'd never have to shoot anything more than a snake, but it would be nice to feel more competent, and it might make Jacob worry less about me."

With a shiver, Megan said, "I'll try to teach you if you want, but you must promise never to mention snakes to me again. I despise those things! They scare me silly! Blake was bitten by one once, and I thought he was going to die right before my eyes!"

"Guns scare me," Tori admitted sheepishly. "Do you really think you could teach me, knowing that?"

Megan shrugged. "We won't know until we try, will we? But I can guarantee I'll be more tolerant than a man would be. Maybe that was part of your problem. I'm beginning to suspect that all men are born impatient and only get worse as they grow. Lord help me if I have a son this time! Alita is enough of a scamp!"

Tori's eyes widened in wonder as she gazed at her new friend. "You're expecting another child?" she questioned in an awe-filled voice.

Megan nodded and patted her flat tummy. "He or she is due around February, as near as I can calculate. Alita will be two years old by then, and hopefully out of diapers."

"But you don't look—uh—you don't appear any different."

"I keep forgetting what an innocent you still are," Megan said with a laugh. "It's too soon yet to show, but in another couple of months I'll look like a waddling buffalo."

"Shouldn't you be lying down or resting or something?" Tori asked curiously. "Surely you shouldn't be traveling and riding all the time."

"Tori, I'm pregnant, not deathly ill!" Megan

shook her head and chuckled. "I feel fine. Don't start coddling me. I got enough of that the first time around with Blake."

"But don't you hurt or feel sick or something?" Tori persisted, trying to recall some of what she had heard from friends and acquaintances.

Relenting, Megan decided to tell Tori what she wanted to know, what Tori would need to know for herself someday when she found herself bearing Jake's child. "When I first get up in the morning, I'm a little queazy; and the smell of coffee, which I dearly love as a rule, almost turns my stomach. After that, I'm usually fine for the rest of the day. I try to eat well, drink enough milk, which I thoroughly detest, and dry crackers help calm my stomach. At least this time I don't seem prone to being so light-headed at odd moments, as I was with Alita.

"As far as hurting, my breasts are more tender now, and enlarging a bit already, but I am not in pain. Expecting a child is not a trial, Tori. It is a joy, the greatest joy a woman can experience. The only real pain is when the baby is actually being born, and even that is fast forgotten once you hold your child in your arms for the first time. I cannot begin to describe how marvelous that moment is! I can only hope that you, too, will know it for yourself someday."

"I hope so, too," Tori whispered softly, her eyes glowing. "I love children. I want lots of my own to care for."

"Lots?" Megan chuckled. "How many is 'lots'?"

"Oh, five or six, at least," Tori answered confidently.

"Then I sincerely hope Jake likes children as well as you do," Megan suggested with a teasing grin. "It might help if you could manage to give him a son or two in the bargain, just to ease the strain on him a bit."

Caught up in the fantasy of having her own children, Tori answered vaguely, "Oh, Jacob is very good with children. He practically raised me, you know."

Jake was more than a little relieved to have Blake around these days. While he trusted all of the ranch hands, only a handful of them were truly as devoted to the Lazy B as Jake was. They would help him defend it, but it was his home, his inheritance and responsibility.

Blake Montgomery understood all this, and more. Not only was he a rancher, well aware of the problems involved in tending a spread of this size, but Blake was also an ex-gunfighter and one of the few men Jake knew who had successfully walked away from that perilous profession and gone back to what most people considered a "normal" life. Blake knew just how difficult this could be, the prejudice that clung for so long, the constant worry that your previous life would one day catch up to you and threaten your family and your precarious newfound peace.

"Nice spread you have here," Blake commented. He and Jake had ridden out to look over the ranch, and Jake had shown his friend the poisoned water hole and the new river channel they had labored to dig.

Jake nodded. "It'd be a whole lot nicer if I could catch the no-good polecat who's causin' us all this grief."

"Any ideas?"

"Nothing sound. Could be just about anybody. I thought at first it was someone local, maybe someone wantin' Dad's land, or with a grudge against Dad. That makes the most sense, since I didn't even think about coming home until Gill wired me about the fire." Jake had been at the Montgomery ranch in Arizona when the telegram had come. He had been helping Blake and Megan get their ranch running smoothly again, after recovering it from Blake's thieving cousin. Now, it seemed, Blake was about to return the favor in kind and aid Jake in solving his problems, if possible.

"Seems reasonable," Blake said.

"Yeah, I thought so until I was in town the other day and heard that young gunslinger, Reno, was askin' around about me. He showed up in town just a week or two after those men shot at Tori and me on our way down from the mountain. Now I wonder if it could've been him or someone like him."

"Hmmm. You think so? From what little I've heard, that's not Reno's style."

"That's what's so damned confusin'!" Jake grumbled. "He might have shot at us that day, maybe, but I don't think he's the one who poisoned the water hole or set fire to the house."

"Have you considered the fact that you might have two separate sets of problems on your hands here? Then again, Reno was down around the border recently. I hear he made a real show out of gunning down a man in Tombstone just last month. It might just be a coincidence, him arriving in Santa Fe just when you are up to your eyeballs in problems already."

"I don't know what to think anymore, Blake. I just wish I could get my hands on the slimy bastard who killed Dad and have an end to all this worry. Carmen's on the mend now, and I'd like to take a weddin' trip with my new bride before we're both too old to enjoy it! Damnation!"

Tori had never met Blake Montgomery's Aunt Josefa. "You're in for quite a treat," Megan advised with a chuckle.

Even so warned, Tori was not completely prepared. Josefa was a sweet-tempered, elderly lady, but every bit as feather-brained as Megan had said. The house, closed up as it had been for a year and a half, had a stale, musty smell. Cobwebs hung like lace decorations from the corners of the rooms, and the furniture resembled stooped ghosts with its protective coverings of sheets. Throughout, the place was crowded to the rafters with stacks of old papers, bric-a-brac, clothing, and various items of no use or value to anyone but Josefa. As Tori gazed about her, she shook her head in wonder. It would take weeks just to make a dent in all this, let alone decent order.

The women definitely had their work cut out for them, but Blake was not entirely excluded. While they waded through the cluttered interior, Blake and a couple of hired helpers set about making small repairs to the outside of the house. The lawn, choked with weeds, had to be cleared, and the house freshly whitewashed before it would be ready to sell.

It also fell to Blake to clear out the small family of rattlesnakes that had taken up residence under the house during Josefa's extended absence. This was a chore he dreaded and approached with extreme caution, having once been badly bitten and not wanting to repeat the harrowing experience. Megan was a jittery case of nerves until he had successfully evacuated the snakes without mishap. To Tori, who was fast coming to admire her new friend, it was amazing to see Megan react so boldly to other situations, yet turn stark white at the mere mention of the word "snake."

To Tori's delight, Blake escorted her to the orphanage school two or three mornings each week, returning to pick her up again and take her to Josefa's house. Once in a while, Megan would go along, bringing little Alita with her. "She needs to get used to being around other children," Megan explained. "Being an only child, Alita has absolutely no notion of how to share. With a new brother or sister on the way, she needs to learn how to play nicely. She's altogether too spoiled for her own good."

"But she is so darling!" Tori said, cuddling the sweet-smelling toddler to her.

"Pretty is as pretty does, and Alita is a little terror when she can't get her own way."

"I don't care. I think she's perfect just the way she is," Tori insisted.

Megan wrinkled her nose at Tori. "You're just a doting godmother," she accused with a wry laugh. "You're only helping to spoil her more rotten than she already is, you know. Luckily, you can get away with it. Blake and I will be gone in a few weeks, and you won't have to put up with her tantrums, but just wait until you have a child of your own! Then it won't be so cute when your little darling decides to be a hellion."

Tori's eyes sparkled. "I can hardly wait," she confided. "I want a child of my own so badly that I ache inside sometimes." Then, with a pretty blush, she added shyly. "And Jacob is doing his very best to oblige me."

A delighted laugh bubbled from Megan's lips. "What else are husbands for?" she quipped, then winked. "Besides, the trying is so much fun!"

Chapter 14

Tori was blissfully happy. She was teaching, her mother was almost completely well, and she was deeply in love and loved in return. It seemed that nothing could destroy her happiness, that glow of love that colored her days in rainbow hues. When she began feeling nauseated each morning, only to have the disturbance disappear later in the day, she could have crowed with delight. Though it would be a while before she could be absolutely sure, Tori would have bet almost anything that she had gotten her final, treasured wish. She was expecting Jacob's baby.

Not wanting to tempt fate by announcing

her good fortune before it was a positive fact, Tori confided in no one. Rather, she kept her glad suspicions to herself. If she wore a silly grin on her face at times, no one seemed to think it odd. She was young and in love, and new brides were often a bit strange until the novelty wore off. If anyone suspected at all, it was Megan, though she did not say anything to Tori or ask any pointed questions. She merely observed with raised brows and a speculative look as Tori continued to glow with good humor.

It was Saturday, and the Banners and the Montgomerys had gone into town together. The two young women had their entire day planned. First they would take care of purchasing necessities for the ranch. Then, their chores out of the way, they intended to spend the rest of the afternoon indulging themselves in a glorious shopping spree. That finished, they planned to meet their husbands in the hotel dining room, where the men had vowed to buy each of them a syllabub and a fancy dinner. It promised to be such a marvelous, carefree day, and Tori was determined not to let anything ruin it, not even the snide remarks and sideways glances of some of the townspeople.

"Are you sure you two will be all right alone?" Jake asked for the third time in as many minutes.

"Jacob, you are turning into a regular worry wart!" Tori answered with a laugh. "Blake, please get him out of here, will you?"

"We're not exactly alone," Megan hastened to point out. "The town is teeming with people, and I have my little derringer right here in my reticule. We'll be very careful, Jake. I promise you."

For Tori, who had not been shopping like this with a friend in so very long, the day was like a trip to the circus. She and Megan giggled like schoolgirls, especially when Tori related how Jacob had bought her such daring underthings on their last shopping expedition. Just seeing the look on the proprietress's face as she and Megan entered the milliner's shop brought a fresh flush to Tori's cheeks, and an unfortunate recurrence of giggles.

As a lark, Megan suggested they each purchase the most outrageous item they could find, provided it was not too expensive. Megan boldly selected a daring black corset, trimmed with blazing red ribbons. "My husband just adores me in black," she told the gaping saleslady in an exaggerated drawl. "Of course, he prefers me in nothing at all, but a woman has to add a little spice to the game, don't you agree?" The shopkeeper merely nodded dumbly, her eyes bulging.

Still much more conservative by nature, and knowing she would have to shop here again in the future, while Megan could safely return to Tucson, Tori purchased two of the gaudiest garters the store had in stock. One was a shocking pink, with purple lace; the other so bright a green it nearly hurt the eyes to look at it. "One for each leg, you know," she said with a sly wink at the astonished lady. By the time they left the shop, Tori and Megan were almost doubled over with laughter. Tori could not recall when she'd had such hilarious fun.

She and Megan were still giggling as they stepped off the boardwalk, headed for the dress shop across the street. "Look, there are our loving spouses just coming out of Speck's Saloon." Megan pointed to the drinking establishment a few doors down from where they stood. "Do you suppose we ought to waylay them long enough to show them what we've just purchased for their entertainment?"

"Oh, no!" Tori disagreed with a shake of her head and a devilish grin. Tugging at her friend's arm, she urged her into the street. "It would be so much nicer just to surprise them tonight, don't you think?"

Before Megan could reply, a man almost at Tori's elbow shouted, "Banner!"

Startled, Tori nearly jumped out of her skin. She stopped short and stared at the man who had called out. Dressed all in black, with a red silk bandanna knotted about his neck, he was just standing there in the center of the street, his gaze not on her, but on Jake.

Megan took one swift look and nearly swallowed her tongue. The man's hand was hovering mere inches from the butt of his gun, his stance one of coiled readiness. "Oh, sweet hell!" she exclaimed softly, accurately reading the situation. With a reaction that was almost instinctive, she grabbed at Tori's arm, literally dragging her off the street and out of the line of fire.

One minute she was standing in the center of the street, and in the next, Tori found herself shoved through the open door of the dress shop. Stumbling and gasping for breath, she turned on Megan, confusion written on her face. "What in the world are you doing, Megan? Why are you suddenly in such an all-fired hurry?"

The look Megan gave her was a mixture of incredulous wonder and acute sympathy. "You really don't know, do you, Tori? You have no idea what is about to happen out there!"

Immediately wary, Tori started back toward the door, only to find her path blocked. "No, Tori! Don't! For God's sake, don't watch! Don't put yourself through this!" Megan thrust her arms out, prepared to stop her young friend from witnessing the coming spectacle.

Her heart now thundering in her breast,

Tori suddenly knew. Even without seeing it, she knew that the man who had shouted at Jake was another gunfighter. Even as she stood here, practically rooted to the spot, he was challenging her husband to a duel—a deadly game of skill from which only one of them would walk away alive!

With a pained cry, Tori brushed Megan's arm aside, nearly toppling her friend into a display of dresses. Megan grabbed for Tori's arm, holding her back. At that instant a shot was fired, the sound echoing through Tori's head. A second later another shot rang out, and the blood seemed to congeal in her veins.

Tori screamed and jerked free of Megan's hold. Dashing out the door, she lurched onto the boardwalk, her eyes frantically searching the nearly deserted street. To her left, standing alone, gun still smoking, was Jacob. At the sight of him, tall and strong, her heart resumed beating once more. Only one thought raced through her brain. "He's safe! Thank God! He's still alive!"

Then unwittingly her eyes searched out the other gunman. He lay sprawled in the dust not ten feet from where Tori stood, gaping and appalled. His hat had fallen off and his fair blond hair had tumbled across his forehead, making him seem even younger than he had first appeared. He lay so still that Tori knew at a glance that he was dead, even before she saw his pale blue eyes staring sightlessly at the clear sky overhead, or the bright red stain that marked the front of his shirt.

"No!" she moaned. "Oh, dear God, no!" Immediately her stomach revolted, and she stumbled off the boardwalk, retching violently, not even aware of Megan's tender assistance or the many avid eyes that watched. As she straightened once again, still white and trembling, the world began to spin about her. Just before the encroaching darkness claimed her, Jacob's face swam before her unfocused gaze. With a soft, pitiful moan, she fainted in his arms.

When Jake heard Reno call his name, he and Blake had just stepped out of the saloon. Pulling his hat down to shade his eyes from the glare of the sun, he had just started to scan the street, hoping for a glimpse of Tori and Megan, simply to assure himself that they were still all right. He spotted them mere seconds before Reno shouted at him, and seeing that Tori and Reno stood, at that moment, almost elbow to elbow, Jake's heart flew into his mouth, then plummeted to his feet. Only years of strict self-discipline kept the fear from showing on his face as icy fingers raced down his spine. Of all places for the women to be, this had to be the worst!

Next to him, Blake felt him stiffen. "Just concentrate on Reno, Jake," he said softly through his teeth. "I'll take care of the girls."

Before Blake could take three easy steps away from his friend, Megan had grabbed Tori's arm and was dragging her hurriedly toward a nearby store. "Thank you, Megan," Jake breathed, hearing Blake draw a deep breath of relief. All around them, sensing what was about to take place, people were scurrying for cover.

Even as he kept his attention on Reno, Jake felt his friend melt into the background and stop, watchful and ready in case Reno had decided to pull something dirty, like bringing along several friends, perhaps hidden in windows or alleys. Jake didn't think Reno would do anything like that, simply because the young braggart would not want to share his glory. Still, he was glad to have Montgomery backing him, if for nothing more than moral support.

Jake's sharp golden gaze riveted itself to Reno's face and stayed there, never wavering, studying the other man's eyes. Slowly, easily, as if he were taking a Sunday stroll and had all the time in the world, Jake stepped from the boardwalk. Those who watched him saunter toward the middle of the street could not help but admire how calm he seemed.

Indeed, Jake had focused all his concentration on this deadly confrontation, mentally blocking out all other thoughts from his mind. As he walked into the street, he took a deep breath, letting it out slowly; then another, consciously relaxing his tense muscles. The fingers of his right hand flexed slightly as they hovered near the butt of his Colt. His eyes were slightly squinted beneath the brim of his hat, not so much against the glare of the sun as to prevent himself from blinking at the wrong moment. Slowly he walked into the street, heading toward Reno at an angle that would prevent him from having to draw and aim across the width of his own body. In this perilous contest of skill and speed, even a single lost second could easily cost one's life.

"I been lookin' for you, Banner," Reno drawled. "You been avoidin' me, hidin' like the coward you really are?"

Jake did not bother to respond to Reno's ridicule. This was one of the oldest tricks in the book, to taunt your opponent into making a rash move, and Jake had learned to ignore it long ago. The only insult here was that Reno actually thought Jake might fall for such an obvious ploy.

Jake had not quite reached the center of the street when a shadow seemed to flicker in Reno's eyes. Jake's Colt was drawn, his bullet speeding its way straight and true toward Reno's heart, in the time it took Reno to draw his own pistol from his holster. A stunned look of disbelief crossed Reno's face as the bullet tore into his body. For a moment he just stood there, incredulous. Then his legs buckled and he fell into the dusty street. As he fell, his finger reflexively tightened on the trigger of his gun. The shot went wild, ripping a strip of wood from the railing of an upper-story veranda over the saloon, but Reno didn't see this. He didn't even hear the discharge of his own weapon. He was already dead.

Jake was still standing there, legs braced and feeling a flood of relief wash through him, when Tori raced from the store. He saw her glance his way, noted the terror on her face easing as she saw him there. Then she looked toward Reno's fallen body, and even at this distance, Jake could see the sick revulsion on her face. Jake couldn't reach her fast enough to help her as she bent forward to empty her stomach. Loping toward her, holstering his gun as he ran, he reached out to her just in time to see her look at him vaguely, her body weaving unsteadily. Without a word, she pitched forward into his arms in a faint.

It seemed an eternity before the doctor came out from the small examining room where Tori now lay. Leaping to his feet, Jake asked anxiously, "How is she, Doc?"

Doc Green somehow managed to smile and frown at the same time. "She's awake, and she's pretty well shaken up, but with rest and a bit of coddling, she and the baby will both be fine."

Jake's jaw nearly dropped to his knees, alerting the doctor that this announcement of his impending fatherhood was new to him. "Baby?" Jake choked out.

"I take it you didn't know yet," Doc said wryly. "Well, don't feel bad. I'm not sure your wife knew for sure either, until I told her a few minutes ago. She might have suspected something was going on, but I don't think she was certain. You're a lucky couple, you know. Victoria has had a pretty bad shock today, and I've seen women miscarry with less cause. She's still fairly stunned. My advice would be to take her home and cosset her for a few days. Just as a precaution, don't let her do anything strenuous. In about a week, if nothing goes amiss, she should be ready to resume her normal activities."

"How soon could she travel, Doc?" Blake asked, earning a strange look from both his wife and Jake.

"Give her a nice, quiet week, and I'd say travel would do no harm. It might even do her some good to get away from here for a while, see new sights and take her mind away from all that has happened today, if you take my meaning. I'd advise a leisurely trip by stage or train, not on horseback, if possible." The doctor's shrewd gaze leveled itself at Jake as he spoke. "And no more gunfights, if they can be avoided. One more severe shock like this one, and she could very well lose that child she's carrying."

* * *

It was a very quiet, subdued Tori who rode home with her husband and friends late that afternoon. None of them had felt like staying in town for the dinner they had planned. Instead, they went directly home from the doctor's office.

Tori made no objections when Jake insisted on carrying her out to the buggy. In fact, she still looked dazed and sat like a frozen statue all the way home, not uttering a single word to any of her companions. Once back at the ranch, Jake again insisted on carrying her to their bedroom, where he laid her gently on the bed and pulled the blanket up over her, tucking it in as he had done when she was a child. "Rest, darlin'," he whispered, kissing her brow.

Tori's only response was to turn her back to him, curling herself up into a tiny ball beneath the blanket. In a part of her mind that was still functioning, she realized that she was hurting him, but she was hurting, too. Huddling beneath the covers, Tori gave in to the violent trembling that assaulted her. Inside and out, she was shaking with emotion. And yet, it seemed as if she were two persons at this moment. One who was quivering on the bed, trying to block out the memory of the young man lying so still in the dirt; another standing outside herself, calmly observing everything. She felt bruised to her very soul; she felt numb and so very weary.

Though she did not sleep, Tori lay quietly, hardly moving. Some time later, Jake returned with a supper tray. Tori did not pretend to be sleeping, but neither did she in any way acknowledge his presence in the room. When he could not get her to sit up or eat, Jake left.

Not long afterward, Tori's mother crept into the room. "'Toria, you must eat, *pequeña*," she coaxed gently. Sitting on the edge of the bed, she brushed the hair from her daughter's forehead. "For the baby's sake, if not for your own. Please."

The tenderness of her mother's voice, the gentle understanding, seemed to melt the block of ice that encased Tori's heart. A sob shook her slender frame, then another and another. Hot tears scalded down her face. Wordlessly, she rolled over, hiding her tortured face in Carmen's lap, her arms tightly clutched about her mother's waist. She cried then, snuggled securely in her mother's embrace; cried as if her heart were broken.

When there were no more tears to shed, Tori allowed her mother to feed her. Propped up on the pillows, she ate what Carmen spooned into her mouth, tasting none of it, not caring what it was. At last she pushed the spoon away, feeling that if she took one more bite, she would become ill again.

"Do you want to talk about it, 'Toria?" Carmen asked softly. Jake had already related to her what had gone on in town, sparing himself nothing. Knowing her daughter, Carmen knew that Tori must have been deeply affected by witnessing such a scene. "It might help to talk about it," she repeated.

Tori merely shook her head, refusing, not wanting to bring it all to mind again any more vividly than it was already. "I'm tired, Mama. So very tired."

Tori was relieved when Carmen did not insist but sat quietly with her in the gathering gloom of nightfall. Her loving presence was a balm to Tori's torn spirit. "Sleep, *mi angelita*," Carmen murmured. "Sleep, my sweet angel."

Hovering somewhere between sleep and wakefulness, Tori heard her mother light a lamp and tiptoe quietly from the room. A while afterward, she heard Jake come in. This time she did feign sleep, trying to keep her breathing regular and light, her wet lashes from fluttering as he bent over and lightly kissed her tear-stained cheek. "I'm so sorry, my love," he murmured near her ear. "There was nothing else I could do."

She listened tensely as he blew out the lamp, then removed his clothes and settled onto the bed beside her. Only when he draped an arm across her waist and tried to draw her stiff body close to his did she give any sign that she was aware of him. Jerking herself away from him, she curled up as close to the opposite edge of the bed as she could. "Do not touch me, Jacob," she whispered past the huge lump in her throat. "I do not wish for you to touch me."

The shudder that quaked through her was echoed by a deep sigh from Jake, but he let her be. Lying flat on his back, staring up at the dark ceiling, Jake wondered how long it might be before his young wife would once again welcome his touch. At that moment he could have gladly killed Reno all over again for ruining his brightest dream, the dream he and Tori had shared so joyously just hours before.

To everyone's surprise, Tori was up and dressed early the next morning, and demanding to be taken to church. She faced them all with a stiff, unsmiling face and a determined glint in her eyes. "I am going to Mass if I have to walk every step of the way," she said in a chilly voice made more brittle from all her crying.

At first, Jake stubbornly refused, insisting that she rest as the doctor had ordered. "Do you want to chance losing the baby, Tori?" he asked, all the hurt he felt blazing from his eyes.

"I feel fine, Jacob," she told him curtly. "Please allow me to be the judge of what I can and cannot do without harming our child."

Jake finally relented, but only after Carmen had talked with Tori privately and determined that she did, indeed, feel well. "I think it would upset her more not to go this morning than it would to risk the ride into town again," Carmen told him gravely. "I think she needs this, for her soul, Jacob."

The ride to the mission church was a silent one. Again Tori sat stiffly in the seat next to Jake. He could almost feel the waves of condemnation radiating from her. Maybe this trip to church would be good for both of them, if it helped Tori work through her feelings. Perhaps once she had talked with one of the sisters or Father Romero, she could see reason again.

Jake spent an hour in the saloon nursing his woes and a single glass of whiskey. After the day before, no one dared bother him as he sat in solitary misery, a dark look clouding his face. At last he returned to the church to collect his wife, only to find she had closeted herself in the convent and was refusing to come out. "What do you mean, she refuses to leave?" he asked in astonishment.

"I am sorry, Señor Banner," Father Romero said. "I tried to reason with Victoria, but she would not listen. Finally, all I could do was to let her go with the other sisters, hoping that one of them could succeed where I have failed. Why don't you talk with the Mother Superior? Perhaps she can help you more than I can. The sisters all respect her wisdom, and she has great sway over them. I am sure she can advise Victoria wisely and make her see what is right."

Wounded with a pain greater than any he had ever before known, Jake soon found himself being admitted to the Mother Superior's office for the second time. Those great gray eyes that had shown such determination before now registered sympathy toward him as the woman came forward to take his hand. "We are making quite a habit of this, it seems, Mr. Banner," she said quietly, leading him to a chair.

"Will you talk with her, Mother?" Jake asked humbly.

With a nod, the woman said, "Yes, I will speak with her if you will wait here and promise not to search the halls for her as you did the last time. The other sisters still have not completely recovered from the shock of that experience, I fear."

She was rewarded for her efforts with a small smile as they both recalled how he had invaded their private domicile when first he had come to take Tori home with him. "I'll wait as long as it takes," he promised.

The clock on the mantel marked the time as Jake waited, downhearted and with growing impatience. Upstairs, in one of the small cubicles that sufficed as sleeping quarters for the sisters, Mother Superior was counseling her former charge. "Victoria, you made your choice some weeks ago, and like it or not, now you must live with it. It is unfortunate that things have turned out this way for you, but Father Romero tried to warn you. Now it is too late. You have a husband, who seems to care a great deal for you, and I have learned that you have a child on the way from this union. You have a responsibility to your new family now, one you cannot turn your back upon."

Turning tear-filled eyes toward her mentor, Tori whispered emphatically, "He killed a man, Mother! He shot him down in the street! How can I go back to him, knowing that? How am I supposed to bear his touch, when he has taken the life of another man with the very hands that touch my flesh?"

"You knew he was a gunfighter when you married him," Mother Superior pointed out gently. "You have known this for years, and yet you have always loved him, even when it was a sisterly love. What is so different now? Why do you suddenly condemn him now, when he is no different today than he was a year ago?"

"I saw it!" Tori exclaimed softly, all the horror of the day before reflected in her vivid green eyes. "I saw that man, so young, not much older than I, lying there on the ground, his life pouring out of him! His eyes were so blue, like a clear mountain lake, just staring blankly at the sky! And Jacob was responsible for that! It was his finger that pulled the trigger, his gun that fired the shot that killed that poor boy!"

"So," the older lady reasoned. "While you knew in your head what Jacob was, it was always removed from you before. Is that it? Before, it seemed no more than a passing thought, but yesterday it was more real, more terrible than you had ever imagined?"

Tori nodded, gulping back her tears. "Yes, that is part of it," she conceded.

"And could your husband have done any differently? If I understand correctly, it was the younger man who challenged Jacob on the street. Do you think, in your heart, that your husband could have refused this challenge and walked away alive? Would he be here now, sitting down there in my office waiting for his wife, if he had done so, or would your tears be for him today instead of yourself as you stood over his grave? Tell me what you think about this, Victoria."

Meekly, her head bent to hide her shame, Tori admitted, "No, Jacob probably would not be alive today if that had happened."

"And would you rather it had been your husband lying dead in the street than the young man you feel such pity for?"

"No! I would never wish that! I only wish that he did not have to kill that man, to waste a life so young. Perhaps it would not have seemed so awful if Jacob had merely wounded him, but he shot to kill. His bullet went straight to that man's heart.''

"The man was old enough to know what he was doing, Victoria. I am sure he knew what a deadly game he was beginning when he challenged your husband. He was no innocent novice with that gun of his. It might have been better for you, for Jacob perhaps, if he had shot to wound, but who can be certain? Perhaps if the man had lived, he would have come gunning for Jacob another day, and perhaps that day Jacob would have been the one to die. Who is to say? Only God knows what might have been, and what will come to pass.''

"Are you saying that God planned it all this way? That Jacob was meant to kill that man yesterday?" Tori asked incredulously.

The older nun shrugged. "What I am saying, Victoria, is that you must cease all this wailing and feeling sorry for yourself.''

At this, Tori's eyes widened, her mouth opening to immediately refute the Mother Superior's statement, but her words were waved aside before she could speak them. "Yes, Victoria. Admit it only to yourself, if you must hide the truth from others. All this sorrow, all this anger inside of you is directed at your husband for something he had no choice in. Even while you voice pretty sentiments regarding the death of that young gunfighter, he meant nothing to you, and you would not have your husband change places with him, would you? You do not feel pity so much for either of them as you do for yourself.

"Meanwhile, your husband, to whom you have promised your love, sits downstairs waiting. He is hurt, too, Tori, perhaps much more than you. He is the one who has taken a life; he is the one who must always bear that burden on his soul, and I think it lies heavily on his heart. He needs succor, Victoria, such as he can only get from you, the person he loves and trusts most in this world. It is your duty as his wife to provide this for him."

"My duty?" Tori echoed stupidly.

"Yes. Upon your marriage, you pledged to love, honor, and obey this man, but above and beyond this, St. Paul admonishes wives to further commitments. He tells them, 'Let not the wife depart from her husband,' which you have done this day. He also says, 'Wives, submit yourselves unto your own husbands, as unto the Lord. For the husband is the head of the wife, even as Christ is the head of the church. Therefore, as the church is subject unto Christ, so let the wives be to their own husbands in every thing.'

"These are not words to be taken lightly, Victoria. I ask you to consider them carefully and search your own heart for an answer. Perhaps most importantly, I think you must ask yourself if you truly love this man, and if you do, you must find it in your heart to forgive him all that you think he has done to wrong you. In turn, you must also be prepared to ask his forgiveness, for I am sure your defection and lack of trust in him has caused him great distress."

It was a greatly humbled wife who presented herself to her anxious husband a short while later. "I am sorry, Jacob," she whispered contritely, her eyes begging his forgiveness. "In my heart, I know you had no other choice, but seeing it was such a shock. I doubt I'll ever forget the sight of that man lying there with your bullet in his chest."

At her words, he winced, and she knew she had hurt him more deeply. "I'll never forget it, either, Tori," he answered gravely. "No matter how many times it happens, no matter how many men I'm forced to kill, each and every incident stays with me, clingin' to the back of my mind like a hauntin' ghost, as vivid as the day it happened. It never goes away. I get no pleasure from killin', Tori, if that's what you've come to believe."

"Oh, Jacob! I know that, darling!" Tears fell like raindrops from her eyes as she threw herself into his arms and embraced him with all the love in her heart. "I know the man you truly are, and I love you more than my next breath. I would take the pain and the memories away if I could, Jacob. I would heal your scars with my tears, if that were possible. I love you, and I promise I'll try very hard never to disappoint you again."

His heart felt as if it were about to burst with thankfulness and joy. He held her tightly to him for a timeless moment, then put her gently away from him and tenderly wiped the tears from her face with his thumbs. "Let's go home, little angel."

Chapter
15

For the next week, Jake made certain that Tori rested. Of course, he had a particularly juicy carrot to dangle before her as incentive. If she followed the doctor's orders; and if her health seemed perfectly fine; and if nothing else drastic occurred around the ranch, he had decided to take her on a wedding trip, a late honeymoon to New Orleans.

Tori was ecstatic! In her entire life, she'd never been further than Albuquerque, and she was looking forward to the trip like a miner looked forward to sunshine. She spent hours in the small library room, researching all she could find about New Orleans. It sounded a bit wild, slightly wicked, and an ever so wonderful place to visit. Her days prior to leaving were filled with eager anticipation, and she found herself hoping that nothing would happen to prevent their departure.

When the sheriff came out to the ranch on Monday afternoon, Tori's heart sank to her shoes. She was sure he had come to arrest Jacob for shooting Reno. She was in a nervous dither until he had left, without Jacob. It seemed he had come to ask Jake to leave Santa Fe, and for a moment Tori feared that Jacob would suggest delaying their departure, just to spite the sheriff.

"No, darlin'," he assured her. "I just told him I would come and go as I pleased, and there was nothin' he could do about it. I didn't call Reno out the other day; I merely defended myself. The sheriff has about as much chance of makin' me leave as he did of catchin' the men who killed Caroline. He's too old, he's too scared, and he likes his whiskey too much to ever be a good lawman again. He might have been once, when he was younger, but no more. Come election time, it wouldn't surprise me if he loses to someone who can do Santa Fe some good for a change, if there's anyone like that who's willin' to run for the office."

"You aren't thinking about it, are you?" Tori asked with big, anxious eyes.

"Honey," he told her with an amused look, "I've got my hands full right here. You and this ranch are almost more than I can handle at one time."

Tori was relieved. Their lives were fraught with enough peril right now. They certainly didn't need to add to it by having Jacob decide he wanted to wear a badge and be the target of any outlaw who wandered into town.

The day for their departure arrived at last, and as excited as Tori was, she could sense that Jacob was having second thoughts. This had not been an easy decision for him to make, and the timing was definitely not the best. Resting a hand on his arm, she looked up at him with sympathy and understanding. "You've taken every precaution, Jacob. I'm sure Blake will take excellent care of things here until we get back. Megan and Josefa will be here to look after Mama and keep her from doing too much. It couldn't have worked out better for us. Without the Montgomerys, we couldn't even think of leaving now."

Jake nodded. Tori was right. If not for Blake, he wouldn't even consider leaving the ranch. Things had continued to be quiet, no more incidents to ranch property or livestock, but that didn't mean it was over. In fact, Jake would have bet his boots that they hadn't heard the last from their attackers. But for some reason, they had decided to bide their time.

"Maybe they're just waitin' until I leave," he'd suggested worriedly to Blake when they'd first discussed the trip and Blake had volunteered to watch the ranch for him.

"Then this is a good opportunity to find out, isn't it?" Blake had countered. "Look, Banner. The doctor has said that this trip would be good for Tori. You said before that you wished you two could go away together. If the culprit makes himself known while you're gone, so much the better. Your men and I can handle it as well as you would, and the problem will be solved by the time you get back. Don't look a gift horse in the mouth, *amigo*. Go; enjoy yourself; show Tori a fabulous time and leave the worrying to me. Besides, I owe you this for saving my hide and my ranch for me."

"Hold off on the fall roundup. We'll be back in time to save you the trouble of that, at least."

Blake shrugged. "If you are, then fine. If not, we'll manage without you. Just go, and try not to worry about things here."

With a final kiss from Carmen, a hug and a smile from Blake and Megan, Jake and Tori were on their way at last. They were taking the train to Albuquerque, then the stagecoach south to El Paso before heading east. "We'll take it real easy," Jake told her solicitously. "There's no hurry. Anytime you get too tired, we can stay over at the way station for an extra day."

But Tori was anything but tired. Even the long, boring hours bouncing about in the stagecoach could not lessen her eagerness. Everything about this trip, right from the start, was a grand adventure to her. Her sunny smile invited others to return her good humor in kind. The only thing that disappointed her even slightly was having to share a room with the other women travelers at some of the smaller way stations, but even that did not discourage her overmuch.

It took five days to get to El Paso. When the stage pulled up in front of the hotel in what was probably the roughest cow town in the West, inhabited or frequented by some of the toughest hombres on either side of the border, Tori found out just how protective and possessive Jake could be. While she was so excited she wriggled like an exuberant puppy, Jake suddenly became a bear with a sore paw.

"We'll stay overnight and catch the morning stage," he informed her grumpily.

"Oh, do we have to leave so soon?" she complained, her head turning this way and that to catch a glimpse of the town as Jake hustled her into the hotel lobby.

"Why? Aren't you feelin' well?" he asked, his eyes dark with sudden concern.

"I'm fine," she made the mistake of saying, before she even considered what a handy excuse it might be. "I just thought we might take a day and see some of the sights. Goodness, Jacob! Do you realize that this is the largest town we've been through since leaving Santa Fe?"

"Forget it, Tori. This is the saddest excuse for a town you could ever want to see. It's no place for a lady, believe me. It's not safe on the streets before *or* after sundown, though it does manage to get worse at night. They've got five undertakers workin' 'round the clock just to handle all the business they get every day."

Tori shivered at this, her enthusiasm severely dampened. Still, she was disappointed, and it must have shown on her face. "When we get to San Antonio, I'll be glad to let you take all the time you want to look around and shop," he promised. "We'll both be ready for a rest from travelin' by then." When she still looked discontent, he said placatingly, "C'mon, sweetheart, spruce up a bit and I'll buy you the best dinner the hotel has to offer. And tonight we've got a room all to ourselves. No more smellin' somebody's dirty feet, or havin' some stranger snorin' in your ear. Just you an' me in that big ol' bed!"

"Well, all right," she agreed with a tempting smile that melted his bones, "but you've got to promise not to snore, and you have to wash your feet!"

A roguish grin transformed his rugged face. "You've got yourself a deal, little darlin'."

The dinner was, indeed, delicious; or maybe it was just so superior to some of the meals they had eaten at various way stations that it seemed fabulous. Long after their meal was finished, they lingered over drinks, Jacob nursing a brandy while Tori sipped a mild sherry. She enjoyed just watching the variety of people who patronized the hotel dining room. Jacob had eyes for no one but his beautiful young wife.

They talked and laughed softly, enjoying this relaxing time in one another's company. At least they were enjoying it until a young woman stopped at their table. She was tall and trim, with an abundance of red hair, and Tori could not help but notice how bountifully she filled out her rather tight, low-cut gown.

"Why, as I live and breathe!" she purred, leaning over just enough to give Jake an unobstructed view of her ripe breasts and generous, perfumed cleavage. "If it isn't Jake Banner! Why, honey, it's been so long since you've hit this dusty old town, I was sure you must be dead. You've never neglected little ol' Iris this long before!" At this, she cut a quick, vicious look in Tori's direction, the first she even acknowledged Tori's presence at the table. When she turned her dark eyes once more on Jake, there was not a hint of the chilliness she'd directed at Tori. She batted long, darkened lashes at him and smiled sweetly through rouged lips.

Tori was speechless. Darting a glance across the table, she was surprised to see her usually unflappable husband actually blushing in embarrassment. This was too much! It was simply too mortifying! Who did this floozy think she was, to flaunt her overblown body at Jake this way, right before Tori's eyes!

Finally getting some control over his own tongue, Jake cleared his throat and managed to say, "I think you'd better leave, Iris. You've just interrupted a private conversation between me and my wife."

For a fleeting second, a horrified look crossed Iris's face, swiftly replaced by haughty disdain as she once again swung her gaze toward Tori, who was now glaring openly. "I never figured you for the marryin' kind, Jake," Iris cooed cattily. "Especially to someone so obviously prim and proper. Why, she looks as untaught as a babe in arms!"

For Tori, jealousy was an unknown emotion, until now. Suddenly it jolted through her with the force of a lightning bolt. Before Jake could come to her defense once more, Tori's temper boiled over. "Look, you brazen hussy! I'll give you exactly three seconds to leave this room, or I'm going to smear your painted face all over this table!" she hissed.

Throwing her head back, Iris had the temerity to laugh. "That'll be the day, sweetie," she crowed.

"Then this is the day," Tori promised. Before Jake could move to stop her, she reached out and grabbed Iris's dress by its revealing decolletage, yanking the woman forward over the table. "This should really make your face glow!" Tori predicted nastily, as she pushed Iris's face into the cold, greasy remains of her meal, now congealed on her dinner plate. "Call it grease paint," Tori taunted smoothly. "It's sure to be an improvement over what you are wearing!

"Oh, and we must do something about that tawdry perfume of yours!" Tori added hatefully, disregarding the stares now aimed their way. "It absolutely reeks!" With a strength born of fury, she held the squirming woman down long enough to dump what was left of her sherry and Jacob's brandy over Iris's head. Then, with all the dignity of a queen, she rose from her chair and swept regally out of the room. Behind her, the dining room erupted in cheers and guffaws, muffling the sounds of Iris's irate shrieks.

Jake caught up with her as she reached the foot of the stairs. As he grasped her arm, she tried to shrug it loose, so angry with him that she could have spit in his eye. "Oh, no you don't!" Jake warned darkly. "You're not going to lay the blame for this at my feet!"

"She was your—your doxy!" she hissed for lack of a better word.

"I never claimed to have lived the life of a monk," Jake reminded her tersely, nearly dragging her up the stairs in his rush to get to their room before they created another scene. Unlocking the door, he pushed her into their room and slammed the door. "All right," he said. "Yes, I have slept with her. I've slept with a lot of women over the years."

"I don't imagine 'sleep' had much to do with it," Tori inserted smartly.

"True, but that was before we were married. You can't hold against me what I did before then, Tori."

"Did you love her?" Tori asked in a small voice, her lower lip quivering treacherously. Even in the dimly lit room, her eyes glimmered like pale green stars as tears filled them.

"No, sweetheart," he answered softly, enfolding her trembling body in his strong arms. He kissed the top of her head. "I've never loved anyone but you. I never will."

"Oh, Jacob!" she wailed into the front of his shirt. "I'm so ashamed! I made such a spectacle of myself down there! I honestly don't know what came over me! All of a sudden I just saw red! I wanted to tear her tinted hair out of her head!"

Jacob chuckled and held her close to his heart. "Honey, I think you did enough damage as it is. Not that she didn't deserve everything you dished out—if you'll forgive the pun!" he added hastily.

Tori started to laugh. She couldn't help it. Jake joined in, and soon they were clinging to one another, laughing hysterically. Wiping tears of mirth from his eyes, Jake gulped. "You really should've stayed long enough to view your handiwork, Tori," he gasped. "It was such a sight! It'll be a long time before I forget it."

"If we encounter many more of your paramours, it will become a common enough sight, I promise you," she warned.

"If that should happen, just remember that it's you I love, with all my heart and soul. I'll never stray, Tori. How could I, when the very thought of you makes every other woman fade from mind? You make me burn in ways I never knew existed."

"It must be my Mexican heritage," Tori answered with a teasing smile. "All that spicy food."

Her tongue crept out to peek between her gleaming teeth, the sight of it tempting Jake as a flame lit in his golden eyes. "Tease me, would you, my sweet?" he said gruffly, pulling her after him as he backed toward the bed. "Come let me show you what I do best with a hot little green-eyed pepper like you."

As he toppled backward onto the mattress, Tori fell atop him, his arms trapping her there. Her breasts pressed invitingly against the top of her gown, exposing a good deal of flesh to his eager gaze. "Just the thing to tempt a man's hunger," he growled low in his throat. "Such tasty treats."

Tori gasped as his hot, wet tongue swept across the top of her breasts. With his teeth, he tugged gently at her bodice, pulling it down to expose her nipples. Circling each with the point of his tongue, he teased her unmercifully, a wicked chuckle echoing her moans of desire as passion rose within her. "Mmmnn," he crooned, nuzzling one rosy tip. "Ripe cherries, ready for pluckin'. I've always been partial to cherries for dessert." His teeth lightly grazed her yearning flesh as his moist mouth closed over her breast, tugging and suckling as if he would devour her.

Hot streams of liquid fire seared through her, centering deep within, where only Jacob could ease the building ache. Somehow, without her being aware, he had loosened his hold on her waist and raised her skirts about her thighs. Now Jacob's hands were caressing the soft, silken flesh high on her legs, urging her closer to his own aching desire. His hands slid upward to touch her through the cloth of her pantalettes, rubbing and teasing until she was warm and damp where he touched, and she could not stop herself from wriggling against him in blind longing.

"Oh, Jacob!" she moaned softly, hiding her flaming face in his dark hair, arching and holding his face to her straining breast.

Suddenly the clothing between them was a barrier to be gotten rid of as quickly as possible. Jake's large fingers fumbled at the fastenings down the back of her dress. Then his patience deserted him, and with a hard yank he pulled the hooks from their threads, baring her back to his hot hands. Her strangled yelp came just as the waistband of her gown gave way beneath his urgent tugging. "My gown!" she gasped breathlessly, already drowning in wanton desire, a yearning somehow made more wild by his forcefulness.

"I'll buy you another. I'll buy you ten!" he rasped, pulling the gown free. The ties of her petticoat, then those of her chemise snapped with the strain. A few more deft moves, and Tori lay clothed only in her long stockings and garters. Her breasts, free of any restraints, dangled enticingly just above Jake's mouth. Her legs were wrapped about his, his hands splayed across her back and buttocks.

Once again his lips clamped eagerly about her breast, and he drew it slowly into his mouth. A long, low whimper escaped her arched throat. Her fingers dug sharply into his shoulders. As he released her breast to seek its mate, he asked huskily, "Do you like that, love?"

"Yes," she moaned. "Oh, yes!" She was melting, becoming as absolutely malleable as heated candle wax. His shirt had come undone, and now, blindly, she tugged the tail of it from his trousers, needing to feel his hot bare skin against hers. "Help me," she whispered, her soft breath tickling his ear and sending chills racing down his body.

His shirt joined her clothing in a tangled jumble spread across the bed and trailing onto the floor. Her nails scraped sensuously over his stomach in a search for his belt buckle and the buttons to his trousers, making him shiver anew. "Wait. Wait," he murmured between kisses, his lower lip trailing up her chest, her throat, to her jaw. "My boots," he mumbled, gently tumbling her onto the mattress beside him.

Tori groaned in frustration at the delay as he swiftly pulled his boots off, tossing them noisily to the floor. The rest of his clothes followed suit. Then he was over her, joining their lips in a searing kiss as his body slid itself along her silken curves. Like a cat begging to be petted, she arched against him, loving the way his rough, muscled legs rubbed coarsely over hers, his chest hair lightly abrading her sensitized breasts.

He tasted of smoke and sweet brandy as his tongue dueled with hers, spearing into her mouth and searching out its dark secrets. The musky scent of their aroused passions surrounded them with its erotic perfume. His lips sipped at hers, nipping lightly along the edges—inviting her to do the same. Her fingertips stroked lightly over his heated skin. They dug into the muscled flesh as her desires flamed higher, ebbed slightly, then flared to new heights.

As his lips tantalized hers, his hands sought her breasts, her thighs, the clenched muscles of her taut stomach. Lean, calloused fingers delved through the dark, dewy curls, searching out the core of her passion. Like fiery satin, she felt the throbbing length of him burning against her inner thigh. She reached for him, wanting, needing to give him even more pleasure.

"No, darlin'," he murmured. "Not now." Clasping hold of her hands and bringing them together above her head, he held them there, her wrists gently imprisoned in one large fist. The action made her breasts rise higher, as if imploring his touch. His brilliant, tawny eyes blazed down into hers, then caressed her waiting breasts. His hot gaze alone made her breasts tingle in acute anticipation of his touch, the rosy crests hardening even more, becoming almost painfully swollen.

Jake's chuckle was dark and rumbling as his head dipped to taste her sweet offering. "You're makin' a glutton of me, my pet," he swore softly. "I can't seem to get enough of you."

Tori was drowning in a sea of desire, her entire body tensed with agonized longing, but Jake had merely begun. Inch by slow, flaming inch, he worked his way leisurely down her writhing body, nipping and lapping, sensually dragging tongue and lips and teeth over her yearning flesh. It was a delightful torture, made especially so since she could not free her hands to stop him or to return his caresses.

Her heart lodged in her throat as his mouth hovered between her legs, his warm breath teasing through the damp curls shielding her femininity. Then his tongue lashed out to sear her there, and Tori could not stifle the sharp cry that seemed to echo through the room. "Honey and spice," she heard him whisper in a deep, husky growl that sent a wave of pure fire through her veins. "Burn for me, sweetheart. Burn hot and wild, just for me."

And she did, as again and again, until she thought she was surely losing her mind, he sipped and nipped and laved the warm, wet essence of her. Her every nerve was knotted with the most intense desire she had ever known, a delicious torment that had her calling out his name in an endless prayer, pleading with him to come to her and end this pain-pleasure before she died of it.

Then the knots came undone, and she felt as if she were unraveling inside a huge, colorful ball of yarn. Round and round she spun, writhing and whimpering, feeling the rapture lashing through her like rapid shocks of a whip. The spasms were still convulsing within her as Jake moved up over her, thrusting his hot, pulsing spear deep within her satin sheath.

Passion exploded again, more violently than ever. His mouth hushed her wild cries, his tongue dancing with hers in wanton imitation of their bodies. There was a strange thrumming in her ears, like native drums beating in rhythm with her pounding heartbeat. There was no thought, only feeling, only Jacob's body claiming hers in this ancient, passionate rite of life and love and splendor.

At that final moment, the ecstasy became so dazzling, so unbearably wondrous, that Tori felt consciousness slipping away. Giving herself over to it, she floated among pastel clouds, far above her own passion-spent body in a moment out of time, out of body, out of this world—a golden moment of unearthly magnificence.

A short while later, when they had both recovered from the fury of their lovemaking, Tori pushed aside her embarrassment and asked very simply, "Jacob, would you teach me how to please you, as you have done for me?"

Jake was astounded, but pleasantly so, that Tori would want to return the favor. She soon proved an avid student, with a talent he found stunning in one so recent to the arts of lovemaking. As he lay gasping for breath, his body trembling and his teeth tightly clenched in blissful agony, he wondered if he might have unleashed a demoness, an insatiable temptress intent on loving him to death.

Dawn was not long in coming when at last they closed their eyes, weary and replete. Sleep was slipping easily upon him when Tori asked past a yawn, "Jacob, what is it that women such as Iris know that respectable women do not?"

Immediately his eyes popped open, his slack jaw snapped shut, and sleep fled on swift feet. "What?" he choked out, nearly swallowing his tongue.

"You heard me," she said quietly. "What is it they do that is so special, that men go to them and pay for their favors? What do they find with them that they cannot find with their wives?"

"No . . . Nothing," Jake stammered, feeling like a schoolboy for the first time in years. At a loss, he blurted out gruffly, "Go to sleep, Tori. It will soon be time to get up."

"Hmph!" she snorted. "You just don't want to tell me, do you?"

Pounding his pillow with his fist, and bunching it beneath his head, he told her bluntly, "No, I don't. It's not fit conversation for a man to have with his wife. Now, just let it be, Tori."

He could almost hear her mind still whirling. Sneaking a peek at her through slitted eyes, he saw her sitting up and staring at him with a sullen pout pulling at the corners of her kiss-swollen mouth. "You're being a real stinker, Jacob Banner!" she declared in a hurt tone. "I only wanted to know if they possess certain—uh—skills that lure men to them. It's the only reason I can think of that a man would seek out such a woman, especially if he has a perfectly good wife at home."

Jake gave up. He knew beyond a doubt that she was not about to let him have any rest until he had satisfied her curiosity. With a heavy sigh, he sat up in bed, propping his pillow behind him. Settling her between his thighs, he put his palms on either side of her face and turned it toward his. "Listen to me, Victoria Banner. There is nothin' that special about any of those 'ladies of pleasure,' nothing mysterious or especially allurin'. If there were, why haven't they all found husbands of their own? Why are they still earnin' their way on their backs and livin' the lives they are?"

Tori gave a self-conscious shrug. "I don't know," she admitted, biting her lip. "Still, why do men seek their company, when there are so many nice women to choose from?"

Trying to choose his words carefully, Jake said, "Men have urges, honey. They certainly can't approach nice, proper young ladies to fulfill them, at least not before the weddin'. Why, they'd be tarred and feathered, and run out of town by a pack of irate women before they knew what'd hit 'em! No proper lady is gonna let a man bed her without a ring on her finger first."

"So they go to fallen women for their . . . their pleasure?" Tori suggested. When he agreed, she questioned, "But why do married men carry on with them?"

Now it was Jake's turn to say, "I don't know. Perhaps their wives are not as givin' or as lovin' as you are. Maybe they're not as fortunate as I am, to have such a warm, sweet wife. Or maybe they're just stupid, randy beasts who can't be satisfied and don't know how to appreciate what they have at home. But I do, honey. Believe me, I know what a rare treasure you are." He placed a kiss on the end of her pert little nose. "Now, does that satisfy your curiosity, my little cat?"

Frowning up at him, she ventured hesitantly, her eyes solemnly searching his, "What will happen when I'm round and fat with child and can no longer satisfy your 'urges,' Jacob? Will you seek out another woman then, when I'm no longer slim and beautiful enough for you to desire me?"

His eyes widened with shock at her words, and he pulled her to him, hugging her tightly. "Oh, darlin'!" he swore tenderly. "You'll always be beautiful to me, especially then. I'll always want you, with every breath in my body. I'm not some ruttin' beast, that I can't control my desires for a few months. I love you. After you, there is no other woman who could ever hope to satisfy me."

He felt her warm, salty tears dampening his chest. "I love you, Jacob," she answered softly. Then, more timidly, "Jacob, what are those places, those houses of pleasure, like inside?"

Jake closed his eyes and groaned. "Enough, Tori," he begged. "Please just hush up and go to sleep now. I don't think I can take much more of this."

Chapter 16

Several days later, by stagecoach and train, they arrived at last in New Orleans. If Tori had been delighted with San Antonio, where they had stopped over for a day's rest, she adored New Orleans on sight. People were everywhere, going in all directions. The city was teeming with activity, and just watching it made Tori tingle with restless energy.

How Jake had arranged it Tori could not guess, but here they were not to stay in a hotel, though the city boasted many grand and elaborate ones. Instead, they were installed in an exclusive apartment in the fashionable French Quarter. The red brick apartment house, and its twin across Jackson Square, were owned by the Baroness de Pontalba, and it was quite a coup to claim this prestigious address, even for a short time.

It was a time to relax and forget the worries they had left behind in Santa Fe. It was a time for themselves alone; a time to enjoy, a time to love, a time to play. Jake seemed an altogether different man. He smiled and laughed freely. It had been years since Tori had seen him react so openly and in such a friendly manner toward others. Perhaps it was just that they were so far from home, in a place where his name did not strike terror or envy upon mention, where he was just another man intent on giving his new bride a wedding trip she would never forget.

The weather was hot and muggy this late in the summer, but even the steamy days and nights could not dampen Tori's exuberance over this jewel of a city. At first she was a bit overwhelmed by it all, but her curiosity soon overcame her shyness. There was so much to do and see, and Jacob was exclusively hers for the extent of their visit!

The nights were marvelous, sparkling with charm and romance as Jacob courted his lady love. The days, while still abounding in love, were filled to overflowing with sightseeing, shopping, and dozens of new experiences. The restaurants and cafes, with their spicy Creole dishes or fancy French cuisine, were heavenly. The French culture, the unique ambiance of the city, was the frosting on the cake, and Tori soaked it all in like a dry sponge. She dragged Jacob through magnificent old cathedrals, and places she knew he had no true interest in seeing, and he indulged her every whim. He even relented and took her for a ride on one of those dreadfully noisy streetcars that so fascinated her.

In turn, he insisted that she take the time to be fitted for several exquisitely designed dresses, all created especially for her by an exclusive and extremely expensive couturiere. Then, as she was still gasping over the cost, he bought her jewels to go with her new gowns, unconcernedly spending a small fortune on coral, pearls, ivory, opals, and emeralds, personally helping her select pieces which best suited her.

When Tori questioned him about the vast amount he was spending, concerned that they could not afford it, he merely laughed and told her, "Don't worry about it, darlin'. I'll tell you when the well is runnin' dry. In the meantime, I intend to spoil you outrageously, so relax and enjoy it."

One day, as they were riding slowly through the Garden District, having rented an open carriage and driver for the day, a lady along the walkway waved and called out gaily, "Jake! Jake!"

As Tori sat frowning, thinking she was about to have a second encounter with one of

Jacob's tarts, Jake instructed the carriage driver to pull over to the side of the street. He leaped from the carriage, meeting the lady halfway as she rushed to greet him. "I knew it had to be you!" she gushed. "No one else would have the audacity to wear that God-awful stetson with all the grandeur of a king, and actually get away with it."

"Susan, you're a sight for sore eyes!" Jake exclaimed with a broad grin, grabbing her about the waist and planting a smacking kiss on her proffered cheek, "and just as outspoken as I recall. What are ya'll doin' here?"

By now Tori was fuming. Jacob was not in the least reticent in his greeting to this woman. Still seated in the carriage, Tori was feeling very excluded. The least he could do was introduce her, or was his wife and the mother of his child to be ignored now?

"Why, we're living here," Susan trilled happily, "at least for a while. Mark got transferred from the Philadelphia mint about six months ago, and now he's heading the one here. I must say, it's so nice to see a friendly face! We really haven't had time to get acquainted with too many people here, except for a few that Mark is working with. Do you have a place to stay? We have plenty of room, if you need a place. How long will you be here? Oh, Mark is going to be so surprised!"

Belatedly, Jake recalled Tori, who was glaring holes through his back by this time.

"Susan," he interrupted, taking the woman's arm and leading her toward the carriage. "I'd like to introduce my wife, Tori. Tori, this is Susan Armstrong. She and her husband are friends of mine." Wary of the glint in Tori's eyes, Jake stressed the word husband, sensing that Tori was none too thrilled at the moment.

His strategy worked. As the fire left her eyes, Tori could see that this woman was nothing like the one in El Paso. Susan Armstrong was a lady. Her clothing, her walk, her entire manner spoke of good breeding. And pretty though she was, she was no threat to Tori. Susan Armstrong had a husband of her own.

Extending her hand, Tori smiled and nodded a greeting. "So nice to meet you, Mrs. Armstrong."

"Susan," the woman corrected, returning the greeting in almost breathless surprise, "and the pleasure is mine, I assure you. Oh, you can't imagine how long I've waited for this moment!" Turning to Jake, she exclaimed, "My stars, Jake! You! Married at last! How wonderful! When did all this happen? How did you meet? Are you living here now?"

Susan Armstrong reminded Tori of a tightly wound toy, chattering nonstop, her hands moving in time with her mouth. It was all Tori could do to suppress a giggle as Jake replied quickly, before Susan could get to chattering again, "Actually, this is our weddin' trip. Tori and I are stayin' in the French Quarter for a couple of weeks. Then we'll have to get back to our ranch in Santa Fe in time for the fall roundup."

Susan's sunny smile melted. "Oh, no! I was so hoping you were living here now. It would be so nice to have friends nearby." Then she brightened. "I know it is your wedding trip, and the two of you will want time to yourselves, but you must make some time for us while you are here. Why don't you stop by the house now? Mark will be home soon."

"We're goin' to have to pass on your kind invitation, Susan, but we'll visit with you another time before we leave New Orleans," Jake said, politely declining the woman's invitation. "Tell Mark I'll talk with him soon, and we'll all go out to dinner one evenin'."

"Oh, horse feathers!" Susan exclaimed in disappointment. "You know I'm dying of curiosity, and Mark is going to hate missing you." Her pert little nose wrinkled up in thought. "If you must go, why don't you come back for dinner this evening, say around eight? We live just down this street a bit. See that brick house with the yellow trim?" She indicated the house with a point of her finger, juggling her packages to do so.

"I don't know," Jake hedged. "I promised to take Tori dancin' this evenin'."

"Good!" Susan declared. "Talk Mark into taking me, too, and we'll join you. It's been

ages since we've been anywhere just for fun."
Then she colored prettily in embarrassment,
remembering that Tori and Jake were on their
honeymoon and might not appreciate others
barging in on their time alone together. "That
is, if you don't mind us tagging along?"

"Tell you what," Jake suggested kindly.
"Why don't I take Tori back to the apartment
and then go meet with Mark at the mint. If
he's agreeable to the idea, we'll all go out to
dinner someplace special, and then dancin'."

Susan glowed up at him. "That's a marvelous idea, as long as you truly don't mind." Her
apologetic look included Tori.

"It sounds delightful," Tori assured her
with a smile. "I'll be looking forward to
meeting your husband and getting to know
the two of you."

"I'm looking forward to getting to know
you, too," Susan said. Then she admitted
wryly, "I'm incurably nosy, but I don't want to
impose on your wedding trip. There is a time
for friends and a time for lovers, and the two
don't always mix well."

Jake's laughter split the air. "Susan, when
you come to know Tori better, you will learn
that when she wants food or lovin', nothin'
stands in her way."

"Now, Jacob, that's utter nonsense, and you
know it!" Tori retorted, trying to hide the rosy
flush creeping up her neck. "Why, just the
other night, didn't I kindly offer my plate and
drink to that skinny, dowdy woman who

stopped by our table and stared so with those hungry eyes of hers?"

To Susan's astonishment, Jake nearly doubled with laughter, tears of mirth dancing in his golden eyes. He waved a hand at her confused expression. "Don't ask now, Susan," he advised. "Maybe you can get Tori to explain it later, but please don't get her started now. For a nun, my darlin' wife has quite a temper."

"Nun?" Susan echoed stupidly as Jake took his place beside Tori in the carriage. She stared after them as they rode away, dropping her packages in her haste to return their waves of farewell. "Nun? Jake Banner married to a nun?" Still shaking her head, and thinking she had surely heard him incorrectly, or that she had been standing in the hot sun too long, Susan retrieved her packages and walked absently toward her house, her mind spinning. "Surely not! A shopkeeper, a dance hall girl, a courtesan, maybe; even a rancher's daughter or a schoolteacher—but a nun? Mercy! What an odd combination that would be!"

Mark Armstrong was of medium height, sturdily built, blond, and a thoroughly charming young Yankee. With his dimpled smile, his ready wit, and his habit of giving his full attention to the person speaking with him, it was impossible to dislike him. He was a bit quiet, compared with his effervescent wife, and at first it seemed they were a mismatched pair, but in actuality they complemented one another perfectly.

Tori enjoyed their company, and they all soon became fast friends. They went out to dinner together, among other things, and it was through the Armstrongs that Tori discovered a side of her husband she'd not known existed. Listening to Jacob and Mark discussing various ventures, she was astonished to find that Jake was a fairly wealthy man in his own right, even aside from the ranch he had inherited upon Roy's death. In the time he had been gone, he had invested much of his earnings, relying a great deal upon Mark's expert advice. His financial ventures had paid off very well.

No wonder he hardly blinked at the outrageous amounts the jeweler and couturiere quoted! Tori thought to herself.

Still, Tori could not help but wonder why Jacob had continued his dangerous profession when it obviously had not been necessary to endanger his life in such a manner for so long. Had he been drifting, lost and lonely, all those years? Hadn't he cared about his own welfare, or that he might have been killed at any time? Or had gunfighting become so much a part of him that it was almost second nature, so much so that it was difficult to quit until now?

How much had Roy's death affected Jacob's decision to give it up and come home? Most of all, was the love he and Tori now shared a major influence in his decision? Would it, and the child they expected, be enough to keep him home, to keep him safe, to make him more cautious with his life? Tori could only pray that it would; that Jacob would never be drawn back into that treacherous profession, that he would always be content to be a rancher, a father, her husband.

Not only was Jacob financially well set up, but he was not stingy with his wealth. It seemed he was a major contributor to several charities, though anonymously. Few people knew of his philanthropical leanings, and Jake seemed more than slightly embarrassed to have Tori learn this about him now. Mark knew, of course, since he was the person Jake had entrusted to oversee his investments and charitable contributions.

All this was a revelation to Tori, who had thought she knew Jacob so well. Not that his generosity surprised her. In fact it was what she might have expected, had she known he possessed the means, and it endeared him to her more than ever. Tori did, however, wonder how many more surprises were in store for her as she came to know this enigmatic man that Jacob had become, the man he had grown into in his time away from Santa Fe. Last, and perhaps most important, Tori knew how proud Roy would have been of his son had he known all of this. The thought brought tears shimmering to her eyes as she gazed lovingly at him across the table.

Her tears did not go unnoticed. Jake's hand found hers and covered it gently. "Darlin', what is it?" he asked softly. "What's wrong?"

Tori shook her head, her voice wavering as she tried to speak. "I'm just so proud of you, Jacob—so proud of your generous and gentle nature, of the man you are," she managed to whisper. "Dad would have been, too."

"You think so?" Jake asked wryly, one brow raised in self-mockery.

"I know so, Jacob. I know so." Her hand turned to clasp his tightly. "I love you so much."

The crowded, elegant restaurant where they were dining might have been empty for all the attention they paid the other diners as Jake leaned toward her and caught her lips with his for a long, sweet kiss. "Thank you, sweetheart," he murmured, his heart in his golden eyes. "Thank you for lovin' me the way you do."

Of all of New Orleans, Tori liked the French Quarter, where their apartment was located, the best. Beautiful homes stood in dignified splendor, bedecked in decorative lace ironwork. Enclosed courtyards ensured the owners their privacy, though the houses themselves were set close to the street.

Jackson Square, which had in years past

been merely a dusty parade ground, had been transformed into a lovely garden park. Flowers bloomed in a profusion of color and fragrance, delighting the senses, while a fountain sparkled in the sunlight. Birds chirped, children laughed and played, vegetable and fruit vendors hawked their succulent wares in lilting chants from atop their laden wagons.

On many fine mornings, along the wrought iron fences that flanked the square, sidewalk artists took up palette and brush. Beauty surrounded Jake and Tori, whether it was the magnificence of the St. Louis Cathedral, the grandeur of the Cabildo and the Presbytere buildings, the iron-embroidered elegance of the Pontalba apartments, or the glorious brilliance of nature in splendid array.

One mid-morning Jake surprised Tori by contracting one of the sidewalk artists to make a portrait of her. At first she balked, but Jake soon convinced her to set aside her modesty and shyness in order to please him. "I want a portrait of you, Tori, just as you are today, so lovely and filled with delight. Your mama would adore it."

"Don't I have anything to say about this?" she argued.

Jake just grinned at her. "You can say yes and give in graciously."

In the end, Tori was both pleased and embarrassed by the resulting portrait. Right there in the open park, not satisfied with her pose, Jake had pulled her into his arms and kissed her thoroughly. By the time he released her, Tori's face was flushed with color, her eyes soft and dreamy, her lips rosy and trembling with longing.

"That's the look I want you to capture," Jake told the artist. "I want her to look kissed, loved, blushin' with passion."

To his credit, the artist had done just that. The woman in the portrait glowed. Her eyes sparkled with life, and just a hint of hidden sensuality. She was the perfect picture of a woman in love—of Tori.

On Sunday Tori again tried to get Jake to go to church with her. Once more he refused, though earlier in the week he had readily toured the beautiful St. Louis Cathedral with her, admiring its grace and splendor. Today he walked her as far as the doors and refused to go any further.

"Jacob, don't you think it would be nice to attend Mass together, to thank God for all He has given us, to ask Him to watch over us and guide us?"

Jake took her small chin in his palm and tilted her face toward his. "Honey," he told her earnestly, "just because I don't go to Mass or light candles and pray in a chapel doesn't mean I don't thank God for all He has done. He and I have an understandin' of sorts; I don't bother Him with piddlin' things that He has given me the brains and means to handle myself, and I don't pester Him with the nit-pickin' details."

The look on Jake's face was so serious that Tori could not berate him. It seemed he truly believed what he was telling her, and maybe it was so. Who was she to contradict him?

"You see, darlin'," Jake went on to explain, "God has given me the one and only thing I ever truly wanted in this life—you and your love. How could I possibly ask for more, when He's already granted my fondest wish? You were practically promised to the church, when I came along and took you away. He allowed me that. In return, I've promised to love and honor, protect and cherish you till the day I die. God knows, I'll love you beyond that, beyond all eternity. If I died tomorrow, I swear to you that I wouldn't regret one moment spent with you. It's been the happiest time of my life, and I'll always be grateful for it, no matter how long or short it might be. God has granted me an angel to love, and I thank Him for every day spent in the sunshine of your smile. I sure can't ask for more than that."

Tears welled up in Tori's eyes. Reaching up, she stroked his firm cheek with her fingertips. "Oh, Jacob, you say the most beautiful things!" she exclaimed softly. "Still, don't you think it would be a good idea to ask Him to watch over our child, to see that it grows healthy and safe within me, to ask that he or she be brought safely into our care?"

"You ask Him for the both of us, sweetheart," Jake said tenderly. "I imagine He already has His plans made for the baby, but you talk with Him if it makes you feel better. How could He resist any plea from you? I know I can't, but then I'm only human, and I love you more than anything else on this earth. I'll be here waitin' when you've finished with your prayers."

True to his word, Jake was standing at the bottom of the steps when she came out an hour later. Shielding her eyes with her hand, trying to adjust from the dim interior of the church to the bright sunlight outdoors, Tori almost ran into an old woman who suddenly cut across her path.

"Oh! I'm so sorry!" Tori apologized, catching her balance just in time to avoid a fall.

The old woman teetered a bit, then steadied herself. When she raised her head, her shiny black eyes, darker than any Tori had ever seen, sent a shiver down Tori's spine. A gnarled finger came up to point at Tori. "You are the one," the old crone said in a wavering voice.

"The—what one?" Tori stammered.

"The one who needs my protection," the woman answered, as if Tori should have known that without being told.

Before she could explain further, were she

so inclined, another woman came up and tugged at the old woman's arm. "Come along, Mama. These white folks don't believe in your magic, and they don't appreciate your pesterin' them. Do you want them to call the law and have you thrown in that jail you're always visitin'?"

Tori's confused gaze wavered between the two strangers. Both were tall, though the older one was beginning to stoop slightly with age. Tori had been so startled at first that she had failed to recognize that neither woman was white, nor did she think they were Cajun, though their lilting speech sounded similar. They appeared to be a mixture of black and perhaps Cajun blood, for each had the slightly dusky complexion of a ripe peach. Studying them, Tori assumed the mother had once been as beautiful and elegant as her daughter was now, though the daughter was also old enough to be Tori's grandmother.

"What's goin' on here?" Jake's voice broke into Tori's study of the two women, demanding their attention.

The younger of the two strangers pulled at her mother's arm, trying to get her to turn away. "Nothin', monsieur," the daughter answered hastily, a worried frown pulling at her face. "My mother is old, and sometimes she does not know what she does."

Exhibiting a strength far beyond her years,

the old woman jerked free of her daughter's hold, letting loose a shrieking spate of patois that startled them all. Reverting to English, she continued her tirade. "I did not give you permission to touch me, daughter! I am the revered Marie Laveau, more powerful than you can ever dream to become, and I do not need you interfering with my work! Be gone with you!"

The name nudged at Jake's memory from previous visits to New Orleans, but he could not place it immediately. It was not until the old lady pulled a tiny pouch from the bodice of her dress that he remembered who she was. Marie Laveau, though aged and half-senile, had once been the most powerful of the area's voodoo queens.

In her youth she had also been quite beautiful, with an elegance matched by none, if the tales be true. After the death of one of her daughters to yellow fever, a scourge which continued to plague New Orleans from time to time, Marie Laveau had turned her strange powers toward healing, with astounding results. Supposedly, her remedies of bark and roots managed to save ninety-six out of every hundred of her yellow-fever patients, while the medical doctors stood in awe, themselves saving only half of those they treated. In her prime, hardly a day passed that someone was not pounding on her door and pleading with

Madame Laveau for a cure or a charm to ward off illness or evil.

Though her notorious title of voodoo queen, illegal though it was, had passed on to her daughter when age had begun to creep up on her, Marie still haunted the French Quarter. She particularly frequented Jackson Square and the cathedral area, and could often be found consoling the condemned prisoners in the parish prison. Marie Laveau was determined to continue her appointed task until death came to claim her, though many ridiculed her these days, conveniently forgetting those times when they had begged for her favors.

Now she met Jake's dark look without flinching, her black eyes boring into his as he said gruffly, "On your way, old woman. We don't need any of your wicked charms. My wife is a God-fearing woman."

Marie nodded and chuckled, though it sounded more like a cackle. "You think I don't know this?" she queried haughtily. "I know more than you will ever learn." Her burning gaze turned upon Tori as she continued to speak in her singsong voice. "I know that your young wife is carrying your first child. I know that it will be a fine, healthy son, and that his name will be Bretton Roy."

At Tori's astonished gasp, the woman cackled anew. "Yes," she said, waving a gnarled finger at them. "I know all this and more. That is why I am here. This woman needs my protection."

Jake took offense at this slur on his role as husband and protector. "I can protect my wife well enough without your aid."

"So you think," Marie conceded, "but you are wrong. There will come a day when you will thank me for stopping your wife and giving her this added talisman against harm." Marie dangled the charm from its thong, holding it out to Tori.

As Tori reached for it, unable to keep her fingers from reaching out, Jake grabbed at the charm. "I told you we don't need your worthless voodoo magic," he repeated angrily, wanting to yank the charm from Marie's clawlike hand and throw the foul thing into the street.

Old as she was, Marie was still agile enough to prevent this. Snatching the charm from his reach, she glared at him. "Men can be so stupid!" she announced with a superior sneer. "That is why women are accorded the honor of leading the rites. Rarely is there a man who does not let his immense pride make a fool of him. Women have sense enough to realize the powers of that which is not understood. They respect the wonder of things magical and mystical, the dark powers of the unknown."

"Keep your 'dark powers' to yourself," Jake sneered. His hand came up, and for a frightful moment Tori feared he was going to push the old woman down the stone steps. Marie's intense stare seemed to freeze the motion before he could complete it.

Her hand trembling violently, Tori reached out to claim the charm. It seemed to almost burn her fingers as they clenched about it, but she held tightly, some inner spirit compelling her to do so whether she wanted to or not. "Thank you, madame," she whispered in a shaky voice. "What am I to do with it?"

"Wear it about your neck," Marie told her. "Do not tamper with it or you will disturb its magic, and never take it off until the danger has passed."

"And when might that be?" Jake put in, his voice dripping with sarcasm.

Madame Laveau laughed up at him, as though to emphasize his stupidity. "Your wife will know," she answered. Then, without further explanation or decree, she turned and made her way down the steps, her body still lithe and graceful at the age of eighty-seven.

Tori watched until the woman was out of sight. Only then did she raise her eyes to meet Jake's accusing glare. "She is old, Jacob, and she means well, I suppose."

Jake's only reply was a rude snort of disbelief.

Opening her hand, Tori surveyed the oddly shaped charm lying in her palm. It was a weathered piece of some kind of wood, per-

haps driftwood, which had twisted itself into
the resemblance of the female form. In the
center of it, approximately where the belly
would be, was a hollow, within which had
been wedged three large seeds, similar to
pumpkin seeds. High upon the main body of
the piece, in what Tori assumed to be the left
shoulder, was a small hole filled with a sticky
substance. Frowning, Tori tried to figure out
what it might symbolize. Was it the heart?
What?

Shaking her head at herself, she raised the
thong, preparing to slip it over her head, only
to have Jake's sharp words stop her. "You're
not actually gonna wear that piece of mumbo-
jumbo trash, are you?"

She met his glare calmly. "Yes, Jacob, I
believe I am."

"For God's sake, why?" he demanded.

"I don't know. I can't explain it, because I
don't understand it myself. I only know I feel
compelled to do as Madame Laveau has instructed. I feel as though I was meant to meet
her here today, for reasons beyond my understanding, and that I must do this."

"I don't believe this!" Jake exclaimed disgustedly. "If I did, I'd swear that old bat has
put you under some kind of spell." Something
in Tori's face made him stop short his tirade,
and he regarded her more tenderly. "Oh, go
ahead," he growled impatiently. "What the
hell can it hurt? It's only a piece of wood and

some seeds!" *I hope*, he added silently to himself, not at all sure he didn't believe just the tiniest bit, despite himself and all intelligent reasoning, in the aged voodoo queen's dark powers.

"I just hope the damned thing doesn't stink!" Tori heard him mutter grumpily.

Chapter 17

Mark and Susan Armstrong received an invitation to one of the nearby plantations outside New Orleans to help celebrate the engagement of the daughter of a friend. In turn, they extended the invitation to include Jake and Tori. It was to be a weekend celebration at the home of Alex and Emaline Drummond, culminating in a grand ball such as had not been seen since the War Between the States.

Tori was ecstatic! She had never seen a plantation before, and Susan assured her that Moss Haven would not disappoint her. The house and grounds were almost exactly as they had been before the war. Somehow, though the Drummonds had lost two sons in the war, and Alex his leg, Moss Haven itself had escaped the ravages of war. The sugar cane plantation was prospering once more.

The fastest, most convenient means of travel was by riverboat, a novel experience for Tori, and one she greatly enjoyed. They arrived on Friday afternoon and were met at the Moss Haven docks and driven by buggy up to the main house.

From her first sight of Moss Haven, Tori was enchanted. It was everything she had ever imagined a Southern plantation would be like. A long, curved drive led up to a wide portico supported by eight elegant white columns across the front of the house. The house was built of brick, but not the usual red-brown brick or the sandy color that Tori was accustomed to seeing. This was an unusual and very lovely dusky pink. Later it was explained to her that the bricks were custom-made and that chips of ground seashell accounted for the color.

Delicate, intricate wrought iron decorated the windows and formed rails for the many balconies on the second floor of the sprawling house; and all around the perimeter of the house, twelve huge moss-draped oaks provided protection from the sun and heat— thus the name, Moss Haven.

Inside, the place was cool and lovely. To Tori, used to much smaller family homes,

Moss Haven seemed a mansion, which in actuality it was. It contained so many beautiful rooms, including an enormous ballroom, a conservatory, and numerous bedrooms. It had magnificent chandeliers and an elegant iron-bedecked staircase that curved majestically upward like something out of a fairy tale.

Moss Haven was, beyond doubt, the most marvelous home Tori had ever seen, and the Drummonds were delightful hosts. Their entire family and a bevy of servants went out of their way to ensure the comfort of their guests. If they wanted to ride, horses were immediately provided. Freshly cut flowers in crystal vases arrived in their rooms daily. Awaking to a tap on her bedroom door in the morning, Tori was served fresh-baked beignets and steaming coffee as she lounged abed. Then, while she wakened at her leisure, servants prepared her morning bath and laid out her clothing. There was even a girl to arrange her hair.

Tori had never known such luxury. Compared with her austere life at the convent, this was almost sinful! "Enjoy it, honey," Jake told her with an indulgent smile. "Just don't get to like it too much, 'cause I'm not about to play lady's maid once we're home."

"Don't worry, Jacob. This life of luxury is fine for a time, but it's not for me. Already I'm suffering pangs of guilt for being so altogether lazy. I'm having a delightful time, but I'm

beginning to miss working with the children
at the orphanage. I miss Mama and Rosa, and
I wonder how the baby fawn is doing without
me."

Jake brushed the damp curls from her
forehead and kissed her brow. "I'm sure they
are all fine, Tori, or I'd have had word from
Blake by now."

The first evening at Moss Haven, with most
of the guests arriving the next day, was rather
informal. After a delicious dinner, the ladies
repaired to the music room to listen to a
recital. Most of the men preferred a rousing
game of cards over the musical entertainment. Jake and Mark were as playful and
frisky as two young boys, and Tori had to
laugh at them both. She wondered how long it
had been since Jacob had indulged in this sort
of male camaraderie, really enjoyed himself
in a way a man can only do amongst other
men. With the troubles at the ranch, she
suspected it had been much too long.

At breakfast the next morning, it became
obvious that the friendly game of cards had
suddenly turned very ugly when a Creole
gentleman, another guest of the Drummonds', had accused Mark of cheating at
poker. Charles Reveneau had lost quite a sum
in the course of the game, not only to Mark,
but to Jake and a number of other men.
However, since Mark was the big winner, he

was the one to take the brunt of Reveneau's temper. It had taken Alex, Jake, and several other men to calm the Creole, and even now the man was very angry. He clearly wanted to call Mark out, demanding this be settled in a duel of honor. Only respect for his host's wishes prevented him from doing just that.

Susan was aghast, and much relieved that circumstances and decorum prevented such a thing. Even now, when duels were officially outlawed, it was not unknown for opponents to arrange to meet "accidentally" out on Esplanade Road, under the Dueling Oaks, to settle their differences.

Jake caught Tori's eye and winked. "See, darlin'? It's not really all that different in the so-called civilized parts of the world than in the wild, wicked West, is it?"

"I guess not," Tori conceded thoughtfully. She realized she was going to have to adjust her thinking a bit. It seemed that even here, in this supposedly cultured part of the world, men still settled their disagreements with violence. She wondered if it would always be this way, or whether men would one day realize that bloodshed was not the best way to resolve their disputes.

That day, and the one that followed, were wonderful. A picnic luncheon near the river was planned for Saturday, with a bountiful barbecue on Sunday, followed by the ball that evening. There were games for old and young alike, and a horserace arranged as a special event. In answer to Jake's many questions about how he ran his sugar cane plantation, Alex Drummond took him on an extended tour of the fields and the refining mill, located right there on the property. He even presented Jake with a bottle of homemade rum, a delightful and lucrative by-product of the refining process.

Tori was very glad now that Jake had insisted on purchasing such beautiful gowns for her. Just to be safe, since she had not known what to expect upon reaching the plantation, she had packed her new gowns, and she knew exactly which of these would be perfect for the engagement ball.

It was a satin creation of shimmering peach color, with yard upon yard of wide, contrasting cocoa-brown ruffles drawn up and back from the hem of the dress to form the bustle, creating a flow of dark ruffles along each side and all down the rear of the gown. Along the flounced neckline, a row of cocoa lace underlay a deep ruffle of peach. This double ruffle dipped low, forming the bodice that just edged the tops of her breasts. At the outer tip of each almost-bared shoulder, the ruffles came together in a charming little bow. Accenting the nipped waist was a slim peach ribbon, imprinted with tiny chocolate-colored flowers along the entire band.

Tori could hardly wait to wear it—to see Jacob's reaction to her in it. It was sure to stir his blood, not that it needed stirring. Still, Tori particularly delighted in the amorous side of her husband, after so many years of thinking of him as a brother. It also crossed her mind that it would not be long before her waist would begin to thicken with their child and she would not be able to wear such a gown as this, and Tori vowed to make the most of this opportunity.

"Mmmnn. You smell as good as you look, darlin'. Like a ripe little peach, just waitin' for me to take a bite of it." Jake's words tickled along her neck and in her ear as he whirled her across the dance floor to the music.

A shiver made her quiver in his arms as she replied coquettishly, "Why, sir! You are much too bold in such a public place!"

"Then why don't we find someplace not quite so crowded, like my bed, for instance," he drawled, giving her a rakish grin.

Fluttering her lace fan, Tori laughed up at him with twinkling eyes. "A walk in the gardens, or perhaps the conservatory might be more appropriate," she suggested.

"Hmmm," he said, considering this with a raised brow. "I don't recall ever makin' love in either of those places. Might be interestin', now that you mention it."

Tori flipped her fan closed with a quick flick of her wrist and tapped him sharply on the arm with it. "Jacob Banner, you are a rogue, through and through!"

"And you know you love it," he continued to tease. "Well, which will it be, the gardens or the conservatory?"

"In the interest of your tempting white bottom," she whispered, her lips mere inches from his, "I'd suggest the conservatory. There are fewer mosquitoes there."

His eyes went wide with surprise and delight. "Why, you wicked little temptress!" he laughed. Taking her hand, he led her across the ballroom toward the doors to the conservatory. "Don't ever say you didn't ask for this, especially if we happen to get caught!"

With eyes only for one another, and giggling like schoolchildren skipping class, they entered the glass-topped atrium. "Sshhh," he hissed. "Hush, you silly goose, or we really will be caught!"

"With your britches down?" she snickered, hastily covering her mouth with her hand to stifle her giggles.

"No, with your skirts up around your neck, and your bustle used as a pillow!" he retorted, smothering a chuckle of his own.

Winding his way behind a pair of potted plants as tall as small trees, Jake spotted a thick bed of wood shavings covering a secluded section of one corner. "This looks like a good place. Out of the way, fairly clean, and we can still hear the music."

"Oh, Jacob! Should we? Truly, what if we are seen? Maybe we shouldn't." Tori was having second thoughts now that their impulsive behavior had brought them this far.

"Too late to back out now, sweetheart," Jake warned, his voice already thick with desire for her. "Don't worry. It's too dark here in the shadows for anyone who might stumble along to see anything. Besides, the only thing showin' will be your bare bottom and those long legs of yours, and nobody else had better damn well ever recognize those but me."

In the dim light, Tori could see the gleam of his teeth in his dark face as he grinned that devilish grin of his. His eyes glinted like gold coins as he gazed down at her, challenging her to be daring, to be bold. This, combined with the feverish lure of the forbidden, the risk of discovery, acted as a powerful aphrodisiac and made Tori's heart beat rapidly, unevenly. Even before his lips came down to capture hers in a hot, sweet kiss that stole the breath from her body, she felt lightheaded. "If we're found out, Jacob," she whispered as he slowly lowered her to the ground, "I swear I'll shoot you!"

"I'm real worried, honey," he chuckled, his warm lips searing a trail of fire down her throat, even as his fingers found her silken thigh beneath the folds of her skirt. "Especially since we both know you couldn't hit the broad side of a barn if you were standin' three feet from it."

If she had been capable of speech, which by now was impossible, she could have told him that her aim was much improved since she had been practicing with Megan. The words died unspoken, only a low moan of desire escaping her lips as his body covered hers.

A short while later, her color high and wood shavings dusting her curls, Tori followed Jake back into the ballroom. They hadn't been seen, though they had come too close to it for comfort. At one point, they had frozen in awful anticipation as a wandering couple skirted the edges of their hidden corner. Only Jake's mouth over hers had stilled Tori's startled squeal. The strolling lovers had passed by without noticing them, though Tori wondered how they had failed to hear the frantic beating of her heart.

Brushing at her wrinkled skirts, Tori tried and failed to send her husband a glare. The sight of him attempting to surreptitiously rid himself of the itchy wood chips that had worked their way inside his waistcoat turned her glare into a dimpled grin. "Never again, Jacob!" she warned in a whisper. "Never, as long as I live, will I allow you to talk me into anything this ridiculous!"

"Never's a long time, darlin', and as I recall,

this was your idea. I was all set to go upstairs to our room."

"It would have been more comfortable," she conceded. Then she cursed softly and muttered low, "Blast it all! I have wood chips down my drawers!"

Jake's burst of laughter had several heads turning in their direction. "Our bed might have been more comfortable, but you can't deny we had a good time in there, angel face—a rousin' good time!"

"One thing's for sure," she admitted, leaning against him as she shook sawdust from her dancing slippers, "I'll never be able to even hear the word 'conservatory' again without getting a silly grin on my face, and I hope to high heaven Emaline doesn't ask how we enjoyed her beautiful plants."

"Just tell her they smell good, and her gardener needs to replace the mulch."

Tori gave a mortified moan and reached out to pluck a wood chip from Jake's lapel. "You tell her. She's headed this way right now, and I'm taking the easy way out and heading for the ladies' repair room."

"Coward!" he hissed as she took a step away from him.

"Most assuredly!" she giggled, scurrying away as Emaline bore down on them. "I'm counting on you to protect my reputation, darling. It's my right, you know, as the wife of such a big, strong, irresistible man!"

She left him basking in the glow of her sugar-sweet words, and wondering what in blue blazes he was going to say to Emaline should she notice the wood shavings still clinging to his hair and clothing.

For all the luxury she'd experienced at Moss Haven, Tori was glad to be back in New Orleans. She and Jake only had two days left here, and there was still much she wanted to see and do, not the least of which was to go back to the jewelers and buy a wedding gift for Jake. She also wanted to buy a new nightgown for the last official night of their honeymoon in New Orleans. She fully intended to make it a night he would remember for the rest of his life, to fulfill his wildest fantasies.

Early the following evening, Jake stood in the doorway of the bedroom and stared in awe at the beautiful woman he was fortunate enough to call his wife. He had given Tori the time she had requested, to have a bath and prepare for their last night in New Orleans, while he had taken the opportunity to do the same in the other bedroom down the hall. Now, as he gazed at her, he could find no words. There simply weren't any that could properly convey the effect she had on him.

She was stunning, perhaps more assured and alluring than he had ever before seen her. She was always beautiful, especially to him, but tonight there was something different about her, something more devil than angel lurking in those pale green eyes of hers. The wisp of a smile that curved her full lips was decidedly wicked as she boldly met him stare for stare, and that green gown was absolutely the most sensuous garment he had ever had the privilege to view.

She started toward him, and his gasp echoed in the still of the room, the only other sound the sensual swish of her gown whispering to him. With every step, her long, lovely legs were outlined against the sheer cloth of the garment. It was evident that she wore nothing beneath the gown, and somehow this was more alluring than if she had been completely nude. The scent of her, fresh from her bath, wafted toward him, something smelling of vanilla and spice. Unconsciously his nostrils flared, inhaling the sweet enticement, while his eyes faithfully followed the graceful sway of her body as she came closer.

Under his heated perusal her nipples hardened, straining at the cloth that clung to her breasts, the bodice cut low across them. Fully aroused just by the sight and smell of her, his own body tightened more painfully. It was clear she meant to play the seductress this evening, and was doing it quite successfully if the intense ache in his groin was any indication.

Just beyond his reach, Tori stopped, then swirled about, giving him the full benefit of the daring cut of her gown. "Do you like it?" she asked in a low voice that sounded suspiciously like a purr.

He gave a gruff chuckle, aching all the more. "You know I do, minx. A man has a hard time tryin' to conceal his reactions."

Her mischievous gaze flickered downward, taking in the hard bulge in his trousers. "So I see," she teased, her tongue sneaking out to wet her lush lips, tempting him beyond measure.

"Come here," he growled, only to have her shake her head and give him a dazzling smile.

"Not yet, darling." With that, she lazily raised her arms and began plucking the pins from her upswept hair. One by one, they dropped soundlessly to the carpeted floor, as the dark fall of her hair cascaded about her shoulders, showering him with another drift of that sinfully delicious scent she was wearing. She shook her hair loose, then stepped forward to run her hands down the length of his shirt front, then up again to the first button. Slowly, teasingly, she released each button in turn, pausing between them to touch his newly bared flesh.

Jake ceased to breathe. The touch of her fingers on his chest were like tiny branding irons. When, at length, she parted the material and threaded her fingers lightly through the dark mat of hair, finding his flat nipples and grazing them with her nails, he drew in a long, hissing breath. "Woman, if your plans for the evenin' include undressin' me, you'd best be doin' it, or I'm liable to toss you on your back right here on the rug." At this point he was sure they would never make it the few steps to the bed.

Her smile was as old as Eve, and twice as devious. "Just enjoy it, Jacob. It's my turn to play now. Your time will come."

"Sooner than you think," he muttered through gritted teeth as her hands pushed the shirt from his shoulders and down his arms. Delicate white teeth nibbled at his chest as her fingers sought the fastening of his trousers. Her hand brushed his swollen flesh and he groaned, the sound rumbling through his chest.

Blindly, he followed as she led him to the bed and urged him down upon its edge. Kneeling before him, she pulled his trousers off, not having to bother with boots this time since he had just bathed before coming to her barefoot and wearing nothing but shirt and pants. With a few deft strokes, he was completely bared to her eager eyes. "You are so beautiful," she sighed, breathing in the musky male scent of him.

"Men aren't beautiful," he objected breathlessly, feeling her fingers slowly creeping up the inside of his legs.

"You are," she assured him. "Oh, yes! Believe me, you are!"

He nearly lurched off the bed as her tongue suddenly swept across the sole of one foot. Tori gave a wicked laugh and held his ankle firm within her grasp as he protested loudly. "Hey! That tickles! Stop that!"

If that tickled, it was nothing compared with the delightful agony to come. At this moment, he was completely at her mercy. He realized it, and from the sound of her chuckles, so did she. She could hear his teeth grating against each other as he muttered unintelligibly and thrashed about on the covers, but Tori was feeling the full scope of her womanly powers now, and she was not about to show him leniency. Too many times she had lain where he did now, their roles reversed, as he tormented her until she thought she would die. Tonight the tables were turned, and she was taking full advantage. Let him endure, as she so often had to.

With tongue and teeth and lips, she worked her way up his lean, muscled body. His hands clutched at her hair, tearing at it as her mouth closed about the fount of his desire, hot and so very smooth as she drew upon him deeply. Hands and mouth became instruments of torture as she worked her magic in long, silken strokes that drove him wild with blazing desire. For Jake it was heaven and hell rolled into one, a pleasure so great it hurt.

When his deep moans turned to dark pleas, she at last took pity on him, licking and nipping a winding path up his heaving torso. The ends of her hair trailed along his ribs like curling fingers as she inched her way upward to straddle his thighs, the full skirt of her gown flaring out about them. Immediately, Jake's lips sought hers in frenzied yearning.

For just a second, as he forgot his own immense power, she feared he might crack her ribs as he crushed her to him. Then he seemed to recall himself. Long, trembling fingers delved into the bodice of the gown, tugging aside the material that shielded her breasts, gathering the silken orbs and freeing them to his touch. Calloused thumbs and fingers worried the taut peaks, bringing a moan from deep within her, muffled by his mouth hungrily ravishing hers. Hot waves of fire danced through her, making her blood sing and thrum through her veins.

When his hands left her breasts to clasp about her hips, she aided him in positioning herself over him. Then, with one powerful lunge of their bodies toward one another, they were joined in a hot, honeyed, blissful union that stole the breath from their laboring lungs. She took everything he offered, and gave still more as he guided her movements over him, moving slowly at first, then faster, harder, plumbing the depths of her sweet, dark cavern with his fiery spear.

Sparks seemed to fly between them, and

lights danced before Tori's eyes as the final, splendid triumph neared. Tearing her lips from his, Tori braced her hands on his broad chest and arched her spine into a bow, her head thrown back in tingling expectation. A ragged cry tore from her straining throat, matched only by Jake's own exultant shout as together they entered that dazzling realm of rapture.

He was weak, replete, wrung out like an old dishrag, trembling and tingling from head to toe. Almost too lethargic to speak, he mustered his last spark of energy to say, "Darlin', you amaze me. Where did you ever learn all those wonderfully wicked things you just did to me? I know they don't teach such things at the convent."

Rubbing her nose in the springy hair covering his chest, Tori giggled. "I learned them from you, silly man, where else?"

"Lord! I must be a better teacher than I thought!" he exclaimed with a soft whistle. "But what about that bit with the feet, Tori? I never taught you anything like that, and you know it."

She raised her head far enough to give him a peck on the chin and an irritatingly enigmatic smile. "Women need their little secrets, too, Jacob."

"Tori!" he growled threateningly.

"Oh, pooh! All right, but you're not going to

believe me when I tell you." He merely cocked an eyebrow at her and waited. "Emaline suggested it."

He couldn't have looked more stunned if she had hit him over the head with an ax. "Emaline?" he exclaimed on a puff of air. "Emaline Drummond? I don't believe it."

"I knew you wouldn't, but she did, and it worked even better than she claimed. Now, what do you have to say about that, Mr. Knows-Everything?"

She eyed him smugly, laughing aloud when he finally gave her a wry grin. "I think it will take a week for my toes to uncurl! And I can't wait to try it on you, you sassy little witch!"

On a burst of renewed energy, he lunged for her, pinning her to the sheets and grabbing for her feet as she squirmed and squealed. Their laughter rang through the room and out into the still night, disturbing several slumbering neighbors and two stray cats mating in the street. With resigned sighs, the older residents of Jackson Square pulled their pillows over their ears, thankful that the lusty newlyweds were scheduled to leave tomorrow. Perhaps then they could get a full night of uninterrupted sleep once in a while. The younger French couples smiled knowingly at one another and tried to imagine what exactly might be going on in the Pontalba apartment occupied by Mr. and Mrs. Jacob Banner.

Chapter
18

Dawn was still an hour away when a furious pounding on the door awakened Jake and Tori from their dreams. "What the devil?" Jake muttered, trying to find his trousers where Tori had tossed them to the floor the previous evening.

"Who can that be at this hour?" Tori yawned, brushing her hair from sleepy eyes.

"Whoever it is better have a damned good excuse!" Jake yanked on his pants and hollered over the continued rapping, "I'm coming! I'm coming! Hold your pants on!"

Regardless of her confusion, Tori had to laugh as Jake struggled with the buttons of his britches. "It's you who had better hold onto his britches, from the looks of things!"

Curious, she climbed from the bed and searched for her robe as Jake clamored down the stairs to answer the door. Her curiosity rose as she heard Susan's excited voice exclaim, "Jake! Thank God you're here!" Then their friend broke into hysterical tears and cried out, "You've got to come! Oh, Jake, you've got to talk him out of this idiocy! He's going to get himself killed! I just know it!"

Forgetting her slippers, Tori ran down the stairs in time to hear Jake ask, "Susan, what in tarnation are you talkin' about? Please, stop cryin' and tell us why you're here."

Catching sight of Tori, Jake threw her a helpless look, and Tori came forward to lead her ashen-faced friend to the nearest chair. "Susan, honey, calm down. We can't understand what you are trying to tell us. Is it something to do with Mark?"

Susan nodded, gulping back her sobs and swiping at the tears blurring her vision. "He . . . he's going to fight a duel! You've got to help me! Help him! Oh, God, I'm so afraid! He can't shoot worth a tinker's damn, and he still insists on going!"

"A duel? Mark?" Jake asked incredulously, as Tori eyes grew wide with disbelief. "Where? When? Who's he meeting?"

With fists tightly clenched, Susan looked up at him fearfully, fighting to keep herself under some control. "With that gambler person from the Drummonds'," she said on a shuddering sigh. "He's to meet him this morning at the Dueling Oaks."

"Reveneau?" Jake asked.

"Yes, I think that's his name. Oh, Jake, you've got to stop him! Mark won't listen to a word I say! Right now he's trying to find a pair of dueling pistols he can borrow! He's sent one of the servants to ask the neighbors, and he sent me here to ask you if you will act as his second."

Jake's brows drew together in thought. "I'm to act as Mark's second?"

"If you agree," Susan told him, "but you must talk to him, Jake! He can't do this thing! You know he's no marksman!"

"Since Mark has the choice of weapons, I take it he's the challenged party in all this?"

"Yes. You see, we were out to dinner last evening and happened to chance upon this Reveneau man. From the outset, I knew there would be trouble. I tried to get Mark to leave the restaurant, but before we could manage it, this dreadful man accused Mark again of having cheated him at cards that night at Moss Haven. Naturally, Mark denied it, but one thing led to another, and before I quite knew how it all happened, Reveneau was challenging Mark to a duel, or the other way around. I don't really recall all that clearly. Everything seemed to happen so quickly. At any rate,

Mark was agreeing to it, as if this were something he did every other day of the week! My God, I still can't believe he got himself talked into this!" Susan burst into fresh tears, and Tori was trying to calm her.

Jake took charge. "I'll take care of things, Susan. Tell me, where am I to meet Mark?"

"At home. Oh, Jake, you should see him!" Susan wailed. "He's been up all night worrying and pacing the floor! He looks awful! He . . . he even wrote out his will and had one of the servants witness it, in case—" Susan broke down, unable to continue.

Jake was already loping up the stairway. "I've got to get dressed and over there. Tori, you stay here with Susan. Give her some brandy or something and try to get her to lie down."

Tori was torn between comforting Susan, who looked as if she were about to faint at any moment, or going after Jake and asking how he planned to help Mark. Susan chose that moment to slump to the floor, leaving Tori little choice in the matter. By the time she had dragged Susan's limp body to the divan and loosened her collar, Jake was rushing down the stairs again and heading for the door, buckling his gunbelt as he went. "Jacob! Wait!" she called after him.

"Can't!" he yelled back. "No time! I'm takin' Susan's carriage. Try to keep her calm until we get back." His final remark drifted back to her as he muttered, "At least the fool had the sense to choose pistols instead of swords!"

Totally frustrated, Tori uttered an oath she had only heard Jake use when he was supremely upset.

Jake didn't bother to knock when he reached the Armstrong home. He simply barged in, slamming the door behind him. "Armstrong! Where are you?"

He found his friend in the parlor, looking as white as death and staring down at a pair of dueling pistols in a velvet-lined box. "I . . . I don't even know if I'm supposed to load these things ahead of time or wait until we get there." Mark's voice was low, his eyes filled with apprehension when he met Jake's angry glare.

"You're not goin' to have to worry about it, 'cause you're not goin' to be usin' either one of them," Jake growled.

"I have to." Mark swallowed hard and sent Jake a sickly grin. "I can't back out. You know that, Jake. I have to go through with this."

"Oh, you'll be there," Jake assured him, "but not the way you'd planned. First, tell me. You have the choice of weapons and chose pistols?" At Mark's nervous nod, Jake asked, "Did you and Reveneau agree on any special type of gun?"

"No, but the standard weapon is something

like this." Mark held the box in his hands out for Jake to see.

Jake shoved the dueling pistols back at him. "You really are a lucky sonovabitch, Armstrong. You know that, don't you? Reveneau could have waited to challenge you until I'd left town."

Mark's brow furrowed in confusion. "What difference does that make? I'm the one facing him. You'll only be there as my second, to make sure the duel is carried out in the proper manner. Of course, I'm glad as hell you'll be there with me, if only to cart my bloody body back and see that Susan is taken care of."

"Yeah, but if anything should happen to you, makin' it impossible for you to fight, I'd take your place against Reveneau, right?"

"Sure, but as you can see, I'm on my feet, and fairly capable, if I don't embarrass myself by puking my guts up when we get there."

"I don't think you're gonna have to worry about it, old friend," Jake retorted, shaking his head. "Under any other circumstances, I'd really hate doin' this, but you can thank me later. Right now, we haven't got a lot of time to waste." Without further explanation, Jake's right hand, bunched into a fist, came up to clip Mark smartly on the jaw. The man dropped like a felled tree. Kneeling beside him, Jake took Mark's right arm in both hands, grimacing as he twisted it sharply. As the bone snapped loudly, Jake winced. "I really hate to do this," he told himself and the unconscious man, "but it's for your own good."

Mark groaned as Jake lifted him from the floor and carried him to the waiting carriage. They were well on their way to their destination by the time Mark regained consciousness. "Oh, God!" he moaned, clutching at his arm. "What happened? What the hell have you done to me?"

Leaning nonchalantly against his side of the carriage, Jake calmly advised, "Don't move around too much. Your arm's broken, and we didn't have time to get it set. Maybe the doctor will tend to it at the duel. You did arrange to have a doctor standin' by, didn't you?"

"You lousy bastard!" Mark stared at him with pain-glazed eyes. "This is the arm I write with!"

"Glad to hear it," Jake shot back with an arrogant grin. "I didn't think to ask beforehand, and I don't imagine you'd be too happy if we had to pull over while I broke the other arm."

"What kind of friend are you, anyway?" Mark groaned, gritting his teeth against the pain. "How am I supposed to duel in this condition?"

Jake gave a wry chuckle. "Now you're gettin' the idea. And seein' as how I had to get so rough with you, I won't even charge you the usual fee for my services. Now, if I'm goin' up against Reveneau in your place, I need to know, do you want him dead or do you just want me to wound him good? Either way, I can assure you he won't be challengin' you or anyone else again."

Before he could reply, the carriage lurched to a halt and Mark moaned in pain as he was thrown against the door. "We're here, sirs," the driver called down.

"Well?" Jake drawled, eyeing his friend with amusement.

"I suppose you'd better just wound him," Mark grated out. "I wouldn't want it on my conscience if you ended up rotting in jail on my account. Tori would never forgive me. As it is, I'm not sure Susan is ever going to speak to me again."

The driver and Jake assisted Mark from the carriage. Charles Reveneau, his second, and a man holding a black physician's bag stood watching as they approached. "What is this?" Reveneau asked suspiciously, eyeing Mark as he cradled his broken arm with his good hand.

Jake grinned. "Sorry to keep you waitin', but my friend was so anxious to get here that he tripped on a rug and fell and broke his arm. A real shame, but these things happen."

"I think this is just a ploy to delay the duel," Reveneau claimed belligerently.

The Cajun's cocky attitude irritated Jake,

but he answered easily, "Let the doctor decide, but I can tell you the arm is definitely broken."

The doctor stepped forward and proceeded to confirm Jake's statement. "Then I have wasted an entire morning for nothing!" Reveneau spat in disgust.

"Now, don't get your feathers riled, Frenchie," Jake drawled. "As Mark's second, I'm prepared to take his place. You'll get your precious duel." His golden eyes sparked a challenge that set Reveneau's teeth on edge.

Still, the young Frenchman turned his nose to the air in a superior manner. "You?" he sneered, his eyes sweeping Jake from head to toe with arrogance, briefly lingering on the gun strapped along Jake's thigh, and the matching weapon stuck through the band of his belt. Reveneau, in his ignorance, had the temerity to laugh. "What would a . . . how do you say . . . a cow poker like you know about dueling?"

"That's cowhand, or cowpoke," Jake corrected amicably, "and if you want to get on with this duel, I'll have to do as your opponent. Or," he suggested lazily, "if you're too scared to face me, you could always apologize to my friend and we'll all be on our way. I have a train to catch in about three hours, so I'd suggest we quit wastin' time and get on with it."

"It is my right to request that the duel be

delayed until Monsieur Armstrong is well enough to meet my challenge himself," Reveneau stated.

Mark paled even more at this, but Jake merely smiled nastily. "Not to my way of understandin' things. When both parties show up, the duel goes on as set, even when the second is required to stand in for the challenged party. Ain't that the way it goes, doc?"

The doctor nodded. "Well, then, let's get this thing settled once and for all, right here and right now. No more shilly-shallyin' around, Reveneau. Do we duel, or are you gonna apologize?"

Reveneau's chin went up as he glared at Jake with icy black eyes. "We duel. Where are the weapons? I understand it is to be pistols?"

"Yeah," Jake answered lazily. He pulled the pistol from his belt and handed it to the Cajun. "Here's yours. You can check the load if you want before we start. You do know how to handle a Colt, I hope, since I don't happen to own a set of fancy duelin' pistols, and neither does Mark."

"Surely you are jesting, monsieur," the other man said with a nervous laugh, eyeing the weapon Jake had shoved into his hand.

"Oh, I never joke about killin'," Jake assured him, his face now composed into somber lines. "Don't worry. That .45 is deadly accurate, and more than capable of doin' the job. You can take a couple of practice shots first if you want," he offered generously, "just to get the feel of it."

Hefting the pistol, Reveneau studied it a moment. With deft motions that belied his unfamiliarity with the gun, he quickly checked to satisfy himself that it was fully loaded. Then, taking aim at a leaf several yards away, he sighted down the barrel and fired. A gloating smile twisted his lips as the leaf flew from the branch. Once more he tried, with similar results. Turning back to Jake, he announced haughtily, "I am satisfied with the weapon, monsieur. Let us proceed."

"Hold on just a minute," Jake said, drawing his own weapon from his holster. To every·one's surprise, he swiftly removed two bullets from it. "Wouldn't be fair for me to have more shots than you, now would it?"

As they walked toward the grassy area where the duel was to take place, Jake commented, "Now, isn't this more sportin' than usin' one of those sissy one-shot pistols? This way, if you miss me with the first one, you can try again."

"I never miss, monsieur," the Frenchman boasted with a cold smile.

"Good," Jake replied with an equally icy look. "Nothin' I hate more than goin' up against a greenhorn."

The doctor was designated the official monitor. He recited the rules to both men in a resigned tone that led Jake to believe he had done this many times before. "You will stand back to back, and when I give the signal to begin, you will each take fifteen steps away from your opponent with your weapon pointed upward and held against your shoulder. On the final count, you will turn and fire. Should either of you wish to halt the duel before this point, you may fire your weapon into the air, thus constituting an implied apology to the other. Should this occur, the opposing party will accept the gesture by not firing upon his adversary. Are these rules understood and acceptable to both of you?"

Both men agreed, as did their friends who would be observing the duel. With a tired sigh, the doctor instructed, "Please take your places."

Having revived Susan with a stiff measure of brandy, Tori left the sobbing woman still lying on the divan, deciding she really should put some decent clothing on before Jacob came back with Mark. She didn't know how Jacob intended to stop his friend from committing this folly, but he'd had such a determined look on his face when he had left the house that she was fairly certain he would succeed somehow. For Susan's sake, she hoped so. Having been through a similar incident herself, Tori could fully sympathize with her. If she lived to be a hundred, Tori knew she would never forget that awful day when Reno had challenged Jacob.

Tori's hands trembled so badly that she had trouble managing the buttons of her gown. She laughed ruefully at her own clumsiness. She was almost as upset as poor Susan. A terrible guilt struck her as she found herself grateful that it was not Jacob who was risking his life this morning. Hastily she chastised herself for even thinking such a thing. Mark's life was in peril! Though she had only just met him, he was already a dear friend, as was Susan. It was dreadful of her to be so thankful that it was Mark and not Jacob involved in this duel! Humbly she murmured a fervent prayer, asking God to forgive her for such thoughts, and to please spare Mark's life this day.

She had just pulled on her shoes when she heard the front door slam. Thinking it was the men returning, she dashed for the stairs, eager to assure herself that all was well. Racing into the parlor, she stopped with a frown. No one was there. The damp cloth she had placed on Susan's forehead was lying on the floor, and Susan was nowhere in sight. "Oh, dear!" she whispered, as the truth dawned on her. Whirling about, she ran for the door. "Susan!"

Tori spotted her immediately, two doors down from the apartment. Susan was frantically hailing a hackney cab. Gathering her skirts in both hands, Tori dashed down the street. "Susan! Wait!"

Just as the driver laid the whip to his horse, Tori launched herself into the seat beside

Susan. Gasping for breath, she hung on for dear life as the carriage rumbled along the rough street. "Susan! This is ridiculous! Jacob is probably on his way here with Mark right now. He told us to stay, and that's exactly what we should do."

"You don't understand!" Susan wailed. "My husband could be bleeding to death at this very moment! I must go to him! I can't just sit and wait to hear whether he lives or dies!"

"I do understand!" Tori declared, her eyes burning into Susan's. "Surely you know how Jacob earned his living before he came back to run the ranch. He's a gunfighter, Susan. For years, day in and day out, he risked his life. Even now, his enemies hound him. Just after we were married, a gunman came to Santa Fe in search of him. I'll never forget how frightened I was the day that man challenged Jacob to a gunfight! Just thinking about it brings the taste of that fear to my tongue! I know what you are going through. I went through it myself that awful day, and I pray to God that I never have to witness anything like it again."

"I'm sorry, but I must know!" Susan replied with a grimace. "I am going to the Dueling Oaks. If you want out now, I'll tell the driver to stop, and I'll continue on alone, but nothing will stop me from going."

Throwing her head back on the cushioned backrest, Tori wanted to scream. In Susan's place, Tori knew she would feel the same.

Like it or not, she was about to witness more bloodshed. "You can't go alone," she said on a quivery sigh.

It seemed a lifetime before the carriage rattled to a halt alongside the one Jake and Mark had taken earlier. When it did, Tori gasped at the blood-chilling sight that met their eyes. According to custom, two men were standing back to back, pistols raised, but instead of Mark Armstrong, one of those men was Jacob! Frozen in horror, she stared at the deadly tableau before her. She didn't even hear Susan's sharp cry of relief, or her second cry of fright when Susan saw her husband holding his wounded arm. Neither did she realize that their driver had to restrain Susan when she leaped from the carriage and tried to run to Mark.

Then the men began walking away from one another, and the paralyzing numbness vanished. Suddenly all of Tori's senses were sharpened to a painful level. Though her eyes remained riveted on the duelists, she heard the driver telling Susan that she must wait here, that she must not disturb their concentration. Chills of terror chased through Tori, making her tremble violently, but she could not tear her gaze from the sight of Jacob and his opponent as they each abruptly turned and aimed their weapons at one another.

For just a moment, Jake's attention wavered as he heard the arrival of the second carriage, and Susan's frightened cry. If Susan was here, Tori must be, too. "Damn!" he cursed inwardly, knowing how this would affect her. The last thing he needed right now was for her to witness another shootout! The shock alone could cause her to lose their child, even if he were not wounded.

Years of self-discipline came to his rescue as Jake resolutely forced his attention back to the business at hand. With supreme effort, he concentrated soley on the voice of the doctor counting out the steps. "Four, five, six—"

At the count of fifteen, Jake whirled, his Colt already leveling toward Reveneau, his finger even now drawing back on the trigger. In the time it took to blink, he saw Reveneau jolt violently, heard him cry out as the bullet tore into his right shoulder. The man's arm jerked awkwardly, his shot going wild. In amazed disbelief and admiration for the man's determination, Jake watched as Reveneau, despite his pain, made the effort to raise his weapon for a second shot. Before Reveneau could take aim again, Jake fired a second shot, this time hitting Reveneau's gun hand. The man's weapon went flying from his useless fingers as Reveneau howled and clutched at his wrist, falling to his knees in the grass.

Without being told, Jake knew exactly how much damage had been done. He didn't need to hear the doctor's verdict to know that

Reveneau would never again use his right hand—for anything. Unless he trained himself to shoot with his left, and it was doubtful that he would ever be skilled enough with it to challenge anyone, his days of dueling were finished. Never again would the cocky Cajun be a threat beneath the spreading branches of these infamous oak trees that had born witness to so much bloodshed.

His duty as friend done, Jake's immediate concern was for his wife. As he turned toward the carriage, Tori was already alighting from it. Even across the distance separating them, Jake could see how shaken she was, how pale and trembling. He started toward her and saw her stumble, then somehow recover her balance. Then she was racing toward him, her skirts flying. He met her halfway, gathering her quivering body tightly to his, wrapping his long arms securely about her. For a heartfelt moment she rested her head against his thudding chest, then raised her face to his. Their lips met in a tremulous, passionate kiss that spoke of fear and relief and boundless love.

At last, breathless and shaken, she drew back enough to gaze into his beloved face. Bright tears glistened in her eyes, her face now flushed with color in the aftermath of her terror for him. With a catch in her voice, she whispered, "Jacob, I swear if this happens very often, I am going to spend more time in prayer than I would if I had remained at the convent! I thought my heart would burst in fright!"

Her words stunned him. Where were the harsh recriminations, the anger and tongue-lashing he had expected? He studied her face and found tears, but they were tears of relief, of joy. Could it be that she was coming to resign herself to the hazards of his life? Was she beginning to understand just a little, and accept this side of him? Was it possible that her love for him was great enough to withstand even this, that she could love him despite all his faults and failings, though she despised violence of any sort? Could God be this kind, to grant him a mate with so forgiving a heart?

Jake's heart tripped over itself. Never was any man as fortunate as he. Tori's faith in her prayers and her God humbled him. Tears stung his eyes as he held her close. The tiny, almost imperceptible bulge of her tummy against his reminded him of the child she was to bear him, a babe whose life might have been jeopardized by the fright she had endured. "Are you all right?" he asked softly, his eyes searching hers.

She smiled up at him, her lips quivering with the effort. "If I ever stop shaking, I'll be fine. I do wish you could avoid these frightful situations, however."

"The baby?" he queried gently, his hand coming between them to rest on her stomach.

She nodded reassuringly. "Fine." She closed her eyes for a moment, released a trembling sigh, then opened them to gaze up at him achingly. "This child needs its father, Jacob. I don't want to have to raise our baby alone."

"Darlin', I don't plan on dyin' for a long, long time. I'll be here for both of you," he promised solemnly, and sealed the vow with a kiss.

Chapter 19

As the train slowed, preparing for its stop at the station south of Santa Fe, Jake pulled his watch from his vest pocket and checked the time. His fingers caressed the gleaming gold watch chain now dangling from it, a gift from his adoring wife. She had given it to him after the duel, a gesture of her love, and he would treasure it always.

"Only six minutes behind schedule," he told her with a wide smile that warmed her heart. "If they got the wire I sent, someone from the ranch should be here to meet us."

"Home," Tori sighed contentedly, laying her right hand upon Jake's arm. On her ring finger, a delicate carved ivory rose graced her hand with dainty beauty. The ring matched the necklace she had chosen in New Orleans, with a few exceptions. Alongside the rose, resting upon the band on either side, were two tiny emerald leaves; and nestled into the very heart of the flower, amidst the intricate petals, lay a sparkling ruby.

They'd had a good laugh over catching one another outside the jewelers the day they each had gone to buy the other these gifts. When Jake had given the ring to her, he told her that he wanted to give her a ring all her own, since her wedding ring had been Carmen's. He'd called this her "love ring," and Tori had cried soft, shining tears as he slipped it on her finger. How had he known that, though she loved her wedding ring and would cherish it because her mama had given it to her, she still sometimes wished there had been time for Jacob to choose a ring for her, one meant just for her, selected by him with love and attention? Now that wish, too, was fulfilled.

Blake and Megan were there to greet them as they stepped from the train. "How was the honeymoon?" Megan asked, the gleam in her eye matching the one in Blake's.

"Exciting," Jake answered, grinning back at them.

"Wonderful," Tori added, "but it's good to be home again, too."

As the men collected their luggage and loaded it on the wagon, Megan wanted to know all about New Orleans. "But first, how are you? You weren't too sick to enjoy yourself, I hope?"

"Sick?" Tori echoed questioningly.

"Morning sickness, nausea?" Megan prompted. "Weakness, fainting? All the things that often come with those first months of expecting a baby?"

Tori shook her head. "I've been fine. A little queasy now and then, but nothing major."

"You lucky woman!" Megan complained enviously. "I've been feeling especially awful these past weeks. I guess I'm getting your share, too."

It seemed as if she and Jacob had been gone forever instead of just a few weeks, and Tori had questions of her own. "How is Mama?"

"You'll be pleased with her progress," Megan predicted with a proud smile. "She wanted to come to meet the train, and it took all our persuasion to convince her to wait at the ranch. She's so excited about having you home again! And you'll never guess what else has been going on while you've been away. Your mother has a new beau!"

"What?" Tori exclaimed in astonishment. "Who?"

Megan giggled at Tori's stunned expression. "Your neighbor, Mr. Edwards." Eagerly she began to relate the details of the fledgling courtship.

Meanwhile, Blake Montgomery was filling his friend in on the happenings around the ranch during Jake's absence. "We've had a few problems," he admitted, "but nothing really serious. The fence has been cut twice now, in different places. The first time, about ten of your cattle got out and trampled an acre of Señor Mendez's ripe peppers before we rounded them up again."

Arturo Mendez was one of their neighbors, a farmer. He and his family had lived there as long as Jake could recall, and rarely was there any problem between them. "Did you assure him that I would repay the damages as soon as I got back home?" Jake asked with a frown.

With a wave of his hand, Blake assured him, "It's all taken care of. Carmen had the bank send out a draft, and I took it to him personally."

"And the second time the fence was cut?"

"We managed to get back all but five head. I have no idea what became of them, but we rounded the others up. I've had riders patrolling the fences every night, with no more occurrences since then."

"Any other problems?"

Blake started to shake his head in the negative, then grinned sheepishly. "Maybe, I'm not really sure." At Jake's questioning look, he explained. "We found a couple of gila monsters in the barn one night. We don't know if they somehow managed to wander in there on their own, or what, but the horses were going wild until we got those ugly critters out of there. One of the mares bruised her leg pretty badly trying to kick down the stall door. At first we thought it might be broken and we'd have to put her down, but it turned out to be nothing more than a lump."

"Gila monsters?" Jake repeated, surprised and confused. The big, poisonous lizards, despite their fearsome reputation, were really very timid creatures. Rarely did they wander from their desert habitat into populated areas, and they usually stayed in the lower elevations. In all his years at the ranch, Jake had never encountered a gila monster on the ranch grounds or in any of the buildings.

The two men shared a look, and Blake shrugged. "I don't know, Jake. I just don't know. Odd, isn't it?"

"Stranger things have happened, but it does make me wonder," Jake admitted.

"Here's something else for you to wonder about while you're at it," Blake told him. "Your other neighbor, Stan Edwards, has been coming around quite a bit lately. I think he's trying to court Carmen."

Jake's reaction was similar to Tori's. "Court Carmen? My God! The nerve of the man! Dad hasn't been dead but four months! And

Carmen is allowing this?" It didn't seem like something Carmen would approve of at all.

"Well, he's been pretty crafty about it all, and I don't think Carmen realizes what he's up to yet. He rides over 'just to check on things and make sure everything is all right,' or his 'housekeeper just happened to make an extra lemon pie, and since it's Carmen's favorite,' or he was 'just passing by and wondered if she needed anything,' or he's on his way to town and 'can he pick anything up for her'— that sort of thing. Carmen thinks he's just being neighborly since Roy's death, but something smells in Denmark if you ask me."

Jake had to agree. Edwards had never been that good a friend to the Banners before. Why was he getting so chummy all of a sudden? Did it really have to do with Carmen? Or was it something else he was interested in, like the Lazy B, maybe? The man would bear watching, and it would be interesting to see if he continued his friendly little visits now that Jake and Tori had returned home.

Carmen looked so healthy, so wonderfully normal, that Tori burst into tears upon seeing her again. "Oh, Mama! You look so good! How are you feeling?"

Returning her daughter's embrace, Carmen smiled. "I am getting around on my own again, and it feels wonderful, but just look at you! My baby is a woman now, and all aglow!

Tori, Jacob," she held a hand out to both of them. "You look happy."

"We are, Mamacita," Jake assured her.

"We had a lovely time in New Orleans, but it feels good to be home again," Tori added. "We missed you, Mama."

Carmen could not help but be pleased by this admission. "I just hope you did not worry overmuch about me," she said. "Rosa and Megan and Josefa have taken such good care of me that I am quite spoiled now; and little Alita is such a precious angel." Carmen's eyes wandered to Tori's tummy. "She makes me anxious for the arrival of my grandchild."

"Well, now that we are home again, you can help me make baby clothes," Tori said, assuring her that all was fine with the babe.

"Oh, we've already started the layette while you were away," Megan put in. "It gave Carmen something to do while she was recovering. I'm certain I've never seen a woman so eager to clean house. We had a devil of a time trying to keep her from it."

At that moment, sharp heels clacked like castanets in the hallway. Seconds later, the fawn burst into the sala, Rosa close behind and waving a dishcloth at him. "You sneaky beast! Just look what you are doing to my floors!"

"Rosa! Velvet!" Tori could hardly decide who to greet first. The fawn, which had grown to the size of a small pony, took the decision from her. Rushing toward Tori, it threw itself headlong into her, bleating and rubbing against her feverishly, its whole body aquiver with excitement. Tori laughed. Kneeling on the floor, she threw her arms about its neck. "Velvet, you rascal! Are you still terrorizing Rosa?" Aside, to Jake, she declared, "Look how big he's grown, Jacob, but he still has his spots! Isn't he beautiful!"

Jake just grinned and nodded in agreement as Rosa sniffed indignantly. "A beautiful mess he has made of my floors, too! And wait until you see the damage he has done to the back door trying to get in here to greet you! Then he will not seem so cute to you!"

Tori rose and went to give the housekeeper a warm hug and a kiss on the cheek. Joyous tears were streaming down from her shining eyes as she gazed at all of them, dear friends and loving family. "Oh, it's so very good to be home again!"

The master bedroom was now finished and waiting for them to take up residence in it. The walls had been freshly plastered and whitewashed, new draperies hung over the windows, and colorful throw rugs adorned the gleaming floor. Furnishings had been taken from their old bedroom, until Jake and Tori could replace them with pieces of their choosing. Everything looked clean and bright and welcoming, with no reminders of the disaster that had occurred in this very room just months before. Even their bed stood in an entirely different spot from where Roy's had been, and Jake was especially grateful for that.

Later, as Tori lay curled tightly to his side, he said, "We should get a big bed, one large enough for all our children to come pilin' in with us in the mornin's, or when they awaken in the middle of the night and need comfortin'."

Tori smiled sleepily. "Megan's been blabbing, hasn't she?" she yawned. "She told you I wanted at least six of your babies."

"Six, huh?" Jake said with a chuckle. "When am I supposed to get any ranchin' done, if I'm gonna be busy makin' six babies with you, woman?"

"Oh, you'll find time, I'm sure," Tori answered with a smug laugh. "Besides, when the boys are old enough, they'll help out around the ranch, and that will give you plenty of time to give me a couple of daughters."

"Oh, do I get my sons first?" Jake teased.

"Well, at least this one."

"And what makes you so sure this one will be a boy?"

"Madame Laveau said so. Don't you remember?"

Jake snorted in disbelief. "C'mon, darlin', surely you don't really believe what that old crone told you."

He felt Tori nod her head. "Laugh if you want, Jacob, but there was something about her—something strange and powerful and knowing. Yes, I do believe her. Somehow I just can't stop myself from doing so."

They had postponed the fall roundup until Jake's return, and now the entire ranch was humming with activity. Even with much of the land fenced to protect the neighboring farmers' crops, the cattle had freedom to wander into the hills to the north and east. These had to be rounded up and brought down from their summer pastures to lower ground. Brands were checked, cattle carefully counted, and those animals for sale separated from those Jake wished to keep. When all that had been accomplished, they would then drive the chosen cattle to railyards several miles south of Santa Fe, where they would be held in holding pens until they could be shipped to markets in the East.

It was a busy time for all. Blake Montgomery stayed on to help with the roundup, since they had not quite finished packing Josefa and closing his aunt's house. Most of the work left to do there could best be done by the women anyway. It involved sorting and packing small items, and he was just in the way, confusing the orderly process.

While he helped Jake, Megan aided Josefa. Tori had her own hands full just running the house these days, and overseeing hearty meals for the ranch hands as the roundup got under way. Still, twice a week, in the mornings, Blake honored his promise and faithfully escorted her to the convent school so that Tori could resume teaching the orphan children. Much against his better judgment, Jake agreed that Megan should meet Tori when her teaching duties were done, and the two women would go to Josefa's and wait until either he or Blake could accompany them back to the ranch.

Tori had missed her orphans more than she had thought. The first day back, she gathered them to her, listening to their delighted squeals, and had to fight to keep from weeping. Her class gladly forfeited their lessons in exchange for hearing tales of New Orleans. None of them had ever seen a big city, and they listened with wide-eyed attention as Tori told them of street vendors and grand cathedrals and shipyards and buildings rising four stories above the ground.

They all settled into their busy routines, gathering together at the supper table to share the news of the day and their labors with one another. Even Carmen had something to contribute to their lively exchanges. "Señor Edwards came again today. I told him he does not need to bother himself, that Jacob is taking wonderful care of everything, but he says he enjoys talking with me." Carmen wrinkled her nose at this. "I think the man is just so lonely that even I sound interesting to him."

"But you are interesting, Mama," Tori insisted. "Why would you think that you're not?"

Carmen gave a self-conscious shrug of her shoulders. "Perhaps because, since the night of the fire, I have not been away from the ranch. I try to keep up on what is happening by asking my friends when they visit, but it is not the same. There is very little that is happening in my life right now that would interest a man such as Señor Edwards, yet he always asks about everyone here, and wants to know all that is going on around the ranch. There is little I can say, but still he asks."

Across the table, Jake shared a narrowed look with his friend. All of them had joined in a conspiracy to keep their troubles from reaching Carmen's ears, especially now that Edwards seemed to be nosing around. "What kind of questions does he ask, Mamacita?" Jake questioned, keeping his tone casual.

"Oh, he asks how the roundup is coming, whether we need any more help. By the way,

Jacob, I forgot to mention it before, but he has offered to have some of his men come to help out, if you should need them. He assured me that he can spare a few now that his own roundup is completed."

At this, Jake's brows rose slightly. "Next time you see him, tell him thanks for the offer, but we have all the help we need."

"What else does he talk to you about, Mama?" Tori wanted to know.

"Just little things. He talks about his ranch, and how empty the house seems now that his daughter has moved East with her husband. Sometimes I send recipes home with him for his housekeeper to use. It is a shame that his wife died so long ago and is not there to see to his needs. I think he misses her and their daughter. He asks me all about you, 'Toria, as if he is hungry to hear news such as he would hear about his own daughter. I showed him the portrait you brought me from New Orleans, and I have to admit I bragged about you both terribly. He seemed pleased to learn that you have continued to teach at the orphanage, and that you and Jacob are expecting your first child already. One day he hopes to be a proud grandpapa, too."

Two days later, as Megan and Tori prepared to leave the orphanage on their way to Josefa's house, a bright cloth blew across the schoolyard and startled the horses. Megan, who was just climbing into the driver's seat, was thrown to the ground as the horses suddenly bolted. Despite her increasing girth, she managed to roll free of the wagon wheels. Tori, who was already seated and waiting for her friend to climb aboard, suddenly found herself clinging to the wagon seat as it charged pell-mell into the open field next to the convent. Behind her, she could hear Megan screaming at her, but over the rattling of the buckboard and the mad pounding of the horses' hoofs, she could not make out Megan's words.

Tori had been flung hard against the seat, the breath knocked out of her. For several seconds she had to fight the dizziness that robbed her of her senses and her strength, clinging precariously and praying all the while that she would not tumble from the racing wagon. A shriek rose to her throat as she raised her head and saw the countryside flashing by at an alarming speed. The wagon bucked and bounced beneath her as the horses continued their wild flight.

Knowing she must do something to halt them, Tori reached in vain for the flapping reins. Holding on for dear life, she crawled down upon the footrest, laying her body as flat as she could, and grabbed for them as they dangled below the wagon, but they remained out of her reach. Bringing herself upright once more, she pulled with all her strength against the hand brake, only to have it snap off in her hands.

Tori screamed as she was catapulted over the seat and into the short, flat bed of the wagon. Then, as the buckboard continued to jump and bounce along the rough ground, she found herself helplessly rolling toward the open rear of the wagon. She grabbed frantically for a handhold, succeeding only in snagging her hands painfully on long splinters of wood. She hit the side panel with a hard thud, hearing the boards groan with her weight.

Even in her fright, she somehow managed to grasp hold of the board and keep from tumbling off the end of the buckboard onto the ground. Slowly she pulled herself to her knees. Chancing a glance, Tori gasped in horror. Running faster than ever, the horses were headed directly toward a deep gully at the edge of the field. Tears gathered in her eyes as she thought of Jacob and their unborn child, a child she would never live to bear! "No! No!" she shrieked. "It cannot end this way! No!"

Then, as if God had heard and provided a miracle, the wagon swerved slightly from its course. Ahead still lay the gully, but now, between it and the runaway wagon, stood a large hayrack, one of those used to feed the convent cattle during the winter season. It was brimming with fresh hay for the coming winter. Tori had only seconds to prepare herself for her leap to safety, only moments in which to pray for strength and guidance as she braced herself against the lurching wagon. As the buckboard came alongside the hayrack, in one swift movement she stood and planted a shaking foot upon the edge of the top board, launching herself forward with all the strength in her small, petrified body.

As she sailed through the air, Tori closed her eyes and prayed. She did not want to see where she might land if she missed her mark, or to contemplate the pain she might encounter just heartbeats away. Then, miraculously, she tumbled into a deep bed of the softest, sweetest hay she had ever hoped to find. For long, trembling minutes she lay wallowing in it, sucking in deep, terrified breaths, sobbing out her terror, feeling her fear wash through her and ebb gradually away.

Slowly Tori eased herself upright. Even now, she could not believe she was safe. Wiping the tears from her face, she moved cautiously, tentatively trying each of her quivering limbs. Bruises were already making themselves apparent, and her hands were speared with splinters, but otherwise she could discern no more serious damage to her person. She was thoroughly shaken and in danger of losing her stomach, but everything seemed to be in working order. She could only hope all that rough tumbling about in the wagon had not caused injury to the baby, but she could feel no pain in her stomach, and she prayed that the smarting along her back was merely from scraping it along the unfinished boards of the wagon.

She was still sitting there assessing her wounds and thanking God for her timely rescue when Megan and the sisters came dashing across the field. Through the slats of the hayrack, she watched them come. Father Romero and Mother Superior were running with them, and it was the first time Tori could ever recall seeing Mother Superior move faster than a dignified walk. Now, as her senses leveled, the terrified squeals of the horses assaulted her ears. Somewhere beyond the hayrack, the wagon had crashed. Vaguely she could remember hearing it happening, though at the time it had not registered on her terrorized brain. She was not sure she wanted to survey the damage, to see how close she had come to death.

Father Romero was the first to reach the hayrack, and Tori watched in bemusement as he and the others ran right past where she sat watching. Not one of them paused or took notice of her. With a confused shake of her head, she wriggled about and peered through the slats on the far side of the rack. There, she saw her rescuers stop and stare into the gully with looks of dismay. Almost immediately,

Father Romero began to climb down the steep incline as the others watched with mingled hope and horror. Several of the sisters knelt and began to pray, while others wept openly. Megan had one hand clutched to her stomach, the other covering her mouth.

Suddenly it dawned on Tori that they had not seen her leap from the wagon to the hayrack. One and all, they believed she had gone into the gully with the buckboard! "Hey! Here I am! Megan! Sisters! I am here!"

A dozen startled, disbelieving faces turned toward her, searching for the source of her voice. "Here! In the hayrack!" she called out.

The relief that instantaneously crossed those eagerly searching faces was humbling, and astounding to behold. Cries of joy split the air; Mother Superior recovered quickly and called down the glad tidings to Father Romero; Megan laughed, and laughed, and laughed until tears of mirth bathed her face.

The sisters released the side catch on the hayrack and gently assisted Tori to the ground. Mother Superior hovered anxiously, needing assurance that Tori and her unborn child were truly unharmed. Father Romero rejoiced in her salvation, sadly relating that someone would have to come and put one of the poor horses out of its misery. When he had unhooked them from the tangled traces, only one had bounded free. The other was badly wounded and would have to be shot. This announcement sobered everyone, for it clearly displayed what might have happened to Tori if she had not managed to leap to safety when she had.

Despite Tori's objections that she was fine, Megan insisted that Tori see Doc Green, just to be sure. Mother Superior agreed vehemently, and Father Romero hitched up the convent wagon and took both women to the doctor's office.

They were still there when Jake rushed through the door, his face as pale as death. Upon seeing Tori, her dress torn and dirty, but standing on her own, he stopped in his tracks and just stared at her with his heart in his throat. At last he heaved a terrible sigh and came to her, gathering her tenderly into his arms. "Oh, God, Tori! I was so scared for you! So scared! They told me you were all right, but I had to see it myself to believe it."

His anxious gaze searched out the doctor. "She is okay, isn't she?"

"A bit battered and bruised, but no permanent harm done," the doctor assured him. "Your wife is one lucky little mother-to-be!"

"O ye of little faith," Tori quoted, shaking her head at them.

"Really, Tori!" Megan reproached. "I suppose you weren't at all frightened, while the rest of us were screaming our heads off?"

"Are you kidding? I was scared stiff!" Tori readily admitted, "but I prayed. I prayed, and God provided a miracle."

"He provided a hayrack," Jake reminded her dryly.

Tori just smiled.

Chapter 20

With the wagon in a thousand splinters, and no one at the convent having seen anything suspicious, there was no way Jake could prove that the incident with the runaway wagon had been anything but an accident. Still, he could not shake the feeling that someone had deliberately tried to harm Tori. Blake Montgomery agreed, and he was angered as well, for Megan had almost been involved and might well have been injured or killed if she had been on the wagon. Mere seconds later, and she would have been.

Convincing the women of this was another matter, however. Both of them preferred to believe that it was as it seemed, just one of those freak circumstances that sometimes happen. "Blake, I saw that red cloth blow in front of the horses. That and that alone caused them to bolt," Megan argued. "I know that a lot of things have happened around the ranch, and I'm not stupid. I realize that a very real danger exists here, but this was an accident."

When Jake tried to tell Tori that she must give up teaching her orphans, that it was too dangerous for her to continue to go into Santa Fe, she turned on him like a tigress. "You are jumping at shadows, Jacob, and I won't stand for being made a prisoner here over a silly accident!"

"That 'silly accident' almost cost you your life, and that of our child!" he roared back. "You might not survive another such accident!"

"I am going to continue teaching those children, Jacob, if I have to walk to the convent every day!"

"And I say you're not! You're my wife, damn it! It's my right to keep you safe from harm in any way I see fit! I've been sick with worry, constantly thinkin' you might be in danger."

Her laugh held little humor as she faced him defiantly. "The way I have been every time you're involved in a gunfight?" she challenged. "Do you think it has been easy for me, knowing that at any time one of your old enemies might turn up and challenge you again? It's hell, Jacob! Pure hell! The only way

I survive it is to push it from my mind and pray to God that He will look after us."

He reached for her then, wanting to hold her, to comfort her, to erase the pain from her eyes, but she drew back from him. "We can't walk around on egg shells the rest of our lives," she told him softly. "It may be weeks, months, before we know who is causing us all these problems. I know we must be cautious. I realize the dangers as well as you, but just because I stop teaching won't make the danger any less."

"I know, but I can protect you better here at the ranch, darlin'. We can't take chances with your life, especially now. With all that has happened, it's a wonder you're still carryin' the baby. You've got to take care."

"For how long, Jacob?" she asked wearily. "Mama is getting well again. She knows none of this, and she is not going to understand when you tell her that she cannot go to church, or into town to shop and visit with her friends. How are you going to explain this to her?"

"I'll think of somethin'."

Privately, the men debated if it might not be a good idea to send Tori and Carmen back to Tucson with Megan and Josefa. "You could take them with you, Blake, and I could send for them when all of this is settled," Jake suggested.

"If I did, I'd escort them there and come right back," Blake told him. "I'm not going to

leave you to handle this on your own. For one
thing, you have absolutely no idea who is
behind this, or how many of them you are
going up against. At this point, you're shooting
in the dark, Jake."

Jake didn't like it. "No, if you take them, you
have to stay with them. Who's to say you
wouldn't be followed? If someone wants to get
at me through Tori, they could attack her
there as well."

"Then why chance it? Maybe it's best we all
stay here together, at least for the time being.
I'll tell Tori and Megan that I can't take them
into town until after the roundup is over.
Maybe by then we'll have a better idea of who
and what we're dealing with here."

Jake's eyes scanned the skies, a frown darkening his hard features as he noted the buzzards hovering in the distance. His gut
tightened. Last night, despite all their precautions, the fence had been cut again. This time,
thirty head of prime beef had been taken.
Now he and his men were trying to find them.
Something told Jake he had just found his
missing cattle, that all he had to do was head
in the direction of those scavenger birds.

With a signal to his men, Jake kneed his
horse into a ground-eating lope. Why was it
they could never catch these marauders, he
wondered grimly. Hell, you'd think they were
dealin' with ghosts, the way they seemed to
come and go at will, with hardly a trace. It was

odd how they always seemed to know just when and where to hit without getting caught.

His thoughts turned to Edwards, who was still making frequent visits to the ranch. With Tori at home now, Jake had asked her and Megan to keep a sharp eye on the man. Of course, Jake was also making certain that the ranch house was well guarded, especially while Edwards was coming around. He had the feeling he was letting the fox into the henhouse, but what could he do, except to make sure that none of the women were ever alone with him or unguarded? So far, the man had done nothing wrong. Supposedly he came to see Carmen. While Jake didn't like it, he had decided to take advantage of the man's visits, hoping to learn something from the questions Edwards asked Carmen, or a chance comment he might let slip.

Now, as he rode ahead of his men, Jake had another thought. Was it possible that one of his own men was in on all this? The idea had come to him when the trouble had first begun, but most of the ranch hands had been with the Lazy B for years, some since before Jake had gone away. Not one had been hired on since Roy's death. In fact, it had been nearly a year since any new help had been hired, and Gill had assured him that all of them, even the ones Jake did not know personally, were hard workers, as reliable as they came.

Jake had dismissed that suspicion, but now he had begun wondering about it again. Wouldn't that explain how the buckboard might have been tampered with? How the gunmen had known that he and Tori were up at the mountain meadow? Maybe how those gila monsters had gotten into the horse barn? Why no one strange had been seen around the ranch the night of the fire? And how their attackers always seemed to know where best to strike?

Who had been guarding the cattle last night? Who was supposed to be patrolling that section of fence? Gill had seen to scheduling the work details. He would know who was supposed to be on watch at the time the cattle were taken. Then, when Jake had names, he would check back and try to determine exactly what those particular men had been doing on the other occasions, where they might have been when the other attacks had occurred.

Damn, but he hated to think that any of his men, men he had come to know and respect, had been responsible! But what else did he have to go on? Something had to break soon; this couldn't go on indefinitely.

With his mind centered on his dark suspicions, Jake almost failed to see the gunman hidden atop a small knoll. At the last instant, his eye caught the gleam of sunlight reflecting off of the rifle barrel. As he threw himself to the side of his horse, letting the animal's body shelter his own in a move adopted from the Indians, his hat flew from his head. Clinging with his left hand, Jake drew his Colt with his right.

He fired from beneath his horse's neck. Almost simultaneously, his horse whinnied in fright and, jerking and stumbling, almost lost its footing. Jake's hand slipped, and he clutched at the saddle with a strength born of desperation. The stallion reared, its eyes rolling white in its head, as Jake grabbed for the reins, trying to control the beast. A barrage of gunfire and a hail of bullets told him that more than one man was firing from the rise.

As Jake swung back into the saddle, exposing himself as a target once more, Blake raced past, placing himself between Jake and the gunmen. Guns blazing, three more hands arrived on the scene, giving Jake the time he needed to gain control of his mount. Dodging bullets, they raced toward the ambushers, who were charging up the hill and briefly taking cover behind small trees and boulders. One of the gunmen gave a shout of pain, another toppled silently from his perch atop a pile of rocks.

Return fire had ceased by the time Jake's men reached the crest of the rise. A cloud of dust and the fading sounds of hoofbeats announced the retreat of the ambushers. Immediately they gave chase, but the effort was fruitless. Within half an hour they had lost the gunmen in the twists and turns of the many hills. All they knew for certain was that three of them had gotten away, and one of the three was wounded.

Backtracking to the point of attack, they found the fourth member of the gang lying face down in the dirt. While the others stood watching, Jake nudged the body over with the tip of his boot. Varied exclamations of shock and surprise echoed from the men as they stared down into the frozen features of one of their own. "Frank!" "Damn! I see it, but I don't believe it!" "Who would've thunk it?"

Jake's grim gaze locked with Blake's. "Well, here's our traitor, at least one of them."

This terse statement brought several heads up. "One of 'em?" Red questioned, his eyes going to those of his fellow ranch hands. "You think there's more than one, boss?"

Jake rubbed his fingers over gritty eyes. "I don't know, but I'm damned sure going to find out before this is over. And believe me, Frank's death will seem easy compared with that of the next man I discover has been a threat to my family!"

"What do we do now?" Jeb asked uneasily.

Jake drew himself up, his eyes fierce as he answered stiffly, "We see about those missing cattle."

"Sure, boss, but what do we do with Frank here?"

"Leave him for the buzzards," Jake growled,

turning on his heel and heading toward his horse.

Blake reached out a staying hand. "I know how you feel, Jake, but we can't do that."

"It's no more than he deserves," Jake stated flatly.

"Maybe, but we should take the body back to town, if for nothing else than to prove to the sheriff that we caught one of the men who are behind some of this trouble."

Blake was right, as much as it irritated Jake to admit it. He nodded. "See to it for me, will you?" He mounted and looked down at his friend. "You know what really eats at me, Blake? The one man we managed to catch has to go and die before we can question him. You can't get answers from a dead man!"

If Jake's temper was already flaring, it blazed further upon locating his cattle. They were found in a small box canyon not far away. Thirty head of prime cattle, months of work and worry, all neatly destroyed. Each and every one of them had been shot, killed and left to stench the countryside with putre- fying flesh. Even now the stench was rising, buzzards feasting on the carcasses. It was a gruesome sight, enough to enrage even the calmest of men, and Jake was not calm by any means. If he could kill that damned Frank all over again, he would do so after seeing this! If Blake's suggestion didn't make so much sense, he would gladly throw Frank's worthless body in among the dead cattle and let him rot with the carnage he had helped to create.

The ranch hands shook their heads in dismay at such destruction, such blatant waste! It was bad enough to rustle cattle, to steal the fruits of another man's labor, but it was sheer stupidity and waste to do something this mean. It made no sense! Why kill the cattle and just leave them to rot? Any man with an ounce of brains knew the price of cattle these days. Why go to all the bother of stealing them and then not sell them?

Jake knew why, he just didn't know who. He knew that whoever was behind this had no intention of trying to change the brands and sell these cattle. The bastard was shifty. He was taking no chances on getting caught attempting to sell cattle that weren't his. No, he had succeeded in his original intent. He wanted to cause havoc at the Lazy B. He'd wanted to set an ambush, knowing that Jake would be out here looking for those missing cattle, and he'd hoped to kill Jake Banner. Someone wanted the Lazy B, and to get it he first had to eliminate its owner, just as someone had killed Roy, thinking perhaps that Jake would not return to claim his inheritance.

They'd been wrong. Jake was home, and he meant to stay. No one was going to run him from his land, from his family! No one was going to threaten his home and those he loved! He was going to find those responsible for this, for Roy's death, for the attempts on Tori's life, and he would make certain they paid dearly for his trouble!

As if things had not gone badly enough, Jake's nasty mood was not improved when he discovered that one of the bullets fired at him had lodged in his saddle, tearing deep into the leather. No wonder his horse had shied so terribly! All in all, this had not been one of his better days, and he had no hopes for improvement until they caught the culprits and put an end to these disasters once and for all.

Within days, the remainder of the cattle had been herded together. Expecting that if trouble were to occur it would hit now, Jake doubled the guard on the herd that last night at the ranch. Perhaps his precautions paid off, or perhaps the troublemakers were not planning on an attack with so many drovers alert and armed. The night passed peacefully, and the two-day drive began early the next morning.

As the herd lumbered toward Santa Fe, clouds of dust filled the air. The loud bawling could be heard for miles around. All day, with few breaks, the cowhands directed the herd, kept busy heading strays back into the main body of cattle. Inevitably, there were a few stragglers that needed extra urging, and those animals that proved beyond doubt where the term "bull-headed" had come from. Generally thought to be dumb beasts, there were always one or two bulls that proved to be mean, too.

With much of the land now fenced, it proved easier to herd the animals along the main roads and right through town. It bothered Jake that this was such a predictable route, but it was also the most convenient and the fastest. When they reached Santa Fe, the drovers had their hands full trying to keep the herd from veering off onto the side streets or careening up onto the boardwalks and into storefronts.

To the residents and shopkeepers, this was a common occurrence in summer and fall, and when word came that another herd was on the outskirts of town, they simply cleared the streets and waited for it to pass. Women grabbed their children out of harm's way, old men gathered in the barber shop or the lobby of the hotel to watch, store owners brought in any wares they had displayed outside.

While almost everyone else stayed indoors, out of the dust and noise, the cattle drive seemed to be a signal for the girls in the bawdy houses along the main route to put on their most alluring costumes and hang from the windows and upper verandas, calling down encouragement and invitations to the passing cowhands. Knowing that the men would pass this way again after the drive, their pockets filled with pay, the ladies took this opportunity to drum up business by displaying their enticements.

As busy as the men were keeping the fractious herd in line, they found time to admire these "evening doves," laughing and yelling up at their favorites. Shouts of "Keep the bed warm, Sally!" "Practice that pucker, honey!" "Have a bath and a bottle waitin'!" could be heard over the thunder of hundreds of hoofs.

They bedded the herd a couple of miles south of town. One more night and most of the next day, and this year's trail drive would be done. For Jake it couldn't be over with soon enough. With most of his men tending to the herd, only a handful had been left to guard the ranch, and this worried him. It would be a golden opportunity for anyone who wanted to attack the Lazy B. He wished Tori knew how to defend herself better, that she had taken better to the shooting lessons he had attempted to give her. From the look on Blake's face as they shared a supper of beef and beans, he knew his friend was worried, too.

Back at the ranch, the women were too busy to worry about how their men were faring. No sooner had night settled upon them than trouble struck. Out of nowhere, it seemed, a band of wild, whooping Indians had descending upon the ranch. They raced their ponies around the ranch buildings, brandishing torches and shooting at everything. Bullets crashed through windowpanes, sending showers of glass through the rooms. The men left behind to guard the ranch quickly returned fire, while inside the house the women scurried to secure the doors and find weapons to defend themselves with. The servants were screaming in fear, gunfire was exploding all around, men were shouting, and the savages were hollering. All was chaos!

Poor Ana was beside herself, and she gathered little Alita to her and screamed, "*Los Indios! Los Indios!*"

On the floor near the window where she sat loading her rifle, Megan sniffed, "Indians my granny's fanny! Those yahoos are no more Indian than I am!" To Rosa, she called, "Douse those lamps! No sense making better targets of ourselves than we already are!"

Tossing the loaded rifle to Tori, Megan said, "Just do like we practiced. Aim and fire. Carmen, do you think you and Rosa can reload for us?"

Carmen nodded and hunched down on the floor near her daughter, her eyes wide with fear. "Why do you say these raiders are not Indians, Megan?"

"For one thing, they're riding horses with some pretty nice saddles, and most of them are wearing boots, not moccasins. Besides, we all know that most of the tribes are on reservations these days. Even those that aren't are such rag-tag bands that they can barely hold body and soul together. These men don't look hungry enough or poorly dressed enough to me to be Indians. Those I saw were some of the saddest looking savages you'd ever care to see."

Without further ado, Megan steadied her rifle on the windowsill, took careful aim, and fired. One of the so-called Indians toppled to the ground. At the next window, Tori poked the barrel of her rifle out of the window, but she could not bring herself to pull the trigger.

"Fire the blasted thing, Tori!" Megan yelled at her. "Hesitate now, and you and your baby could be dead in the next hour!"

"I can't!" Tori wailed. "I can't bring myself to spill another human being's blood."

"Well, they won't think twice about spilling yours! If it bothers you so much, just think of them as moving targets. Think of them as the snakes they truly are, but fire that gun and make it count!"

Drawing her courage about her, and asking forgiveness for what she was about to do, Tori did as Megan instructed. Over and over again, as she aimed and fired the rifle, she told herself that this was for the life of her unborn child. Each time she drew a bead and pulled the trigger, she immediately closed her eyes, not wanting to see if she hit her target or not, not wanting to know if she had wounded or killed another person. Despite her efforts to avoid this knowledge, she knew she hit at least two of the men, because Megan called out, "Good shot, Tori! Do that again!"

At one point, Rosa shrieked, "*Dios mío!* They are setting fire to the barn!" As Tori watched, torches were thrown into the barn, and thick smoke immediately began rolling out of the doors. Nausea clutched at her as she thought of the horses inside, and the fawn, but there was little they could do about the barn at the moment. First they had to deal with their attackers. Beside her, Megan got off another shot, and Tori forced herself to do likewise.

It was with relief that she saw one of the ranch hands make a successful run into the barn, and even as flames flared up, frantically neighing horses began to bolt from the barn. He was setting the animals free from their stalls.

Then, as suddenly as it had begun, the attack was over. Thick smoke was rolling in waves across the ranch yard, obscuring their vision, but they could see the remaining marauders quickly collecting their fallen comrades and riding away. The shooting and yelling faded. They were gone!

Cautiously, rifles ready, Tori and Megan crept from the house, not yet sure that the attackers were really gone, and not just lurking about waiting for the unwary to expose themselves. They could see Gill and the other ranch hands slowly coming forward from their cover. Then everyone seemed to be running at once. While Megan and Tori manned the pump near the barn, the men began a bucket brigade. Tears streamed from smoke-smarting eyes, arms ached, backs groaned in protest, and still they worked on. Ana and Rosa took over the pump, giving the other women a respite. Carmen, who had been forbidden to do anything strenuous, held Alita and watched as the others fought the blaze.

At one point Tori looked toward her mother and was relieved to see the fawn standing at Carmen's side, nuzzling her skirts. Someone said all the horses had safely escaped the barn, and for this too she was grateful. By the time the fire was out, Tori was so weary that she dropped where she stood, too tired to walk to the house. For long minutes she just sat there, gasping for breath, gazing in dismay at the smoldering ruin of the barn. "It's not as bad as it looks," she heard Gill say. "Most of the damage is to the front, and part of the roof. It could have been worse. The whole thing could have burned."

The sun was rising as they dragged their aching, soot-smudged bodies off to bed at last. Glancing behind her as she headed for the house, Tori shuddered to see several of the ranch hands dragging four dead "Indians" out of the ranch yard.

Once in her room, she fell to her knees,

covering her blackened face with blistered hands. With tears streaking dirty paths down her cheeks, she prayed a mixed prayer for forgiveness and of thanksgiving that all of them were safe. Only two of the ranch hands had been wounded, not seriously. They had come through this latest attack with few casualties. She could only hope Jacob and his men would fare as well or better in their attempt to get the herd to the rail station.

Dirt, smoke, and all, Tori tumbled into bed. Before she could pull the covers about her, she was asleep—a fitful, exhausted sleep filled with strange dreams fraught with danger and threatening shadows. In her sleep she cried out and reached for Jacob, but he was not there to comfort her. It was with bleary eyes and an anxious heart that she finally woke to face the day.

Chapter 21

It was that darkest time of night, just before dawn, when the stars and moon were no longer lending their soft light to the sky and the sun had yet to send its golden rays over the horizon. The cattle were bedded down, quiet now, with only an occasional lowing. The guards were slowly riding the perimeters of the herd, gauging the time before they would be relieved by now-sleeping comrades, wishing they could grab an hour in a bedroll or at least a hot, strong cup of coffee.

Suddenly the silence was split by gunfire. Riders galloped in from all directions, appearing out of the darkness like magic. At the first burst of gunfire, the cattle stirred, slowly rising to their feet, snorting and bellowing. Then, as shots were fired directly into the herd, the cattle panicked. Some began to run over the top of those still struggling to rise. Confusion reigned. Long, curved horns swung in frantic reaction, gouging and prodding as the herd surged in several directions at once. Then the lead steer charged forward, others followed, and the run was on.

Stampede! As prepared as the men thought they had been, the attack still took them by surprise. Shouting orders from horseback, Jake could hardly make himself heard over the din. As the herd gained speed, the ground shook with their pounding hoofs. Dust and chunks of dirt flew into the air, making it all but impossible to see anything. Yanking their kerchiefs over their noses, the cowboys squinted and tried to take aim, hoping they wouldn't shoot one another in the melee.

"Sam!" Jake yelled, spotting his head drover. "Head off the herd!"

Sam nodded and kneed his horse into a gallop. While some of the hands tried to control the stampeding herd, the rest would concentrate on holding off the rustlers. At the head of it all, Jake and Blake were trying to return fire and create some kind of order in the process.

By the light of the campfire, Jake glimpsed one of the rustlers. For just a second, as his finger instinctively tightened on the trigger,

Jake's eyes widened in disbelief. Damn! On top of everything else, he was starting to imagine things, because he could swear he saw an Indian! He blinked, trying to clear his vision, then ducked reflexively as a bullet whistled past his head.

The barrage of gunfire continued. Grunts and groans were heard as men on both sides were hit. A few minutes later, Jake spotted another Indian. This time his aim was true, and the fellow literally flew over the head of his horse as he fell to the ground. Though he couldn't take the time now to check, Jake had seen the man long enough to know that his eyes weren't playing tricks on him. He hadn't really seen an Indian, but a white man dressed as one. "Sneaky bastards!" he growled, swinging his horse around to give chase to another. "Who do they think they're foolin'?"

As the eastern sky began to lighten to pearl gray, Jake was thankful for those disguises, poor as they were. At least now, with darkness beginning to lift, it was easy to distinguish his own men from the raiders; they wouldn't be shooting each other by mistake.

Evidently their attackers realized this as well, for as sunrise drew closer, they called a hasty retreat. With Lazy B cowhands hot on their trail, they turned tail and ran, not even bothering to collect their dead and wounded.

Side by side, their guns drawn, Jake and Blake raced through the waning darkness after the rustlers. "I want one of them alive!" Jake shouted to his friend.

Blake's answering grin was evil and determined as he urged his horse faster.

As they drew almost even with the rear of the fleeing band, the two friends split up. A lone rider lagged slightly behind the rest, his winded horse unable to keep pace. While Jake approached slightly to the left, Blake took the right side. The rider shifted in his saddle, casting a wary look back at Jake. His pistol came up even with his shoulder as he tried to draw a bead on his pursuer.

Blake was quicker. While the rider was concentrating on Jake, Montgomery aimed his own weapon and fired. The man cried out, grabbing frantically at his right shoulder. The pistol flew from his hand as he lost his balance and tumbled from his horse.

With a quick glance at the retreating band of outlaws, Jake knew he didn't stand much of a chance of catching any more of them. His horse was tired, and they had ridden quite a distance from the camp already. He would have to be satisfied with just this one, and any others who might still be alive back in camp.

Leaping from his saddle, he stood glaring down at the fallen man. "Get up!" he growled. As the man groaned, clutching his shoulder, Jake reached out and yanked him to his feet. The man yelped in pain, his face turning pasty-white, and Jake's features twisted into a sneer. "You haven't felt pain yet, pale-face. I've learned a trick or two from the Indians myself. Before I'm through with you, you're gonna pray for death; but first I want some names."

"I don't know nothin'!" the man cried out, his eyes wild as he stared back at Jake. "Honest, I don't!"

"You know plenty!" Jake snarled back, shaking the man like a dog.

The man screeched in pain. "Please, mister! I'm bleedin'!"

"He does have a point there," Blake drawled, leaning crossed arms on the horn of his saddle. "Wouldn't want him to bleed to death right here and ruin all our fun."

Jake grunted a curse. Tearing the bandanna from his neck, he thrust it at his prisoner. "Hold this over the wound." This was all the further his charity extended, as he pointed the way back to camp with the barrel of his Colt. "Start walkin'," he ordered.

Their prisoner's name was Tandy, and they were lucky to have caught him. In the confusion of stopping the stampede and tending to their own wounded, the cowhands had not concerned themselves with the injured raiders. Four good men were dead, six others shot. Those attackers who could manage it had escaped; those who couldn't were either dead or soon would be. Tandy was the only one still capable of answering Jake's questions. The camp cook bound Tandy's wound to stop the man from bleeding to death before he could be questioned. Then he was tied hand and foot and tossed into the bed of the chuck wagon until they had time for him.

The first order of business was to round up all the cattle and get them back on the trail to the railyards. The wounded ranch hands were sent back to Santa Fe, to be patched up by Doc Green. Though this left them short-handed, Jake was thankful that the injured men were still capable of riding and could get themselves back to town. He tried to cheer himself by telling himself that it could have been worse, but when he thought of the four men who had died, it was a hard pill to swallow.

The delay put them behind several hours, but they finally reached the railyards just before dusk. By the time it was completely dark, all the cattle had been herded into the stock pens, and the final tally was only eight shy of the number they had started out with. The bank draft in his pocket, Jake hated telling his hands that he couldn't pay them until the bank in Santa Fe opened in the morning. After all the trouble they'd been through with him, he felt bad having to disappoint them, knowing they had planned on a big night in town.

There were a few grumbles from the men, but they were a loyal bunch for the most part.

When Jake offered each of them a bonus to make up for their troubles, they brightened considerably. Then, when he drew out of his own pocket, with Blake's help, five dollars for each of them, telling them to ride on into Santa Fe and have a drink on him, they thumped him on the back and cheered him. Only Red, who volunteered to drive the chuck wagon back to the ranch, stayed with him and Blake.

"What now?" Blake wanted to know as they slowly made their way back along the trail. "The women will be watching for us, and we're gonna be late as it is." Even riding steadily, it would be midnight before they reached the ranch. "We taking Tandy back to the Lazy B with us?"

"Nope. We're gonna stop out there somewhere, where no one but the coyotes can hear him scream, and I'm gonna get some answers to a lot of questions. Then, if two and two still add up to four, I think I'll pay old Edwards a visit."

"What about Red?"

"We'll send him ahead with the chuck wagon, and he can tell the women not to worry, that we'll be along later."

A few miles further, not far from where the stampede took place, Jake reined in his horse. He signaled to Red, who was following in the chuck wagon, to stop as well. Jake dismounted and headed back toward the wagon with a determined stride, Blake following just steps behind him. "Now don't get carried away and ki—" Blake's words were lost in a blast of gunfire.

Caught by surprise, Jake's legs buckled beneath him as a bullet seared his skull, another tearing a hole in his thigh. Through the initial shock, his mind registered what was happening. Red had shot him, taken him totally unaware and unprepared! One of his most trusted men!

A red mist clouded Jake's vision; a loud ringing sounded in his ears; the stars were spinning above his head. He was falling, twirling like a child's toy top. Waves of darkness washed over him, sapping his strength. He tried to find his gun, but his hand would not seem to obey his mind's commands; his fingers seemed to have gone numb. There was pain—such mind-rending pain! He could hear nothing except his own screams of pain, echoing through his pounding head. His last thoughts were, "I'm dying! I promised Tori I wouldn't!" Then the earth opened up and swallowed him in a deep, dark pit.

Sheltered behind Jake, Blake had time to throw himself out of the direct line of fire and draw his gun. He saw his friend fall, heard Jake's startled cry of pain. Blake hit the ground and rolled, firing as he went and dodging a hail of return fire from Red and Tandy. It didn't take a genius to figure out who was responsible for untying and arming their prisoner! Traitorous bastard!

Dirt flew up at him as bullets skimmed the ground all about him. He heard Tandy scream as he fell back into the wagon. Blake felt his ribs catch fire as he took a bullet in his left side. Ignoring the pain, he took careful aim, hitting Red in the arm. The man's gun flew from his hand.

Red cursed, feeling along the wagon seat for the rifle before he realized that he had given it to Tandy. As Blake pointed the barrel of his Colt point-blank, Red threw himself down on the wagon seat. Grabbing the reins, he brought them down hard over the horses' backs. The crack of the reins came simultaneously with Blake's final shot as the wagon lurched forward.

Red didn't wait around to see how badly the two men were injured. He knew he'd hit Montgomery, and it was a sure bet that Banner was dead; but with no weapon and Montgomery still breathin', it was time to quit while he was ahead and get the hell away from there while the gettin' was good! He called back to Tandy, but there was no answer, not even a groan as the wagon barreled across the rough ground. A quick glance into the back of the wagon told the story. Tandy was sprawled in a pool of blood, his eyes staring straight up at nothing.

An evil smile creased Red's face. Tandy was

just one more problem he wouldn't have to bother with later. Right now, while Montgomery was busy with his friend, and before the Banner women suspected anything, Red had plans of a different nature. All he had to do was make it back to the Lazy B and not let anyone catch on.

Blake put his head down on the ground and sighed. "Oh, God, that was close!" For a moment, as he had taken that last shot and heard the firing pin click sharply against the spent cartridge, his heart had stopped. He couldn't believe that Red hadn't realized his gun was empty, that the red-haired man had whipped the horses into a gallop and kept right on going! "I must have an angel on my shoulder," he thought gratefully.

He raised his head and gazed over at his friend. Jake hadn't moved since he'd fallen. Was he dead? Holding his burning side, Blake crawled the few feet that separated them. "Jake?" he called softly. Receiving no response, Blake feared the worst. Blood was splattered over one side of Jake's face. Pulling himself up into a half-sitting position, he put shaking fingers to the side of Jake's neck, just below his ear. To Blake's surprise and relief, he felt a pulse. His long-time friend still lived, but for how long was anyone's guess. Here in the dark it was hard to tell just how extensive either of their injuries were, though Blake assumed that his own were far less life-threatening.

"Horse," he muttered to himself. "Got to get the horses." Gritting his teeth against the pain that lanced through his ribs, Blake levered himself to his feet. He stumbled and lurched his way over to the horses. Though they shied a bit at his fumbling and the smell of blood, they settled as he spoke soothingly to them.

With halting steps, leaning against his own horse for support, Blake led them to where Jake lay. "Now the tricky part," he murmured, steadying himself as the world took a spin. Stooping over his friend, he tried to lift Jake's upper torso far enough to get his own arms around him. Jake was dead weight, too much for him to lift with his injured side. Blake slumped back, gasping for breath, clutching his ribs. His hand came away red and sticky with his own blood, but Jake was bleeding, too. He had to think of something quickly. He had to get them both on those horses and out of here before they bled to death where they lay!

He had an idea, but he wasn't too sure how it would work. A lot depended on just how well trained the horses were. Pulling at the reins of Jake's stallion, he coaxed the horse to its knees. At first the animal was confused, not understanding what this man wanted of it. Then, after several tries, he sank to his knees. "Bless you, you big black beast," Blake sighed. "Now, just stay down here and don't move."

Turning to Jake, Blake rolled him over on his stomach. Grabbing him under the arms, he dragged Jake across his lap and half onto the saddle. The big horse snorted and started to gather his legs under him to stand, but Blake jerked at the reins and commanded sharply, "No!" It took three more attempts before he could get Jake completely across the saddle. Urging the horse to its feet, he then used the lariat hanging from the pommel to tie Jake securely over the horse's back.

Blood dripped from the wound on Jake's head. "Got to stop the bleeding," Blake thought blearily, shaking his head to clear it. It took every bit of willpower to keep himself from passing out as he eased his shirt from his body. Using his teeth, he ripped it into several strips. Some he wrapped tightly about Jake's head, feeling with his fingers to try to locate the wound and make sure he covered it. The remainder he bound about his own ribs, clenching his teeth as waves of agony undulated through him.

Tying the reins of Jake's horse to the tail of his own mount, Blake then used the last of his strength to haul his battered body into his own saddle, slumping forward as the effort drained him. "Giddap!" he groaned, hoping he could stay conscious long enough to guide the horse toward Santa Fe and help.

* * *

Tori awoke to a light tapping on her bedroom door. She and Megan had waited until past midnight, and still the men had not come home. Finally, her eyes too heavy to stay open much longer, Megan had gone to bed. Shortly afterward, Tori had done the same, thinking she would not be able to sleep until Jake was home safely. But her body had demanded rest, and she had drifted off to sleep, still dressed and lying atop the covers. Now, what surely was just a short while later, she was being summoned. Groggily she rose and went to answer the door.

Ana stood on the other side, a worried look on her sleepy face. "I am sorry to wake you, Señora 'Toria, but Red has just brought the chuck wagon back from the trail drive, and he says he must speak with you. He has a message from Señor Jacob."

"A message? What kind of message?" Tori mumbled, still not able to shake the sleep from her brain.

"I do not know, Señora. He would not tell me. He says he must speak with only you. He is waiting at the kitchen entrance."

Tori frowned, her heart starting to thud within her breast. Something must be wrong! "All right, Ana. I'll take care of it. You go on back to bed. I'll wake you if I need you."

Tori was to regret those words sooner than she could guess. Quietly, careful not to disturb the others, she made her way to the kitchen. She thought it odd that Ana had not left a candle burning there. No sooner had the thought crossed her mind than she was grabbed from behind, a hand clamped roughly across her mouth. Her startled shriek of terror was muffled by the fingers pressed tightly over her lips. The smooth, round barrel of a gun pushed into her ribs caused her to cease her wild struggles.

"Now you jest calm down, little lady," a voice rumbled close to her ear. "We're gonna walk outta here nice and easy like, and you're not gonna give me any trouble or your blood's gonna get splattered all over this clean floor. You understand what I'm tellin' ya?"

Tori nodded jerkily, as best she could with her head held so tightly. The man chuckled low. "I knew you'd see things my way." His voice hardened once more into a gruff command. "Let's go!"

He shuffled her out the door ahead of him, careful not to take his hand from her mouth. Keeping to the shadows, they edged close to the house until they rounded the far corner. There, through terror-glazed eyes, Tori saw a horse tethered. Lifting her against his chest, her feet dangling off the ground, the man somehow managed to mount and drag her up on the horse before him. He kneed the horse into a quiet walk, and within minutes they had left the ranch yard.

With his hand across her mouth and her

fear mounting by the minute, Tori could scarcely breathe. In panic, she clawed at the burly arm encircling her waist, trying to free her arms. She had to get his hand from her mouth! She couldn't breathe!

Just when she was certain she would faint, or die from fright, he stopped the horse and pulled his hand away. Gratefully, weakly, she dragged sweet, precious air into her aching lungs. Before she even had sufficient breath to scream, he promptly tied a filthy rag over her mouth. "Can't have you wakin' all those unsuspectin' folks, now can we?" he taunted. With a short length of rope, he tied her hands together and lashed them to the pommel. When they started off once more, he urged the horse to a faster gait.

Tori wrapped her fingers about the pommel and clung for dear life, trying to make some sense of what was happening. Though she wouldn't have recognized his voice otherwise, she could only assume that the ranch hand known as Red was her captor. Ana had said he was waiting at the kitchen door, wanting to speak with her. But why was he doing this! Why had he grabbed her and taken her off like this? What did he want?

The only answer that came to mind was not comforting. Red was going to kill her! Immediately, Tori's mind shied away from this idea. If he meant to kill her, why hadn't he done so at the ranch? she reasoned to herself. It made no sense to think that he wanted to keep his identity a secret, that others might not guess it was him—Ana had already spoken with him. Ana would know! Did he mean to hold her for ransom? Was that what all this was about? The remaining alternative that sprang to mind was even more frightening. Did he mean to assault her? Was he going to rape her? Is that why he wanted to take her from the ranch, so that he would have the time and chance to do so without interruption?

A violent quiver raced through her, like icy fingers trailing up her spine, and she fought the nausea that assailed her, knowing she would choke and die right here if she did. Not that death would not be preferable to rape by this creature, but Tori did not intend to give up her life, or that of her unborn child, without putting up a hell of a struggle first! She would fight him with every ounce of her strength, with every breath in her body! And she knew without doubt or qualm that if the opportunity arose, she would kill this man— with her bare hands, if need be; and she would take great pleasure in doing so!

Surely God would understand and forgive her. Surely He would not let this man kill her baby! Surely He would help her, show her a way to defend herself against this terrible beast! Even now, help could be on the way!

Then Tori remembered that she had sent Ana back to bed. Oh, why had she done such a stupid thing? It could be morning before anyone missed her! Ana was a sweet girl, but a bit slow in her thinking at times. Told to go to bed, that's exactly what she would do! Red probably knew this too, just as he had relied on Ana's dimwittedness to bring Tori to him. After all, Red had worked for the Lazy B for two years. Ana knew him; they had all trusted him. Why would the girl suspect anything now?

Tori had to survive until morning. Somehow she had to delay whatever Red might have planned for her until the others missed her, until they could learn from Ana that Red had summoned her. One other thought gave her hope. If Jake was to come home and not find her there, he would immediately rouse the household. He would save her. Surely he would find her—but would it be in time? She had only herself to rely upon at this moment, her own wits to aid her. She could only pray that she could keep her head, and that an opportunity would somehow present itself.

Chapter
22

Not a soul was stirring in the sleeping town as Blake directed the horses through the dark streets of Santa Fe. He drew up at last in front of the doctor's office, breathing a shaky sigh of relief. Thank goodness the doctor's office was at the front of his residence, because Blake didn't think he had the strength to go any further. He'd be darned lucky if he managed to wake the man before passing out.

Literally falling off his horse, Blake steadied himself, drawing a shallow breath before lurching for the door. Through a haze of pain, he pulled the bell cord, summoning the doctor from his bed. As he waited, he slumped against the door, and when the physician answered, what seemed a lifetime later, Blake almost tumbled into the man's arms.

"Mr. Montgomery!" the doctor exclaimed, catching Blake before he fell on his face. Despite just being awakened, the doctor's sharp eyes noted Blake's pallor, his groan of pain, the way he clutched at his ribs. "Let's get you inside where I can take a look at you," he said.

"No!" Catching his breath, Blake said more calmly, "No, Doc. I can make it. You see to Jake. He's outside, tied over his horse."

Doc Green's brows rose in surprise. "Jake Banner?"

Blake nodded. "He's hurt pretty bad, Doc. He hasn't made a sound since he was hit."

For an average-built middle-aged man, the doctor was stronger than he looked. All on his own he managed to untie Jake from the horse, lift and carry him into the examining room, and lay him gently on the table there. Blake followed, falling into a chair to watch as Doc Green began to examine Jake. "Is he still alive?"

Doc nodded, his face grim. "Yes, but he wouldn't have lasted much longer without care. What happened?"

"To make a long story short, we got ambushed by one of our own men, caught completely unaware. It's a miracle Jake and I are here at all."

"He's got a bullet in his leg, and a gash the

size of a canyon on his head," the doctor commented as he surveyed Jake's injuries. "The leg I'm not so worried about. It's that head wound that really concerns me. It looks pretty nasty, especially since he hasn't regained consciousness in how long now?" He slanted a glance in Blake's direction.

"What time is it now?" Blake asked.

"Somewhere around three in the morning," came the answer.

"Then he's been out for about five or six hours, I'd guess."

Shaking his head, the doctor said, "That's not good."

"Doc, as soon as you get a chance, we've got to get someone out to the ranch to warn Gill and the women. They've got to be warned about Red, in case he decides to try something else. Unless they know what he's done, they have no reason not to trust him, like always."

"I'll get Billy to ride out," Doc promised. Hearing a thud behind him, he looked back to find that Blake had finally lost his battle with consciousness. He lay on the floor next to the toppled chair. "Times like this I wish I had an extra pair of hands," Doc muttered to himself. "Should have gotten married and raised half a dozen sons to help out."

They were riding up into the hills, going at an easy pace only because it was too dark to push the horse any faster over the rough, unfamiliar terrain. It would be daylight soon. Tori was glad. Perhaps in the daylight she could better control the terror gnawing at her.

When dawn came at last, it was a spectacular display of color. It seemed ludicrous, under these circumstances, to view the eastern sky and think that it was perhaps the most beautiful sunrise she had ever seen. A chill chased through her as she wondered if it might be the last she'd witness.

Red drew the horse to a halt in the midst of a small copse of pine trees, dismounting and pulling Tori down after him. Her legs, numb after many hours of riding, collapsed beneath her, and she fell into a heap at his feet. He laughed, an ugly, evil laugh that sent fear racing down Tori's spine. "That's where I like my women," he sneered down at her. "On their knees."

Reaching down, he grabbed a handful of her hair and yanked her head up painfully, forcing her to look at him. "You're gonna be real nice for old Red, aren't you, missy?"

She glared up at him. "What's the matter, girl?" he taunted. "Cat got your tongue? Here, mebbe this'll help." With his other hand he pulled the cloth from over her mouth. "Can't kiss you with that thing coverin' those sweet lips, can I?"

His grip tightened on her hair, bringing a moan of pain as he pulled her to her feet. His lips, open and wet, ground down on hers. His tongue pushed its way into her mouth, making her gag. She held her breath against the stink of his, crying out when she felt her tender lip split beneath his brutal mouth. His hand, like a huge paw, came up to grab her breast, tearing the bodice of her dress as he fumbled for her pink flesh. She tried to hit him with hands still bound before her. "Go ahead and fight me, girlie," he laughed, at last pulling his mouth from hers. "I always liked a good tussle, myself!"

With a strength born of fear, Tori wrenched away from him, leaving a good portion of her bodice still clutched in his hand. She ran, stumbling and gasping for breath, toward the cover of the trees. Almost there, she screamed and leaped aside as a shot rang out and a bullet kicked up the dirt at her feet. Whirling about, she faced him, panting, giving no thought to her exposed breasts.

Red walked slowly toward her, a leer twisting his lips, his gun drawn and pointed directly at her. "Now, that wasn't real smart, missy. You don't want to make me shoot you before we've had our fun."

Tori backed slowly away from him, almost crying out again as her retreat was suddenly halted by a tree at her back. "Why are you doing this?" she whimpered.

His laugh was as ugly and rough as he was. "Can't ya guess?" he cackled, rubbing himself in a lewd, disgusting manner that made her wince.

"If . . . if you hurt me, Jacob will kill you."

"He's the last of my worries now," Red sneered, almost preening. Thoroughly terrified, Tori did not stop to wonder why Red would not fear Jake's retaliation. Over the mad pounding of her heart, it was all she could do to comprehend Red's next words. "I've had my eye on you for quite a spell now. Too bad I have to kill you afterward. You and your gunslinger husband should've both stayed away."

"But, why?" she repeated, her voice but a shaky whisper. "I don't understand."

Red just grinned and shook his head. "I'm tired o' talkin'. I didn't bring you all the way up here to talk. I jest wanted some time to enjoy that sweet, temptin' body o' yours for a while, all to myself like, ya know? And if you're real nice about it, I'll make sure ya die quick and easy afterward."

His big, hairy hand reached out, and she twisted her head aside, eyes shut as she cringed from his touch. When it came, it was not what she had stiffened herself to expect. "What's this thing?" she heard him ask.

His hand was clasping the voodoo charm that Marie Laveau had given her, a curious, almost wary look on his face. Squaring her shoulders, Tori met his gaze unflinchingly, a gleam coming into her unusual green eyes as an idea suddenly occurred to her. Her voice was uncommonly calm, low, as she answered softly, "You shouldn't have touched that, Red. It has sealed your doom."

"That's bull!" he replied gruffly, but she saw him struggling just to swallow. "You're makin' all this up!"

"Then why do you think I talked Jacob into taking me to New Orleans on our wedding trip?" she persisted, cocking a haughtily raised eyebrow at him. "While he was gambling with his friends, I spent the evenings in secret rituals with my fellow priests and priestesses, practicing spells and incantations in the bayous."

She took another step nearer, and his gun came up suddenly, aimed at her heart. It took all her courage not to falter now, to produce a truly wicked-sounding laugh that sent goose-flesh over Red's skin. "That won't save you, Red," she laughed. "Nothing can save you now. You touched my charm. You are going to die!"

"No!" he choked out, his eyes going wild with fear. "No!"

"Yes, Red. Do you want to know how you are going to die?" He shook his head from side to side, not wanting to hear what she might say, but she told him anyway. "Have you ever seen a rabid animal, the way they foam at the mouth? That's going to happen to you, Red. In fact, I believe it has already begun. I can see the drool starting at the corners of your mouth.''

Tori almost laughed again as, against his will, his tongue came out to lick at the corners of his lips. "That is only the beginning, though. Has the fever begun yet? The chills?" She saw him shake again. "Soon you will be down on all fours, howling with pain. Your eyes will swell until they pop from their sockets. Can you feel them swelling yet, Red?

"It's really a shame you had to touch the charm before I could warn you against it," she lamented. "I might have been able to prevent this from happening. I like your hair, you know. I could have cast a spell over you and changed you into a pet—a dog, I think. You would have made a nice dog, Red, and I'm very good to my pets. I could have kept you with me forever and ever."

He dropped the charm as if his hand had been burned. Now it was he who backed away. "What do you mean? What is that thing?"

"It's a charm—a voodoo charm," she answered in a tone that might have been construed as provocative at any other time. "You do know what voodoo is, don't you?"

He began to shake visibly. "It . . . it's evil!" he whispered. "Bad magic or somethin'."

"Black magic," Tori crooned, stepping toward him and hiding her glee as he hastily backed even further from her.

"Wha . . . what you doin' with somethin' like that?" he blustered. "You ain't no witch! We all knew you was at that convent studyin' to be a nun!"

"Was I, Red? Or was that what I wanted you to believe?" Her voice was soft, soothing, almost hypnotic now. "Do you think I wanted it known that I'm really a voodoo priestess?"

By now, Red's eyes were almost rolling back in his head. His hands were trembling so badly that he dropped the gun, not even realizing it as he backed away from her. With a scream of pure terror, he turned and ran for his horse.

The minute his back was turned, Tori dived for the gun, aiming it at his retreating back. She didn't want to kill him, but now that she had the gun, maybe she could wound him, stop him long enough to get the answers to some questions. His foot was in the stirrup as she fired. With her hands bound together, her aim was slightly wide, the bullet ripping across the top of the horse's tail. With a shrill whinny, the animal reared, tossing Red, who was only half mounted, to the ground. Red's leg twisted, his boot catching in the stirrup, as the frightened horse bolted into a run. His screams bounced off the hills, echoing and multiplying as the horse dragged him in its wake over rocks and thistles.

Tori turned away, unable to watch as Red was flung against rocks and trees, the horse continuing its wild flight. Her hands came up to cushion her ears from his repeated screams. Bracing herself against a tree, she vomited violently. Weak and shaken, she sank to her knees and sobbed out her terror.

Some time later, Tori rose on trembling legs. The sun was further up in the sky; soon it would be midday, and she had a long, treacherous walk ahead of her back to the ranch. She knew the way, having grown up in this area. She had walked perhaps an hour and a half when she suddenly became aware of the sounds of an approaching rider. Her heart flew into her throat and lodged there as terror found its grip again. What if it was Red? What if he'd managed to get his foot loose and catch the horse? Her face paled at the thought, and she scurried to hide behind a tree.

Quivering with fear, Tori peered cautiously around the trunk, almost fainting with relief as she recognized the rider. Quickly she stepped out into the path again. "Gill!" she cried weakly, tears streaming down her face. "Gill!"

Gill, his face twisted in anguish, held her while she sobbed. "It was Red! It was Red!" she cried over and over again.

"I know," he soothed, running his rough, gnarled hands over her trembling back, smoothing her flyaway hair. "It's all right now, Tori. It's gonna be okay."

When she had quieted some, he put her gently away from him, gathering the torn ends of her dress and holding them to her chest to cover her. "Did he . . . uh . . . did he hurt you?"

"No! No! But he was going to—he wanted to!" she gulped. Once more her eyes went wide with fear. "Gill! We've got to get out of here! He might come back! He might—"

Gill hugged her to him. "He ain't comin' back, Tori, gal. He ain't goin' nowheres but to hell!" Gill's voice held anger and satisfaction. "I come across his horse makin' tracks back for the ranch, still draggin' that coyote along behind. He's dead, and he ain't gonna cause anybody no more trouble again." Reaching for the knife in his boot, he cut the rope from her wrists.

"Oh, it was horrible, Gill!" Tori exclaimed, turning her tear-ravaged face up to his. "The horse bolted, and Red's foot got caught, and —oh, God, it was just awful!"

"Now don't you go sheddin' no tears for that varmint," he told her sternly. "He was evil, Tori, pure evil, and we got a lot more to cry about than his worthless hide!"

It was the tone of his voice that caught her attention, that rang a warning in her brain. Her bright green eyes searched his face. "Jacob!" she whispered in horror. "Something's happened to Jacob!"

Gill nodded sadly, hating what he had to tell her now, after all she had been through. "He's in pretty bad shape, gal. He and Montgomery got ambushed and shot on their way home. Montgomery took a bullet in the side, busted a couple of ribs, but he got hisself and Jake to the doc's place in Santa Fe."

"And Jake?" Tori asked hesitantly.

"It don't look good. He got shot in the leg, but that ain't the worst of it. He got hit in the head, and Doc's plenty worried about that."

"What do you mean, 'hit'? You mean with a bullet? He has a bullet in his head?" Tori's voice rose hysterically.

"No, it just creased him, sort of, but bad enough that he ain't woke up yet."

"Do they know who did it?"

Gill nodded, his eyes blazing. "It was Red, so don't you go feelin' sorry for that snake. He got what he deserved, though I wish I coulda been the one to do him in."

Tori took a deep, quivering breath, trying to calm her racing heart, trying to stem the scream that was threatening to escape, knowing she needed to think clearly now, for Jacob's sake. She couldn't let herself go all to pieces, not now. Later, after she had seen Jacob, after she knew that he was going to be all right, she would lock herself in her room and have a good, long cry. But not now. Now Jacob needed her.

"Tori! Tori!" Jake groaned her name over and over again, calling for her, needing her.

His head hurt, his leg hurt, even his hair seemed to hurt. He tried to remember what had happened, where he was, but when he tried to think, his head hurt worse. As he rolled his head to the side, pain lanced through it, making him gasp with the force of it. Colored lights danced in his head as it seemed to explode. Then darkness swirled the colors into an endless pinwheel, and Jake let it take him with it, down . . . down . . . down

The next time he woke, he opened his eyes to darkness. Wherever he was, it was dark. Somehow, Jake didn't think he was outdoors. He couldn't feel any air moving; there were no night sounds. A peculiar odor assaulted his nose. Jake concentrated on it, trying to block out the continual pounding in his head. Then he knew! It was the smell of medicines, of alcohol! He must be in the doctor's office!

He tried to move, but at the slightest movement, his head throbbed until he thought it would burst. Slowly, easily, he brought his hand up to his head and felt the bandage. Yes, somehow he must have gotten to the doctor's, though he couldn't recall how or when. Blake. It must have been Blake. He remembered being shot, but he didn't remember anything after that, until now. He tried to concentrate, to recall everything that had happened, but the effort was too much. He couldn't seem to recall how he had come to be shot, or who had done it, but he remembered the lightning bolt of pain and knew without doubt that he had, indeed, been shot.

There was a sound, the creak of wood nearby, and Jake stiffened. Someone was near. Who? Where? Damn! Why was it so dark in here? He strained to hear, and his ear picked up the sound of a leather sole squeaking as someone moved. "Who's there?" Jake called out softly.

"Banner! You're awake!" Doc Green's voice came out of the darkness, moving closer. "About time, son. I thought you were going to sleep the clock around, not that you can't use the rest, mind you, after taking that crack on the head. How are you feeling?"

Jake's curse described exactly how he felt. The doctor chuckled. "Doc, why don't you light a lamp or somethin'?" Jake asked. "It's as dark as the inside of a goat in here. You savin' money on lamp oil or somethin'?"

There was an odd silence following his words, and Jake felt the hair on his neck begin to stand on end. He couldn't quite figure it out, but something wasn't right about all this.

"Jake," the doctor asked quietly, "can you see anything at all right now?"

Cold fear clutched at Jake's stomach. "No. Why?" When there was no immediate answer, he asked more forcefully. "Why?"

"Jake, I don't know how to tell you this. It's probably a result of the gunshot to the head, and chances are it might not be a permanent thing. I want you to understand that."

"Blast it, Doc! What are you tryin' to tell me?" In his gut, Jake thought he already knew, but he needed to hear it put into words. His hands clenched into fists at his sides as he prepared himself for the worst.

"You're lying in my office and the curtains are open. Jake, it's bright daylight outside, and the sun is shinin' right into the room."

Even braced for it, the news was devastating. Jake felt as if he'd been hit in the stomach with a sledge hammer. Like an animal caught in a trap, he howled with the ripping agony of it. "No! No! No! Damn it, nooooo!" Tears gushed from his eyes, eyes that saw nothing. His hands flew to his face, wanting to tear those sightless eyes from his body. Then mercifully, the intense pain in his head, combined with the pain in his soul, was too much to bear. His hands fell to his sides as he lost consciousness.

"You've got to see her, Jake," Blake told his friend hours later. "She's out there going through hell worrying about you."

"See her!" Jake barked out a humorless laugh. "That's good, Montgomery. You really know how to cheer a fella up!"

"Blast it all! You know the doctor said this blindness might only be temporary. Once the swelling goes down, you might see again. It'll just take time, but you can't ignore your wife in the meanwhile. She loves you."

"I don't want her to love me. Not now. Not while I'm like this."

"You're talking nonsense, Banner. You need that woman's love now more then ever. If nothing else, you owe her your gratitude for killing the man who put you in this position."

"What?" Jake exclaimed, his jaw going slack in surprise.

"Thought that might get your attention," Blake said smugly.

"She killed Red? How?" This time, when he'd awakened, Jake had remembered most of the shooting. He had worried that Red might harm Tori next, or Carmen or Megan. His relief was great when he learned that they were all safe, that Tori was waiting in the next room to see him.

Blake proceeded to tell Jake everything that had happened, how Red had kidnaped Tori, how she had frightened him away with her wits and the voodoo charm, how her wild shot had caused the horse to bolt and drag Red to a gruesome death. He also informed Jake of the "Indian" attack that had occurred at the ranch just hours before the stampede, and how the women and the ranch hands had held off the raiders and saved the barn from burning.

"She might be small and delicate, but that wife of yours is one of the bravest little ladies I know. You should be real proud of her," Blake concluded.

Jake shivered just imagining the danger Tori had been in, how frightened she must have been. "I just hate to have her see me so helpless," he admitted. "How am I supposed to protect her when I'm blind, Blake? What kind of husband will I be now? I'll be nothin' but a millstone tied around her neck, about as much use to her as a two-legged horse!"

"The danger is over for now. Red was the culprit, and he's dead," Blake reminded him.

Jake shook his head, wincing at the pain the slight movement brought with it. "I don't know, Blake. Has anyone gone through Red's personal things? Did they find Dad's gun?"

"No, Roy's gun wasn't there."

"It wasn't among Frank's belongings, either. Blake, there is still another killer out there. I know it."

"Maybe. It could be they sold the gun, knowing it could tie them into Roy's murder. Or they might have hidden it somewhere, or lost it," Blake suggested. "Just because it hasn't turned up doesn't mean they didn't have it."

"Okay, what about all those other men, the ones who raided the ranch and stampeded the cattle? Has it occurred to you to wonder who's payin' them? You can bet it wasn't Red or Frank, or Tandy either. None of them had that kind of money. No, there's someone else behind all this, Blake—someone with money —someone like Edwards, maybe," Jake persisted with a frown.

"Could be you just don't like the man courting Carmen so soon after Roy's death. Maybe you just have your mind dead set against him from the start, and want to find something to hold against him. The man hasn't actually done anything wrong that we can point to or prove. Have you considered that he might be innocent after all? Maybe the others threw in with Red for reasons we haven't even thought about. If Red was heading up the trouble, maybe now that he's out of the way, the others won't bother anymore. Maybe it will seem too risky, with so many of their own dead now."

All this thinking was making Jake's head hurt worse. "We'll know for sure if the trouble stops now, I suppose," he sighed. "I hope to hell you're right, 'cause I don't know how I'm supposed to protect Tori and the baby when I can't even see trouble comin'."

"Give it a chance, Jake," his friend advised. "Maybe the doctor is right. Maybe your sight will come back."

"Soon enough to prevent us all from bein' killed?" Jake muttered with a grimace.

"Hey, you might have died out there on the trail," Blake reminded him. "Count your blessings!"

"I'm supposed to be thankful to be blind?"

Jake asked incredulously. "Don't make me laugh, pardner! My head's splittin' as it is!"

Jake finally agreed to let Tori see him, though he cringed inwardly at the thought. Damn, he hated to have her see him like this, lying helpless as a turtle on its back! He heard her light tread hurrying across the floor toward him, and a moment later her arms came tenderly about him.

She put her cheek next to his, and he felt her hot tears wet his face. "Oh, Jacob! I've been so worried! They said you were unconscious for so long. I was afraid I was going to lose you, darling! I was so afraid you were going to die!"

"It might have been better if I had." The bitter words were out of his mouth before he could stop them.

"No, Jacob! No! Don't ever say such a thing! Don't even think it!"

"I'm blind, Tori!" he told her bluntly. "As helpless as a babe. What sort of husband am I going to be to you now? I'll tell you," he said before she could answer him. "I'll be a burden more than anything. It won't be long before you come to hate me, to resent me for tyin' you down when you need a whole man to look after you."

Tori swallowed back the pain his words brought to her aching heart. "But you might see again, Jacob. The doctor told me so."

"And maybe I won't. Maybe I'll be blind for the rest of my life."

"Even if you are, that won't make me love you less," she argued. "Jacob, do you love Mama less now just because her legs are scarred from the fire?"

"No."

"Would you love me less if I were to lose a leg or an arm, or if I couldn't give you any more children?"

"Don't be silly, Tori," he grumbled.

"Why not?" she countered. "*You* are! Jacob, I love you with all my heart. I love all of you, not just your eyes, beautiful as they are. I'll love you till the day I die, and there isn't a thing in this world that can ever change that."

His arms came up to hold her near, his lips searching blindly for hers. "Oh, God, Tori! I'm just so scared," he admitted, his tears mingling with hers. "I don't know what I'll do if my sight doesn't return."

"We'll manage somehow," she promised. "You and I, together, can do anything, overcome anything. I'm praying, Jacob. I'm praying real hard."

He managed a weak chuckle. "You prayin' to those voodoo spirits again, darlin'?"

She blushed, though he could not see it. "Oh, you heard about that?"

"Yeah, and I'm real proud of you, honey. You kept your head in a tough situation."

She drew a deep breath and blurted, "If I

thought it would help you, I'd pray to the devil himself, Jacob. I'd trade my soul in exchange for your eyes."

He hugged her tightly, his heart about to burst with love for her. "I'd never want you to sacrifice anything that precious, little angel. I've already robbed God of enough when I stole your heart."

Chapter
23

They took the two invalids home three days later. Doc Green had warned against jostling Jake's head too much, so they piled mattresses in the bed of the wagon and walked the horses the entire way back to the Lazy B. A day bed was set up in the master bedroom for Blake's use.

"So you two 'wounded warriors' can keep one another company while you recover," Megan said with a grin.

"But, honey, you're supposed to keep me company," Blake objected plaintively. "You're a mean-hearted woman to keep me cooped up here with this grouch. Jake's as mean as a riled snake these days."

Megan was not moved by his pleas. "I've got work to finish at Aunt Josefa's, now that it's safe to go back and forth to town again."

Both men frowned at this. "Megan, I'd still feel better if one of the ranch hands went with you," Jake suggested. Blake agreed. Frank, Tandy, and Red were dead, but that didn't mean there weren't others involved, others just waiting to strike again. Neither of them wanted to take any chances with the women's lives until they were absolutely certain it was safe. After all, as Jake had pointed out, there was still the matter of Roy's missing pistol.

In the days that followed, Tori wondered if her orphans weren't older, if not in years than in patience, than the two men left in her care. If one of them didn't want something, the other did, and they were running her ragged with their incessant demands. She had given them a bell to ring to summon her when one of them needed something, and now she was severely tempted to shove it down their throats, if only she could decide which of them deserved that honor more. They were behaving like spoiled brats, and she told them so.

"Spoiled brats!" Jake objected in a wounded tone. "A man needs a little sympathy now and then, darlin', especially when he's laid up. I wouldn't say that makes us brats!"

"Yeah," Blake agreed. "A little tender, loving care makes the pain more bearable."

Tori rolled her eyes heavenward, praying for fortitude. "Your constant complaining is a bit hard to bear, too, you know," she told them both. "The sheets are wrinkled, the bed is lumpy, the coffee's too weak, the soup is too hot, the covers need to be straightened, your pillows need to be fluffed, the room is too hot, it's stuffy, it's too cold! Shall I go on?"

They both had the grace to look sheepish. "Have we been that bad?" Blake asked.

"Yes."

"I'm sorry, angel, but I get bored just lyin' here all day," Jake said. "I like your company."

"Meaning you don't care for mine?" Blake suggested in a huff.

"Well, it's nice to hear a sweet, feminine voice now and then, instead of you grumblin'."

"If anyone is grumbling these days, it's you!" Blake countered. The two of them were squabbling like children.

"At least you have other things to occupy your time," Jake hastened to point out. "You can look out the window, or read."

"Feeling sorry for yourself, are you?" Blake questioned.

"Yeah, I am. I think I have the right. If it was just the lame leg, or just the blindness, I could handle it better, but both at the same time is too much! If I have to be blind, I'd like to be able to move around a bit; and if I have to be

laid up in bed, it would be nice to see somethin'. I could read, or do the ranch books, or
admire my wife!"

"Is this all the thanks I get for keeping you
company?" Blake shot back. "Hell's bells, I've
read aloud to you till I'm hoarse!"

"Yeah, Shakespeare! Not all of us are as
intellectually inclined as you, Montgomery. A
dime novel wouldn't kill you, you know!"

Blake groaned audibly. "Ugh! Tori, how can
you stand living with such a plebeian?"

"Because he makes me look smart by com-
parison?" she teased, a giggle erupting from
her before she could stifle it.

"You'll pay for that remark," Jake growled.
"Just wait until this leg heals. I've paddled
your behind before, and I can certainly do it
again!"

His words brought a vivid blush to her
cheeks as Tori recalled the last time he had
spanked her, and how that particular episode
had ended. While Jake could not see the color
rise sharply to her face, Blake could, and he
spent an interesting few minutes contemplat-
ing just what it meant.

All in all, Jake was taking his blindness
fairly well. There were times when he was
despondent and moody, refusing to be cajoled
into good humor. Self-pity often claimed him,
but he tried, for Tori's sake, to shake free of
that pitfall lest it become a habit.

He despised having to be fed like an infant, and soon demanded to feed himself. Tori bit her tongue and quietly changed the bed linen when he made a mess of his food, knowing he must be allowed to manage on his own. She could not fall into the trap of coddling him, though it was tempting at times. He even insisted on bathing himself, allowing her to wash only those areas he could not reach because of his injured leg. At least he was trying to find ways to be self-reliant, though his choices were severely limited.

Blake's presence helped tremendously. When the two men were not bickering back and forth, they fell to reminiscing about old times. It helped make the long hours pass more pleasantly. Drawn by their bursts of laughter, Tori discovered, much to her shock, that they also traded off-color jokes and bawdy tales. After suffering the first embarrassment, Tori took care to make her approach known, practically stomping down the hallway to alert them to her arrival.

Aware of her tactics, Jake couldn't help but tease her about it. "Puttin' on a little weight these days, Tori?"

She was, but his teasing only caused her to blush even more. However, it was a small price to pay to hear him laugh.

Out of desperation and boredom, Blake marked a deck of cards—but not for the purpose of cheating. He marked them in such a way that Jake could tell the face value of each card by touch. Jake quickly memorized the formula and the men spent many hours gambling for matchsticks, a table erected between their beds.

For this, Tori was grateful. It occupied Jacob's time and mind and freed a few hours of her busy days. Despite the fact that Madame Duvalier had created gowns for her expanding girth, those garments were not designed for everyday wear about the ranch. She used the extra time to sew a few plain dresses for herself, as well as making tiny clothing for her baby. She also devoted many an hour to prayer, asking God to restore Jacob's sight, that he might know the joy of looking upon his child when it was born.

With Megan busy finishing up Josefa's packing, it was left to Tori to monitor Stan Edwards' continued visits to Carmen. One day, as he was leaving the house, Tori cornered the man for a private word. "Mr. Edwards, I hate to seem forward or disapproving, but I must ask you, what is the meaning behind all of these visits to my mother?"

The man stared at Tori in disbelief for a moment before a smile crept slowly over his face. "Victoria, are you asking my intentions toward Carmen?" he asked, humor lacing his voice.

Tori did not think she cared for his condescending tone. She answered stiffly, formally. "Yes, I suppose I am. You must agree, sir, that it is unseemly that your visits are so frequent lately, and that they come so soon after Dad's death."

"Are you worried that I might be courting her? Do you disapprove of me so heartily?"

Tori picked her words carefully. "It's not that I disapprove of you, exactly, sir. It's your timing, if you are, indeed, courting my mother. There is such a thing as a proper period of mourning, you know."

"Then let me set your mind at ease," Edwards replied just as formally. "I enjoy your mother's company. Carmen is a delightful woman, and it has been a long time since I have spent so many pleasant hours in the company of such a lady. We enjoy talking with one another, and as amazing as it might seem to you, we find one another very interesting. I have no intention of courting Carmen until she gives me some indication that the time is right, that she is past her grieving. Does that satisfy your curiosity?" He stood there almost laughing at her, the sides of his jacket flaring out as he faced her with his hands on his hips.

It didn't, for she didn't like him or his attitude in the least, but what else could she do but agree? "I suppose so, Mr. Edwards. Thank you for your time." In a fit of temper, she dismissed him as one might a servant. "Good day, Mr. Edwards."

"Good day, Mrs. Banner," he returned, his smile widening as he doffed his stetson toward her as if it were a top hat. The caustic humor glinting in his eyes made her suspect that he wanted to sketch a dandified bow, but resisted the urge only because it would further enrage her.

Tori honestly did not know what to make of Edwards. There were not many people she disliked on sight; she tended to give almost everyone the benefit of the doubt, but something about this neighbor of theirs rubbed her the wrong way. She could not put her finger on what it was about him that irritated her so, besides his gloating air of superiority. There was something sneaky about him, something sly in his eyes that brought forth a deep-seated and intuitive feeling of distrust.

Besides that, there was something about him today in particular that nagged at her, something he might have said or something about his appearance—she wasn't quite sure. It was just a feeling she had that she had missed something, or perhaps noticed something amiss, but now it eluded her. It was like misplacing an item about the house—you knew you had seen it lying about somewhere, but you just couldn't recall where, and it continued to bother you until you found it. "Oh, well," she thought with a sigh, "I suppose it will come to me sooner or later."

Two weeks passed. In that time, Megan finished closing Josefa's house, and no other problems cropped up. As soon as Blake's wound healed sufficiently, the Montgomerys would be on their way back to their ranch outside Tucson. Megan was halfway through her term now, and eager to get home before travel became too uncomfortable for her. Blake's ribs were beginning to mend nicely, as was the gun wound in Jake's leg. Fortunately none of the bones or major muscles had been damaged. It was merely a matter of the flesh mending itself again.

Jake was on his feet, walking with the aid of a cane, soon thereafter. His curses could be heard throughout the house as he repeatedly stumbled into furniture and walls, the leg making it even more difficult for him to retain his balance, especially without the use of his eyes. His stubborn nature refused to let him give up, however. He was determined to regain some measure of self-reliance again, despite his disabilities. The first time he actually negotiated his way without assistance from the bedroom to the inner patio, without knocking anything over or bumping into a wall, he was so pleased with himself that it brought tears to Tori's eyes. After that, he could often be found outdoors, soaking up the autumn sunshine, reveling in the tug of the breeze through his hair.

Of course, he had to take care not to aggravate his head injury. All of them were supremely aware that any further damage could result in permanent blindness, if that were not already the case. Each time Doc Green came to examine him, he seemed more pleased with the way the swelling was gradually decreasing around the head wound.

Though Blake was also recovering rapidly, he was still much too weak for extensive travel. He was, however, well enough to move into the guest bedroom with Megan now. With Jake up and around these days, there was no need for the men to conduct their conversations and card games in the bedroom. They were both heartily sick of that one room, and glad to be able to escape it at last.

In fact, the only time Jake entered that room now was to dress or bathe or to sleep at night. When Tori expressed concern about sharing the big bed with him, afraid she would bump his leg or injure him while they slept, he stood firm. "You are not going to sleep in that day bed, Tori. If you even suggest it again, I'll take an ax to it myself, and relish every swing. It seems like an eternity since

I've had the pleasure of sleeping with you, and I'll be darned if you're going to cheat me out of it now."

"But what if I hurt you? Your leg is just beginning to heal so nicely."

"You won't hurt me. If anything, I'll rest better with you at my side. I've missed you, love. I want to feel your warm, silky flesh next to mine. I want to smell your hair on my pillow and my skin. I want to hear your soft sighs when I touch you. Blast it all, if I'm to be denied the sight of you, at least let me hold you and make love with you."

"Jacob, we can't make love yet, darling. I'm sure the doctor would not approve of such activities until your wounds heal further."

What he suggested the good doctor do with his restrictions made her gasp aloud. "If I'm well enough to want you this badly, I'm well enough to do something about it," he told her.

He proved it to her that very evening, in some very interesting and innovative ways that thoroughly delighted them both. As they lay gasping for breath, totally replete and still glorying in the love that had just passed between them, Jake sighed, "I can't remember when I've felt so absolutely relaxed! Sweetheart, you're just what the doctor ordered."

"I doubt that," she answered with a sleepy chuckle. "He'd probably chew your ear off if he knew what we've been up to."

Jake laughed and searched for her lips once more, the length of his body caressing hers. "I think I'm up to it again," he murmured softly. She could not doubt it as she felt his arousal, hot and firm along her thigh.

"Already?" she squealed. "Honestly, Jacob! You're randier than a stag in rutting season! Isn't there anything that will slow you down?"

"Not much, I guess. You complainin', woman?"

"Never."

As word got around about Jake's injuries, friends and neighbors came to call and express their sympathies and best wishes for his recovery. And Stan Edwards continued his visits with Carmen. He also offered assistance. "If you need any more help around the place, I have several good men I can send your way."

Jake immediately declined. "Like I said before, thanks for the offer, but we can handle things fine with the help we've got here."

"Just tryin' to be neighborly," Edwards claimed. "Now, if you need any help with the ranch books, don't be embarrassed to ask. I know it must be a trial to you, trying to cope with this blindness, and women aren't real good at business and figures."

With great effort, Jake held on to his rising temper. Edwards would be tickled pink to get his grubby hands on those books, he was sure. "I'll take care of it," he repeated sternly.

"You know, you're more like your pa than most folks would have guessed," Edwards said. Somehow, Jake got the impression this wasn't meant as a compliment.

Jake's friend Ben Curtis also offered assistance. "If there's anything at all I can do, Jake, you just ask."

Poor Ben felt so awkward trying to avoid the subject of Jake's lost sight that Jake finally had to say something to put the man at ease. "Ben, it's okay to mention that I'm blind. God knows, it's not somethin' I can hide all that well, and I'm tryin' to come to terms with it. Now quit dancin' around the subject and trippin' over your tongue thinkin' you're gonna offend me. Hell! I know I'm blind, but there's still a lot of things I can do—like beat the pants off of you in a game of poker!"

His grin was an open challenge to his friend, and when Doc Green and Wayne Neister, Jake's lawyer, arrived shortly thereafter, they put together a rousing poker game that lasted until the wee hours of the morning. The other men were so intrigued with Blake's ingenious system of marking the cards that they couldn't resist closing their eyes for a few hands and trying it Jake's way—by feel. It was a congenial gathering, and Tori was glad to see Jake opening up more and really enjoying himself for once.

Through this adversity, Jake was discovering that he had many more friends in the community than he'd thought. Some of the shopkeepers and folks around Santa Fe who had shied away from him when he'd first come home now came out to the ranch to visit. Of course, they had nothing to fear from him now. Who had ever heard of a blind gunslinger?

But Tori suspected it was more than that. Many of them probably felt guilty about the way they had treated Jake at first, and were now trying to make amends, to welcome him home the way they should have done earlier. There were still others who would resent him for a long time to come, but it was heartwarming to see how many of the residents of Santa Fe were softening toward him now, and would no doubt remain friendly even if Jake regained his sight.

The afternoon following the card game proved that Jake's suspicions were correct. Their troubles were not yet over. Gill presented himself at the house with a grim look on his weathered face, and Tori's heart sank. Didn't they have enough to cope with now, especially Jacob? Reluctantly, she invited Gill into the house to speak with Jake.

"More trouble, Jake," the older man announced in his forthright manner.

"I've been expectin' something. What is it?"

"We got about a dozen sickly head of cattle in the north pasture."

Jake's brow furrowed. "More poison?"

"Not like before," Gill told him. "This time it's locoweed."

"Locoweed?" Jake was baffled. "There's no locoweed in that area. Never has been, as far as I know."

"There is now, but it ain't growin'. Someone deliberately put it there, where the cattle could get to it."

Jake sighed heavily, his fingers going to his temples to ease the tension building up. Since the ambush his wounds were healing, but he got such throbbing headaches at times. The doctor had assured him that this was normal, under the circumstances, and that the headaches would come less frequently and intensely as time went by. "Separate those cattle affected from the rest of the herd and move them all to another location. Get a few of the men to go out there and clear out any locoweed they can find, and post extra guards if you have to."

"They're already workin' on it," Gill assured him. "I jest thought you'd want to know."

Jake nodded dispiritedly. "Thanks, Gill. I don't know how I'd manage without you."

Shifting his feet in pleased embarrassment at Jake's praise, Gill said, "Jest doin' my job."

"And mine," Jake added. "I really do appreciate it, Gill. Keep me informed, and I want to know if anything else looks suspicious."

"I'll keep a sharp eye peeled." As soon as

he'd said it, Gill could have torn his tongue out for making such a blunder.

The tense silence following his words alerted Jake to Gill's mortification. "You keep one eye peeled for yourself and the other peeled for me, Gill," he told him. "Right now I need all the help you can give me."

When Blake learned of this latest development, he promptly asserted that he and Megan would be staying on at the Lazy B. "I'm not leavin' until this thing is settled," he told Jake. "I don't care if it takes till spring!"

"Blake, you've got your own ranch to run, and Megan to consider. She's not gonna be fit to travel much longer."

"I've got good help, thanks to you. My foreman is as honest as the day is long, and he knows ranching. If he needs me, he knows where to reach me; he sends a wire every week to keep me informed. I'm not worried. As far as Megan is concerned, she agrees with me about staying. We've already discussed it between us." Jake could hear the grin in his voice as Blake added, "You couldn't get rid of us if you tried, so don't wear yourself out thinking up ways to do it. You'll just give yourself another headache, and nothing you could try would work anyway."

Tears glazed Jake's sightless eyes, and he had to clear his voice before speaking, he was so touched by his friends' unselfish loyalty.

"What did I ever do to deserve friends like you and Megan?" he asked humbly.

"Probably something terrible!" Blake answered with a hearty laugh. Then he quipped, "We sinners have to stick together, you know."

Chapter 24

Jake stirred sleepily, nestling his head more comfortably between Tori's breasts. Lord, he loved waking up this way, breathing in the sweet scent of her body. Strands of her hair tickled his forehead. It had grown so fast in the past months, now lying in soft curls down to her shoulder blades in back, and just brushing the tops of her breasts like a dark veil. His hand trailed slowly over her bare thigh, coming to rest on her stomach, now rounding with the swell of their child. Her breasts, too, were enlarging in anticipation of the baby's arrival in little more than five months.

Though he could not see the changes taking

place, he could feel them, and he treasured sharing them with her. Soon they would be able to feel the babe move within her, and Jake impatiently awaited that priceless moment when they would first feel the precious life their love had created.

Slowly, lazily, his lashes fluttered open. His inner clock told him it was morning, and though he could not see, habit made him open his eyes whenever he was awake. Suddenly Jake stiffened, almost afraid to believe what he hoped was happening, afraid to move for fear it was only an illusion. He held his breath, then cautiously blinked, praying the images would not disappear. His heart leaped within his breast. It was real! Through the dark curtain of Tori's hair, he could see the curve of her breast, the pert nipple cresting it. The vision was shadowed, blurred, but it was definitely there!

Easing his head from his fleshy pillow, Jake glanced warily about the room, still unsure of what to expect. His eyes picked out vague outlines of the furniture. Though it was hazy, he could discern the lighter squares of the windows from those of the walls. He could see again! Not well yet, but he could see! Joy brought tears to his eyes, blurring the images further, and he hastily brushed them away. He wanted nothing to interfere with what little vision he had! It had been so long since he had seen anything at all.

A sob shook his broad chest as the magnitude of this miracle washed through him. If this were just another dream, he didn't want to wake from it. This time it was real—it had to be real! He could feel Tori lying next to him, hear her soft breathing, hear someone in the kitchen preparing the morning meal. He could smell freshly brewed coffee. This was no dream! He could actually, truly see! "Thank you, God!" he whispered fervently. "Oh, thank you! I know I probably don't deserve this miracle, but whatever your reasons, thank you for giving me back my eyes!"

Tori awoke with a start; something had disturbed her slumber. Her sleepy eyes found Jacob sitting up in bed, his back to her. His shoulders shook, and she heard the raw sob that escaped his throat. "Jacob!" she cried softly, rising to wrap her arms about his waist and lay her head upon his broad back. "What is it, darling? What's wrong?"

He twisted to pull her into his arms and hold her tightly to him. "Nothing is wrong, Tori!" he declared triumphantly. "Everything is finally right again!" Gently he held her away from him, his eyes avidly scanning the features of her face, stroking them, adoring them. "You have the most beautiful eyes I've ever seen, but they've never been more lovely to me than they are right now, at this moment."

Her eyes went wide with shock and hope,

her jaw dropping slightly. "You can see!" she exclaimed, her hands flying up to cradle his face in her palms. "Oh, Jacob! You can see!"

He nodded. "Yes! It's not real clear yet, and maybe it never will be, but I can see!"

"Oh, Jacob! I could dance on clouds, I'm so happy!" Joyous tears streamed down her face, falling onto her bare breasts.

"I can think of a better way to celebrate," he told her. Bending his head, he licked the tears from her breasts, his tongue sweeping roughly over the rosy crests. "A bit salty," he murmured, "but still delicious."

She was sobbing and laughing all at once, unable to control the intense emotions rioting through her, and now Jacob was adding to the turmoil. It was almost more than Tori could bear.

They fell to the sheets, his laughter joining hers as they rolled and tumbled about in ecstatic delight, the weight of the world lifted from their shoulders. Even the pain in his leg did not deter him as he nipped and licked and kissed every inch of her body, cherishing the sight of her silken body, her long legs, her blushing breasts and gleaming eyes, her lush, smiling lips.

It was a wild and gentle joining, a mating of hearts as well as bodies, an exuberant celebration of life and love. In their delight, their desire reached new heights, pinnacles of passion never before attained. Spent and gloriously happy, they lay at last staring into one another's eyes. "I can't express my joy at knowing that those wondrous golden eyes of yours can see again," she told him tenderly. "It broke my heart to think that you might never see our child when it is born."

A wide smile lit his face. "I suppose we should go tell the others the good news, but I just want to savor it a few minutes more, just the two of us," he admitted. "I need to look at you, to fill myself with the sight of you. It seems so long since I've seen your smile."

When they broke the good news to the others, there were shouts of joy and sighs of relief. Broad smiles wreathed the faces of everyone at the ranch. Doc Green was nearly as thrilled as the rest of them, and his predictions were encouraging. "I'd say you should regain full vision in a few days, if all goes as well as I expect. The blurring should clear and colors become brighter, but I'd still advise you to take it easy for a while. No riding or straining to read, and no bumps to the head. No sense courting disaster until you are completely well."

Jake agreed wholeheartedly. He wasn't about to take any chances that might land him right back in that eternal darkness. Nearly four weeks of that had been almost enough to make him lose his mind. Throughout all of it, the only thing that had kept him going, kept him from the absolute depths of depression, had been the slim hope that he might see again—that, and the love and encouragement of his family and friends.

For the next few days, as his vision steadily improved, Jake was like a child in a candy store. He couldn't seem to get enough of looking at things. Because of those dark weeks, he was now looking at the world through new eyes, reveling in small things he had taken so much for granted before. A sunrise took on new colors; sunsets had never been so glorious! Even the barn, desperately in need of paint, was beautiful to behold, just because he could see it with his own two eyes. Leaves, blades of grass, puffy clouds, the delicate wings of a butterfly—all were marvelous new wonders.

He'd never before stopped to realize how many shades of green there were, or brown, or blue. Everything intrigued him as he gazed about, noting shapes and tints and patterns. Never again would he take his God-given senses for granted, as he had in the past. Now he could truly appreciate the meaning behind the old saying that you never miss something until you've lost it. He'd been granted the gift of sight for a second time, and he would never look at things in quite the same way again.

Within a week, Jake's vision was as sharp and clear as ever. Though he still walked with a slight limp, favoring his injured leg, he had cast the cane aside as a nuisance he could do without. With renewed determination, he set himself to the task of bringing his body back to its former state of health, honing his muscles and his skills with his gun. He wanted to be fully prepared to defend his family and home, ready for anything that might come along, whenever the next bout of trouble might occur—and something told him it would not be long in coming.

Carmen wanted to go to church. She hadn't attended Mass since before the fire. Tori, too, desired to go. Her last confession had been in New Orleans, and a lot had transpired since then, including the "Indian" attack at the ranch and that terrifying episode with Red. Guilt lay heavy on her soul, knowing she had wounded, if not killed, at least one of the disguised Indians, and was responsible in large part for Red's death. No matter that they might have deserved to die; Tori still felt the need for absolution.

Also, she and Carmen wanted to thank God for providing such wonderful miracles; for saving Tori's life when the horses had bolted with the wagon, and for restoring Jacob's sight. He had been very good to them, and they needed to offer up their thanks in His house, to sing His praises for all to hear.

Jake was not thrilled with their request, but after having received such favors from his

Maker, how could he deny it? He would have felt like an ungrateful worm. As luck would have it, Sunday morning arrived and Jake was hit with another of those debilitating headaches that still plagued him from time to time. Knowing that Jake had planned to escort Tori and Carmen to church, Blake and Megan had made plans of their own. They were going to spend the day taking Josefa around to visit several of her old friends she would not get to see again before long. As a result, Jake had to arrange for two of his best men to escort the women to the mission church. Like it or not, there was no other recourse.

Carmen was welcomed back into the fold like a long lost soul. Both before and after Mass, friends came up to greet her, to ask about her health. They also exclaimed over Jake's miraculous recovery, telling the women how they had prayed and lit candles on his behalf, and how thrilled they were that he could see again. Father Romero heard Tori's confession, assuring her that her soul was not in jeopardy, and she felt tons lighter with that worry off her mind. It had been tormenting her more than even she had suspected.

The priest shared her joy over Jacob's regained sight. Father Romero had made several visits to the ranch while Jake had been blind, and he and Jake had held a few deep, private discussions, the contents of which Tori did not know nor ask about. She considered it a matter between her husband and the priest, and if Jacob wanted her to know what was discussed, he would tell her. Now Father Romero told her, "Tell Jacob I'll be out again to see him soon, and that I am pleased to hear his good news. One day, before I am an old man, I hope to see him here with you in church."

For Tori, the one bad moment came when Stan Edwards approached them. He took Carmen's hand in his and raised it to his lips in a gallant gesture that set Tori's teeth on edge. Carmen seemed quite disturbed that he would do such a thing right here in church, with so many people about. He politely inquired about Jake's health, mouthing an appropriate response before asking Carmen if he might escort her home.

"My daughter and I have made other arrangements, Mr. Edwards," Carmen told him, rebuffing him lightly.

Though he frowned at this, he accepted her refusal with seeming good grace. "Perhaps another time," he replied, then sauntered off to speak with other friends. Tori noticed, however, that he kept glancing back in her and Carmen's direction, as if to assure himself of their whereabouts.

It was as she was watching him from the corner of her eye that Tori noticed the way he was standing. Again, as he had on the day she had spoken with him at the ranch, he had his hands on his hips, his jacket flaring out at the sides as he did so.

Suddenly it came to her! In her mind, she could see him standing there in the hallway at the Lazy B. Just now, in church, he wore no guns, at least not visibly; but that day, when he had posed as he was now, he had been wearing a gun. She had seen it quite clearly with his jacket pulled back. Since then she had often puzzled about what it had been about him that bothered her so on that particular occasion. Now she knew! The pistol he had been wearing was Roy's! It had been the revolver with the special pearl grips that Jake's father prized so dearly!

In her mind's eye, Tori could now recall even having seen Roy's initials engraved on the grips of the gun Edwards was wearing. It simply had not registered with her at the time, but her subconscious mind had stored the information, and now Tori was almost physically ill at what this meant. Edwards had been the one who killed Roy! He was the one who had set the fire that almost caused her mother to die! And now he had the temerity to come sniffing about the ranch, making a show of courting the widow of the very man he had murdered!

Tori's eyes were wide with shock at this startling revelation. For several seconds she stared at the man in mute horror. Then, as her gaze traveled up from his waist to his face, she found him staring back at her. His eyes were glowing with malice and mutual recognition! "He knows!" she thought in terror, trying to stifle a gasp. "He knows that I know what he's done!"

Just as Carmen turned to ask Tori what was wrong, having heard her daughter's sharp gasp, Edwards started toward them. Panicking now, Tori grabbed her mother's arm, tugging her toward the door. "Come, Mama! Hurry!"

"Child, what on earth is wrong with you?" Carmen asked as Tori pulled her along.

"I don't have time to explain! Just believe me, Mama. We're in great danger! We must get out of here! We have to get home to Jacob!"

They'd reached the doors, and Tori glanced frantically about, trying to locate the ranch hands who were supposed to escort her and her mother back to the ranch. They weren't there! Where were they? Oh, dear heaven, where were they when she needed them so desperately?

Her eyes scanned the church yard, lighting upon two unsavory characters lurking under a nearby tree. Both wore guns and mean expressions, and both were looking directly toward the open church doors. They spotted her at almost the same instant she saw them, and Tori knew they were waiting for her. "Dear God!" she exclaimed on an indrawn breath. "What are we going to do now?"

" 'Toria! You must not take God's name in vain!" Carmen remonstrated.

"Mama, trust me. I wasn't! I was praying most sincerely!" Tori dragged her mother back from the door, the two of them scurrying in a direction that would prevent them from encountering Edwards as he pushed his way through the crowd just inside the entrance of the church. Crouching down, and urging Carmen to do the same, they tried to lose themselves in the throng.

Suddenly Tori spotted a couple of the nuns. Could she ask them for help? Dare she risk involving the sisters in this treachery? Dare she not? Already the crowd was thinning as people left the church. "Sister Teresa!" she hissed.

The woman looked around, frowning slightly when she saw Tori bent over and looking so frightened. Carmen was also behaving strangely. Then Tori put her finger to her lips in a gesture for silence and motioned for Sister Teresa to come near. Careful not to arouse suspicion, since Victoria was being so secretive, Sister Teresa walked casually to where Tori stood hunched over.

"Sister Teresa, we're in danger! Our lives are in peril! Can you aid us?" Tori whispered frantically.

If Sister Teresa wondered at the odd look Carmen shot at her daughter, she said nothing. Victoria was obviously very frightened, and Teresa recalled that day not long ago when Victoria had almost lost her life in the runaway wagon. "What can I do?" she asked softly.

"There are men waiting outside the church to harm us, and Mr. Edwards is also involved. Can you hide us from them, until word can be sent to my husband?"

At this, Carmen gasped and stared at Tori. " 'Toria, surely you are mistaken! Mr. Edwards has been a guest in our home!"

"Mama!" Tori hissed desperately. "Please! I know what I'm saying! He murdered Dad, and now he has discovered that I know it!"

Carmen clutched at Tori's arm to keep from falling, her face suddenly ashen. "Are you certain?"

Her eyes on Sister Teresa, waiting for her answer, Tori nodded wordlessly.

"Wait here, sister," Teresa said, unconsciously addressing Tori as one of the order, as in days past. "I'll be right back."

"Hurry!" Tori called back in a hushed voice. She watched as Sister Teresa approached several of the other sisters, whispering quickly to them. As a group, they moved toward Tori and Carmen.

"Come," Teresa said when the sisters had gathered round them. "We shall walk slowly to the back of the church and into the ante-room. Stay down and do not make any noise. Mr. Edwards appears to be searching for someone, most likely the two of you, and we do not want to alert him to our deception.''

In their fright, it seemed to take eons to reach the anteroom, moving at such a snail's pace. Once there, one of the sisters shut the door. Two of them immediately began to disrobe. ''You will dress yourselves in these good sisters' habits,'' Teresa explained as the garments were handed to them. ''I would suggest that you put them on over your other clothing, so that if anyone searches the church, they will not find your clothes and guess that we have disguised you.''

''What about Sister Agatha and Sister María?'' Tori thought to ask, quickly donning the familiar habit. ''It will appear just as strange if someone should come across them standing back here in nothing but their undergarments.''

Teresa smothered a laugh as she assisted Carmen in dressing. ''Don't worry. Even now, Sister Sarah is collecting habits for them, and will smuggle them in under her own clothing. We merely thought it more imperative to get you properly disguised as quickly as possible, without wasting precious time.''

''Thank you, sisters,'' Tori told the group.

''Do not thank us yet,'' Teresa said gravely. ''Now we must smuggle you into the convent, and to do that we must walk past the men who are looking for you." More for Carmen's benefit than Tori's, she explained, "Keep your eyes cast downward, as if in prayer. You two will walk on the inside of our group. We do not want anyone to see your faces clearly."

A soft knock sounded on the other side of the door, and Tori nearly leaped from her skin. Carmen was visibly trembling. Teresa opened the door to admit Sister Sarah. "We'll go now," Teresa said, leading the way.

To Tori it felt strange, and yet so normal, to be walking among her fellow sisters again. She fell into step with them, easily recalling the words to the prayer they began to recite as one. Beside her, Carmen mimed the unfamiliar words in order not to appear conspicuous. Tori stiffened slightly as they came abreast of Edwards, standing just outside the entrance. Hastily, she averted her face as his gaze raked over them.

In her fright, Carmen stumbled, but quickly recovered herself. It was then that Tori's downward glance caught a glaring error in their hasty plans. While Carmen's black shoes blended perfectly with the sisters', Tori's yellow pair stood out like a shout! Hoping no one had yet noticed, and that she would not appear too odd by her actions, Tori scrunched down until the hem of her habit dragged the ground, hiding her shoes from view. Realizing something must be amiss, the sisters next to her and immediately behind closed ranks even further.

On they walked, serenely and sedately, practically beneath the noses of the two men still waiting outside. When they at last gained the sanctuary of the convent, Tori allowed herself her first full breath. Carmen almost wilted with relief, too confused and upset to demand an explanation at this point.

Mother Superior met them just inside the convent doors. Word of their predicament had already reached her sympathetic ears. "Come, sisters," she told them. "We will go into our private chapel and continue our meditations there, just in case unexpected visitors intrude upon us." Aside to Tori and Carmen she added, "Father Romero has sent a trusted friend to inform Mr. Banner of your circumstances. Until he arrives you will remain in our care."

"I don't want to place any of you in danger, Mother Superior," Tori hastened to say. "I just didn't know what else to do!"

With a smile, the woman responded calmly, "God has brought you to us today, Victoria. He has His ways of protecting His own. Trust Him, my dear. He does not make mistakes."

Tori recalled her shoes once more, and mentioned this to the Mother Superior. The other woman shook her head in amused dismay. "Unlike Him, we mortals are prone to

making many mistakes." She directed one of
the sisters to take Tori's shoes and hide them
well, and to bring her a more appropriate
pair.

They had been in the small chapel perhaps
ten minutes when they heard the commotion
in the outer hall. Suddenly the doors flew
open with a crash, and two men strode into
their midst. Edwards was not with them,
probably preferring not to have the church
aware of his involvement. The two would-be
attackers said nothing as they searched the
room for Tori and Carmen, who kept their
heads lowered in prayer. Up and down each
row of nuns they went, until they were finally
satisfied that the women they sought were not
there.

Throughout the invasion of their private
domain, the sisters remained silent, continuing their prayers as if nothing untoward were
happening. Only as the men were exiting the
chapel did Mother Superior speak up. "Gen-
tlemen, is there something you seek? Can we
aid you in any way?"

The taller of the men turned a nasty glare
upon her. "Just go on about your prayers,
lady. We're gonna search this place, and then
we'll be on our way. No one tries to stop us,
no one gets hurt. You savvy?"

She gave them a terse nod of her head and
promptly turned her back to them. Tori had to

admire the woman's serenity before such crude behavior, the almost regal way she had responded to the situation.

It was several long, tense minutes before they heard the men leave the building. Tori was not the only one who sagged and drew in a ragged breath. White-faced and trembling, Carmen turned to her daughter. "You may explain all this now, please—from the beginning."

Chapter 25

Edwards was running scared. The game was up, and he knew it. When his men had not been able to find either Tori or Carmen after Sunday Mass, he beat a hasty retreat. Now that the Banners knew he was the one behind all the attacks, his life wasn't worth a plug nickel. Jake Banner could see again, and Edwards desperately needed to stay out of shooting range now.

Despite his throbbing head, Jake had come for Tori and Carmen at the church, bringing several of his most trusted men with him. By the time they arrived, Edwards and his two thugs had departed, depriving Jake of immediate revenge. Once safely back at the Lazy B,

it was all Tori could do to keep Jake from
charging off in a rage. It took the combined
efforts of Tori, her mother, and Gill to convince Jake of the wisdom of waiting until his
temper cooled enough to formulate a work-
able plan. To just ride off in a huff with no plan
would be foolhardy, especially since Edwards
would be waiting for him and have all his men
alerted.

Jake waited until Blake returned. Then they
closeted themselves in Jake's study and, between them, debated what their best chances
would be. It was Blake who talked Jake into
waiting until late that night. "We'll beard the
bastard in his own den," he said. "Let them
stay on guard all day. Let him worry and wait,
and sweat it out. Then, when he's decided we
aren't coming after him, we'll slip past his
guards and give him a little surprise party
tonight."

That had suited Jake just fine, but now he
wondered if their delay would not cost them
the killer they sought. They had, indeed, managed to sneak quietly past the guards at
Edwards' ranch, but when they at last reached
the man's bedroom, they found it empty.
Drawers were pulled open, clothing scattered
about. They had searched the whole house,
finding it deserted except for the sleeping
housekeeper. Awakening her, they had proceeded to question her, learning that Edwards
had hurriedly packed and left earlier in the

day. The frightened woman told them that her employer had mumbled something about visiting his daughter back East. To the best of her knowledge, he intended to take the train.

Now the two gunfighters were racing into the night, toward the train station several miles south of Santa Fe, in the same little town where they had driven the cattle for shipping. There were no night trains heading east, and only one hotel in town, so if Edwards was there, he wouldn't be hard to find.

It was close to three in the morning when they pulled their lathered horses to a halt near the hotel. They didn't ride right up to the building, not wanting to alert anyone to their presence if they could avoid it. Slipping through the shadows as silently as ghosts, they approached the darkened hotel. If their luck held, everyone would be sleeping soundly within.

While Blake climbed the back stairway and let himself in through the second-story doorway, Jake tiptoed into the deserted lobby. The small establishment had no night desk clerk. Instead there was a bell on the counter for patrons to ring if they needed service after midnight, and the owner and his wife slept in a room directly behind the main lobby.

Quietly, Jake examined the hotel register, noting the room number. With a silent sniff of disgust, he thought to himself, "The dumb sonovabitch doesn't even have enough sense to use another name." Edwards had signed in as Stanley Edwards, plain as the nose on your face.

In the mail slot allotted to that room number, Jake found the extra room key. It was all so easy! Now they wouldn't even have to make noise getting into Edwards' room.

"He's in room twelve," Jake whispered, meeting Blake in the shadows of the upstairs hall. He dangled the key for his friend to see, and the smile on Jake's face would have sent the devil himself dashing for cover.

They were in the room and standing on either side of the bed before Edwards was aware of anything wrong. In the darkened room, the cold steel kiss of a gun barrel on his bare neck was the man's first indication of danger. "Who's there?" he whispered anxiously, his heart thudding in his chest.

"Now, who do you suppose?" Jake drawled lazily. "You didn't run far enough or fast enough, Edwards. It was almost laughable how easy you were to find."

"I didn't do it!" the man said excitedly. "I don't care what your wife claims to know, I didn't do it!"

"Now, have I accused you of anything yet?" Jake asked in that cool, deceptively calm tone that made shivers run riot over Edwards' skin.

"You can't prove anything against me!" The man panicked, making a move to reach his hand beneath his pillow. The sound of the hammer being cocked back on Jake's Colt almost echoed in the silence of the room. "I wouldn't if I were you," Jake warned darkly. Leaning over, he pulled the pistol from beneath Edwards' pillow—Roy's pearl-handled revolver.

"This is all the proof I need. Say your prayers, Edwards. You're about to meet your Maker."

"Now, just hold on a minute, Jake," Blake put in softly. Despite the gun held to his head, Edwards jerked his startled face about to stare at Blake. This was the first he was aware that he and Banner were not alone in the room. His surprise and dismay were obvious. "I've got some questions I'd like to hear the answers to before you blow this bastard's brains all over the wall."

"Get up, Edwards," Jake ordered. The man rose warily from the bed, his long white nightshirt making him easy to see even in the darkness. "Light the lamp, Blake," Jake suggested. "This might take a while, and we might as well make ourselves comfortable."

While Blake lit the lamp standing on the table before the room's only window, Jake kept his gun leveled on his quaking prisoner. Jake chose a chair and indicated with a jerk of his gun barrel that Edwards was to stand beside the table. "If anyone happens to notice the light, I want you to be the only one they see in this room."

Blake settled himself on the edge of the bed. "Let the trial begin!" he quipped.

"Trial?" Edwards managed to choke out. "This is no trial! It's cold-blooded murder!"

With a nonchalant shrug of his broad shoulders, Jake commented casually, "You should know, Edwards. Now tell me, why did you do it?"

"Do what?" the man blustered.

"Let's start with the fire that killed Dad, and don't try tellin' me you didn't do it. The only way you could have gotten hold of Dad's revolver was to be in that room the night he died."

Edwards stared back at him, refusing at first to answer until Jake leveled the gun barrel toward the area between Edwards' legs. "You know, with the light shinin' through that nightshirt, I can pretty well pick any part of your body I want and be fairly sure of hittin' it. I don't have to kill you with the first shot. In fact, the more I think about it, the more I think I'd enjoy seein' you suffer a while first," Jake threatened softly.

"Well, shoot him once for me, then, if that's your plan," Blake suggested with a sneer.

The man paled, his throat working spasmodically. "There are other people in the hotel," he said finally. "They'll hear the shots. You won't get away with this."

A smirk curled Jake's lips. "But you'll be

dead before they even throw back their bedcovers," he pointed out. "Now talk."

"I wanted the Lazy B," Edwards admitted at last.

"Why?"

"For the land; for the water. That, combined with my own property would have given me one of the largest, richest spreads in New Mexico."

Dark brows winged upward as Jake considered this. "Thanks for the suggestion, Edwards. Once you're dead, I'll have to see about acquirin' your land, since it runs right alongside the Lazy B."

"You won't have much use for my land or yours, swinging from the end of a rope," Edwards reminded him in a show of bravado.

"But I don't intend to be caught." Jake's eyes gleamed with naked malice. "I suppose all the trouble and the attempts on my life were for the same purpose, to get the Lazy B for yourself?" he surmised.

Edwards concurred with a nervous nod. "You never showed much interest in the ranch in the past, and I was hoping, with a little encouragement, you could be made to leave again."

"But you misjudged me, Edwards. Everything you tried just made me more determined to stay, especially once I was sure Dad had been murdered.

"But what about Tori?" Jake went on. "She was the innocent in all this. Why all the attempts on her life?"

Edwards hesitated with his answer, but a dangerous glare from Jake had him babbling again. "I just wanted to scare her at first, get her to run back to that convent of hers. It wasn't until I learned she was going to have your brat that she became any real problem. The child could inherit the ranch, you see. Suddenly there were just too many people in line to inherit the land I wanted for myself. At the start, I thought it would be so simple. The fire got rid of Roy, and even if Carmen lived, I thought I could talk her into selling the place."

"Or marrying you," Jake guessed. "Then I came home and ruined all your fine plans. What a pity, Edwards. Of course, you had your spies working from inside the ranch all the while, or we would have caught you sooner. You should have hightailed it when Red failed to kill Blake and me, and then Tori."

Just the thought of Tori all alone at the mercy of that lecherous son-of-a-snake made Jake's fury rise even further. "You've threatened my family for the last time, Edwards, and without you to pay them to do your dirty work for you, I doubt I'll have too many problems with the rest of the men you've hired." While they were talking, he had let the hammer of the Colt back down. Now he cocked it again.

Edwards jerked at the sound, his arm flying out as he turned away in panic, seeking someplace to run, but there was no such place. The long sleeve of his nightshirt hooked the oil lamp, yanking it on its side and immediately catching the cloth on fire. Before any of them could move fast enough, the lamp rolled to the floor, splashing oil on the table, the floor, and all over Edwards.

Within seconds, the man was a living flame, from head to toe! His agonized screams made Jake wince despite himself. Even as Jake reached for the pitcher of water on the bureau, instinctively wanting to douse the flames, he tried to tell himself that this was the way Edwards had killed Roy—it was the ultimate justice that Edwards was now suffering the same fate as Jake's father. As Jake's fingers wrapped about the handle of the pitcher, Edwards reeled blindly. In the next instant, he threw himself out of the window, shattering the pane and falling straight down to the stone patio below. Almost immediately, his screams ceased.

The two friends rushed to the window. Two stories below, they could see Edwards' body. It was twisted at odd angles, still flaming, a dark patch of blood staining the light-colored stones near his head. Even as they stared downward, they could hear other lodgers stirring from their beds. Edwards' screams had awakened them.

Tugging at Jake's arm, Blake pulled him back from the broken window. "Come on, pardner. We've got to get out of here if we don't want to get blamed for this. Personally, I've got a passion for breathin'." As he spoke, Blake jerked the pitcher from Jake's hand and tossed the water on the spreading fire. With a blanket, he quickly smothered the remaining flames. While they didn't want to get caught here in Edwards' room, or anywhere near the hotel if they could manage it, neither did they want to be responsible for taking the lives of any innocent persons staying in the hotel, or for letting the owner's livelihood burn to the ground.

With their hats pulled low over their faces, the two men ran into the hallway and down the back stairs of the hotel. Though others were now awake, they encountered no one on their way. Most of the patrons were still busy gaping out of their windows, still puzzling over what might have happened. Not one person glimpsed the two men loping away from the hotel, dashing from shadow to shadow as they swiftly made their way back to their horses.

Two days later, the *Santa Fe Weekly* carried the story of Stan Edwards' death. It seemed the man had somehow caught his hotel room on fire, and in the process of trying to douse the flames had caught himself afire. In his pained frenzy, he had either leaped from the window or stumbled through it, dashing his skull on the patio below. He had died before anyone could reach his broken, flaming body. His remains, so the newspaper stated, were being shipped East for burial. His daughter and only living relative had been wired about her father's death and was presently making the arrangements.

Carmen read the news item with a somber face. Knowing her mother was distressed, Tori tried to comfort her. "I'm truly sorry, Mama. I know you were coming to care for the man, with his many visits and all the time you spent together."

Shaking her head, Carmen denied this. "No, 'Toria. That is not entirely true. Yes, it was nice to have him visit while I was recuperating and couldn't get out of the house. It gave me someone to speak with, and it was a pleasant way to spend a few hours, but I did not care for him in the way you are suggesting. If anything, I felt pity for the man, living all alone with no wife or children to brighten his days."

"Then you do not grieve for him?" Tori asked, hoping her mother was speaking the truth and not trying to hide deeper feelings from them just to make them all feel better.

"I grieve for his soul," Carmen said sadly. "For his evil deeds, he will burn in hell for all eternity. I regret his twisted mind that has caused us all such pain and loss. But may God forgive me, I also feel relief and a sense of peace that Roy's murderer has met with divine justice. Roy was never an easy man to understand, as both of you know. Nor was he always easy to live with. He had many faults, but underneath that gruff exterior and the harsh words, he meant well. He did not deserve to die in the manner he did."

"I'm glad you're not sufferin' over Edwards' death, *Mamacita*," Jake said, bending to kiss her cheek. "I'm just sorry it took so long for us to catch him. I thought all along it might be him, but I couldn't prove it, and in the meantime he was deceivin' you, makin' you think he cared for you."

Carmen's mouth turned up in a gentle, curious smile. "Don't let it bother you so. I could never have loved that man, whether he was innocent of wrongdoing or not." Her dark eyes took on a teasing gleam as she added, "The rest of you have been too busy to notice, I suppose, but I have another admirer who more appeals to me."

Several jaws dropped, and they all chorused, "Who?"

Laughing at their shocked faces, Carmen announced smugly, "Owen Green. He has already asked if I would take offense if he courted me once my mourning period is finished."

"Doc Green?" Jake exclaimed, then chuckled wryly. "Why, that sly old goat! I *thought* he came around more than necessary when Blake and I were laid up!"

"Jacob Banner! I'll have you know that Owen is only three years older than I, and I resent you calling him old!"

"Does that mean he's a young goat?" Jake teased, wagging his eyebrows at her. His a-mused gaze swung toward Tori. "We're gonna have to keep an eye on those two or we're gonna have a baby sister or brother younger than our own child. Wouldn't that stand all of Santa Fe on its ear!"

"Go ahead and laugh," Carmen said with a serene smile. "You may end up eating those words yet!" Tori and Jake just stared at one another.

With Edwards dead, the problems at the Lazy B were at an end. It was with mixed feeling that Megan packed their bags and prepared for their return to Tucson. "I'm anxious to get home," she admitted to Tori, "but on the other hand, I'm going to miss all of you dreadfully. I wish we lived closer to one another. You've become a special friend, Tori."

Tori echoed Megan's sentiments. "I'll miss you, too. It's been so nice to have someone else around who is also expecting a child, someone I can talk with about it and compare feelings with. It would be lovely to raise our babies together, to watch them grow and become friends. Mother is going to especially miss Alita. We all adore that child!"

"Promise that you'll write often, and that you'll let me know when the baby is born. Already I'm dying of curiosity to know which it will be, a boy or a girl," Megan said.

"Oh, it's definitely going to be a boy, and his name will be Bretton," Tori stated confidently. "Of course, we'll probably call him Brett most of the time."

Megan laughed, giving Tori a strange look. "What is this? The rest of us have to wait until our children are born to find out, and you know? How, Tori? If you've got a crystal ball hidden around here somewhere, how about letting me use it?"

"No crystal ball," Tori said, "but something just as good. Madame Laveau, the old voodoo priestess who gave me the charm, told me this child would be a son. She even told us what we would name him."

Megan gaped at her. "And you believed her?" she asked incredulously.

Tori nodded, not at all upset with Megan's blatant skepticism. "Why shouldn't I? After all, she was right about the charm. It did save my life."

"I don't doubt that," Megan came back. "It sure as heck scared the drawers off of Red! Still and all, Tori, I wouldn't get my heart set on a boy. You could be greatly disappointed."

"I don't think so," Tori answered, laying a hand over the small bulge of her tummy.

Megan shrugged. "Well, I tried. I still want you to write and let me know when the baby is born."

"I promise, and you must do the same."

Megan agreed, then asked curiously, "Are you still wearing that odd charm?" When Tori nodded affirmatively, she said, "Now that Edwards is no longer a problem, don't you think it's safe to remove it, or are you planning on using it to ward off evil for the rest of your life?"

Tori hesitated, then tried to explain to her friend. "I know the danger from Edwards is past, but Madame Laveau told me I would know when the time was right to remove the charm. So far, I haven't felt that. Somehow I feel much more secure with it on right now. I can't explain it any better than that." She shrugged self-consciously. "Maybe I'm just frightened that something will go wrong while the baby is being born—I don't know. All I know is that I want to wear it a while longer."

"Blake, I know you've stayed longer than you intended, and got wounded to boot, but I hate to see you go. You're like a brother to me. Not many men really know what it's like to go from being a gunfighter to tryin' to have a wife and family and a normal life. Only someone who's been through it all himself understands just how hard it is to do."

Blake nodded. "It does have its rough spots. Reno was proof enough of that. I really don't think he had anything to do with this other business with Edwards."

"Neither do I," Jake admitted. "Reno just happened along at the same time everything else was happenin'."

"Write and let us know how things are going from time to time," Blake said, holding out his hand to Jake. "And you know you're always welcome at the ranch, if you get over our way."

"You, too." The men shook hands and thumped one another on the back. "Thanks for bein' here, Blake—for lookin' after the ranch, for escortin' Tori around, and for cartin' my carcass in to Doc Green's like you did. You saved my life, and I'll always be grateful."

Blake laughed. "You didn't sound too thrilled when we were cooped up in that bedroom together day in and day out," he reminded his friend.

Jake grinned. "You snore like a buzz saw. How could I be expected to be cheerful all day, when I hardly got a wink of sleep at night for all the racket you were makin'? Now I can really sympathize with Megan. How does she stand it night after night?"

"She's too busy snoring right along with me

to notice, I guess," Blake joked, "but don't ever tell her I said that. She's kind of sensitive about it, and she'll never admit to it. Makes her mad as a hornet when I mention it!"

The Banners and Montgomerys all gathered together in the *sala* to bid their final farewells. There were hugs and kisses all around, and more than one pair of damp eyes. At last the bags had all been loaded into the wagon, and it was time to leave. Gill was taking their friends as far as the rail station, where they would continue on their own.

"Take care now," they called as Jake and Tori walked them to the wagon.

"Have a safe trip home."

They were in the wagon, heading down the drive toward the main road to Santa Fe, and Jake and Tori were standing arm in arm, waving goodbye, when the first shots rang out. For a moment Jake was almost too shocked to react. Then he pushed Tori toward the house, shielding her with his own body as he drew his Colt and provided cover fire for the two of them. Bullets whizzed past their heads, slamming into the house behind them as they dashed for the door.

In the wagon, Blake shoved Megan, the baby, and Josefa down, throwing himself over them as Gill whipped the horses around and sent the wagon careening back up the drive, headed for the rear of the house. Beneath her husband, Megan was screeching, "Get off of me, you big galoot! Blast it, Blake, give me a gun!"

They made it to the house, forsaking their baggage as they ran for safety. Tori threw open the back door, grabbing Alita from Megan's arms as they came tumbling into the kitchen through a barrage of gunfire. Windows could be heard shattering all through the house. With Gill and another of the ranch hands guarding this end, Blake and the women practically crawled into the *sala* to join Jake and Carmen. The friends shared a look of confusion.

"What in blazes is going on?" Jake asked, voicing what all of them were thinking.

Chapter
26

Another hail of gunfire peppered the house. "Banner! Come out and face me, eyeball to eyeball!"

Blake frowned, his gaze holding Jake's. "That voice doesn't ring any bells with me. Do you have any idea who that is out there?" he asked softly.

Jake nodded grimly, his golden eyes glittering with malice. "That, my friend, is the man I've been tracking for almost seven years now. He's the only one of Caroline's killers I haven't been able to kill."

He heard her indrawn breath and turned to find Tori staring at him, her eyes huge and frightened. "Jacob?" she breathed shakily. "What's he doing here?"

"Probably heard I was looking for him and decided to beat me at my own game, darlin'," Jake guessed.

"Banner? You hear me?" came a second call.

"That you, Rowan?" Jake shouted back.

With an evil laugh, Rowan answered, "Yeah, Banner! You surprised to see me here? Sort of turned the tables on ya, didn't I? One thing I don't like is havin' to look back over my shoulder all the time. Makes me jumpy, ya know?"

Jake laughed, a chilling sound that carried easily on the breeze. "Obligin' of you to save me the trouble of trackin' you down, Rowan. I won't even have to set foot off my own property to kill you."

"You gonna talk all day, Banner? Me and my boys got better things to do with our time. Quit hidin' behind your woman's skirts and come on out. You're the one that's wanted this showdown for so long now."

"There's a whole world of fools, Rowan, but I'm not one of them," Jake called back.

"Well, that gives us some idea of who and what we're up against," Blake put in. With a jerk of his head, he gestured toward the study. "Gill and Sam have got the back covered. Megan and I will take the south side, if that's all right with you."

Jake nodded. "Fine. Can't let those sons-of-snakes sneak up on us. There's no tellin' how many of them there are out there."

"I'd judge about eight, maybe ten at most." Blake winked at Megan. "Just a fair morning's work between us, eh, darlin'?"

A smile creased Jake's face as he recalled the time Megan and Blake had held off five desperados in Blake's mountain cabin. "Maybe we'd better give her a skillet to work with, Blake," he suggested wryly.

"What's all this about Megan and skillets?" Tori asked. This was the second time this subject had been mentioned, and she still didn't understand it.

"Remind me to tell you about it another time," Megan told her. "Suffice it to say that I can do more damage with a cast-iron frying pan than most men can handle."

"Tori, Mama, you two go with Blake and get rifles from the cabinet in the study. Bring back enough ammunition to last a while," Jake instructed briskly as more gunfire erupted. "We three will cover the front. Oh, and drag Ana out from under her bed, where she's probably hidin'. She and Rosa can help load for the rest of us."

As the others scampered off to take up their positions, Jake returned fire. The battle was on in earnest now. From the side of the house where the barn was located, Jake heard several shots. He smiled grimly to himself. At least the ranch hands would handle things from that end. From the sounds of things, they were armed and had stationed themselves in and around the barn. He, Blake, and the women were not alone in this.

To Tori, this was almost a repeat of the night when she and Megan had fought so hard to hold off the "Indian" attack, with a few exceptions, of course. Now their husbands were here beside them, for which Tori was grateful. As she aimed her rifle through the broken window and fired again and again, however, she wished that this attack had also come at night. Granted, she could see their enemies better now, but she could also see the damage she was inflicting, which she would rather not have known.

As dangerous the situation, and as awful as her aim was, Tori still tried to shoot to wound. She didn't want to take another life if she could avoid it, and she didn't want to know about it if she did. After Red, she didn't think she could bear the guilt. The old adage "Ignorance is bliss" came readily to mind, and just now she agreed with it wholeheartedly.

In reality, the fighting lasted only about fifteen minutes, though it seemed much longer as bullets were flying back and forth. Then, suddenly, there was a cease to the firing coming from the outlaws. A shout went up, and Tori recognized Sam's voice as he called out triumphantly, "Boss! We got 'em pinned down like rats in a hole! Looks like they want to surrender!" Not another shot was heard to refute Sam's announcement.

Jake exchanged a broad grin with Tori. She trailed along beside him as he left the house. Behind her came Blake and Megan, still carrying their weapons. They found the small, disarmed group of outlaws banded together, surrounded by ranch hands standing guard over them. At least five of the desperados had been wounded. Another lay a few feet away, dead.

"What you want us to do with 'em, Boss?" Sam asked, his chest puffed up with pride at having helped capture these men.

"Take them to the barn and tie them up good and tight," Jake ordered. "We wouldn't want them to escape after you've all done such good work at catchin' them." His eyes, glistening proudly, swept over his loyal hands, letting them know how much he appreciated their help.

As the men prodded their captives toward the barn, Jake frowned. "Wait a minute! Where's Rowan?"

At that moment, a prickling along her neck made Tori turn away and look. Her eyes went wide with fear! To one side, just stepping out from behind a tree, was an evil-looking man with his gun trained straight toward Jake's chest! His finger was already tightening on the trigger! Her gasp of alarm alerted the others, but it was too late. Jake turned just as Tori launched herself in front of him. The report from the gun sounded a split second after he felt her jerk violently. Tori was shot!

Stunned, Jake caught her as she slumped against him. He heard a second shot, and with a part of his mind he realized that Blake had fired at Rowan. The man cried out and dropped his weapon, but did not fall. Through a red haze, Jake raised his pistol, fury seething through him. With one arm, he held Tori to him, her blood already staining the front of his shirt. With the other he leveled his Colt at Rowan, his eyes narrowed and blazing as he aimed to kill.

Then she stirred against him, moaning. Her eyes opened and stared up at him imploringly. "Don't!" she begged raggedly, tears of pain streaming down her pale cheeks. "Don't kill him, Jacob!"

Her plea tore through him, ripping his heart apart. Relying on Blake and the others to handle things, Jake swept her small body into his arms. She groaned, her eyes closing for a moment as she fought the pain. Jake's face twisted in agony. "Tori! Don't die!" His tormented cry rang out. "Please, don't die! I couldn't stand it! Please!"

Though it must have cost her a great effort, her hand came up to stroke his cheek as he carried her swiftly toward the house. Once more her gaze found his. "It will be fine,

Jacob," she comforted with a soft sigh. Then her hand fell to his chest, her lashes drifting shut, as she let the swirling mists surround her.

Jake was like a wild man. He hovered over Tori, refusing to leave her side as Carmen and Megan tended the wound high on her left shoulder. A rider had been sent into Santa Fe to fetch Doc Green, and every two minutes Jake would fly to the window to see if they had arrived yet, though Blake assured him it was much too soon to expect them back. He promised to let Jake know the minute he heard them coming.

Though he realized he was behaving irrationally, Jake could not help himself. Tori, his darling Tori, had been shot! Her blood covered the front of his shirt! Her face had been so pale as he carried her into the house! And now she lay so quietly, almost peacefully, as Carmen gently cut the blood-stained dress from her upper body, peeling the cloth away to reveal the bullet wound. Never squeamish, Jake's stomach lurched at the sight of the gaping hole in her shoulder. Her pain became his, and he wanted to howl in agony. This was his love, his very life lying here! If he lost her, he didn't think he would want to go on living.

He turned shakily away as Carmen took the damp cloth Megan handed her and began to tenderly cleanse the wound, then bind it tightly to stop the bleeding until Doc Green could get there and remove the bullet from Tori's torn flesh. Never before had he felt such pain for another person. In all his days, he had never experienced such freezing terror, or felt so utterly helpless. She could be dying! What was taking that doctor so long? Didn't he realize that every moment he delayed might cost Tori her life?

Alternately he paced and stood anxiously over the bed, willing Tori to fight for her life, and that of their child. On one hand, he desperately wanted her to awaken, if for nothing more than to assure himself that she could; on the other, he hoped she would remain unconscious, merely to save her the pain that came with waking. Throughout it all, he prayed as he had never prayed before.

At last, when Jake felt he could not stand another moment of just letting Tori lie there, the doctor arrived. He immediately ushered Jake from the room. When Jake protested, the physician stood firm, enlisting Megan's help in getting him out of the room so the doctor could tend to his patient. For Jake this was another version of hell, this waiting outside the bedroom door, not knowing what was going on behind it. He paced; he cursed; he prayed.

When Carmen, too, was evicted from the room, leaving only Rosa and the doctor in attendance, he fell upon her like a vulture, firing questions right and left. Finally, Blake and Megan made him sit down in the *sala* and stop tormenting the poor woman, who had no answers for him. "I'm sorry, Mamacita," he muttered, dragging trembling fingers through his dark hair. "I'm just so scared—so damned scared!"

Carmen nodded wordlessly, her worried eyes turning toward the hallway to the bedroom.

Blake shoved a glass of whiskey into Jake's hands. "Drink it," he commanded. "Maybe it'll help take the edge off."

They were still waiting there, almost an hour later, when the doctor walked into the room with a stunned look on his face.

Thinking the worst, Jake groaned, throwing back his head in agony. "She's dead, isn't she?" he asked through trembling lips, shutting his eyes against the sting of tears.

"No," the man replied in a hushed voice. "No, she's going to be just fine!"

Carmen issued a joyous cry, a heartfelt prayer of thanks to her Lord. Megan grabbed hold of Blake's arm and let out an unladylike whoop of delight. Blake grinned broadly. Jake just sat there, almost too stunned to believe the good news. Then, with a glad cry, he was out of his chair and dashing for the hallway. Doc Green caught hold of his sleeve, holding him back. "Wait, Jake. She's resting now, and I need to talk with you before you see her.

There is something odd going on here, and I'm hoping one of you can explain it to me."

"What's to explain, Doc?" Jake asked impatiently, needing to be near his wife. "She was shot!"

The doctor nodded, leading Jake back to his chair. "Sit down," he urged. "There's more to it than that."

Jake paled. "The baby?" he whispered fearfully. "Is she losin' the baby?"

Shaking his head, the doctor denied this. "She and the baby will be just fine, as far as I can tell. Tori doesn't appear to be in shock. The strange thing is, there is no exit wound in her shoulder, and none of you removed the bullet, but I'll be darned if I could find it!"

"Doc," Megan declared excitedly, voicing all their fears, "you've got to find it! You can't just leave it in there! She'll die!"

"You don't understand," the man replied with a puzzled look. "I've probed the wound; I've examined it thoroughly—and the bullet simply is not there! It's gone!"

Jake shook his head, trying to comprehend what the doctor was saying. "It can't be!"

"Believe me, there is no bullet in that wound, and what's even more strange, the wound has already stopped bleeding completely. In all my years as a doctor, I've never beheld anything like this!"

Four stunned pair of eyes met his, questioning his statement. "I don't blame you for looking at me like I've lost my mind," he said with a shaky laugh. "Maybe I am, but I know what I've just seen. The bleeding had stopped before I even removed the bandage. All the time I probed for the bullet, no blood welled up. I tell you, it's the eeriest thing I've ever seen!"

"And Tori," he continued in amazement. "Well, I've seen grown men with less grit! It was all I could do to convince her to stay in that bed! She's acting like being shot is no worse than stubbing her toe! Her color is good, she's not in shock, she has no fever, and according to her, the pain isn't too great. To top it all, she's asking for something to eat— says she missed lunch and she's famished! I just don't understand this at all."

In the silence following the doctor's words, Megan's gasp was loud. "The charm!" she exclaimed with wide eyes. "It's that charm!"

All eyes swung toward her, surprise reflected on their faces. Poor Doc Green looked more confused than ever. Jake's jaw hung slack until he finally recovered himself enough to snap it shut again. "Megan," he began skeptically, but there was doubt in his tone, too, and wonderment.

"It's got to be, Jake!" Megan insisted, defending herself. "What else could it possibly be?"

"What charm?" Doc Green asked, completely baffled. "Would someone please explain to me what the devil you are talking about?"

Jake left it to the others to explain, as best they could, for at that moment, Rosa stepped into the room. "Señor Jacob, Señora Tori is asking for you. I'm afraid if you do not come now, she will try to get out of bed and come to you."

Jake raced to Tori's side. When he entered their bedroom, she was sitting up with the pillows propped behind her back. "Oh, Tori!" he sighed, his eyes devouring the glorious sight of her, knowing how close he had come to losing her. Wrapping her tenderly in his arms, he drew her close, a shudder racking his big frame. "Oh, dear God! I was so frightened, love! I was so afraid I was going to lose you! You're my life, Tori! You're the air I breathe!"

With her good hand, Tori stroked his dark head, her eyes glowing with her love for him. "I'm all right, Jacob. Really. Nothing is going to happen to me, at least until after I birth this son of ours."

"I wish I could be so sure of that," he said shakily. "Megan is convinced that the charm saved your life."

"So am I," Tori admitted with a smile. When he opened his mouth to refute this, she shook her head and said softly, "Jacob, there are some things in this world that simply cannot be explained. This is one of them.

Sometimes you just have to believe, without questioning why."

Tori had a request to make, one she was certain would not be easy for Jake to accept or understand. "Jacob, I want your word that you will not kill the man who shot me. I'll not have his life on my conscience, nor his blood on your hands, knowing that you've killed him to avenge me."

He stared at her, aghast at what she was suggesting. "I can't just turn him loose, Tori, to try again!"

With a shake of her head, she said, "I don't want you to release him, darling. I just want you to turn him over to the law, and let justice take its rightful course."

He could not stop the snort of disgust. "With the sheriff we have, Tori?" he asked incredulously.

"There will be an election in just a few weeks," she reminded him. "As you said, we will probably get a new sheriff, and hopefully he will be an improvement over this one. Regardless, I want your promise that you will not take vengeance into your own hands this time, that you will let the law handle it."

She was waiting for his answer, her eyes shining up at him with hope and trust. "You have my word," he promised.

Within two short days Tori was out of bed; within five she was walking about as if nothing had happened. Her wound was healing at a miraculous rate, showing no signs of infection. She swore she felt almost no pain at all. One evening, as if to prove her point to them all, she showed them the charm. Holding it out to Jake, she said, "Look, Jacob. Do you notice anything different about the charm?"

Jake took the charm from her. Warily, he glanced at it, his eyes going wide at what he saw. "It's gone! The hole in the figure's shoulder! It's disappeared!"

As the others gathered round to exclaim over this, each wanting to see for himself, Tori nodded. "Yes, and so is the wound in my shoulder, which was in the exact spot as that on the charm. It's as if it all never happened!"

The six occupants of the room stared at one another in dumbfounded wonder. First, Tori had recovered so quickly, so easily—now this thing with the charm changing! Who would ever believe such a thing! They were all wondering exactly what kind of awesome power this voodoo charm contained. It was frightful to imagine, even worse to believe!

"If I really thought that charm saved your life, I'd get down on my knees and kiss that old crone's feet!" Jake finally admitted on a huge sigh.

"I'm going to have to take a trip to New Orleans myself one of these days and find out what kind of magic that voodoo woman uses," Doc Green said, still amazed at what had transpired. "Maybe we could join forces and save the world!"

"And maybe you'd better take Mama with you to protect you from Madame Laveau's evil clutches," Tori teased him. At her words, the doctor and Carmen shared a tender look.

Carmen was still baffled. " 'Toria, how could you possibly believe in such a thing?" she asked, shaking her head. "It's sinful! Surely God would not approve of this!"

"I did not go to Madame Laveau, Mama. She came to me. Has it occurred to any of you that perhaps God sent her to me with this charm? After all, the Lord works in mysterious ways, and who are we to question them?"

Who were any of them to question the strange events they had witnessed lately?

When he handed the charm back to her, she slipped it into the pocket of her dress. "Aren't you going to wear it any longer?" Megan asked curiously.

"No. There is no longer any need." That, more than anything, convinced them all that the danger was really and truly past this time.

The Montgomerys finally caught their train, a week delayed, and were on their way home at last. When Jake and Tori eventually found time enough alone together, he held her tenderly to him and told her, "Tori, I could search the world over until the day I died, and I would never find another woman as loving or compassionate as you. I thought I knew what love was, but I had only glimpsed a part of it before. It goes much deeper than I would ever have believed. It's all-giving, all-forgiving, completely selfless. You proved that to me when you took that bullet meant for me. I've never known a love so pure, so honest, as the love you give to me, and I'm truly humbled by it."

"Then will you grant me one more favor, Jacob?" she asked.

He stiffened slightly, almost afraid to hear what she might suggest this time. Then he relaxed. Whatever it was, he would try to give it to her. She had been willing to forfeit her life to save his, and he could deny her nothing. "What?" he asked.

"Will you go to church with me sometime? I know you won't always be able to attend with me, but will you try to make it once in a while?"

"I'll be there with bells on, if it will please you," he agreed, making her laugh aloud.

Her gleeful laughter was music to his ears. "You do that, Jacob!" she chuckled. "The nuns have formed a bell choir, and if you really show a talent for this type of thing, Mother Superior just might let you join their group!"

His laughter joined hers. It was good to be alive! It was good to be standing here holding her so close to him, to feel her heart beating next to his. Then, suddenly, he felt a tiny, fluttering movement in the stomach pressed up close to his. Their eyes met in mutual wonder and surprise. "The baby!" he whispered softly, as if to speak louder would disturb the infant nestled in her womb.

She nodded joyfully. "Your son."

This time he did not refute her words.

Several months later, on a blustery day in late March, Bretton Roy Banner made his way into the world. His mother's labor was neither short nor long, hard nor easy, but something in between. When it was done, and he lay cradled in her arms, clean and new, his father came to watch him take his first meal from his mother's breast.

"Isn't he beautiful?" Tori breathed in awe, admiring the tiny, perfect fingers curled upon her breast.

Jake smiled his crooked smile. "If you're partial to bright red prunes, I guess you could say that."

Tori wrinkled her nose at him playfully. "Really, Jacob! Admit it, now. You think he's the most marvelous thing since the invention of the wheel!"

"Of course, he is! He's my son! But I wouldn't go so far as to say he's beautiful. On the edge of handsome, maybe."

"We'll have to write Blake and Megan and let them know," Tori reminded him. "I was so pleased to hear they had a boy this time."

"Yeah, but I'll bet Brett is better lookin'," Jake announced, his paternal pride taking over.

The baby had finished nursing, and Tori placed him gently on the bed at her side. When she started to rise, Jake motioned for her to lie still. "Tell me what you want, and I'll get it for you. You've done more than your share of work today, just bringin' our son into the world."

With a grateful smile, she told him, "In the top drawer of my bureau you'll find the charm Marie Laveau gave me. Would you bring it to me, please?"

Jake frowned. "Why, darlin'? You aren't worried somethin' is gonna happen, are you?"

"Oh, no! I'm just curious about something, and I wanted to look at it a moment."

With a shrug, he did as she asked. When he had handed it over to her, a strange smile crept over her face. "Just as I suspected," she murmured.

"What is it?"

Showing him the charm, Tori said, "One of the seeds is missing, and I'd bet almost anything you can search that drawer and this entire house and you'll never find it."

Sure enough, as Jake examined the charm,

one of the seeds from the center of it was gone. "What do you suppose it means?"

"It means," she told him with a knowing smile, "that you are not going to get those six children we talked about." She paused a moment. "There will only be three, if Madame Laveau is correct—three to match the three seeds in the charm. One is missing now because Brett has already been born."

"Three will be just fine, darlin'," Jake agreed. By now he wasn't about to argue the strange powers of either Marie Laveau or the charm.

He studied the charm more closely. "These two seeds are not alike," he noted. "Do you think that means that we'll have at least one girl among the three?"

"Perhaps. I think that would be nice, don't you?"

Jake bent close to claim a kiss. "I think it would be very nice," he told her softly, his lips brushing teasingly over hers. "I would adore a daughter, a tiny replica of my favorite lady, my special fallen angel."

ForeverGold

CATHERINE HART

**"Catherine Hart writes thrilling adventure...
beautiful and memorable romance!"**
—Romantic Times

From the moment Blake Montgomery holds up the westward-bound stagecoach carrying lovely Megan Coulston to her adoring fiance, she hates everything about the virile outlaw. How dare he drag her off to an isolated mountain cabin and hold her ransom? How dare he steal her innocence with his practiced caresses? How dare he kidnap her heart when all he can offer is forbidden moments of burning, trembling esctasy?

__3895-1 $5.99 US/$7.99 CAN